The Good Child

The Good Child

S.C. Karakaltsas

Karadie Publishing
Melbourne

A catalogue record for this book is available from the National Library of Australia

ISBN: 97809945032-9-9 (print)

ISBN: 97809945032-8-2 (electronic)

Book Cover Art & Design: Anthony Guardabascio from Continue.com

For my mother

Also by S.C. Karakaltsas

Climbing the Coconut Tree
Out of Nowhere: A collection of short stories
A Perfect Stone

1

LUCILLE

HAMMONDVILLE, JUNE 1992

It wasn't as if the house was about to burn down. Yet, Lucille anxiously checked she had everything she needed. In her handbag: an envelope with a small bundle of photographs, her most precious memories; her medication; and her bank book holding details of the only money she had left.

Everything else was hardly important.

She glanced around the small timber cottage, its quaint prettiness now lifeless. It was more from habit that she double-checked the window locks and backdoor one last time. She'd got rid of most things, trying to sweep away her past so she could come to terms with her present, or what was left of it.

If anyone had enquired, they would have seen from her sunken eyes and thin frame that she wasn't doing well. But no-one cared enough to ask. She pulled a hand-knitted beanie over her ears, tucking away stray wisps of white hair before wrapping a grey woollen scarf around her neck.

"You got the money, didn't you?" Tom had asked on the phone the night before. "I sent you a cheque."

She noted the concern in his voice. "No."

"You must have. Come on, Mum. Have you been checking the mail every day?"

She heard the growing frustration in his voice. "Of course I collect the mail, but you haven't sent me any funds for more than five months." How else did she know the electricity was to be cut off today?

"You're kidding. Why haven't you told me?"

"I thought you might have rung me when you reconciled your cheque account and realised that these so-called cheques hadn't been cashed."

"I have no idea what you're talking about. As if I don't have enough to worry about. It seems to me like you're not looking after yourself. Jesus Mum, what have you been living on if you haven't even cashed the cheques?"

She faltered. Perhaps he had sent the money. Then a sudden thought: perhaps they'd been stolen. There were people in this town desperate enough to do that.

"I've been under a lot of pressure, Mum. You of all people know that." His voice softened. "I'm worried about you. I'm glad you're coming."

She stared at the giant eucalyptus tree just outside her window; the wind buffeting the top branches.

"What else are you losing?"

"I'm not losing anything."

"Can I can trust you to get here on your own."

She rolled her eyes. "I'm perfectly capable of taking the train."

Tom had decided five years ago that she was too old to drive, and so had sold her Mercedes. At the time, she'd only been sixty-seven and hardly considered herself old. One minor car accident doesn't make you a danger on the road, she'd protested. Her son had thought otherwise.

She couldn't even remember when he'd started to take control of her life, how much she could spend, where she should live. She'd let him look after her finances. What did she know about paying bills and managing money? That had been drummed into her for as long as she could remember from all the men in her life. Tom was quick to take on the task after his father died. She should have learnt, but it seemed easier to let her son deal with it all and drip-feed her funds when she needed them. And she didn't need much. Except now, she wished she could have driven herself in the luxury of leather and warmth, instead of taking the train.

So much for worrying about her when he hadn't asked how she was. Didn't he wonder how she'd coped all this time? It was pointless telling him. He'd have manipulated the discussion and made it about him – how hard he worked, the pressure he was under. It was always someone else's fault when things went wrong. She kept her mouth shut as she'd always done. It wasn't worth the aggravation.

"Don't worry," she said. "I'll be there."

The sigh in his voice reminded her of how confident and arrogant he'd always been.

"I'm glad," he said. "It really means a lot to me to have you here for moral support, you know."

His words hung between them, then found a place deep inside her as they always did. The mother and son bond could never be broken no matter how much it had been stretched. Now it was at the very limit. He didn't need her, had never needed her. So why now? Bring out the old mother to gain sympathy? Perhaps he'd sent that journalist.

"I know. I'll see you tomorrow," she said finally, then hung up.

She didn't want to be there, with him. Yet, she didn't want to stay in this town, and the town didn't want her either. That much was clear. His worried concern for her supposed forgetfulness niggled at her.

Over her black pants and hand-knitted grey jumper, she put on her old camel-coloured coat, expensive ten years ago. Her black ankle boots weren't new but would keep her feet warm enough. Then she glanced in the bathroom mirror before checking the cupboards for anything she might have missed. Grabbing her handbag and canvas overnight bag, she locked the front door, side-stepping the smashed eggs – which regularly peppered the cottage – and walked past her garden of spent roses. Marching along the street she prayed she wouldn't see anyone, ignoring the weight of her bag and the growing ache in her arm. Was it her imagination? Did the curtains move as she passed Shirley Brown's house? The town's gossip could be counted on to pull the other old girls from the bowls club into a huddle to talk about what she'd seen, then speculate, analyse and tut-tut.

Lucille hurried across the bridge, glad of the new barriers hiding the gorge below. She'd been as shocked as anybody when the emergency services had winched up the wet sludge-covered body of Sammy Briggs. Her condolences and beef casserole had been gratefully accepted by his parents until they'd found Sammy's note. After that, everything had turned pear-shaped, and fingers were pointed at her.

Glad to get to the other side of the bridge, she headed up the slope next to Hammondville railway station, trying to ignore her aching knee. At the top of the hill, the full force of the wind whipped up debris, stinging her face. Flustered, she dabbed her watery eyes, shading them from the sun as much as from the wind, and peered into the distance to see if the train was coming. It wasn't.

Dead twisted twigs, shaken loose by the wind, fell from the eucalyptus trees. She tramped back down the hill, glimpsing the wild sea beyond the railway station, the sky a brilliant blue except for the dark clouds headed towards the town.

At the railway station, she set down her worn canvas bag on the cracked concrete, stood in front of the counter and removed her gloves, slipping them into her handbag. The cold bit painfully into her knuckles. Slowly, she drew the cash from her purse, suspecting the notes were probably still musty from where she'd hidden them in an old jam tin in the shed.

"Melbourne," she said, glancing nervously at Stan Briggs on the other side of the counter.

Stan glared. He'd worked there for years as the Station Master. She shouldn't have been surprised; it was stupid of her to think that, after everything that had happened, he wouldn't be there. Her gaze flickered from his shrunken, hollowed face, to the grubby white shirt under his open jacket.

"You're actually going then?" he said.

It had been almost two years since anyone in the town had spoken a civil word to her. She'd been too afraid to venture out of her cottage for long, and careful to avoid neighbours or people who'd once been friends.

"Yes." She lowered her eyes and slid the cash across the worn timber counter towards him desperate to keep her hands from shaking.

"One way?"

She held her breath, not wanting to have this conversation, but met his fierce dark eyes. "Yes. For now."

His top lip curled, and when he leant in closer, his breath was rank with stale alcohol. "You know he's gunna get what he deserves."

She dug her nails into her palms and stared at his thick fingers resting on the ticket, like a ransom, waiting for something from her. The wind whipped the bottom of her unbuttoned overcoat, thrashing the edges against her legs. She pulled it tight around her, folding her arms against the cold. Stan had been a friend once, but that was before he and his wife, Meryl, had lost everything, including their son. Her own son and Sammy had been good friends. No amount of apology or sympathy could undo what had been done.

The train's approach ended the standoff and Stan flicked the ticket at her, sneering, his teeth yellow and black, like old piano keys.

He glanced past her to see if anyone was around. "How does it feel to know that you've raised a murderer? You've got a lot to answer for, and I hope you fuckin' rot in hell with him. Don't bother coming back."

Lucille turned away, forcing herself to breathe slowly and keep her shaking hand steady enough to slip the ticket into her purse. With no-one to help, she picked up her bag, straightened her shoulders and entered the nearest passenger car.

Towards the front of the carriage, near the exit, she found two vacant bench seats opposite each other. The three other passengers on board ignored her struggle to lift her bag. Taking a deep breath, she hoisted it with all her strength, lumping it onto the rusted metal luggage tray above. She sat next to the window, careful to avoid the ripped aisle seat, clasped her large brown handbag protectively in her lap, and waited for the train to leave.

Her hearing aids beeped a warning. Batteries flat again! She searched in her handbag for new ones. There were none, and when she removed the aids to place them in her bag for safekeeping, she touched the envelope of her most precious memories. She couldn't resist pulling them out and shuffling through them. Hank, young and handsome in his uniform, was on top of the small pile. Sighing, she didn't need to turn it over to know what was written on the back. Next was a photo of her parents on their wedding day, their expressions guarded, which contrasted sharply with the one of her own wedding day – gazing wide-eyed, filled with hope and love for the man next to her – now buried in the town's cemetery beyond the railway station. She touched each photo of her babies until she picked up the photo of Tom. He sat on his father's knee and she, kneeling down beside her boy holding his chubby hand. Looking at the family picture her face was worried and tense.

The loudspeaker crackled, and she carefully gathered and replaced the photos while straining to hear. Her stomach tightened. What if it was something important?

Perhaps the middle-aged man a few seats behind her had heard the announcement. Turning around, she opened her mouth to ask, then snapped it shut. It was her face on the front page of the newspaper and with her was Tom and the Premier. The photo was old, taken more than six years earlier when Tom had asked her to host a lunch during the election. Her heart thumped.

She turned back and fumbled in her handbag for a tissue and when she found one, she held it under her nose hoping the man hadn't seen her.

How had the paper got the photo? The journalist had accosted her a few months ago when she'd been walking home from the shops. Charming at first, she began hounding Lucille, asking her how she felt to have such a son. The headline made her sick: *Doomsbury attacked for recklessness: Ruling tomorrow.*

Trying to calm herself, she focussed on breathing and began to relax. The man couldn't have recognised her. Back then, she'd dressed smartly for the occasion, her hair dyed with blonde highlights and her face smoothed with carefully applied make-up. She stared outside at the old railway building, pockmarked with neglect, yellowing paint peeling off the walls. Now her hair was grey, her face lined much like the sea-salt rust stains spreading tentacle-like along the building and fence outside.

Glancing at her gold watch – her twenty-fifth wedding anniversary present – her heart sank at the delay. She'd been the only passenger on the pot-holed platform. Why had a five-minute stop turned into fifteen? She wanted it over, and the sour heaviness in her stomach to be gone. Loosening her scarf, she removed a woollen glove and scratched her neck.

Outside on the platform, Stan stood proudly like a major general and blew his whistle loudly. A young woman blustered into the carriage, and of all the empty seats available, flopped breathlessly into the one opposite Lucille. The train shuddered and jerked forwards as the woman in worn jeans and windcheater blew into her cupped hands.

The light outside suddenly dimmed as the train went under a bridge, long enough for Lucille to catch her anxiety in the window's reflection as red splotchy blotches on her face and neck. Just as quickly, her reflection faded. The sun had gone,

and now grey light revealed a landscape of blackened trees –
remnants of a fiery summer three years before.

The town's outskirts disappeared. Once large and bustling
during gold rush times, the town had shrunk when the area's
gold had run out. Soon dairy farmers grew fat off the rich
dark soil. Later, empty nesters brought their wealth for the sea
air.

Twenty-two years ago, Lucille and her husband had settled
in a charming double-storey mansion amid expansive
manicured gardens, built by a wealthy landowner in 1890.
Five years ago, after her husband died, Tom had helped her
sell the house and move into a small cottage. Then two years
ago, Solid Rock Building Society collapsed, the recession
happened, and Tom had done his worst.

Yet her life hadn't turned out the way she'd hoped. When
she was fifteen, she and her best friend, Bethany, went to
a fair and saw a fortune teller. The woman, shrouded in
colourful scarves, lifted a spindly cold hand and studied
Lucille's palm, silent, her face serious except for a slight twitch
of her brow. Lucille shivered nervously, waiting for the
woman to look up, and when she did, her eyes bore into her,
as if trying to decide what should be said.

"You will have a long life, marry a tall handsome man," the
fortune teller blurted, "have three children and be wealthy.
Anything else, I cannot say."

At the time, Lucille was pleased with the prediction, not
knowing that the man she would marry was someone she'd

already met and that the life predicted would twist unexpectedly.

She thought of more recent times – the hurtful whispers on the street from people who'd been friends for years. She'd felt their stares, curious, angry, and disgusted as she'd walked the short distance to the supermarket with her trolley. Blaming her – as if it were her fault, as if she'd had any control over what had happened.

Perhaps Stan Briggs was right. Maybe she and her son did have a lot to answer for. She knew one thing for sure: her grandmother had been right all along. If only she'd made a different choice. When she thought about it, the fault had to lie back there, when she was a young woman. Perhaps she should have told the journalist the whole story.

Lucille's grandmother had warned that her life would turn out the way it had, though not the detail. Not the pain of it, or even the happiness.

The fortune teller had been right too. She had married a tall handsome man and had three children. She'd been wealthy, but the fortune teller had told her only half of her story.

In 1938, when Lucille was eighteen, her grandmother, whom she'd only met that one time, had predicted the rest. It was she who'd laid out the cold, hard prophecy of what Lucille's life would look like. Her grandmother had no special gifts, not like the fortune teller, just her conservative, old-fashioned values passed on as advice. And for a split second, Lucille had seen what her grandmother envisioned for her.

With one single thought, she'd rejected everything her grandmother had said. Love made her do that. And being young, made her stupid, blind and naive. The lure of happiness had been intoxicating.

But the prophecy had got under her skin, digging at her, year after year, until it took hold, haunting her, as it gradually became true. Despite Lucille's fight to throw the weight off her, like a curse, the words uttered more than fifty years earlier had unknowingly guided her life.

Regret had settled in and Lucille blamed only herself.

*

She stole a look at the fair-haired woman opposite, daring her to say something and steeling herself for the abuse she knew would come. The woman dug around in her backpack. She lifted her head and Lucille waited for the look of contempt, disgust even, like all the others. Yet the woman's bloodshot blue eyes expressed something else, something Lucille couldn't quite pinpoint at first, and then recognised – misery, like her own.

2

QUIN

JUNE 1992

Quin looked for the banana she thought she'd packed, disappointed it wasn't in her backpack. She settled into her seat and looked up at the woman opposite her. She was terribly thin, and her gloved hands fidgeted with the tassel on her scarf. Her skin was remarkably smooth over high cheekbones, and the wrinkles around her hollow eyes reminded her so much of Nan.

She folded her arms to keep warm. Her stomach rumbled. She'd like to have been inside with a fire warming her, eating hot porridge washed down with a cup of tea, not sitting on this train taking her back to the place she'd run from. But then she wanted a lot of things – her old life back for one, with her brother and Nan. And going back further, her parents. Be a good child, were her mother's last words. She'd tried. She really had tried.

She had to stop thinking; it was doing her head in. What

was done, was done. All she could do was look forward, make a new life. She had to stop blaming herself. Tomorrow, when justice was served, she'd let it all go, put everything behind her, maybe study and start again.

She wriggled around to find a spot where the springs weren't uneven and put her elbow on the window ledge leaning her head into her hand. The bush had moved on, replaced by blackened grassland dotted with run-down weatherboard houses, broken-down windmills and dried-out dams. The train slowed through the next town, and there was an endless array of shattered billboards and boarded-up shop fronts covered with faded graffiti. A handmade wooden sign, announcing the population numbers – declining from one hundred and thirty-five to the lonely number of three – shuddered in the wind. Someone had painted underneath in big white letters: *It was bloody great here once.* It saddened her to think that Solid Rock had probably killed that town.

Her gaze shifted to the other passengers. A middle-aged woman with dyed-blonde hair and leathery skin, a youth in torn jeans and red flannelette shirt and a man in sports jacket and slacks – a farmer perhaps. A large felt hat on his head, his knees were splayed, as he held his newspaper aloft taking in the space around him. Quin caught the headline about the ruling tomorrow. There was a photo of a man and woman on the front page. She squinted. It was Tom.

She got up to go to the rest room and passed by the man, steadying herself to get a closer look at the front page. She never read newspapers much anymore – bankruptcies, collapsing companies and rocketing unemployment. And "the recession we had to have" according to one self-righteous politician. She'd already had enough of that herself without reading about it. But her heart lifted to see Tom's picture on the front page. He'd hate it. He could no longer manipulate the story in the media. He'd call it a witch -hunt and it pleased her to think about him squirming in court. After what he did to her, he deserved everything that she hoped he'd get.

When she'd resettled into her seat, the train pulled into a station, and the youth in the flannelette shirt got off. It wasn't much of a town, and the train didn't pause long, blowing its whistle before crossing a road with a waiting line of three cars and two trucks. Then a man's voice boomed from the door at the end of the carriage. The old woman sitting opposite looked frightened, tilting her head in his direction. Removing her right glove, the old woman pulled out a well-worn leather purse, and her pale blue eyes landed on Quin who began searching the pocket of her torn jeans.

The ticket inspector stopped in front of the blonde. Quin's hands fumbled as she hunted through her windcheater's pockets, then her backpack. It had to be somewhere. She searched again.

She was almost certain Stan had given her the ticket. "The machine's on the blink," he'd said. "Bloody government's dragging their feet gettin' us new trains, new stations …"

She'd stood, impatiently moving her weight from one leg

to the other, realising there was no time for a toilet stop. The train had arrived. Stan had waved the ticket in the air.

Quin pushed a strand of lank hair behind her ear and plunged her hand into her pocket again. Her heart thumped. *Had Stan given her the ticket?* She glanced at the exit, then out the window. The train was moving too fast to jump off.

"Tickets! Tickets."

The man was in front of the old woman. His huge pot belly hung over his belt straining against the buttons of his shirt. He took the ticket with a hardened, blistered hand and punched it with a little metal clipper. He returned it, then planted his two feet flatly in front of Quin.

"Ticket, Miss." He looked bored.

A broken memory of a fear she'd wanted to forget brought out a prickle of sweat across her body. "I bought the ticket at Hammondville, but I don't think the guy at the station gave it to me. He said the machines were broken."

He stared at her with the piercing eyes of a hunter. "You can't travel without a ticket."

"I know, but I don't seem to have it. It's not my fault your staff are incompetent and can't do a simple task."

"So ya tryin' to be a smart-arse and travel for free?" He bent over, his coffee breath strong, and dug his fingers into her arm. "Get up!"

Quin glanced around the carriage. The farmer had his head in the newspaper. The blonde's attention was on the landscape, but the old woman's mouth had tightened into a grim line.

"Get your hand off me." A kernel of rage pushed through her as she pulled away and raised her voice. "Don't you dare try to manhandle me."

The farmer put down his newspaper, and even the blonde stared.

"I wasn't." The man looked surprised as he put his hands behind his back.

"Excuse me, but is that the ticket? Under your boot?" The old woman pointed to the floor.

The man stepped back.

"Yes!" Quin retrieved it and smiled gratefully at the woman, thrusting the ticket in front of the man.

He grunted and punched her ticket before moving into the next carriage.

"Thanks for helping me," Quin said.

"What's that dear? I'm a little hard of hearing."

"Thanks for your help," Quin said slower and louder.

"You're welcome."

"Oh god, that was lucky. I don't know what I'd have done. It must have fallen out of my pocket. These inspectors act as if not having a ticket is the worst thing in the world."

The woman looked surprised when Quin thrust her hand out. "Quin," she said, her voice cracking.

"Lucille."

"I can't stop shaking," Quin said. "He was horrible. That's the problem with these guys. The power goes to their head." Someone was yelling in the next carriage, and she craned her neck to see. "He probably gets off on catching people without a ticket. Makes him feel like a big man when people are down and out."

"I guess that's his job. But he seemed a bit overzealous. I wasn't sure what he was going to do to you."

"Me neither." Quin pulled up the sleeve of her windcheater and looked at the red mark on her arm. "Look at that."

Lucille leant forwards. "You should complain. I'd be more than happy to be your witness."

"Thanks. Maybe I should." Quin knew she wouldn't but liked the fact that Lucille was on her side. "Where did you get on?"

The woman looked surprised.

"What station did you get on?"

"Oh, at Hammondville."

"Me too. I nearly missed the train. To be honest, I'm glad to get out of there. No offence, but it's a bit of a shithole, if you ask me." Quin didn't know why she'd said that. The ticket inspector had rattled her, and here she was prattling on and on.

"I agree with you, dear," Lucille said with a hint of a smile.

Quin smiled back. "Too cold and miserable."

Lucille nodded. "But can be nice in summer."

"I was there in January and got two hot days. That was about it."

"Our last summer wasn't good."

"Do you live there?"

"Yes. Would you like a mint?" Lucille said, bringing an open packet from her large brown handbag.

"Thanks. I didn't get a chance to have breakfast." Quin reached into the bag.

She noticed the woman stare at her hand. Her nails looked terrible, like chewed down stumps

"Take the whole packet. I've got another one."

"Oh, I couldn't. Are you sure?"

Lucille nodded and hugged her handbag even closer. Quin unwrapped the mints shoving them in quick succession into her mouth.

"Be careful," Lucille said. "They're extra strong."

Quin stopped chewing and nodded, then read the packet. "Yeah, you're right. My nose is burning." Her eyes were watering. "Whew! They're really hot."

"These days, there's not much left of my tastebuds or smell, and they're the only thing I can really taste."

Quin folded the packet and shoved it into her windcheater pocket, then looked up and smiled. "You look familiar."

Lucille seemed startled and held a tissue up in front of her face as if to wipe her nose. "I worked at the Koffee and Kettle for a little while. Maybe you came in?" Quin said.

"Perhaps. I really don't know."

The clouds were heavy, and rain streaked horizontally along the window. She had to stop talking. Goodness knows she'd be divulging everything to this woman, a perfect stranger. Shame had stopped her from telling anyone. Maybe it was because Lucille reminded her of Nan. Shouldn't families trust each other? Nan and Ben had believed in her completely and they shouldn't have.

Quin folded her arms tight to keep warm. She'd made mistakes. If only she could go back in time and make things right.

Lucille's eyes seemed lost and sad, and Quin wondered why she looked so miserable. Perhaps Solid Rock had touched her too. For a moment, she forgot about her own troubles and wondered about the woman opposite her.

3

LUCILLE

OCTOBER 1937

Steam from the boiled kettle spiralled along the windowsill's flaking paint and animated the grimy streaks on the sunlit glass.

Lucille rested her elbows on the kitchen table, her hands around her cup, and stared at her father. His nose, thin and pointed like a lead pencil, thankfully hadn't been passed on to her. His hair, once light brown like hers, was now mostly grey. He wasn't a tall man, and his unshaven face accentuated deep lines and hollow bags under his eyes, hiding the once-handsome man in her parents' one and only wedding photo.

"It's just a dance," she said.

"Like a coming-out ball?" he said.

Pushing the newspaper to the side, he removed his spectacles taped together with sticking plaster, picked up his toast and took a bite. "It's high time you were introduced to society," he said, spraying crumbs onto the table.

Lucille had kept the notice about the ball from him, but he'd found out from a school parent at the second-hand car yard where he now worked as a salesman. She hadn't expected this reaction. She'd hardly allowed herself to care whether she went or not.

She cocked her head. "Pa, it's school, not society. It's not a debutante ball."

He grunted and picked up his paper and spectacles.

Debutante balls were for the rich, she wanted to say. At seventeen, she should have been a debutante by now and probably would have if her mother hadn't died. She tried to picture her – the face she'd loved, which had been lost back on Christmas day of 1929. Lucille had been sent to her Aunt Mavis's farm in the Mallee, while her mother died giving birth to her stillborn brother. By the time she returned home six weeks later, she found a father who'd lost his car dealership business, sold their home in affluent Toorak, and who'd become angry and lost in alcohol. Her childhood slipped away as she took over her mother's job, looking after the house and keeping out of Pa's way. Somehow, they'd settled into their uncomfortable roles.

"Besides, I already know everyone." She put her cup down and eyed him. "Did you know parents or chaperones have to come?"

He pulled his gaze from the paper, his spectacles low on his nose, and frowned. "Are Bethany's parents going?" His hand shook as he picked up his cup.

"Yes." She gnawed on a hangnail to free it. "But I'm not going."

She had nothing to wear and little money to buy anything. It was all very well for her best friend, Bethany; her parents were rich. Lucille had never invited her friend to their derelict house in Port Melbourne, and whenever the subject came up, she made excuses. The simple fact was Lucille was ashamed of her father and how they lived.

"Then I'll be going with you!" Pa declared, grinning. "Get yourself something nice to wear, and I'll buy a new suit. You'll be the belle of the ball. You're going and that's final." He put the newspaper down looking pleased with himself.

There it was again in the pit of her stomach – hope – like a dog wagging its tail waiting for food. There were times when her father showed he cared, like now, but just as suddenly, he loved the bottle more, leaving a crushing despair and resentment to wedge itself further inside her.

"I'm not going," she said, inching her chair back. "I haven't anything to wear."

He reached into his trouser pocket and pulled out a one-pound note. "Do you think you can get something with that?" He pushed it across the table as if it were small change and he had money to spare.

"What about the rent?"

He ran his hand through his thinning hair, the elated smile

evaporating before one last burst of enthusiasm. "Hell, I'll work overtime. Now, you're going and that's final."

Commission was the life-line in a used-car sales yard, not overtime. She'd worked odd jobs after school in the local milk bar to help out, but the work was irregular. When she'd reluctantly suggested she get a fulltime job, Pa had been adamant that she stay at school and finish. It was her mother's dying wish.

He reached for a beer from the icebox. It was only nine in the morning. There'd be no more coherent conversation for the rest of Sunday, so she pocketed the money.

The following week, she went to the city to shop for a dress to wear. She found what she needed in a thrift store – years of being frugal with a meagre housekeeping budget had taught her to economise. She would go to the ball after all – Bethany had been even more persuasive than Pa.

Lucille ran through the drizzle to catch the tram in Collins Street, cursing herself for not bringing an umbrella. She'd almost reached the tram when her heel slid on the track and she fell. As she wiped dirt from her hands, people gathered around her. Certain her face had turned a bright red, she lowered her head, completely embarrassed.

"Are you all right?" a softly-spoken man asked, his voice buttery and warm.

"Yes," she said, brushing herself down. "I think so."

Her head began spinning and she moaned. The man, holding her elbow, led her to a bench on the footpath. Her shoe, parcels, handbag and hat appeared on the bench beside her. Her stomach swirled, and she closed her eyes.

Forgetting herself, she lifted her skirt. "Oh dear!" Dirt and stones were embedded in her knee. "I'm bleeding."

"Should we call a doctor?" someone said.

Staring at the blood oozing through her only pair of good silk stockings made her dizzy, and she felt herself sliding off the bench. Strong hands gripped her before she hit the gutter.

"Poor lass," she heard through the haze of noises.

Once she was comfortably seated, a hand gently pressed on the back of her head. "Now just lean over. A bit more." The man's voice calmed her. With her elbows on her knees, she obeyed, watching the blood seeping slowly down her leg. She promptly threw up splattering some on the man's shoes as well as her own.

"Strewth!" he said.

She was horrified.

"Just keep ya' head down love."

"How awful for her."

"That's right, girl. Get it all out. It's just the shock. She fell over pretty hard."

"Did you see it?"

"Yeah. A car just missed the lass."

"She just has to sit tight for a minute or two, then she'll be right as rain soon enough."

Lucille closed her eyes, too embarrassed to face the voices.

"It's all right. I'll look after her." The man sounded genuine, comforting.

"If you're sure," a woman said.

"Gawd, I'm gunna be late," another man said. "C'mon. She'll be right."

Lucille stared at the ground, her cheeks burning. Some of that morning's toast lay in congealed lumps.

"Here you go. Just have a sip of this."

She gulped the water from the glass thrust in front her, wondering where it had come from. "Thanks," she murmured.

A freshly laundered white handkerchief materialised, and she patted her lips and wiped her hand.

"Ah, thank you. I'm feeling much better," she said, wishing everyone would go away, before she lowered her head again.

"Does she wanna 'nother drink?"

She shook her head, and someone took the empty glass from her. She pulled her skirt down below her knees, the blood already drying.

"Are you feeling a bit better?" the man asked, hopefully.

She nodded, wondering about the voice. It sounded familiar, and she tried to remember where she'd heard it.

"What's your name?" he said.

"Lucille." She finally raised her head and looked at him. The eyes and mouth were the same. His hair, dark brown, was slicked smooth except for the indent from the hat he'd removed. "Max?"

He looked confused. "Yes." His brown eyes squinted at her. "I'm sorry. I've been away, so forgive me if I can't ..."

His eyes widened as he looked at her, closely. "Lucille? Of course. You're all grown up. Well, I'll be."

"Yes," she said, managing a smile.

He beamed. "Back on the farm?"

"My first day with Aunt Mavis. You saved me from your attacking geese. I was terrified."

He nodded. "I remember."

She had stayed with Aunt Mavis, Pa's oldest sister. And Max, her cousin did save her, in more ways than he knew. He'd been home for the university holidays and looked after her in the weeks following her mother's death. She'd been almost ten and he, seventeen or eighteen. She'd trailed after him, sunk her hands into mud while digging for worms, then with his help, hooked them, still wriggling, onto her own fishing line. She'd squealed when the yabby she caught jumped back into the dam's murky brown water. They'd hidden behind a bush to watch a cheeky joey jumping away from its mother. Holding his hand tightly, she'd stood frozen as a brown snake slithered slowly away. When there was work to be done, she handed him nails while he fixed the barbwire fences. He'd told her stories, giving names to the trees, the sheep and the roos and showed her where his favourite wombat lived.

And when she'd returned home, she prayed Max would come. All those years ago. She'd missed him terribly. What were the chances she'd run into her cousin now, her idol from when she was a child?

"I'm sorry I lost contact with you. It must have been hard for you and your dad. How have you been getting on?"

She nodded. "Fine. Just fine." She lowered her eyes. "Oh dear, I've ruined your shoes."

"It's only a splash. I've had worse things. Remember, I grew up on a farm." He smiled again, and she remembered the dimples on either side of his face.

"Thanks."

He took the handkerchief she held, wiped his shoes, then threw it in a nearby bin.

"There. I've got plenty of others. Can you sit up a bit so I can take a good look at you?"

All she wanted was to go home.

He put his hand gently under her chin, turned it towards him and studied her face. "How do you feel?"

She nodded, blinking from the glare of the sunlight. "I feel better."

"I'll get a taxi, and we'll get you home. Okay?"

She nodded, suppressing her nauseousness.

He was more handsome than she remembered, slim-framed and even taller. He must be about twenty-five now, she thought. He held up his hand with authority and self-assurance, whistling for a taxi. Glancing around, Lucille was relieved not to be the centre of attention anymore and slipped her damp stockinged foot into her shoe, trying not to think about the splash of vomit.

A taxi pulled up and Max opened the door. "Dear girl, your carriage awaits."

She glanced at him and murmured, "Thank you." Then she slid onto the bench seat as he gathered her parcels and placed them in the boot. Before she had a chance to think, he was in the seat beside her.

"You've done enough," she said meekly. "You don't have to come with me."

"Where to, Miss?" the driver said.

"Um, Pickford Street, Port Melbourne please," she said. "I'm feeling much better, really."

"Nonsense! I'll make sure you get home in one piece. Goodness, what would your father say?"

She bit her bottom lip. It was after four, so he'd probably be at the pub or at home drinking.

"Now just roll down the window just in case you feel the need to … ah …"

"Yes," she said, quickly opening the window, her face burning again with shame.

Max had raised his eyebrows when she'd told the taxi driver the destination, so it seemed that Pa hadn't told anyone, especially Aunt Mavis, that they'd moved. Lucille lay her head on the back of the seat, closed her eyes and welcomed the cool rush of air.

With few visitors since Ma died, she and Pa had become friendless and alone. Pa had lost many jobs, and they'd moved countless times over the years, yet somehow, they'd survived. He'd vowed to stop drinking dozens of times but never did. At least he'd held onto a job for the last twelve months.

How could she stop Max from seeing the way they lived?

What if he insisted on coming in to see Pa? She wasn't sure what state Pa would be in, but she frantically hoped he might not be home. Perhaps if she just ran from the taxi? And then there was the matter of how to pay the driver.

"A day out in the city?" the driver said.

"Just a few things I had to attend to," Max said. "Is that an English accent, I detect?"

Lucille listened.

"It is indeed," the taxi driver said. "All the way from Camden."

"I've just returned from England."

"You don't say? How long were you there?" The driver stopped at the lights and turned his head. Lucille opened one eye then closed it. Max rested his arm on the back of the seat.

"About five years. I went there to study."

"I came out here just after the war in '19." The driver accelerated. "Where'd you study?"

"Oxford."

"My sister lives just outside of Oxford. Let me guess? I reckon you studied medicine."

"Chemistry."

"Oh," the taxi driver said.

A truck roared past, belching fumes through the open window.

"Looks like your wife has been taking in the sales," the driver said after a while. "Is she okay back there? Bit too much for her, I expect."

Lucille's eyes sprung open. "I'm not his wife!"

Max laughed. "She's my cousin."

Lucille sat upright and wound the window up.

"How are you feeling now?" Max said.

"Better, thank you." She clasped her clammy hands on her lap and peered past the driver to see how close to home they were.

"Thanks for your help, Max, but I feel terrible that I've dragged you away from your errands."

"I've finished, and it's the least I can do."

"Driver, can you drop me just at that next corner? I have to get a couple of things, and I can walk from there."

The driver slowed as they approached the corner milk bar.

"You're in no condition to walk," Max said. "Driver, please continue on."

"But I'm fine."

"You still look pale to me."

"Really, I'm all right."

"What number, Miss?" the driver said as they turned into the street.

"Fifteen," she muttered.

"What?"

"She said fifteen, mate."

Her heart beat wildly.

"Is that it?" Max said. "The yellow house?"

She stared straight ahead, not needing to see his face to tell he was surprised or maybe even shocked. The taxi pulled up in front of a weatherboard cottage, its paint peeling away from the window-sills as if even it couldn't stand to be there.

The letterbox on its stick leant towards the footpath as if trying to escape. The only thing that seemed content to live there were the weeds in what were once flower beds.

She quickly opened the car door before Max had a chance to get to it. Both men got out of the vehicle and stood at the boot – Max plucking out parcels, and the driver tucking his fare into his pocket before pulling out a cigarette.

"I can take them." Her hands grasped at the packages as if in a tug of war. "There really is no need for you to come in, Max."

"Nonsense," he said, clinging to her possessions. "I wouldn't dream of it. I'll come and say hello to your father. It would be terribly rude if I didn't. I'll just say hello, then go."

"You want me to wait then?" the driver asked, pulling a remaining package from the trunk, then holding it out for one of them to take.

"Yes, thanks." Max put the package under his arm, and with the rest of the bags in one hand, held Lucille's elbow and steered her to the door.

He must be noticing the cracked footpath, she thought. And the battered wooden door encased by a concrete barricade for a porch. It seemed like she was walking a gangplank.

She glanced at her watch. Four-thirty. Pa finished work at three. Please god, let him be at the pub.

She unlocked the door and opened it, hesitating on the doorstep before turning. The driver, leaning against the car, was still smoking his cigarette. A stale mustiness greeted her from the dark hallway.

"Unfortunately, Pa isn't home." She took the parcels from him, grateful that he let her. "It was good seeing you again."

"That's a pity."

"He works quite late sometimes," she said.

Max frowned. "Perhaps I could visit again at another time?"

"It's quite difficult to pin him down. Shift-work, you know. Well, thanks again. I mustn't keep you. I'll send you some money for the taxi. To Aunt Mavis's house?"

He frowned again and his eyes narrowed. "You haven't heard then?"

"Heard?"

"She died five years ago."

Her hand flew to her mouth. "I didn't know. I'm so sorry. She was wonderful to me after Ma died."

"I know. She was a great mum, and I still really miss her." He sighed.

She reached out and patted his arm, not knowing what to say. Then she glanced at the taxi driver who watched them while he smoked.

"Goodness, the taxi meter will be ticking away. You better go."

He ran his hand over his chin. "Yes. Yes of course. It was good seeing you."

"Thanks again for your help," she said.

Minutes after the taxi disappeared, she heard her father's familiar slurred singing and tensed.

4

QUIN

JUNE 1987

Quin fidgeted with her blouse to make sure it was still tucked into her skirt as she stood in the doorway to the kitchen. Nan and Ben were sitting at the kitchen table eating breakfast.

"Is there a cup of tea for me?" she asked.

They both looked up. "Sure, there is, love. Sit down. I'll get it for you. How about I pop a piece of bread in the toaster?" Nan said, putting down her cup.

"What did your last slave die of? She can get her own breakfast." Ben laid his hand on Nan's arm. "You finish yours."

"I just meant if there was any still left in the teapot." Quin reached into the cupboard for a cup and poured herself a tea. Not that she felt like it, but she thought it might settle her stomach.

Ben leant back in his chair and whistled. "Well, well, don't you look the executive in your new suit."

Quin stiffened and gave him a withering look. "It's what you're meant to wear." She smoothed her blazer over her skirt and checked the back of her pantyhose for snags.

Ben grinned. "So touchy."

"Don't mind him. You look perfect for your first day, darl," Nan said, her silver hair glimmering wet from the shower.

"Are ya nervous?" Ben, in blue overalls lifted a booted foot and rested it on the chair nearby as he bit into a piece of toast. His sun-bleached hair around his face reminded her of a shocked scarecrow.

"Ben, boot off the chair." He quickly moved his foot. "You're not, are you?" Nan asked, scrutinising her. "There's nothing to be worried about."

Quin's stomach churned and suddenly she couldn't face the tea, pushing it aside. "I'm okay. Do I look all right?"

"Waddya think?" Ben taunted. "Everything falls into the lap of the golden child."

"Why don't you just grow up? Aren't you running late for your dead-beat job as a shitkicker?"

Ben's eyes flickered with anger, and he flung a crust at her. Nan frowned.

Quin brushed the crumbs off her sleeve. "You're a ..."

She stopped herself. It had been a low blow. She knew how much he hated his job as a mechanic and would do anything to leave. But their grandfather had forced him to take the apprenticeship. "It's a good job," he'd said. "There's nothing else." A memory forced its way through – Ben feigning sickness and coming home early. It was only after her persistent needling that he confessed he'd worked on a truck that day, the same model and colour as the one that had struck their family car. Their parents were gone and their family had changed.

She bit her lip. Why couldn't she have shut up, today of all days, when she needed to be calm and prepared? She looked at them, waiting for his retaliation and Nan's admonishment. Neither happened, so she studied her sleeve where the toast had collided. Should she change? Again?

"Gotta be going. Break a leg," he said, without looking at her.

Nan put on her cardigan. "Come on then. You ready? I'll drive you to the station. Don't forget your lunch."

Quin took a deep breath, grabbed the paper bag and shoved it into her handbag.

*

The building loomed high above her. Eyeing the revolving door, she waited for the right beat to snatch her chance, like jumping through a skipping rope. Metal doors opened and closed capturing people like prey. A nervous glance at the tattered piece of paper again – Level 32. Then her watch – seven minutes to get to her new job.

What was a western suburbs girl like her doing in the financial hub of the city? Ben was right; she'd never fit in. She should have been a hairdresser. But she'd learnt from Ben's mistake. Touching the oily scalps of women, making inane conversation, wasn't for her.

After a couple of years working for a department store,

then a year of travelling, she'd worked for a bank in London and liked it. But Nan had said it was time to settle down, get a permanent job, find a nice boy, marry and give her some great-grandchildren. Quin agreed, only about the job. Banking was a good, solid career. Nan had seen the ad for a job at Solid Rock, a long-established building society. They were expanding and looking for staff.

And now she was riding the lift to a successful and prosperous career.

She wiped her sweaty hand on her new skirt. The doors opened at every level letting more people out until she was the only one left in the lift. She looked at her watch. One minute to go. Her floor was next. Her nerves tingled. She sniffed her underarms quickly, did the button up on her blazer, walked out of the lift and pushed through double-glass doors into a reception area with deep-purple couches and Australian landscape paintings. "Solid Rock Building Society" screamed for attention in large chrome lettering on the wall behind the receptionist – a thin woman called Debbie, according to the name plate on the black counter.

"I'm Quin Schmidt," she said. "And I'm here to see …" She fumbled, trying to open the piece of paper.

Debbie looked at her watch, her unsmiling face framed by a mass of blonde frizzy hair. "Yes, we've been expecting you."

Was the woman judging her? She was on time, wasn't she?

Debbie picked up her phone, told someone on the other end that a Quin Schmidt had arrived, then rose from her chair. "This way to Larry's office."

Quin followed her through a door into a large open-plan office. In stark contrast to the foyer, it was plainly decorated with several brown laminate desks in rows of three, behind which, sat men in a uniform of white shirts, wide ties and brown gabardine slacks. Their knowing glances seemed full of pity.

"At least, you're better to look at than Bruce." She turned to see the smirk under the dark, bushy moustache of a man who was walking out of an office, towards her. She assumed he was Larry. "You must be the new girl," he said, not looking at Quin's hovering hand. Ben had warned her that men wouldn't shake a woman's hand unless she offered it first. But he hadn't told her what to do when her hand was ignored.

"Yes, I'm Quin." Her hand fluttered back to the safety of her handbag strap as she followed the man, around the room, past the assembly line of desks, each adorned with an in-tray, out-tray, ashtray and telephone. Debbie disappeared. A dispirited-looking man glanced up and smiled before burying his gaze in a thick cream-coloured manila file. Others barely noticed her, too busy imploring the people on the other side of the phones to make a payment. The only other woman there, whose face was caked with make-up, fixed a stare at her.

"Okay, Quin. Here you go. This is where you'll sit," Larry said. "Next to Janie, my secretary."

"Janie, can you take Quin around and introduce her, and you know, show her where everything is? Quin, come and see me after you're done." He winked, then yelled, "Dave, bring me the Linden file," before marching into his office.

Janie smiled half-heartedly. "You're going to brighten up things around here," she said, raising her eyebrows as she checked out Quin's suit and bright-red polished nails.

Quin gave her a "happy to be here" smile, but Janie hardly noticed as she picked up her ringing phone. "Hello, Loans Department."

As she put her handbag under the desk, the smell of curried egg sandwiches wrapped in wax paper wafted into her nostrils. Quin quietly cursed Nan.

"Come on," Janie said, when she'd put the call through to someone. "Bring your handbag. I'll give you a locker."

Had she smelled the egg?

Janie was a chatterer, telling Quin that she was twenty-eight, engaged to be married, hated Larry the boss, was scared of the big boss, Tom, had worked in Loans Department for eight years and was glad there was another girl around besides the ones in the typing pool.

Quin's jaw was stiff from smiling so much. She remembered only one name, Dave, after the whirlwind of introductions to an array of staff, short and tall, straight and bent, and alert to the shrilling phones. Then she sat in Larry's office, forcing herself not to fidget, and waited for him to finish with Dave.

"Get her to make a payment today. Tell her if she doesn't, we'll come down there and take that bloody Ferrari off her so fast she won't know what's hit her."

"She said she would, boss," Dave said scratching his head, revealing a yellowing sweat stain under his arm.

"She says that every day. She knows you're a soft touch, mate."

"But boss …"

"Get out of my office and get it done!"

He thumped his hand on the desk. Quin jumped and Dave scurried out.

"Sorry about that, love. I'll be with you in a minute." Larry stood, walked to the doorway and yelled. "I want all phone calls done by ten. Don't go to tea until you've finished. Warren, get in here."

Quin smoothed her skirt as Larry sat behind his large wooden desk. There was nothing on it except a cream-coloured manila folder marked with her name. He opened it, picked up a piece of paper and read while she waited with clammy hands clasped on her lap. As she stifled a yawn, she hoped her gritty eyes weren't too red. She'd barely slept the night before, nervous about the new job.

Warren walked in with an armful of files clutched to his chest like armour and sat in the other vinyl chair.

Larry looked at her, ignoring Warren. "Right. You're a Loans Officer Category A, which means you'll be putting together deals for small businesses. You'll have a portfolio of clients, and most of all, you'll be expected to bring in some new business. Reckon you can do that?"

She stifled her surprise. "Ah, yes. I think so."

She thought the job was a loans assistant, helping with

administrative work, filing, and property searches. Did he say she had a portfolio of clients? What did she know about getting new business?

"Um," she said. "I …"

"You've met Warren already?"

She nodded and smiled at the slightly built man with sleeves rolled up and dark eyes darting around the room.

"Mate, I want you to take Quin under your wing and show her what to do." He looked back at Quin. "Waz is an expert and one of our best trainers."

They were going to train her. Relief.

"Okay boss." Warren put the files in the in-tray, stood and so did Quin.

"What's this then?" Larry said.

"These are the files for your sign-off."

"Not so fast, mate. Walk me through them. Tom'll be in later, and he'll want a full briefing on Pacific Development's loans."

"But he's at the funeral."

"He's driving back this afternoon, and he's got another deal."

"Jesus, even at his own dad's funeral he brings in business."

"He'd mortgage his own granny if he had one." Larry smirked.

Warren looked grim faced as he pulled out a thick file. "Quin, I'll be out in a minute. Why don't you get yourself settled at your desk?"

She nodded, relieved to escape. Janie had disappeared.

No-one seemed to notice her. She'd already explored the drawers — empty except for two ballpoint pens and a notebook, which she took out and began doodling paisley designs. How was she going to handle the job? Who was she kidding? She was out of her depth. She turned around to see if Warren was still in the office with Larry. But she couldn't tell from where she sat. Could she sneak out and disappear?

"Hello, I didn't meet you before. I'm Pete." She dropped the pen and closed the notebook, then looked up at the tall young man whose shirt hung on his thin frame.

Standing, she thrust her hand out. He stared at it, looking uncertain, then held her fingers as if they were a pair of stinking socks.

Quickly letting go, she smiled. "I'm Quin."

"Do you want to come down to the cafeteria for morning tea? A few of us are going early … got our calls done already." He straightened his black-rimmed glasses and pushed his hands into the pockets of his dark-brown slacks. His blue tie hung loose enough for her to see that the top button of his shirt was missing.

"Ah … I better not. I'm waiting for Warren."

"Waz? He's already gone down there with the boss."

"Oh, well I guess I could go," Quin said, looking around for someone to give her permission.

Janie walked back to her desk. "Do you think I should go to morning tea?"

"Yeah, I suppose you could." She seemed to be enjoying Quin's discomfort. "But …"

But what?

"Hang on, we're coming," Pete yelled. "Hold the lift."

She followed Pete, leaving Janie to pick up her ringing phone.

The smell of brewed coffee greeted them as they entered a large windowless room in the building's basement. Chatter from the fifty or so people seated at white tables bounced off the walls. While Quin and Pete waited in the queue for their tea, Pete pointed out the tables of staff and what departments they worked for.

Quin shuffled behind him in the queue, scanning the sea of unfamiliar faces, mostly men. The loans area, where she worked, the conveyancers, the valuers, the title custodians, the accounting and human resources departments. It was a large company of more than two hundred in the head office, according to Pete.

"Do you want anything to eat?" he asked.

"No thanks. I'm good." She couldn't very well tell him that she'd thrown up from nerves once already this morning. She couldn't risk eating anything just yet.

Pete grabbed the teas and a scone from the bench, put it all on a grey plastic tray and slid it along the metal counter. He took his wallet out of his back pocket. "Just one of the perks of working here. Isn't it, Mary? This is Quin, and it's her first day."

"Welcome." A plump woman in a navy uniform smiled from behind the register. "Tea's on the house for all first-dayers."

"Thank you," Quin said, smiling back, kicking herself for forgetting to bring her purse, yet relieved.

"How about we sit here?" Pete said. He put the tray on a table and pulled out a white plastic chair.

She nodded, trying to take everything in. Warren and Larry were nearby, deep in discussion.

"It's nice to get a few perks, like a subsidised cafeteria. Tom likes to keep us well fed," Pete said, buttering his scone.

"Janie mentioned him too. Who is he?"

"He's the boss and the owner. You'll meet him soon enough. He's pretty cutthroat when it comes to business, but he's fair with his people.

"Janie said he's terrifying."

Pete rolled his eyes. "He's demanding, that's all. He wants everything done yesterday, but he's got a vision for the business, and it'll go places with him. We're meant to be moving into a new building soon. It's going to be state of the art, and we're going to have our own computers too. Someone said the bathrooms will have gold-plated taps."

Quin picked up her cup. "Larry said Tom's at his father's funeral today."

"Yeah, his old man died last week. Heart attack, I think." Pete leant in closer. "Didn't even take any time off, just today for the funeral."

"He's coming back this afternoon."

"Shit. Is he? I've got a deal for one of his buddy's, and he'll expect it this afternoon."

"Should we get going?" She gulped the tea, scalding her tongue.

"Nah, we've got plenty of time. I haven't finished my cuppa yet."

"Do you like working here?"

His doe-like eyes rose from the scone plate. "It's good. I really enjoy it."

"And what's your job?"

"I put loan applications together for Waz. He's the approval officer for loans up to two mil. Then once it's approved, I organise everything from the documents through to the funding for the client."

"I think that's what I'll be doing too."

"Yeah, you've got Bruce's job. He left to join one of the big banks. I don't know why. I've worked for those guys, and you have to be old and grey before they'll promote you. I was a lead teller for four years until I was in a hold-up. After that, I left."

Quin put her hand over her mouth. "Oh my god! What happened?"

Pete ran his finger around the plate, finding the crumbs and pushing them into a pile.

"I'm sorry. You don't have to tell me."

His smile had come unstuck, and his lips tensed. He blinked large brown eyes, which seemed to see through her, and she immediately regretted saying anything.

"It's okay." He pulled at his collar and his Adams apple bobbed when he swallowed. "The bandit had a balaclava over his head and told everyone to get down. He got me to put all the money in a bag. It happened so fast. It was over almost as soon as it began."

He leant back. "Anyway, I left and got a job here and have had two promotions already. It's a progressive company, and Tom's great. He listens to new ideas and wants everyone involved in the business. We get bonuses, and so far, this year is looking really good. I reckon you'll like it here."

"And where's his office?"

"On Level 33, just above us."

At the nearby table, Warren was on his feet, pushing in his chair.

"I suppose we should get back," Quin said.

Pete drained his teacup. "We better."

They were quiet in the lift, and Quin's head was in a spin from everything she'd learnt that morning, or perhaps lack of sleep. Pete's arm brushed against hers in the crowded lift, and the hairs on her arm stood on end. As the lift rushed upwards, she tried to slow her breathing and control the rise of her stomach contents.

5

LUCILLE

1937

At first, Lucille didn't hear the knock. She was in the kitchen, clearing away the lunchtime dishes while Pa lay on the couch in the lounge room, listening to the wireless. The vegetable stew she'd made that day had burnt hard on the bottom of the pan. She'd scrubbed so vigorously her apron was damp from the splashes of water.

"Will you get that?" Pa yelled.

She caught a glimpse of her reflection in the kitchen window, her hair limp around her sweaty face, and grimaced.

"What's that?" she yelled back trying to budge the burnt-on food while Pa was drinking and singing along to the wireless. She glanced around the kitchen and groaned. The stove was smeared with stew from the ladle her unthinking father had let drip.

"Get the door. There's someone at the door."

She rolled her eyes and muttered under her breath. "There's

no-one there, you stupid old coot. We don't get visitors, ever."

"Are you getting the door? Maybe it's one of those kids after his ball? They're making a racket out there."

"For goodness sake," she muttered, wiping her hands. She thumped along the worn linoleum hallway towards the front door, poking her head into the lounge so Pa could see she was going. "Are you satisfied now?" she said under her breath.

She opened the door and reeled back when she saw who it was.

Max stood in front of her, smiling, the dimples on either side of his mouth on full display. "I'm glad you're home."

Lucille gaped, utterly flustered. "Yes." Her hands flew immediately to her hair to pin the loose strands.

"I told you," Pa yelled out. "Who is it?"

While she tried to compose herself, Max walked right past her and into the lounge room with their second-hand mismatched furniture.

"Hi, Uncle Clarry. It's only me, Max."

Lucille whisked off her apron and flung it into her bedroom on the opposite side of the hallway, before following Max into the lounge room.

Pa had got himself into an upright position on his bare feet. "Max? Mavis's son?" He shook Max's hand. "Well, I'll be."

A smile of recognition lit up Pa's face.

"How are you?" Max said. "It's been a while."

"Sit down, son. Lucy, get rid of those things." He pointed

at a pile of newspapers on the armchair and a couple of empty beer bottles on the floor.

She rushed to grab what she could, then went into the kitchen.

"I'm sure Max would like a cup of tea, love," Pa yelled out. "Pop on the kettle."

She clenched her teeth before pulling herself together, then gaily called out from the kitchen. "Won't be long, Father."

She stared at the pot in the sink happy to abandon it and put the kettle on. She found Ma's best cups and saucers, saved from when they'd sold almost everything. Not that they'd ever been used. They'd never had visitors, except for the debt collectors in the early days.

When she took the tray into the lounge room, the two men were happily chatting about England. Pa had been born there and had come out with his parents when he was ten.

She poured the tea and listened.

"Is the countryside still green and lush?" Pa asked.

"It's very beautiful."

"London could be awful though. The fog used to roll in at night, and it was so cold. Your mum and I would go to the country in spring, then to the seaside in summer."

Lucille stared at this man – her father – so wistful and almost normal. She said nothing and sipped her tea, watching them both.

"How is Mavis? I should have told her where we were. But we moved around a lot, didn't we love?"

Lucille nodded.

"It's been tough ever since the depression when we lost everything, but we pulled through. We're getting on our feet. Lucy's at one of the best schools now. Mac.Robertson Girls' High. Do you know it? Doing well, she is. Her mother always wanted her to have an education. She's as smart as a whip."

"Pa," Lucille said, her face burning.

"She's off to a ball next week. A girl of her age should have a coming-out ball."

He looked over at her and winked. She squirmed. Why was he telling Max all this?

"Your daughter has spirit and courage. I could tell that from when she was young. She was a tremendous help around the house with Mum, when she stayed with us. Even helped me mend a few fences too."

Why were they talking as if she weren't there?

"I was pleased to have run into her last week. All grown up now."

Pa and Max both looked at her, and she placed her teacup onto the side table.

"Yes. Max was kind enough to help me. I'd fallen over, and he helped me get home. I told you, remember?" She hadn't told him. He'd been on a bender, and it hadn't been important. Pa looked puzzled.

"That reminds me. What do I owe you for the taxi fare? We really should pay Max back."

She recognised the stiffening in Pa's neck as he bent to study a blood blister on his thumb.

"No, no, no. I wouldn't dream of it. It really wasn't much," Max said.

Pa lifted his eyes, relief spread across his face.

"Are you sure?" Lucille said.

"Yes, of course."

"To make up for it, you can come round for dinner one Sunday. My girl's a great little cook."

"I'd like that. Thank you." Max looked at Lucille.

"Of course," she said, wishing her father would stop talking. "And what brings you back from London?"

"I've just got a new job at CSIR," Max said. "It stands for Commonwealth Scientific and Industrial Research. You might not have heard of it, although it's been around for more than thirty years. I'm a chemist there. Or will be from next week."

"Well, son, that calls for a celebration. Lucy, get two glasses."

She began gathering the cups and saucers.

"Let me help." Max picked up the tray and followed her into the kitchen while her father searched for two glasses in the crystal cabinet, the only piece of Ma's furniture that hadn't been sold.

"Just put the tray there, on the sink," she said.

"That was a really nice cup of tea." Max smiled, and she admired how straight his teeth were. A lock of dark hair fell charmingly over his forehead.

"Thank you. I'm sorry we didn't have any biscuits to give you. And I'm sorry about Pa."

"Nothing to be sorry about." He ran his hand through his hair. "You haven't told him about Mum?"

"No. I couldn't."

"I better do it."

He turned and walked back into the lounge room. She followed and sat on the other armchair.

"Here you go. Whiskey?" Pa said.

"Yes, thanks."

"Straight all right?"

"Yes."

"Cheers. To your new job. A chemist in the family. It sounds important."

"I'm going to be doing some research to formulate a pesticide. They've been working on something like this in England for some time now. If we can use it effectively, we could double food production right around the world."

Lucille frowned. "How will pesticides double food production?"

"Well, if we kill the pests that eat or damage the crops, we'll have more crop to harvest," Max explained as if he were a teacher and she, a student.

"But doubling production isn't just about pests, is it? There are other things like drought and flood, which will have an impact on the crop outcome," Lucille said, thankful for her geography lesson the week before.

Max looked at her, raising his eyebrows, and her face burned. She'd been rude and should have kept quiet. It wasn't her place to speak out about a subject she knew nothing about. She was just a schoolgirl, and he was an important scientist.

"Of course. You're absolutely right. But if we can get this off the ground, it will have an enormous impact on our agriculture."

Pa raised his glass. "Well, that sounds like a noble and important thing to be doing, son. Here's to progress."

Max stared into his glass, the liquid barely touched, his knee jiggling. He cleared his throat. "Uncle Clarry, I tried to find you to let you know."

Pa looked confused. "Let me know what?"

Max sipped. "About Mum." His knee jiggled faster. "She passed away after a sudden stroke, just after the bank foreclosed on the farm."

Pa's face paled, and he leant forward, head in his hands, elbows cutting into his skinny legs. "When?" he said without looking up.

"About five years ago. I'm really sorry."

The sound of children laughing outside cut cruelly through the silence.

Pa rubbed his head then looked at Max.

"I'm sorry too, son. I should have been there for you … and for her." He heaved himself up and paced. "After Beatrice passed away and I lost the business, I was too busy feeling sorry for myself to care much about anyone." He stood in front of the flameless fireplace, placed his hands on the mantelpiece and looked down. "I've been a bad brother, uncle and father." He turned around, swayed slightly, then straightened. "But that's going to change. I'm going to get myself sorted out."

Lucille folded her arms, unmoved. He'd declared this many a night since Ma had died.

Max looked relieved. "Glad to hear it, Uncle Clarry. I'd be happy to help in any way I can."

"The farm. What happened to the farm?" Lucille asked.

"It was sold. The bank took most of it, and the little that was left over, I invested. Then I went to England. I was lucky and got a scholarship to study."

"Here's to your lucky break." Pa moved across the room, poured another whiskey and downed it. "You said you'd like to help? I was thinking. Maybe you can go to the ball next week with Lucy. Be her chaperone. I'm not up to going."

"Pa! I don't need a chaperone. It's not the 1920s, and besides, I'm not sure I want to go."

"You will be going. No daughter of mine is missing out. Your mother, god rest her soul, would be turning in her grave if she knew I hadn't done a good job."

He'd conveniently forgotten that he'd already done a lousy job. She was the one who kept the household going, stretched the budget, cleaned, cooked and looked after him and had done so since she was ten, but she said nothing.

"I'd be honoured to accompany Lucille." Max grinned and winked at her.

"That's settled then. Next Saturday at six o'clock you can pick her up. She deserves to spend time with some young people and get out of the house. You work too hard love, looking after me."

She was dismayed. Not because Max was lumbered with the job of her chaperone, but at what Pa had said. Did he really mean it? For years she'd hoped for his attention, his approval or even a word of praise. She closed her eyes, hoping her prayers would finally be answered – that she'd have a father who cared.

6

QUIN

AUGUST 1987

The view was so clear across the bay, from her desk, Quin could see a sailing regatta as she dialled her client's number. They'd moved into a brand-new building down the street the week before, and she was still getting used to the environment. She absent-mindedly tapped her blue pen on the open manila folder in front of her. It had been almost two months and every day at Solid Rock had been different. She had learnt quickly, getting to know each of her clients.

"Hello," a woman's voice said. "Jan Bellows speaking."

"Hi, Mrs Bellows. My name is Quin Schmidt, and I'm calling from Solid Rock Building Society. How are you today?"

"I'm okay. What happened to Bruce?"

"Um, he left. I'm looking after your account now."

"Right. So, what are you after?"

"I'm ringing about the outstanding balance of your

business overdraft, which is over the agreed limit. Are you expecting to put some funds into it today to clear it?"

"Ah, well I'll have to talk to my husband."

"As you are aware, there's no approval to overdraw your account, so unless you have the funds, we won't be able to honour the cheque of $2384.15 made out to Simpson Wholefoods. For your information, there'll also be an overdraft fee of twenty-five dollars, so you'll need to deposit for that today too."

There was silence on the other end of the phone.

"Mrs Bellows?"

"Look, can you give us a couple of days? We've had to pay our suppliers. They want their money in fourteen days and our clients are only paying in thirty. And some of them aren't paying on time."

"I'll need it cleared today, I'm afraid. There's not much I can do. If funds aren't in there by eleven am, the cheque won't be honoured."

"You people are unbelievable. When we need support, you don't help. All I want is a couple of days. If you bounce that cheque, we'll be in trouble. Have some heart for god's sake." She heard the woman sniff and her voice, completely miserable, lowered to a whisper. "Listen, my husband has a gambling problem and … well, I need you to understand. I'm trying to feed my kids, and I'll get the money, but I can't get it today."

"Oh," she said, thrown by the woman's plea. "Look, I'll see what I can do. Can you hold? I'll talk to my manager."

"Thank you. I'd appreciate that."

Quin walked over to the other side of the open-plan office and found Warren bent over a file.

"Have you got a sec, Warren? Mrs Bellows says she needs a couple more days."

He looked up wearily, then frowned. "Bellows Foodie account?"

She nodded.

Warren shook his head. "This happens all the time. The answer is no."

"But she told me her husband's a gambler, which must be awful, and she's doing everything she can to feed her kids and get the money, and that she's trying really hard …"

"Not our problem. It's no. The sooner you tell her, the sooner you can finish your calls."

"It's only for a couple of days."

Warren picked up his pen and opened another folder, his voice strained. "It's still a no."

Her stomach churned as she walked back to her desk. She took a deep breath to compose herself before picking up the receiver. "Mrs Bellows, I'm afraid we can't see our way clear to assist you and will require the funds to be deposited by eleven this morning. I'm sorry."

"You, Miss Schmidt are an evil, nasty human being with no heart."

"She hung up on me," Quin said to no-one in particular. She leant back in her chair dumbfounded and a little shaken.

"She's a cow."

Quin jumped. Warren was behind her.

"She's been doing this for years. She and her hubby live the high life, drain the account, then expect us to lend them the money to get out of it. Did she tell you she's waiting on clients to pay over thirty days?"

"Yes, she did."

"Think about it. They run a grocery store, it's a cash only business. She fed you bullshit because you're new. You gotta be tough with these jokers."

Quin nodded and wrote, *Not to be honoured* across the name of the account in red. She looked at the file and wondered if what Warren had said was true. But then he hadn't heard the desperation in the woman's voice. What if the woman was in real trouble? She read through the file. No, it was a pattern, as Warren had described. What a fool she'd been.

After she finished her calls, she picked up a new file from her in-tray. She had to review the loan to make sure the business was meeting its required repayments. The latest financial statement figures swam across the page. An expense of fifty thousand dollars was listed as miscellaneous on the profit and loss statement. Miscellaneous? What did that mean? Her head ached and she stretched. She'd done high school accountancy, but she was struggling to interpret financial statements on some of the files. Perhaps she should do a course.

"Do you have any qualifications?" she asked Pete one morning during their break.

"No. I did year eleven, then left school and joined the bank. But I'm doing an accountancy course, now and Solid Rock's paying for it."

"Has it helped?"

"Yeah, it has. Quite a lot actually. Why? Are you thinking about doing a course?"

"I think I'd like to do a course so I can make sense of the figures."

Pete grinned. "You gotta remember. They have a set of financials for us, another for the tax department and one for themselves. And none of them tell the same story."

She shook her head. "Why? It's crazy."

"The only real ones are theirs, but we never get to see them. Look, I'm happy to help you. Next time a set of financials doesn't make any sense, come and see me, and I'll check it over for you."

"Oh really? Thanks, Pete. That's so nice of you."

He gave her one of his gentle smiles. "Happy to help. And if you want to do a course, I'd recommend the one I'm doing. Two hours of lectures after work on Tuesdays and Thursdays. The mid-term intake starts next week. Put in an application. You'll get in for sure, and then apply for a bursary. Tom will approve it. He wants us to upskill. You get study and exam leave, and the cost of your books will be reimbursed."

She liked the idea of someone else paying for her to do a course "Thanks. I'll check it out."

She could see herself studying, climbing the corporate ladder, raking in the big bucks as Ben liked to say.

The following week, Quin enrolled in the two-year Diploma of Accounting course. The week after, she caught the tram with Pete for her first lecture. She was excited and nervous. It had been years since she'd studied, and part of her wondered if she'd like it, even if she could understand it. Ben had told her it was a stupid idea, telling her it was hard work, that she'd have no time for anything. She'd have to give up netball, and her weekends would no longer be free to see her friends. It wouldn't be for long. It'd be worth it, she told herself. She needed extra qualifications to advance her career.

They found a seat on the tram.

"Deb gave me a letter just as I was leaving. It's probably the bursary approval," she said, ripping open the envelope.

"That's good," Pete said. "Every bit helps. How about we meet afterwards for a bite to eat."

The words seemed to blur: *Your application for a bursary is declined.* She shoved the letter into her handbag and took a deep breath as they got off the tram. "Sorry, what did you say?"

"How about a meal after lectures?" Pete said, "Meet me here at eight?"

"Look I'm going home."

"What, why?"

"There's not much point doing a course I can't afford. I'll see you tomorrow."

He held her arm. "I don't follow."

"The bursary was declined."

"Declined? That's impossible. You must have missed something on your application. We'll talk to Larry. Apply again."

"What makes you think I stuffed up the application? I filled it out correctly. There's nothing you can do."

Pete frowned. "Sorry, I didn't mean …"

"It's very sweet of you to offer to help. It's all right." Quin glanced at her watch. "You better go, or you'll be late."

"Don't worry. You'll get that bursary. I'll help you."

"You're going to be late."

"Hey, before I forget. I'm going to a party tomorrow night after work. Some of the other guys are coming, Deb, Janie and I think Waz. Would you like to come too?"

Why was he being so nice? Was he trying to cheer her up? "I'm not sure."

"Come on. It'll be fun and might help to take your mind off things. Friday nights should be for going out and relaxing. You gotta live a little."

She hadn't any other plans. "I'll think about it."

"It'll be fun. I better go. I'll see you at work tomorrow."

She left him and crossed the street to wait for the return tram. She was more disappointed than she realised. What was the bursary worth anyway? It was a government funded course so there were no course fees, just books to pay for. Maybe she could borrow them. The tram was approaching. She could take annual leave for the exams if she had to. It stopped and the doors opened. She'd have a couple of days owing by then. The tram doors closed as she hitched her handbag over her shoulder and sprinted across the road and into class, only a couple of minutes late.

7

LUCILLE

1937

Lucille lifted the second-hand dress to her nose, satisfied the smell of the thrift store had been washed away. She slipped it over her head and looked in the mirror. The soft pink organza lifted in an arc around her feet when she twirled. Picking up her mother's green satin sash, she ran it through her hands, before tying it around her waist. Its silky softness, and how it matched the tiny green leaves embroidered on the bodice, delighted her, conjuring a memory of her mother dressing to go out. Ma had tied the same green sash into a bow around her small waist and together they stood in front of the mirror and twirled. Lucille sighed. How she wished her mother was here with her.

The low-heeled beige sandals she'd bought from the same thrift shop weren't the latest, but the dress was long enough to hide them. The whole outfit had been cheap. The money Pa had given her wasn't quite enough, but she'd saved the extra over time from leftover change from the housekeeping. She'd never taken much, just a ha'penny or threepence here and there in the years since Ma died. Pa was often so drunk he never noticed, so she'd squirrelled it away in a jar under her bed, in case she ever needed it.

She ran her hands down her dress and touched the sash again making sure it sat perfectly. Like Ma had done, she brushed her light brown hair one hundred times until it sat with a natural curl on top of her shoulders. She practised in the mirror what she'd learnt from novels. "Oh hello," she'd say, and gaily wave. "Yes, I'd love to dance." Then she'd smile. Could she pull it off?

*

She'd been nervous all week about the ball. The girls at school had been talking non-stop about what they were wearing, who would be there, how their hair should be done. They talked about the boys who were going. There was one in particular, Michael. She and Bethany had met him at the local cricket ground. He and his friend Patrick were still in their cricket whites, and Patrick, who was sweet on Bethany, introduced them. Michael seemed like a nice boy, and Lucille hoped to see him again.

Lucille jumped when she heard the knock at the door. Five-forty-five. Too early, yet Max's voice greeted Pa.

Pa seemed different since Max's visit. He'd been drinking less and worked more. He spoke little, but when he looked at her, he smiled as if to say how sorry he'd been. She prayed that his promise to stop drinking wouldn't be broken.

Hearing his laugh from the next room lightened her heart. She had her cousin to thank for that.

She would have preferred to go to Bethany's house to get ready and be driven by Bethany's father in his flash new car. Pa couldn't trust himself without a drink, so she was thankful he wasn't going. But now that Max had been forced on her as a chaperone, there was nothing she could do. How would she explain him to the others? She didn't know why the girls at school mattered. It wasn't as if she was particularly friendly with them. Unlike her, most of them came from well-to-do families. They weren't embarrassed by their parents like she was of her father.

She pinched her cheeks, licked her lips, then looked at herself full-length in the mirror before going into the lounge room.

Max, in a dark-blue suit and crisp white shirt, stood when she entered the room. He beamed. "Wow! I mean, you look really nice."

Pa gave a long low whistle. "You look wonderful, love, just beautiful. Give us a twirl."

The attention made her self-conscious. "We better go," she said. "The girls will be waiting." She turned abruptly, grabbed a shawl from her bedroom, then walked out of the front door. She stopped at the leaning letterbox, uncertain what to do next.

"Wait up a sec," Max said. "What's the hurry?"

"It starts soon, and I don't like to be late. We have to catch the bus and then the train." Suddenly she wondered how she was going to walk in the sandals, which were already pinching her toes.

"We're not catching a bus and a train."

She whirled around. "A taxi is too expensive, even if you do have a swanky new job."

He grinned. "We're not going in a taxi."

"Oh?"

He stepped around her to the footpath and opened the door of a gleaming royal-blue sedan. Why hadn't she noticed it? It was the most glamorous-looking car she'd seen since Pa had sold his in '29.

"Where did you get a car from?"

"I bought it. You're the first person to ride in it."

Pa had followed them out and stood admiring it. "You ended up getting the Riley. It's a beauty. Four cylinders?"

"Yep, second-hand. I thought you'd like it. It's almost like Dad's. Thanks again for sending me to Morrie."

Lucille settled herself in the front passenger seat, carefully pulling her long dress around her. Max closed the door, and when she rolled down the window, she admired the polished wooden trim.

"He's a top bloke. You picked up a good one. Pity we don't have any of those models in our yard. I haven't seen one for a long time. They reckon it can get thirty-five to the gallon."

"And up to ninety miles an hour."

Pa ran his hand over the hood. "Would you mind if I checked under the bonnet?"

"Pa! We're going to be late."

Pa lifted his hands off the bonnet as if it were hot and stepped back onto the footpath. "Another time. You better get going. Have fun."

"I should be home by eleven."

Pa nodded, and she wasn't sure if his wistful expression was for her or the car.

Lucille and Max didn't say much on the way. She wondered what she should do about him. She shot him a look. He had a strong jawline. He glanced at her, and she quickly looked away smoothing her dress. As they got closer to the ballroom, she had an idea.

"It's very nice of you to take me. And I know it's a bit of a nuisance for you to babysit."

"I'm happy to come. It's no bother at all."

"You'll be sitting on the sidelines with the other parents, which will be incredibly boring for you."

He frowned. "With the parents?"

"Yes. So, I have an idea. Why don't you drop me off, and you can go and do something you'd rather do? I'll get a ride home with my friend's father."

"Have you got a beau?"

"No! What gives you that idea?"

"You must have if you're trying to get rid of me."

"Well, I haven't! I don't know why you'd say that. I'm only thinking about you and giving you the opportunity to get out of this frightful ball. I don't see why you need to suffer."

Max laughed. "You really are funny. I think I'll take my chances and see what happens. After all, I imagine you might need protecting from all the lads who'll be asking you to dance."

Her face burned. "I won't be dancing with anyone."

"If you say so," he said smiling. "I promised your father I'd look out for you, and that's what I'm going to do."

She folded her arms and looked out of the window, worried. Why would she need protecting? Surely, he wouldn't stop Michael from dancing with her?

When they arrived, she pulled her shawl around her shoulders while Max opened the door for her. Some of her school friends were standing near the building entrance. As Max took her arm, they stared at him, then at the car, and for a moment her confidence soared.

Approaching, she smiled at the girls. "Oh, hello there."

Bethany pushed her way through the group. Wearing a silver clip that swept her dark hair to one side, her emerald-green satin dress glimmered.

"You look amazing," Lucille said.

"So do you. Like Ginger Rogers with brown hair."

"Do I?" Lucille said, smiling.

Max cleared his throat and Lucille introduced him.

"Come on. We better go in. Father and Mother are already inside."

The ballroom was teeming with people, and Lucille soon became separated from Bethany. The boys, mostly from Melbourne Boy's High, looked smart in their suits. Lucille wondered where Michael was. After introducing Max to Bethany's parents, she went off in search of her friend.

Lucille was soon surrounded by a group of girls who usually thought themselves too good for someone like her.

Liz grabbed her arm. "Who did you bring, Lucy? He's gorgeous."

Vivian smirked. "You sly thing. I saw you come in that car."

"How on earth did you snag him? An older man too."

Lucille decided to say nothing and instead smiled, leaving the group with their mouths open. She was beginning to enjoy herself.

When she found her, Bethany was breathless. "God, you've created a stir."

"Why?"

"You know why. Max. They all think he's your date. You have to admit it. He's very handsome."

"He's a bore. My father, who should have been here, forced him to come instead. He's my chaperone. I'm going to tell him to go. Look at him standing there with that stupid grin on his face. It's embarrassing."

"What's embarrassing is having *both* your mother and father at your first ball." Bethany clapped her hand across her mouth. "Sorry, I mean, I didn't mean that the way it sounded."

"It's fine."

"Look at Loopy Liz and the others, ogling him. Has he got a girlfriend?"

"I've no idea. He's only been back in the country for a couple of weeks."

"Where does he live?"

"Does it matter?"

Bethany shrugged. "Take a look at Mrs Plumpton. What's she got on her head? It looks like a strangled bird."

Lucille wasn't listening. Liz was standing next to Max, deep in conversation. She wasn't sure why it bothered her.

The music started up and David, whom she knew vaguely, stood in front of her and asked her to dance. She was too distracted staring at Max to say no and found herself on the dance floor. Bethany was dancing with a boy she didn't know. Lucille caught her eye and grinned when Bethany grimaced.

Then she noticed Max dancing with Liz. She was sure there was a rule that chaperones couldn't dance with students. Yet there he was. The dance ended, and David mumbled something as he led her off the floor. She started to make her way across to Max to tell him about the rule, when Michael asked her to dance.

On the dancefloor, she noticed Max talking to Bethany's parents, so she relaxed, turning her attention to Michael.

"You look nice, Lucy."

"Thanks, so do you," she blurted, then couldn't think of anything else to say. Luckily, he was too busy concentrating on his steps to the waltz.

"Ouch!"

"Sorry," he said.

"That's all right. It didn't hurt," she lied. The balls of her feet ached, and her left little toe stung from where Michael had stood on it.

"Isn't the band good?"

"Yes. They are."

His hand was sweaty in hers.

"I really like this song," Lucille said.

"I haven't heard it before. What's it called?"

His hand felt damp against her back.

"Uh, not too sure."

Flecks of dandruff sat on his shoulder, and she couldn't wait for the song to end. What had she seen in him?

"Thanks for the dance. I'll just go and get a drink," she said.

"Good idea. I'll get one too."

He followed her, and before they left the dancefloor, she felt a tap on her shoulder. Max.

"How about a dance?"

"Oh … yes … I suppose." She smiled apologetically at Michael. "Sorry."

Max slid one arm around her waist, held her hand gently and pulled her close. He smelled pleasantly of soap.

"You're a good dancer," she said.

"Thanks. Mum would be proud to hear you say that."

The song was "They Can't Take That Away from Me" by Fred Astaire and she was swept along with the music. It was wonderful. Some of the other girls stared from the sidelines at them. Then she caught sight of Michael gawking. He's just a boy not a grown man like Max, she thought.

After the third dance, he stopped. "I better let you dance with someone else."

"Yes. I suppose so." She didn't want to dance with anyone else. She wanted only to dance with Max. She found Bethany getting a drink from the punch bowl and feigned interest in what her friend was telling her. Every now and again, she glanced over and met Max's eyes. He smiled and nodded as if urging her to have a good time.

The band started up and Michael stood in front of her, wiping his hands down his trousers. "How about it?"

She nodded, reluctantly.

8

QUIN

AUGUST 1987

It was unseasonably warm for a Melbourne winter's day. Quin regretted coming as soon as she stepped through the gate of the little Victorian terrace booming with music. She should have stayed home, curled up on the couch in her pyjamas and slippers to watch an old movie with Nan.

Greeted with loud music, she hesitated at the open front door then hitched up her black halter-neck top and peered into a long corridor filled with people she didn't know. She squeezed herself past a barrel of a man to peer into the packed front room, hoping Pete was in there. The air was heavy with cigarette smoke and she sighed. Her freshly washed hair and clothes would stink.

"Quin! Over here."

She squinted in the dim light. Deb was standing in front of an unlit open fireplace. Quin waved and pushed her way through.

"You scrub up well," Deb said, waving a can of rum and coke.

"Thanks, so do you."

The compliments between them were hardly sincere. Quin's blonde hair was limp without a twist of a curl and perhaps she should have made more effort than just mascara and lip balm. But she only came because Pete had been so insistent. Deb's heavily made-up face was almost dwarfed under a mountain of blonde frizzy hair.

The music stopped. Perhaps she could stay for one drink, then go.

Deb nodded at the woman next to her, who looked almost breakable she was so thin. Her arms were covered with long white lace gloves, and her bright-blue eyeshadow made the black circles under her eyes stand out. "This is Quin. She's new at Solid Rock. And this is Dimi, she used to work there."

"Hi," Quin said, tucking her hands into her jean's pockets. She tried not to stare at Dimi's wild black curly hair, which seemed to stand out in all directions.

Dimi nodded. "Nice earrings. You one of the typists?"

Quin lifted a hand to touch her large gold hooped earrings. "No, a loans manager."

They regarded each other. Everything about Dimi seemed hard, even the lines running around her mouth. "Breaking through outta the typing pool?" Dimi said with a sneer.

Quin wasn't sure what the comment meant but left it. Instead, she turned to Deb. "We haven't seen you much since your promotion. What's it like working for Tom?"

Deb's eyes flickered nervously to Dimi, then back to Quin. "It's okay. Same shit, different boss."

Dimi's eyebrows shot up. "*You're* his secretary?" Dimi folded her arms. "How come ya didn't tell me you're working for the scumbag?"

Deb shrugged and fumbled in her handbag, probably to avoid looking at Dimi. "Didn't think you'd want to know." She kept searching for something in her bag.

Quin didn't know what to make of Dimi but was sure Deb was being careful around her.

"What did you do at Solid Rock?" Quin asked.

Deb stopped rummaging and her head jerked up. Quin caught the frown and the slight head shake, too late.

Dimi narrowed her eyes as if weighing up what she should say. "What does it matter? I'm happy where I am now." Then Dimi leant in close to Quin. "Just watch your arse is all I can say, especially from—"

The song "Smoke on the Water" by Deep Purple started up so loudly Quin didn't catch the last part of what Dimi said. There was an awkward pause between the trio, Deb still rifling through her large bag with Dimi looking pissed off.

"I'll go get a drink, I think, and see where Pete is," Quin yelled over the music.

"Drinks in ice-buckets, out the back." Deb drained her can. "Bring me one too? Rum and coke."

"Sure," Quin said. She turned to Dimi, who'd turned sullen. "You want one too?"

"Nup."

After fighting her way through the crowded, smoke-filled corridor, Quin found the back door and a concreted courtyard filled with people. Locating a couple of bins filled with ice and drinks, she bent, selected a can of beer and a can of rum and coke. A hand tapped her bare back.

"Would you mind grabbing a VB?"

She found another one in the ice before she turned to see Pete, pushing up his glasses, grinning. "Glad you came." His white shirt and blue jeans sat on him comfortably.

"Here you go then," she said, giving him the can.

He smiled his thanks, pulling off the ring-top before flicking it into an empty box nearby.

"For Deb," she said, explaining the two cans in her hands.

"She's here?" His eyes travelled across her cleavage.

She nodded. "In the front room."

The pounding beat of Madonna's "Papa Don't Preach" came on. "Great song, better than that heavy metal shit," he said. He moved closer, not quite touching, and swayed to the music.

"Yes, I love it too." Still holding the drinks, she closed her eyes and moved in rhythm with him.

The song ended, and the way he looked at her gave her goosebumps.

"I better get this to Deb. I'll be right back," she said.

He held up his can and winked. "I'll be here. It's too stinking hot in there."

She pushed her way through the crowd.

"Is that for me, darlin'?" A bulk of a man blocked the corridor. "Allow me to introduce myself. Kevin's the name."

He moved closer, trapping her against the wall. The bass thumped through her body. Another Madonna song, "Like a Virgin".

"It's for a friend," she yelled, glad of an excuse to get away.

Kevin, in low-slung acid-wash jeans and a black t-shirt rested a muscled arm on the wall next to her head. He leant in closer, his beery breath hot against her ear. "What did you say your name was?"

"I didn't say."

"Come on now." He pressed his body against her. "Don't be like that. How about we go into the bedroom?"

"How about you fuck off?"

He stepped back and she twisted away from him, pushing through the crush until she found Deb. Quin handed her the can. "That was like running a marathon."

Deb snorted. "Why'd you think I sent you? I wasn't going to fight the lechers for a drink when you were going."

"Thanks a lot." Quin pulled the ring-top on her can, sipped, then rested it against her chest to cool down.

"Are there any cute-looking guys out there?" Dimi asked.

"I didn't notice," Quin said, sipping her beer. "There's a few dickheads though."

Deb plucked out a cigarette.

"I didn't know you smoked," Quin said.

"Honey, there's a lot you don't know."

Deb offered the packet to Dimi who took one. Quin shook her head.

"Did you find Pete?" Deb asked.

"Yeah, he's in the courtyard. He's the one who asked me to come."

Deb raised her eyebrows. "Did he now? I think he likes you. Watch out for that one."

"Watch out for what?"

Dimi sniggered.

Deb leant over, her breath reeking of smoke. "Let's just say he's had quite a few girlfriends, and it never ends too well. Besides, going out with work colleagues will always end up being messy. You know what I'm saying?" She leant back and dragged on the cigarette.

"We're just friends," Quin said.

She had no intention of telling Deb what she thought of Pete. He was nice, they got along, and if something developed, well, she wouldn't mind. She also knew secretaries were the source of all information and gossip in an organisation, and although she liked Deb, she'd be careful what she said.

"I've seen you at morning tea," Deb teased. Elbowing Dimi, she winked. "They're very chummy."

"Just friends, Deb. Don't read anything into it." It suddenly felt oppressive. "I think I'll go outside and get some air."

Deb laughed. "Yeah, you go back to Pete. Tell him we'll see him later."

Quin opened her mouth to say something and instead smiled.

She found Pete in deep discussion with someone she didn't know.

"Sorry. Don't mind me," she said. Pete stopped talking, turned to her and smiled.

"I'm glad you're back. Quin, this is Eric. Eric, Quin."

The man stared at her, clutching a beer can in one hand and a cigar in the other, which showed off a thick gold wedding band. He looked ridiculous with a cowboy hat on his head.

"Quin works at Solid Rock too."

Eric smiled, tapping cigar ash onto the concrete. "G'day."

"We were just talking about Solid Rock's loan rates. Eric's a property developer looking to do expansion out in the northern suburbs. He thought he might give Solid Rock a go."

Eric's eyes bored into her. "Enough business talk in front of this beautiful lady."

"And what suburb are you thinking of?" She hid her irritation and smiled.

"A place called Greenvale. But you wouldn't have heard of it yet," Eric said.

"It's farmland on the outskirts of Melbourne, but it's going to be a suburb after Eric finishes with it," Pete said.

"There'd be a lot of acreage out there," she said.

"I guess you pick up a lot of info when you type up all those loan applications?" Eric blew a smoke ring.

"Quin's actually a very capable loans manager in our office," Pete said.

It was nice of Pete to say she was capable. She was pleased how well she'd done in a couple of months and had even brought in a new client – her brother's boss who owned a car repair business. Warren had been ecstatic, although Larry had only been mildly pleased.

Eric's expression didn't change. The creep wouldn't take his eyes off her, and she shifted about on her feet wondering how she could diplomatically get away.

"How about you rustle up another drink for me, Pete?' he said. "We'll talk business on Monday."

Pete looked flustered. "Yeah, Monday. I can take a formal application."

"I'll get it. You keep talking," Quin said. She hoped she hadn't ruined Pete's chance to get the deal.

"It's okay. I'll get it. You got the last one," Pete said. "Another beer? Quin what about you?"

She shook her head.

"VB thanks, mate," Eric said, his voice smooth. "I'll keep Quin company."

She watched Pete as he walked away so she could avoid eye contact with Eric.

Then suddenly, she felt his breath, hot on her neck. "Now, Quin. That's an unusual name."

"Yes, it is," she said, edging away from him. "A family name."

How many times had she been asked about her name,

her great-grandmother's surname? An early feminist, great-grandmother had decided her surname should be passed down to her daughter, who took it as a second name. Quin's grandmother had then passed it onto Quin's mother, who had taken the next step and named her daughter Quin. She doubted this leering man standing too close would be interested anyway.

He leant in again, then jerked his head towards Pete. "He your boyfriend?"

"We're work colleagues."

He touched her bare shoulder with his thumb. "That's good."

What did he mean "good"? He was towering over her, inching closer.

"You're very pretty to be working for a building society." He ran his fingers down her arm brushing her breast and lingering. "Perhaps you'd like to talk to me about my developments."

"Do you mind?" she said, taking a step backwards and searching the crowd for Pete. First Kevin and now this sleaze. It was time to go.

"Relax." He sucked on the cigar, then blew a smoke ring over her and laughed. "That almost went right over you." He lifted both hands and skirted her body from top to bottom to illustrate what he'd wanted the smoke to do.

"Yeah well, I'll leave you to Pete."

She turned away from him, threw her half-full can into

a nearby box of empties and pushed her way through the crowd. She caught sight of Pete who raised his eyebrows.

She mouthed that she was leaving.

He mouthed, "Wait," and headed towards her. "Why are you going?"

"I'm tired."

"You're not mad about what Eric said are you? He's old school that's all, but he's harmless."

"Eric may be married, but he is anything but harmless."

His eyes widened. "What did he do?" She looked at his hand on her arm, and he let her go. "Did he do something?"

"I wasn't about to find out. Anyway, thanks for asking me to come. I'll see you on Monday."

She pushed her way through the corridor, wondering where the phone was so she could call a taxi. She asked a couple of people and eventually found a phone in the kitchen, dialled, then fought her way back to the front door. Music was blaring Joy Division's "Love will Tear Us Apart". When she glanced in the front room, Deb was slow dancing with Kevin. Perhaps he was her type.

She stepped outside into the cool.

"Quin. Quin, wait."

She turned to see Pete looking hot and flustered.

"Phew, I'm glad I caught you. God, it's bloody hot in there. I'm coming with you. If that's okay?"

"I'm going home."

"Yeah, I figured you might like some company, and I'd like

to share the ride too." He grinned. "Share the cost. Is that all right?"

"Sure," she said. "If you like."

The taxi arrived. "Flinders Street train station," she said.

The driver pulled out, leaving the sound of the music pulsing behind them.

"Are you catching the train home?" Pete said.

She nodded. Her ears were ringing.

"It's not safe. I'll come with you."

"I'll be fine, really."

"I'm sorry about what happened."

She felt his eyes on her in the dark. "It's no big deal."

"It's a big deal to me. Getting Eric's business isn't worth it if he can't treat people properly."

She met his eyes. "So, you'd give up a multi-million-dollar deal and the huge bonus?"

"Ah … well," Pete stuttered. "I would."

"Because he's not nice?"

"Yeah. I would."

"Bullshit," she said.

He sat up straight. "Bullshit?"

She regretted trapping him when she saw his crestfallen face. She reached over and touched his hand.

"I'm playing with you. I'm a big girl and can take care of myself. It's all right. Business and pleasure shouldn't mix. See him on Monday, get the deal and screw him down. The more loans we bring in, the better the bonus for all of us. Isn't that right?" She quoted the line Larry repeated every week, and they both laughed.

"Hey, I met Dimi. Do you know her? She worked for Solid Rock."

"Yeah. She left under suspicious circumstances."

"Really?"

"She was Tom's secretary. They say she was after him, and when he turned her down, she got a bit vengeful. She ended up resigning."

She frowned. "That's an interesting story."

"Well, that's what I heard from Larry. Although the girls in the typing pool reckon it was the other way round. But I'm pretty sure Tom's not like that. He goes out with super models and actresses.

"Mmm." Quin pondered. "Don't you think the girls would know?"

"Dunno. I suppose. But then Dimi might have made up a story."

They pulled up at Flinders Street and Pete paid the driver before she had a chance to get out her purse.

"How much?" she said, getting out of the taxi.

"Hardly anything."

"Pete!"

"You can buy me morning tea on Monday," he said grinning stupidly. "What line are you on? I'll come with you."

"Werribee. I live in Werribee." She turned to him. "Where do you live?"

He looked stunned. It was a good hour and half, there and back. "Brunswick."

"In the opposite direction. It's ridiculous for you to come with me. I'll be fine. Nan will pick me up from the station."

She pecked him on the cheek. "Thanks, anyway. It was a sweet offer."

They looked at each other. He put his arms around her, to hug her goodbye she thought. His strong arms lingered. And then they were kissing.

She finally pulled away, breathless; he was a great kisser. "That was a surprise," she said. He grinned as he leant in again, but Quin glanced up at the train times. "Shit. I've got to go. The last train leaves in five minutes." She turned and sprinted.

"Okay then," he called out. "See you Monday."

9

LUCILLE

1937

Saturday. Next-door's dog yapped constantly as Lucille read the same passage in her textbook over and over, trying to force the words into her brain. Pa's footsteps padded down the hall, past her bedroom to the front door.

She froze when she heard the voice; she hadn't heard a knock.

"Come in, come in," Pa said. "Lucy! Max is here. Get the kettle on."

She jumped off the bed, glanced in the mirror and swept her hair into a bun. Her floral housedress would have to do. She snuck into the kitchen and put the kettle on the stove before she presented herself in the lounge room.

Naturally, Max had been the topic of conversation at school the previous Monday and Lucille had been bombarded with questions: Where did he live? How old was he? What did he do? Some girls were more direct, asking when he was coming to her house and could they come over. She'd shrugged them off and tried to concentrate on her studies. Exams were only weeks away. Surely, it was just a schoolgirl crush? *He's my cousin for god's sake,* she told herself.

"Hello," she said, shyly.

"G'day," Max said, standing and smiling. "Hope I'm not disturbing you?"

She had to admit she'd give up study to see him again. "It's okay. I needed a break."

The kettle whistled. She stood unmoving, noticing the upturned corner of his collar. She quashed the urge to walk over and fix it.

"The kettle's done," Pa said, staring at her.

She tore her eyes away from Max, then looked at Pa and nodded before returning to the kitchen to make the tea and bring back a tray.

"Your daughter is quite a good dancer," Max said, taking the teacup from her and leaning back in the armchair.

Pa laughed. "She won't be getting it from me."

"We have dancing lessons at school," Lucille said quietly, settling into the armchair opposite Max.

Pa shifted in his seat and cleared his throat. "Did you bring your car? Didn't get much of a chance to take a good look at it last week."

"I did." Max jerked his head in the direction of the street. "I remember Mum told me that you'd actually built a car yourself. Is that right? Wasn't it one of the first to use petrol?"

This was news to Lucille. Was her father not just a used-car salesman?

Pa looked pleased. "Yep. It was 1912, and I don't know how I drove the thing across the Nullarbor to Perth. You know I was famous for about two minutes." He chuckled.

Lucille sat forward in her chair. "Really?"

Pa scratched his head and grinned. "Don't you know this story? I met your mother at a party thrown in my honour by your grandfather."

"You never told me." They'd barely had conversations about anything other than what was for dinner and how was school.

Pa lifted a shoulder in a half shrug. "Ma was only seventeen when we met."

"How old were you?" Lucille asked.

"Me?" Pa tilted his head towards the ceiling trying to remember. "I suppose I was about twenty. Yeah, twenty. Anyway, we defied your grandparents' wishes and got married and drove that car all the way back to Melbourne. It was lucky we made it in one piece. I wanted to build cars but had no money and no backers. So, I sold them instead and set up my own business, importing the latest models from America." He scratched his chin. "Then people stopped buying fancy cars when the crash happened and well, we lost everything."

Lucille sipped her tea and thought about all the questions she'd asked Pa and the answers he'd never given. She didn't remember any mention of grandparents and now she knew why.

"Are my grandparents still alive?"

Max looked from Lucille to Pa.

"Oh, my parents died before your ma and me married."

"What about the disapproving ones?"

Pa scratched his head and frowned. "Ah … only your grandmother. I believe she moved to Sydney." Pa set his cup down and jumped to his feet. "Let's take a good look at your car, son."

First Max, Aunt Mavis and now a grandmother in Sydney. What else had Pa kept from her? She glanced out the lounge room window. Both men had their heads under the hood, Max's lean body stretching as he reached in to show her father something of interest. When they'd finished and Pa walked towards the house, she scurried from the window, ran into her bedroom, grabbed her textbook and threw herself into the armchair.

"Max and I are going for a drive. Leave you to study in peace. Be back soon."

She heard him grab his hat from the hallway hook and slam the door behind him. She tossed the book on the floor and curled her legs up under her. She was in no mood for studying. How could she when she had all these distracting feelings? Was it a passing phase? Max was here for Pa, not her, and the two men got along so well. And what about her grandmother. What was she like and where was she now?

*

The following Saturday, Max and Pa went out in the car again, while she tried to memorise the chemical properties of phosphate. Pa had said a girl shouldn't be studying such a useless subject, and now she was beginning to think he might well be right. Deep down, she knew he begrudgingly let her stay at school only because of her mother's dying wish. And there were many times when she'd wanted to leave and earn money, her own money. But what really stopped her was that she'd have to give up all her earnings to Pa and the drink.

It wasn't long before they returned. "Love, how about a cup of tea?" Pa called out.

She heard them move into the lounge.

"I don't know where that girl is. Lucille?" Pa yelled out. "A cup of tea!"

Footsteps. A knock at her door.

"I'm studying," she said.

Her door opened. "Sorry to interrupt," Max said.

"Yes?" she said without turning around.

"I'll make the tea. I wondered if you'd like a cup?" he said.

"No, thanks," she said, her eyes on the page. She didn't trust herself to look at him. Was he looking at her? Lying on her stomach, her books spread around her, bare legs kicking to and fro? Did he judge her for her very unladylike behaviour? She didn't care.

He left without a word.

The men's voices murmured quietly in the lounge room until, finally, she heard the front door close and footsteps fade away. The car's engine started. It was only then that she sat up and stared through the old lace curtains to watch as Max drove away.

*

By the following Saturday, after her final exam, she was relieved school was over and the summer holidays beginning. School was behind her and a new life to be planned. The sun was hot, the first of the summer's heat having arrived early. And like clockwork, Max showed up again. Only this time, he asked Lucille to go for a drive.

"I reckon you deserve a break,' Pa said. "You've been hard at it for the last couple of weeks, haven't you?"

"If you're sure?" Here was her chance to be alone with Max. It's just a drive.

"It's so hot out there. Why don't you put your bathing suit on?" Max said. "And we'll go to the beach."

Pa smiled his encouragement.

"I'll get changed then."

He'll see her in a swimsuit. She thought of the determined heroine in the last romance novel she'd read. It was only a swim at the beach. What harm can come from that, she wondered?

It was hot in the car, but Max smelled fresh, like the expensive soap she'd sniffed at Bethany's house. She glanced sidelong at his close-shaved firm jaw and wondered what it would feel like to touch his face.

"How do you think you went in your exams?" he said, interrupting her thoughts. They'd barely spoken since the dance.

She shrugged. "All right, I suppose. I probably passed." She glanced out of the window, saw a girl from school and waved. The girl looked at the car, then at Max, then back at Lucille. Her hand fluttered up to wave back, and Lucille enjoyed the look of envy. It was going to be a brilliant day.

"What's your best subject?"

She looked across at him. "Oh, I suppose, English and chemistry."

"Really? I could have helped you with chemistry. Why didn't you ask?"

Why hadn't she asked? She couldn't very well say, "I think I'm a little bit in love with you." It was best to keep their distance, wasn't it? "I … I didn't really need any help."

"What are you planning to do now that you've finished school?"

"I'd like to do teaching. I've applied for a scholarship, which will help. It's only a two-year teacher training course."

"Teaching is a great job. Here we are." He parked the car scattering a handful of seagulls.

The sand was white against the crisp blue of the sea, and already, quite a few people were on the beach. She opened the car door before he got to it.

From the boot, Max took out a picnic rug, towels and a basket. "Provisions," he said, grinning.

"Looks like you're well prepared. I forgot about bringing a towel. What if I'd said no?"

He stared at her. "You have an enchanting smile. Did you

know that?" He handed her the picnic rug. "I knew you'd come. Why wouldn't you? It's a perfect day."

"Yes, it is," she said. "But I might have been going out on a date."

She enjoyed his look of surprise. Why had she said that? Was this what the magazines called flirting?

He unpacked egg and lettuce sandwiches and orangeade. "Shall we eat first?"

She nodded. "May as well."

"What are you going to do during your holidays?"

"I've got a job in the milk bar for a few weeks, full-time. Then, I hope, part-time while I'm at Uni. If I get in, of course." She needed the money. Pa wasn't bringing in enough, so they were struggling to pay the rent, but she couldn't tell Max that. "The sandwiches are good. Did you make them? I'm actually starving."

"I can't lay claim to making them. I bought them from a little place around the corner from where I live and that's all they had. I'm glad you like them." He held out a glass with orangeade to Lucille. "Yes, Uncle Clarry said it hasn't been easy for you both. I had a job in a menswear store in London while I was going through Uni."

"Ah, that explains why you're such a snappy dresser."

He looked surprised, then realised she was joking. "I'm a bit conservative, I know. I don't go in for black and white brogues and bright ties."

"Maybe you should," she said, smiling.

He shrugged as he handed her some chocolate. It was

delicious. Then he leant over and wiped a bit of chocolate from her mouth just as she licked her lips, and her tongue caught the end of his thumb. He stopped for a minute before putting his thumb into his mouth to suck off the rest of the chocolate. She blushed at the most intimate thing anyone had ever done to her. Then she remembered that he'd done the same thing when she was a kid on the farm. He still thought of her as a child.

"It's getting hot now," he said. "I'll think I'll go and change."

She glanced at him as he packed everything away. He seemed not to have noticed her awkwardness.

"Shouldn't we wait for a bit? You know in case we get a cramp?"

"That's just an old wives' tale. The change rooms and toilets are down further and by the time we change it'll be enough time."

They walked to the change rooms and when Lucille came out, she was suddenly self-conscious of her body clad only in a one-piece bathing suit. Max was already folding his clothes neatly and putting them on the picnic rug. It gave her a chance to run her eyes over his body – an athletic build. He returned the look, his gaze taking her in. Surely, he'd have to see her as a woman. She threw her dress on the rug and ran across the soft white sand to the water's edge.

The beach was filled with other swimmers, children screaming, running and laughing. She waded in, the sea bitingly cold at first, her white arms turning mottled–lilac with goose-bumps. She swam for ten feet or so until she could barely feel the sand under her toes, then turned around. Max was nowhere to be seen. Squinting she could make out their things on the beach, then felt something on the back of her leg. Hands gripped her waist, and she was pulled down suddenly. She lashed out with arms and legs and the hands let her go.

Gasping for air, she struck out towards shore until she could feel the sand under her feet.

Max had followed her. "Sorry. Are you all right?"

"No, I am *not* all right. What's the big idea? I could have drowned."

He looked mortified. "I thought you saw me. It was just a bit of fun."

He pushed strands of hair from her face. Her strap had slipped, and he pushed it back up onto her shoulder.

She stared back at him.

"I'm really sorry. You used to like that when you were little."

Little?

"There!" She splashed him in the face. "Now we're even." And she laughed as he coughed and spluttered.

He grinned. "You're a devil."

"And I'm not so little. Last one to the end of the pier is a rotten egg."

She swam well. Soon the pylons were looming, and she reached the end of the pier where she trod water and watched his smooth, slow strokes coming closer.

They were alone out there, and the beach seemed a long way off. Something touched her leg again, and she looked around for him, but he was a few feet away.

She squealed. "Oh god! Something really did touch my leg."

He puffed when he reached her. "Are you sure?"

"There it is again." She lunged at him, his body strong under her hands, his back muscles tightening.

"I can't see anything. Let's get closer to shore to be on the safe side." He tried to move. "You'll need to let me go," he said gently.

She nodded and released her grip.

"Come on. I'm right next to you. Can you make it?"

"Yes, I think so."

When they reached the beach, Lucille ran ahead and flung herself, exhausted on the rug, wrapping the towel around her, shivering despite the heat.

When Max came out of the water, he stared out towards the pier, shading his eyes. He spoke to another man. They both looked out. Then a third joined them, and the three went along the beach until they reached the pier and began walking along it, looking in the water until they reached the end.

Her mouth dry, she found the bottle of orangeade and took a sip, then lay wrapped in the towel, enjoying the sun, and closed her eyes.

When she woke, Max was dressed, sitting on the rug next to her.

"Are you all right, sleepyhead? You might have been brushed by a jellyfish. Apparently, there were some sighted near the pier."

"Oh?"

"Which leg was it?"

"I felt it on my calf."

She drew the towel away and pointed. He got up and knelt over her right leg, close enough for her to see flecks of sand in his hair.

He looked up. "Do you mind if I touch?"

She swallowed and nodded. His hand ran along her calf lifting it off the blanket. Her body tingled. "Does it hurt anywhere? Like a sting?"

"No, nothing hurts. I wonder what it was."

He leant back. "It might have been a bit of seaweed." His eyes glanced across the V-neck of her bathing suit "It looks like you got sunburnt."

Her hand went up and touched her chest, pulling the towel up and around her. "Is it red?"

"It sure is."

"How long did I sleep?"

"An hour, I suppose."

She groaned. "You let me sleep for that long?"

"You looked peaceful."

She stood, and while Max turned away to gather up the rug and shake out the sand, she slipped her dress over her bathing suit and put on her sandals.

The sun had dipped low on the horizon, and the beach was

almost deserted. She welcomed the warmth of the car as she slid onto the bench seat.

"I had a great day. Thank you." Then she slid over and kissed Max on the side of his mouth. It was meant to be a thank you kiss, but something overcame her. She sought his lips and he responded, his mouth soft as they kissed each other.

Abruptly, he pulled away.

"Sorry," he said. "That shouldn't have happened." Jaw clenched, he started the engine.

She couldn't think of a word to say.

When he pulled up at her house, she smiled. "I really did have a nice day."

He smiled weakly. "So did I. And I am really sorry about before. I don't know what got into me. I guess you really are grown up now."

She frowned, wondering what he meant by that. "I better go," was the only thing she could think of to say. She wanted to lean over and kiss him again.

He didn't move. She opened her own door, and as she got out, took a deep breath and said, "I'm not sorry."

There. She'd said it. But she resisted the urge to see his reaction and, instead, ran into the house. She didn't want to hear his lecture about being cousins or that he was too old for her and they should just be friends.

She was in love; she was sure of it.

10

JUNE 1992

The train slowed as it came into a small town. Tufts of grass grew in the concrete and a thin tabby cat strolled along a stone fence that ran along the railway line. The train came to a stop at a run-down station.

"This used to be such a pretty town," Lucille said.

"It doesn't look much now. Have you lived in the area for a long time?"

"Since the early seventies. There's a cheese factory here, or rather there was one, where we'd buy the most beautiful cheeses."

"It must have been something."

"Yes, it was. And behind that building over there, we played bowls."

There was nothing but neglected old buildings, and Quin couldn't imagine a pristine bowls green. "My nan used to play bowls too. She was quite good at it." Quin bit her lip at the thought of Nan – the woman who'd raised her, supported and loved her. She didn't deserve her Nan's love now.

"It's excellent for fitness. Although golf is very good too. I don't know if you visited the golf course in Hammondville, but it runs along the cliffs, and the view is quite something. Tourists like the kangaroos on the fairways too, although they can be a bit of a nuisance."

"You still bowl and play golf?"

"Not for a while, not since my husband died."

"I'm sorry to hear that. How long ago?"

"It's been nearly five years." Lucille raised a tissue to her nose and for a horrible moment Quin thought she was going to cry. "His health hadn't been all that good."

Quin leant across and patted Lucille's arm. "I'm sorry. Are you okay?"

Lucille nodded. "It's nice to talk to someone."

The poor old thing is lonely. "Yes. It is actually."

Quin had missed chatting to someone who didn't know her and her history. It felt good to forget her sadness and her own loneliness. It had been more than two years since her life had been turned upside down. "Do you have children and grandchildren?"

"Just one son. No grandchildren, and I'm not sure if there will be any."

"Oh, you never know."

"Children aren't always a blessing."

"Oh?"

Lucille winced. "I didn't mean it like that. My son is my

world, but I don't think he wants children. He's ..." She waved her arms. "Oh goodness ... I've lost my train of thought. I'm just a silly old woman."

"Not at all. You seem very sprightly to me." And her chest tightened as her thoughts went to Nan again, when she'd sometimes lose her train of thought mid-sentence. But she always recovered quickly.

"Are you married, Quin?"

"Oh, no. Not married. Not even in a relationship."

"It's important to find the right person to settle down with and have your family."

"I'd like to have children one day, but not now." Was this woman going to be like Madge, nagging her about marriage? "I think you have to be ready to have children, but then, I don't know if I'll ever be ready. It's such a big responsibility bringing children into the world, hoping they'll turn out all right."

Lucille looked thoughtful. "It's a challenge. But I can hardly give you advice. I've made more than my share of mistakes as a mother. But I'm sure your parents would be very proud of you and how you've turned out."

Now it was her turn to feel the tears coming, and she bit her lip. "They died when I was very young. To be honest I don't think they would be terribly proud of me so it's probably for the best."

Lucille raised her eyebrows. "Why? Are you a bank robber or murderer?"

"No of course not."

"Then I'm sure you've done nothing they wouldn't have been proud of. Maybe you set your expectations too high. That's all."

"Maybe, I have. You remind me so much of my nan. She's the one who raised me and my brother."

Lucille smiled. "Do I? I'm glad. Are you going to Melbourne to visit them?"

Quin glanced out of the window. She wished she had family to see, that she wasn't so horribly alone. "No," she said. "Not this time. Just having a break."

A break? She couldn't tell Lucille that she was going to be part of a crowd ensuring justice was done. That she was a nervous wreck just thinking about what would happen tomorrow.

"And you?"

"Just seeing my son."

"Oh, that's nice."

The train began moving again.

"We seem to be going awfully slow. At this rate, it'll take hours to get to Melbourne." Lucille looked at her watch. "I'd say we have at least another two hours."

"Oh, that long?" Quin said, touching her stomach. "Sorry, that was me rumbling."

Lucille pointed to her ears and smiled. "I couldn't hear it."

From her handbag, Lucille pulled out a sandwich tightly packaged in cling wrap, which she held out to Quin. "Would you like to have this?"

"I can't take your food." Quin licked her lips staring at

the squashed white bread in Lucille's hand. "I might get something from the dining car. I think there's a snack bar there."

"I'm not hungry, and if you don't want it, I'll just end up throwing it in the bin. I don't even know why I made the thing. It's not much, just a bit of lettuce, tomato and a slice of cheese. The bread is probably soggy by now. You'd be doing me a favour by taking it … that is, if you're hungry."

"If you really don't want it. Thank you." Quin impatiently picked at the plastic wrap. The smell of tomato filled her nostrils, and she salivated as she sank her teeth into the soft bread. "It's delicious," she said, her mouth full.

"If you don't mind me saying, you look like you should be eating more. I know it's fashionable to be stick thin, but it's not really healthy, is it? I used to tell my son that work shouldn't take precedence over sitting at the dinner table and eating a good meal. Not that he ever listened to me."

"I just hadn't had a chance to get anything." Quin bunched the cling wrap tight and rolled it from one hand to the other.

"Really?"

"Too much of a rush to catch the train. Why aren't you hungry?"

"I'm never very hungry these days. At my age, dear, I have very little sense of smell, and nothing tastes like it used to. That's the price you pay for living a longer life than necessary."

11

QUIN

AUGUST 1987

The night after the office party, Nan wanted Quin and Ben to help with a bingo fundraiser at her bowling club.

Ben tended the bar and Quin helped out at the buffet. They were so busy, she hardly had time to think about Pete and the kiss.

"They can sure put it away," Ben said, sidling up to her with a beer in his hand. The room was filled with people seated at tables, their heads bent over pieces of paper, pen in hand waiting for the announcer in the front to declare their winning numbers.

"You can't have a drink yet. You're still serving. All I've got to do is put away these dishes and that's it. Any chance of a wine?"

Ben slipped back behind the bar and brought out a white wine for Quin. "Surely, they're done? I've gotta get up in the morning to play footy."

"And I've got to study." They both stood watching the rows of men and women tick off their numbers. "Look at Nan. She looks so happy."

"Yeah, she does. The number of times I've heard her shouting 'bingo' I reckon she's really enjoying herself."

"Bingo," someone yelled. It was Nan who was on her feet smiling as if she'd won the lottery rather than a tray of chops.

"There she goes again."

"And here we are acting like we're parents watching kids on a Saturday night."

Ben laughed. "True. Our parents would have been standing here instead."

Quin looked at her brother in surprise. They'd never spoken about their parents. "I wish they were here, and I feel bad because I've lost the memory of them. I can't picture them. Do you remember much?" It was a rare moment between them.

"That's the problem. I remember them. Too clearly." He skolled his beer and left her staring after him, wondering what he meant. She supposed he'd remember more than her since he was ten when the accident happened.

Madge, Nan's best friend came over. "Thanks love, for cleaning up." Her eyes scanned the empty food table. "I don't know what we'd have done without you."

"It was my pleasure," Quin said, smiling.

Madge had been around for as long as Quin could remember. She'd been a great support for Nan when Grandpa died. A widow herself, Madge was like a sister to Nan. She'd even babysat them when they were young. Growing up, she and Ben had played with Madge's grandkids although they rarely saw them now. Madge put an arm around her and gave her a gentle hug. She was much shorter than Quin, stocky with a full head of silver hair that saw rollers every night.

"I don't know how the old girl does it," Madge said. "She wins every time,"

"I know. She's amazing."

"So, how's your love life going?"

Quin could feel herself redden. Typical Madge – never beats around the bush. "So, so," she said.

"You're getting on in years now."

Quin spluttered. "Me? I'm twenty-five, Madge, not forty-five." How was she going to get away from her? She loved her, but when Madge started down this path, Quin needed to escape.

Madge grinned. "Well, the clock is ticking, and your nan isn't getting any younger. Most of the good men are being snatched up. You don't want to be left on the shelf." Then Madge looked over at Ben. "And your brother. It's high time he settled down."

"It'll happen when it happens. I've got a career to work on, and so does Ben. There's plenty of time. It's not the same as in your day. People don't get married and have kids all by the time they're twenty-one."

"Yes, more's the pity. Anyway, love, you don't want to leave it too long. You don't know what's waiting for you around the corner."

"I don't know if I really want any of that. I love my job and these days women have more options for a career."

This was the same argument they'd had for years. Madge lecturing both of them yet singling out Quin.

"A career is well and good, love, but who'll look after you in your old age? You work to live, not live to work."

Quin stared into her wine glass. There was no point going round and round in circles with Madge. That's the problem with the older generation, she thought. They think their way is the best way. They don't have to think about AIDS when they meet someone. Pete had been around, so Deb had said, so she had to be careful.

"What are you gasbagging about, Madge? I hope you're not lecturing my granddaughter again," Nan said, carrying her tray of chops.

"What me? Lecture? I don't know how you can say that," Madge said, smiling. "We were having a nice little chat. Now I hope you're going to ask me round for a barbeque. You can't eat all that by yourselves."

Nan laughed and nodded. "I'm ready to go home. Quin do you want to get Ben?"

*

"Got home all right on Friday? Saw you and Pete left together," Deb smirked as she put a file in Quin's in tray.

Quin put her pen down. "We only shared a taxi. He went one way at the train station, and I went the other."

Deb nodded. "If you say so."

"Did you enjoy yourself with Kev?"

Deb laughed. "I got rid of him pretty quickly. He's a loser."

"And what about Dimi?"

"What about her?"

Quin looked around. There was no-one within earshot. "Why did she really leave Solid Rock?"

Deb looked uncomfortable. "She wouldn't want me to say."

"Pete told me she was after Tom, and that's why he got rid of her."

Deb's face tightened. "I wouldn't believe Pete if I were you! More like the other way round. I've said too much. A word of advice: you don't say no to Tom. I've gotta go."

Quin pondered over what Deb had said. She'd be on her guard around Tom, not that she had any dealings with him anyway.

As she settled into her seat, she looked over at Pete's empty desk. She'd been thinking about that kiss all weekend. Deb was right; going out with someone from work would be too messy. Concentrating on her career was more important. She reached for a file sitting in her in tray and opened it.

"G'day. Glad you got home in one piece." There he was, standing in front of her desk. "It worried me all weekend. I should have got your phone number to check that you were safe."

"You didn't need to worry. I am a big girl." She picked up the phone.

"Yeah, I know. See you later?"

Quin nodded, and dialled, watching Pete head to his desk.

*

After lunch, Pete stopped her on the way back to the office.

"I wondered if you'd like to go see a movie tonight?"

"You mean go out with you?"

"Yeah. You can pick the movie if you like."

Quin swallowed. "You're really nice, but I don't think it's a good idea to take our friendship any further."

"I thought we had a nice time on Friday night?"

"It's not something I'm interested in at the moment. With study and helping out at home and work, I just … well, I don't have the time. Sorry."

She thought she caught a shadow of disappointment in Pete's eyes, or maybe it was her imagination.

"No worries,' he said. "Do you still want to catch the tram to class with me tomorrow night?"

"Sure. I better get back."

Don't have the time. What sort of excuse was that? She felt bad, but it was better this way.

12

LUCILLE

1937

Over and over, Lucille relived the moment in the car with Max, thinking about how soft his lips were. He'd definitely kissed her back. It wasn't her imagination. She was dying to tell Bethany, but of course, she couldn't. Her first real kiss. She could hardly wait an entire week to see him again.

But he didn't come the next Saturday.

Was it the kiss? Had she frightened him away? Perhaps he was repelled by her. She was too young. Or maybe her kiss wasn't any good. She'd read that there were ways to kiss. How could she know? In the end, she convinced herself that his car had broken down.

Saturday, a week later, while mending a hole in her jumper, Lucille looked anxiously out the lounge room window. Pa had started drinking earlier than usual, and she prayed he'd stop before Max arrived. In the last month or so, Pa had drunk less, and she'd been heartened that he was making good on his promise. But here it was, only eleven-thirty, and he'd poured himself a beer. He read the paper while listening to music on the wireless. After the mending was done, Lucille put her sewing away and pulled back the curtain for the fifth time.

"What are you doing?" Pa said, looking over his newspaper.

She let the curtain drop and swung around. "Nothing. I'm wondering if I should clean the windows."

Pa raised his eyebrows and went back to the newspaper.

"Max hasn't come for a while," Lucille said, trying to sound casual.

"He's probably been busy with the government, I expect. He's doing important work." Pa lowered his newspaper and peered at her. "Get lunch on. I'm hungry."

After they'd eaten, she tried to read a book, then a magazine. She mended a hem, washed and scrubbed the kitchen bench and floor, then went for a walk around the block, but nothing could rid her of the sinking feeling that perhaps Max was deliberately staying away. That she'd offended him somehow with her forthrightness. It was simply not done to throw yourself at a man. She knew this from the hours spent in Bethany's bedroom, talking about the romance books they'd read, learning what was proper and what wasn't. Was Max merely tolerating her and her stupid schoolgirl crush? She'd embarrassed herself and him. He must have decided to remove himself from her life.

Later, she and Pa sat to eat the leftover vegetable soup from the night before.

"It's been quiet without Max again today," Pa said.

Lucille stared at her food.

"It's good to have family again. I've missed that," Pa mused. "Max is all we have."

She stopped eating and fixed a glare at him. "Don't I have a grandmother somewhere?"

Pa lurched back in his seat and stared at her as if he didn't know her. The lines on his face, like rivulets after a heavy downpour, moved in waves on his cheek as he chewed. "A grandmother in Sydney, but I haven't seen her since your mother's funeral." He looked pained and scratched his head, avoiding her glare.

"Why Pa? Why haven't we seen her? Is it because she's a long way? I would like to have to met her ... just once. You know it's been hard for me too."

Pa frowned. "It was ... difficult."

"Maybe she didn't know where to find us." Lucille folded her arms and sat back in her chair. She had him against the ropes, like a prize fighter. "After all, Max didn't know, did he?"

She waited for an answer, which of course, didn't come. He'd never open up, no matter how many questions she asked. She pushed her plate away.

Pa went to the icebox and pulled out another bottle of beer.

Lucille cleared the dishes. "Maybe you're the reason Max hasn't visited."

Pa looked at her sharply. "Me?"

"You made such a grand statement about pulling yourself together. And here you are, drinking. He probably feels uncomfortable."

Pa stared at the bottle and seemed about to say something but stopped himself. He turned from her, reached for a glass and walked into the lounge.

She sat and held her head in her hands.

*

The next day was sunny and hot. She formulated a plan. In the kitchen draw, she found the piece of paper where Max had written his address for Pa.

"I'm going to Bethany's place to meet up with some of the girls. I might be quite late."

Pa had barely spoken to her since dinner the evening before, but he'd heard her – he didn't look up from his newspaper. She was used to the silent treatment whenever she touched a raw nerve. Soon, he'd drink and forget all about it. It made no difference. She had other things to worry about.

If Max couldn't come to her, then she'd go to him – a bus to the station, then a train into the city, as she'd done many times before. But this time she was nervous. What if he wasn't there? What if he sent her home?

She got off the train and waited at the tram stop. There was still time to turn around and go home. When the tram arrived, she hesitated. What was she doing? Chasing a cousin who thought of her as a family friend? He only came over out of sympathy and duty. He'd felt sorry for them.

"Are you getting on?" a man behind her said. "Hurry up. We're all waiting."

"Sorry." She boarded and hung on to the railing as the tram lurched up Nicholson St. She peered out the window. A beggar accosted a woman for money. She kept her eyes peeled for the stop she needed. What should she say when she saw him? "Just thought I'd check to see if you were all right." Maybe he had the summer flu and was bedridden, so couldn't get a message to her and Pa. Why hadn't she considered that before? She'd go to him and nurse him back to health. He'd smile at her, and she'd touch his brow …

There was the street. She rang the bell and the tram stopped. Soon she stood on the footpath in front of number ten, a Victorian single-fronted, brick house. His car was parked in the front. He must be home. She licked her lips, patted her hair and ran her sweaty hands down her floral dress before knocking on the grey painted door. She waited to hear his footsteps. Nothing. She knocked again, then pushed her face against the stained-glass window in the door. It was dark and still. Not sick, and not at home. She sighed and walked back to the tram stop.

She didn't have to wait long before the tram home arrived. Just after she boarded, she glanced down the street. There he was, his hand on the shoulder of a young woman who was laughing. Then they disappeared from view. Lucille gasped, clapping her hand over her mouth. The woman opposite asked if she was all right.

"Yes, thank you. I thought I saw someone. But I was mistaken," Lucille said, blinking back tears.

Her worst fear – he'd found himself a girlfriend.

Without thinking, she stood and rang the bell to get off. She had to find out, no matter how much it might hurt.

Her initial resolve began to fade as she walked towards his street. If he had a girlfriend, she'd have to accept the fact. Her hands were sticky with perspiration as she thought about what she would say. "Hi, I was just in the neighbourhood." That wouldn't do. "Thought I'd come to visit, seeing how we haven't seen you for so long. Just checking to see if you're all right."

Soon she was standing in front of his house once again knocking on the front door.

Silence. Then footsteps padding down the hallway. The door swung open.

"Hello," she said.

"Why hello," he said, smiling. "What a pleasant surprise! Come in, come in."

She blinked as she followed him down the hallway, quickly glancing into the darkened bedroom – the bed neatly made, a jacket thrown across the plain bedspread. Then past a second closed door – a bedroom she supposed – and through another door that opened onto a lounge where two people sat on a couch. The woman she'd seen before and another man.

Max grabbed Lucille's hand and pulled her to face them.

"Meet Lucille. This is Harvey and Geraldine."

"Hello," she muttered, trying for a smile.

"Hello," they both said.

"Lucille, sit over here. Would you like a cool drink?" Max said.

She nodded.

"We just got back from lunch," Geraldine said, smiling. "It's a stinking day. So nice and cool in here."

Lucille looked around for Max, but he'd disappeared.

"So, this is the famous Lucille," Harvey said, puffing on a pipe. "Max has told us so much about you."

"He has?" she blurted, wondering what he might have said.

"Told us you just finished school," Geraldine said, picking up her glass. Her fingers were long and elegant, her nails painted a blushed pink.

"You want to be a teacher, hey?" Harvey said.

"Ah, yes I think so. Just waiting to see if I've got into my course."

Harvey sat forwards. "Geraldine wanted to be a piano teacher, but she's too good for that."

Geraldine smiled. "When my fingers are no longer able to fly across the keys, then I'll teach. Lucille, do you play?"

"I remember that you played very well," Max said, coming into the room. He winked at Lucille as he handed her a glass of ice-cold lemonade.

Lucille gulped, not prepared for the hit of fizz. "I don't really play now. I only played …" She couldn't say she'd stopped because Pa couldn't afford to pay for lessons. "… when I was a child."

"So Max, looks like another trip away?" Harvey said.

"Possibly. But I'll let you know sometime next week. It's becoming a bit tedious."

Harvey laughed. "Watch out. They might want you to move."

Lucille looked at Max, alarmed.

"It won't come to that, mate. Enough shoptalk." Max looked at Lucille. "We work together."

"Oh," she said. What about Geraldine? she wondered. A pianist. She would be with those long fingers and her beauty. No wonder Max likes her.

Uncomfortable, Lucille searched for something to say. "Are you working on the pesticide too?" she blurted.

Harvey raised his eyebrows and looked from Lucille to Max, then back. He picked up his glass and drained the last of the beer. "Sort of. Well, I reckon we better get going, old chap. You ready?"

"Yes. I'm ready." Geraldine's pencil skirt hugged her slim body. Her high heels looked expensive.

Lucille felt like the schoolgirl she was, in her floral dress and flat sandals.

"Nice to meet you, Lucille."

She may have imagined it, but Lucille thought she caught a knowing look pass between Geraldine and Max.

"Will you stay while I see them out?" Max asked Lucille.

Uncertain, she nodded. "Nice to meet you both."

"See ya," Harvey said, winking as he put his hat on.

Lucille's mind was in a whirl. Why did Max want her to stay? Perhaps he wanted to explain privately about his new girlfriend. Was that a giggle from Geraldine and someone saying, "Shush"?

They were laughing. At her.

"Thanks for lunch. See you tomorrow," Max called out.

When he came back into the room, she was already on her feet. "I think I better go too. I just wanted to check if you were all right. When we hadn't heard from you for so long, Pa and I … well, we were worried, that's all. But you're fine, so I think I'll go."

"Don't go," he said. "Stay a bit. I've been away. That's why I didn't come. If you had a phone, I would have called."

Lucille picked up her bag.

"Don't go."

He took her bag and placed it beside the chair.

"But I …"

He was silent, gazing at her. What did he see? A foolish schoolgirl?

Then he leant in, his aftershave intoxicating and kissed her. Her arms, at first limp by her sides, found new energy as they encircled his waist. She kissed him back with an eagerness she hadn't known she possessed, giddy in his arms.

"I've been dreaming of those lips," he murmured.

Lucille pulled away.

"And missing you." He smiled.

"But Geraldine? What about her?"

He frowned. "What about her?"

Lucille's heart thumped. "She's your girlfriend, but you dream of me? I can't be here."

This was exactly what had happened in the last romance book she'd read. She turned to pick up her bag.

Max began laughing.

"This isn't funny."

"Geraldine? No, she's not my girlfriend." He grabbed her arm. "She's Harvey's wife. Didn't I say that when I introduced you? I haven't been able to get you out of my mind."

Harvey's wife. Not Max's girlfriend.

He looked at her. "Do you feel the same way?"

She tried to catch her breath and nodded. "Yes! Yes, I do."

Lucile kissed him this time. This was so much better than what she'd read about in her romance novels.

13

QUIN

NEW YEAR'S EVE, 1987

She'd forgotten to draw the curtains and the hot morning sun woke her. Her head thumped, but then she remembered the night she'd had and smiled.

"What's your resolution for the year?" Deb had said above the din of music.

"Finish my course with distinction and get a promotion?" Quin swayed to the music, a can in one hand.

"Climb the ladder, hey?" Deb said. "I'm happy being a secretary, although I'm struggling to get used to the new computer. Give me an electronic typewriter any day."

"You know a lot more than some of those guys. Why not try and do something else?"

Deb smiled. "You know how it works. Once you're pigeon-holed as a typist, there's no way they see you as anything else. Besides, being the boss's secretary allows me to know everything that goes on. In fact, I know things that'd make your hair curl."

Quin laughed. "I can imagine."

"And if you don't mind me saying, the one thing I've seen all year is Pete mooning over you like a puppy dog. I've never seen him like that, ever. Look at him."

Quin turned and Pete's eyes were on her. They'd spent a lot of time together studying, comparing notes, and she liked him. A lot. He winked and she winked back. But they were just friends.

"Stop leading him on."

"I'm not. It's your fault. You're the one who said that office relationships are no good. Besides, I told him months ago I wasn't interested."

"Well, I happen to know he's holding out hope you'll change your mind. At least go and say hello."

"What are you, my nan?" Quin laughed. "I've got to find a bathroom."

"Upstairs to the right."

Quin found the bathroom. It was quiet and a tiredness came over her. While sitting on the toilet she closed her eyes and the room spun.

She was tempted to see out the new year right there, where she could be alone with her thoughts, but now someone was furiously banging on the door.

She pushed her way downstairs and someone thrust a plastic glass of cheap champagne into her hand. Then Pete was beside her, grinning.

Voices merged into one in the countdown to midnight. Quin and Pete joined in. Then she was kissing him, her arms around him, not wanting to let go. But she was pulled away and smothered with kisses by everyone around her – people she didn't even know or want to know. Party popper strings and splashes of champagne sprayed over her. She wondered when her glass had become empty, and when she had put her head against Pete's shoulder, and when he'd put his arm around her, and why her lips had become swollen from kissing.

As she led him by the hand to a bedroom upstairs, she forgot what Deb had said and thought only of what she wanted. To her, this felt right.

*

Whenever Tom Doomsbury walked onto their floor, everyone tensed. Three weeks into the new year, he stopped at Quin's desk and asked how her day was going.

"It's good thanks."

When he pulled up a chair and sat next to her, she tried not to panic as she swivelled towards him. Had she done something wrong? The smell of musk drifted from him. Her eyes skimmed the diamond cufflinks on his white shirt, which showed off his olive skin. Everything about him looked expensive, even his blue paisley silk tie. Correcting her posture, she crossed her legs, then noticed too much of her leg showed and uncrossed them.

"Can you do me a favour?"

His eyes were an intense green, and when he smiled, she relaxed. Not in trouble then. "Yes, of course," she said.

"You're looking after the Sanders Furniture account, aren't you?"

She nodded.

"Can you ring Alex Sanders and ask him if he can get me a couple of couches and have them delivered to my beach house?"

She picked up her pen, putting the end to her mouth before remembering her disgusting habit. "Oh, Okay. What sort of couches?"

He stood and his hand drifted to rest lightly on her shoulder. "He'll know."

"Tom, you gotta sec?" Larry yelled across the room, and he was gone.

Quin grabbed the file for Alex Sanders's company and dialled the number.

"It's Quin Schmidt from Solid Rock calling on behalf of Mr Doomsbury. Could I speak to Mr Sanders please?"

She suddenly wondered what she'd say when Mr Sanders asked for payment. Putting her hand over the mouthpiece, she whispered to Janie. "How will Tom pay for the couches?"

Janie rolled her eyes. "He won't be paying. Tom pays for nothing. He scratches Sanders back and Sanders scratches his."

"Oh," Quin said.

"Yeah? What's Tom after, love?" Sanders asked.

Quin told him, terminated the call and looked at the file. It didn't seem right not to pay for the couches.

The interest rate on the file was at staff rates rather than client rates. Very generous. A couch or two would hardly be anything. Maybe that was the deal. Sanders owed two million for the expansion of three stores, had mortgages over them all, with his house in Toorak and another in Portsea as collateral. The properties were worth two and half million. Was borrowing as much as you can the way to get ahead?

On the train on the way home, she read the Financial Review. "Solid Rock has just completed its most successful year in its thirty-year history. It is now the largest building society in Australia with assets in excess of two billion dollars. Profit has grown by more than a million in the last year alone."

Everyone talked about the results. A bonus would be coming her way, and she wondered if she would get enough to buy a new car. It felt good working for a growing, successful company. But she wanted more. She wanted to work upstairs on the corporate deals instead of the small and medium business loans. Her last chat with Larry had been positive.

"You're doing a great job, Quin. I just want you to bring in more business. That's all you need to round out your experience, then you'll be ready for the next level," he'd said.

It wasn't hard getting new business. Everyone wanted to make money. Her friends sought her advice and sent their parents and relatives to her. Nan arranged group talks at the local bowling club and the RSL – the Returned Serviceman's League. Even Ben sent his mates from the cricket and footy clubs to her. She brought in more than fifty clients, and the biggest deal was more than five million dollars to finance a shopping development on the Mornington Peninsula.

She put the newspaper away, happy with herself.

14

1938

Lucille lay on her bed, daydreaming about Max – the way his brown eyes crinkled in the corners when he smiled, and the dimple that danced on one cheek when he laughed. The week had been tortuous. She was bursting to tell someone, anyone, especially Beth, that she and Max were, well what were they? Was he her boyfriend? He'd been nothing but gentlemanly, and they'd talked for more than an hour about how he felt about her. She felt the same, so perhaps he *was* her boyfriend. Her body tingled at the memory.

He'd asked her out to lunch in St Kilda the following Saturday. "We should do this right," he'd said. "A proper date and permission from Uncle Clarry."

She hadn't said anything, but when she thought about Pa, there was a hollowness in the pit of her stomach. She didn't want him to know, wasn't ready for her father to become involved, so she'd hatched a plan.

She glanced at her watch and sat up suddenly. It was already after eleven. Max was due at twelve. She headed to the lounge and watched for him through the window. Pa was lying on the couch listening to the radio.

"Pa," she said.

"Hmm?" His eyes were closed.

"Max is giving me a lift to Beth's house on his way to an appointment, so he can't come in. I've left you a roast beef sandwich for lunch. Okay?"

She waited for him to ask her how she knew? It wasn't as if they had a telephone. Damn.

Pa's eyes remained closed. He'd already had three glasses of beer. He waved his hand at her and she relaxed.

*

The following Saturday, Max came by to take her out, and she couldn't stop him from coming in.

"Uncle Clarry, how are you?" Max said. "I hope you don't mind if I take Lucille to a dance?"

"No, my boy. You youngsters should be having a good time."

"Now, I just want you to …"

"Max, how's work?" Lucille said.

Pa looked on expectantly.

"There's a lot going on."

Pa and Max talked about pesticide research, while Lucille turned away to get her shawl, relieved that she'd stopped Max telling Pa about them. She wasn't ready yet. But she told herself that it would be soon.

With her shawl over her arm, she interrupted them. "It's time we left. We don't want to be late, Max."

"Ah, yes." Max looked confused.

She had to act fast, so opened the front door, hoping Max would follow her. It was a gamble, but it worked.

"I should have told him about what's going on," he said. "I feel bad about this."

"Don't worry. There will be ample time to talk to Pa. Now, let's just enjoy this evening."

*

Because Pa was drunk and barely coherent most of the time, Max never got the chance to speak to him. The holiday season was the anniversary of her mother's and baby brother's deaths, so especially hard for her father.

"It's too hard to talk to Pa now. Maybe in a little while," Lucille said. "It's just that he drinks himself into a stupor for a few weeks."

"That's awful. I had no idea. Surely there's something I can do?"

"Just coming in and saying hello will be enough. He probably won't even remember that you were there."

"And it's been like this since your Ma died?"

"Yes, every year." Lucille lowered her eyes.

"And what do you do while he's like that?"

She shrugged. "There's not much I can do. I mostly stay in my room, read books, do the chores and keep out of his way."

Max looked at her in alarm. "He doesn't beat you, does he?"

She shook her head.

Max moved across the car's bench seat and held her. "You poor thing. If only I'd known."

Lucille pulled away. "The best thing you can do now is take me out. I don't want to stay at home with him. I want to enjoy life. I've finished school, got an offer to study teaching and have a handsome boyfriend."

He kissed her. "Let's go then," he said.

*

Unlike her other birthdays, most of which Pa had forgotten about, Lucille's eighteenth birthday was filled with presents – a shawl, flowers, chocolates and perfume – all showered upon her by Max. Even Pa seemed to have come out of his slump. He'd gone back to work and was acting normal again. He even gave her a small gift – a silver broach – which she cherished.

After her birthday dinner, Lucille and Max drove to the beach. She sat close to snuggle next to him, when he reached into his jacket pocket and left his hand there.

"I've a special gift."

"Another one?"

His face turned serious. "I've given this a lot of thought and have gone over and over it in my mind. It's going to be so hard. But I can't stand not having you with me. I think we can make this work. And well, do you think you'd like to marry me?"

He smiled and when he pulled his hand out of his pocket, he brought out a small box. She sat up straight and took it, hands shaking with excitement as she felt the soft red velvet. Inside was a ring with a single diamond surrounded by smaller diamonds.

Any strength she had seemed to have left her, and when she tried to speak, words evaporated.

He took the ring out and slipped it onto the fourth finger of her left hand. "So, how about it?"

She flung her arms around his neck and squealed. "Yes. Oh, yes!"

Eventually, he pulled away from her with a worried look. "There might be objections."

"What do you mean? Who on earth is going to object?"

"Well, your father might not be too happy."

"He loves you."

"As a nephew. I'm not so sure how he'll feel about me being a son-in-law.

"He'll be glad to have me off his hands."

"No, he won't. You look after him too well."

She frowned. It was true.

"And we should have told him we were going out. I feel really bad about that."

"Let's get it over with and tell Pa."

Lucille thought about what Pa would say and convinced herself that after the initial surprise, the engagement ring would prove their relationship was serious, and Pa wouldn't be able to do much about it. She stared at the ring and tilted it to try to catch what little light came in from the lamplights outside.

When they reached home, Lucille ran inside ahead of Max. She wanted to get to Pa first.

"Pa," she yelled. "Guess what?"

Her father was, as usual, glued to the wireless and frowned when she bounced into the room, interrupting his favourite radio show.

"Pa, this is important."

"What's so important to interrupt my serial?"

His face softened when he saw Max trailing in behind her.

"Pa, I'm getting married."

"Married?" Pa raised his eyebrows. "Who to?"

Lucille looked at Max who stared at his feet. "Max, of course. Look." She held up her hand with the ring on it.

Pa frowned. "Is this true, Max?"

"Yes, Uncle Clarry. I love Lucille, and I want to marry her. I know I should have asked you first."

"Yes, you should have." Pa stood to turn off the wireless and leant one elbow on the mantlepiece.

"Surely you don't object," Lucille said.

Pa narrowed his eyes.

"Well?" she said. The room was suddenly stuffy. Surely, he couldn't say no.

"I thought there was something going on," Pa said slowly. He studied Lucille, then Max. "I suppose there's not much point objecting. Better to be married than sneaking around."

Lucille glanced down at her ring, then at Max, who fidgeted, pulling his shirt cuffs under his jacket sleeves.

"People aren't going to like it," Pa said, shaking his head. "First cousins getting married."

"Well, that's bad luck. We don't care what people think." Lucille looked at Max. "Do we?"

"Um, no."

The silence was punctuated by the ticking of the clock on the mantlepiece. Pa abruptly left the room and went into the kitchen. Max looked at Lucille, raising his eyebrows in a told-you-so expression. She returned the look with a that-went-well-I-think expression. Max followed Pa, putting his hand up to prevent Lucille following.

But he was met by Pa who was coming back with a whiskey bottle and three glasses. "I suppose we should celebrate."

"You're welcome to live with us," Max said.

"I'm perfectly happy here on my own. I wouldn't dream of living with newlyweds." Pa handed a glass to Lucille.

"One for me?" she said.

"A small one for the bride-to-be," Pa said, pouring. "You're a young woman now. Here's to you both." Pa downed his.

15

QUIN

JUNE 1988

Quin hummed to herself as she left the factory and headed for her fleet car with a spring in her step. It had already been a great half year – she'd brought in twenty small business accounts with the lure of competitive interest rates. And now she'd signed another big deal – a $350,000 loan for her client to buy a bigger factory. She couldn't believe how easy it had been. Using the yellow pages of the telephone directory, she'd rung three potential clients. Two of them had told her they weren't interested, but the third said yes. They'd met, she reviewed the financial statements and put an application together, Warren had approved it, and now she had another new client.

She opened the car door, threw her briefcase and handbag onto the floor of the front passenger seat, got in and started the engine, enjoying her high. Thirty minutes to get back to the office just in time for an urgent staff meeting.

Rushing out of the lift, she bumped into Tom Doomsbury so hard, he grabbed her arms to steady them both.

"Oh god, I'm really sorry." She was so close she could smell his musk aftershave.

He smiled and dropped his hands. "It's all right." His breath was tinged with the sharp scent of coffee. "Been out?"

"Yes," she blurted. "Just signed a $350,000 deal." She jiggled the car keys in her hand. Am I being too forward? she wondered.

He raised his eyebrows as he opened the reception door for her, then followed. "Is that so? How did you get it?"

They both stopped, and she explained, the words tumbling out of her mouth in short bursts of excitement. She'd never really talked to him before, and he'd never shown any interest in her other than to say hello. His green eyes narrowed in concentration for a minute, then his eyes darted away. She was losing him; she'd gone on for too long.

"I see." He nodded and walked off towards Larry's office.

Had he been pleased? She had no idea. He was a busy man, and she'd taken up too much time, telling him about some little deal, which was probably just small fry to him.

She rushed to her desk and put her things down. The staff were gathering, and she craned her neck to catch Pete's eye. He raised his eyebrows as if questioning her about the deal. She nodded and he smiled.

Tom started his speech. "We've proven that we can write large volumes of mortgages for homes and small businesses. Now, we're going to expand our horizons to another lending sphere: corporate and the secondary mortgage market. Plus, we're going to offer even cheaper interest rates. We're going to undercut every other financial institution in this country, and we'll fund it via our retail deposit base."

The announcement was greeted with a murmur in the back where she stood.

"How are we going to make extra profit?" Tom paused and scanned the faces.

Quin looked around. Was he expecting an answer?

"By generating income from the fees we'll charge. Every staff member is to source and secure new clients who have money to invest, as well as clients who want to borrow, by offering them lucrative interest rates. I want everyone to be proactive like Quin. Where's Quin?"

She raised her hand reluctantly and everyone turned to stare.

"Quin rang clients out of the phone book and, with a strike rate of one out of three, managed to bring in a $350,000 loan today. If you want to pick up business, it can be as simple as that. Thanks Quin."

He looked at her, and her face burned.

"This is a team effort," he said. "If Solid Rock does well, so will you."

After the meeting, Larry called Quin into his office. "The boss wants you to go out with him to get a deal he's been chasing. He's taking the client to lunch and wants someone there to take down all the details."

Quin swallowed. "When?"

"Tomorrow. And whenever he needs you. You must have impressed him."

She could hardly wait to tell Pete. Then she thought about her workload. "Uh, how will I get the rest of my work done if I'm going to be out?" she blurted.

"You'll just have to work back, I guess."

Larry picked up the phone and dialled, dismissing her.

That night at dinner in a Malaysian restaurant, she told Pete her news. He leant over and kissed her. "You're amazing."

They'd been going out for six months but had kept their relationship a secret from everyone at work. Not even Deb knew, or at least Quin hoped she didn't. Ben and Nan had met Pete and while Nan approved, Ben was non-committal.

"You know it's a big deal to work with the boss. I'm really proud of you."

"God, I hope I don't stuff it up."

"You'll be fine. He doesn't pick just anybody. I've done it a few times and learnt a lot. He's the master of negotiating a deal. He seems to have a power. Whatever he says, clients believe it. Of course, your job will be to bring the deal together. But you will."

She sipped her wine and pushed away doubts of whether she'd be good enough.

"Now how about we celebrate properly, and you come home to my place and stay the night?"

"I can't. Nan would be furious. I don't want to upset her.

Besides, now I've got all this extra work and study, I don't have time."

He looked hurt. "No time for me?"

"Probably only weekends. I wish I'd already finished the course like you, but it's only six months to go until I have that piece of paper. Then maybe I'll stay over, I promise."

16

LUCILLE

1938

"Urgh." Bethany screwed up her face. "It's almost as bad as marrying a Catholic."

"You liked him," Lucille said, sitting on Bethany's bed. "Why aren't you happy for me? I really want you to be my bridesmaid, Beth."

"I have to get my head around it. People are already gossiping."

Lucille thought back to where she and Max had been. She'd been so vigilant, keeping their relationship a secret. They had gone out without a chaperone, but everyone knew he was her cousin. Still, she'd let her guard down once when they'd kissed at night in the car outside of her house. Did someone see something?

"What people? What are they saying?"

"Why didn't you tell me what was going on? You kept this whole thing a secret. My parents said you were mooning over Max, especially at the dance, and I told them it was stupid of them to say that. Now they're going to be so righteous."

So, it was only Beth's parents at the dance, ages ago. She drummed her fingers on the pink chenille bedspread. She hadn't expected this reaction from her best friend.

Bethany folded her arms. "And I thought you were going to be teacher."

"I don't really care. If I wasn't going to be married, then I would have done it to earn a living. Max is all for it but says we don't need the money." Lucille glanced at her diamond, moving her hand around to catch the light. "I just want to take care of Max and have children. That's my job once I'm a married woman."

Bethany raised her eyebrows. "We all want that, but we don't marry our cousins, do we?"

Lucille stared at Bethany. "That's not very nice. Are you jealous that I'm getting married first?"

"Of course not. Patrick will probably ask me. I think he's the one. But what I'm saying is it's not really the done thing, is it?"

"What?"

"Marrying your cousin. Are you absolutely sure?"

"Look Beth, I'm not going to force you to be bridesmaid, and I don't want to lose your friendship, but I am going to marry Max, and that's all there is to it. Do I have your support or not?"

Beth shrugged. "I'm sorry. I suppose it'll be fine." She

sighed. "I don't want to fight, and I'm happy for you, really I am." She leant over and hugged her. "And I do want to be bridesmaid. Now show me the ring again."

*

The next few weeks were filled with wedding preparations. They had no relatives, so it was to be a small wedding.

One day, Lucille answered the front door to a slight woman dressed in a tailored dark-green suit with a matching felt hat resting on her grey hair.

"Lucille?" the woman said.

"Yes."

The woman stared at her from head to toe. Under the scrutiny, Lucille shifted self-consciously from one foot to the other.

"Um, can I help you?

"You can invite me in. I'm Grandmother Stewart." The woman's chin jutted out, and she made no move to hug her. Lucille wondered if she should at least shake her hand.

"Oh, sorry," Lucille said, swallowing hard. She pushed her hair behind her ears. "Please come in."

She prayed Pa had heard their voices in time to put on his shoes and get himself composed.

Her grandmother was nothing like she'd visualised. The one she'd imagined was plump and jolly. She wondered where she'd got that idea from. It wasn't as if there were any photos. As she stood aside to let her grandmother in, the woman's eyes darted to the peeling wallpaper in the corner. Lucille opened her mouth to say they were going to fix it one day, but the look of distaste on the woman's face made her close her mouth quickly.

"This way," Lucille said. For once, the loungeroom looked tidy. There were so many questions Lucille wanted to ask: Why was her grandmother here? Why now and not back when Lucille needed her? There was a lot to talk about.

"Um, take a seat," Lucille said, her heart sinking at another look of disapproval.

"You mean, please sit down, don't you?"

The woman peered around the room as if it were the last place she wanted to be.

"Um, yes."

"Yes," the woman corrected. "There is no 'um'."

"Yes," Lucille said. "Would you like a cup of tea?"

"Yes, that would be nice. Thank you."

Her grandmother gave a curt nod and perched herself on the edge of the seat as if it too were filthy. She clutched her black handbag tightly on her lap with green-gloved hands.

"And I'll see where Pa is."

Lucille found Pa hiding in the kitchen, trying to put his tie on. "Do you know why my grandmother is here?" she hissed, helping to straighten his tie.

"Because I sent her a note. Frankly, I didn't expect a response, and I especially didn't expect her to turn up here unannounced," he whispered.

"You might have mentioned it," Lucille said.

Pa strode into the lounge room leaving Lucille preparing a tray with their best teacups. She heard Pa greeting her grandmother and making small talk about Melbourne's weather.

Lucille brought out the tray, and her grandmother took a teacup, her hands still gloved. She regarded the tea with suspicion.

"I'm glad to see you're using your mother's teacups, the ones I gave her when she married. God rest her soul."

"Yes," Pa said. "We've missed her."

"We've all missed her, Clarence." Her grandmother's pale-blue eyes darted at him before she set the teacup on the coffee table.

Lucille suppressed a smile, seeing Pa's look of dismay at the use of his formal name, as if he were a boy in front of the headmistress. She sat up straighter herself, waiting for her grandmother to acknowledge her. Her eye caught a lone ant valiantly crossing the coffee table towards the sugar cubes. She held her breath. It made it to the bowl and disappeared for a moment before it reappeared, hovering on the rim of the sugar bowl.

"Is the tea strong enough?" Lucille said, leaning across and picking up the bowl. She deftly squashed the ant, flicked it onto the floor, dropped a cube into her own teacup before returning the bowl to the coffee table.

"It's adequate."

Adequate? Lucille wondered if she should have put more

tea-leaves into the pot. Some people were so pedantic about that.

"Let me get to the point of my visit. I'm here to take my only granddaughter home with me so she can go to a good finishing school. She needs help coming out into society, and I'm the person who can do that for her." The woman glanced at Lucille as if she were a stray dog needing a bath and a good feed. "She should have come to me when Beatrice passed. You weren't capable of bringing the child up. I told you that at the time."

This was news. What might her life have been like if she'd lived with her grandmother? Would it have been better? But how could she warm to this woman who was already trying to control her life?

Pa slumped so far into his seat, he looked as if he'd disappear into the crease if he could.

"I don't know if you are aware, Grandmother Stewart, but I'm engaged to be married," Lucille said. She sipped her tea and grimaced at the extra sugar. She put it down, carefully keeping her hands steady.

"Sit up straight, child," her grandmother said, before turning back to Pa. "This marriage business is nonsense. She needs to go to finishing school."

"I wrote to let you know out of courtesy … not for you to come all this way," Pa muttered.

"She's far too young for marriage."

"Actually, I've just turned eighteen," Lucille said quietly, holding her hands in her lap to stop them shaking. Why was she so nervous about this woman she didn't know and who had no clue about her?

The woman blinked and faltered for only a few seconds before she puffed out her chest in raw composure. "Either way, she needs to be mixing in the right circles and marry the right man. Rest assured Clarence, I won't allow this to happen again."

Lucille looked at her grandmother's determined face, then at Pa who looked like a wild-eyed animal caught in a trap. This was about her parents, not her. It was clear that her grandmother disapproved of her parents' marriage. She shouldn't be forced to pay for that. This was her life and this woman didn't have a say.

"I'm sitting right here. I'm a grown woman now. I appreciate the fact that you'd like to help, but it's too late. I've made up my mind to marry Max."

"Poppycock! You've been stuck in this hovel with a father who should have known better. Moving you around so I couldn't find you and be part of your life. Really, do you honestly say you can call this … this … filthy place fit for a young lady?" She ran a gloved finger along the wood of the armchair and sniffed.

Pa shrank further into his chair, his head low. "We've done all right."

Lucille's anger rose. She watched her grandmother inspect her glove, satisfied the woman hadn't found a grain of dirt.

"Lucille, I don't know what you're thinking. He's your cousin. Your mother would be turning in her grave. You mark my words, marrying your cousin, besides being highly distasteful, will cause defects in your children, even kill them. It's a well-known fact. You'll be shunned by society and you'll have nothing but trouble. And what's more, I'm sure it's illegal. Now pack your things. I have a car waiting. You're coming home with me."

Lucille looked at her father, slumped in his chair. He was no help, but then he never had been. She had to stay calm. "Thank you for the offer to come and live with you, and for your advice. However, I love Max. You're probably not aware, but it's not illegal to marry a cousin, and in fact, many well-known people have done so. Queen Victoria married her cousin, as did Charles Darwin. I won't be coming to live with you. I will marry Max, and there is nothing you can say or do to persuade me otherwise."

Lucille wiped her sweating hands on her skirt. Her grandmother stared at Lucille before she rose to her feet.

"How dare you speak to me like that." Her eyes flashed at Lucille, then she turned to Pa. "Clarence, this is all your fault." Her eyes darted back to Lucille. "Young lady, you should not be marrying that man. You are headed into a life of ruin, and I for one will not give my blessing, nor will I attend any wedding. Think very hard about what you're doing. Mark my words. No good will come from it." Her eyes narrowing, the woman leant forward poking her finger at Lucille. "Do you hear me! Your life will be utterly ruined, just like your mother's was. Sooner or later. And there'll be nothing you will be able to do about it."

She straightened her hat and left without another word, leaving Lucille saddened and Pa sullen.

She and Max were married a month later in a small ceremony.

17

LUCILLE

1992

If only the girl knew it was her anxiety and worry that had shrunk her appetite. Just the waft of tomato when Quin unwrapped the sandwich was enough to turn her stomach.

She watched her eating, envying her youth and the life ahead of her.

"You know you have a lifetime to correct your mistakes."

Quin stopped chewing. "What makes you think I've made mistakes?"

"Everyone makes mistakes, dear. I've made a mountain of them but have no time left to fix them."

Quin looked thoughtful. "I see what you mean. But sometimes we can't always see how to fix things."

"Or maybe we're not given the opportunity." The townspeople would be happy to see the last of her, of that Lucille was sure, and she had no way of fixing what Tom had done. She pictured Shirley smiling with glee now that she'd left. No doubt Stan would have told her first. "But when we're given the opportunity, one should grab it and enjoy life while you can."

"You make it seem as though you haven't had a happy life."

"Oh goodness, I'm just prattling on dear. How did we get onto this?" Lucille forced a laugh. "Let's talk about something else. It'll help pass the time faster."

"Good idea. But first, I'm going to find us a coffee. Would you like one?"

"No dear. But you go ahead."

Lucille sighed as she watched Quin go through the carriage door. She'd scared the lass away with her melancholic talk. She tried to focus on something positive, and her mind drifted to the memories of the photos in her handbag. Her wedding to Max was one of the happiest days of her life. Pa had looked at her proudly, kissed her when he gave her away and wiped a tear from his cheek. In that moment, she'd forgiven him for taking her childhood.

Max waiting for her as she walked down the aisle, his smile, his eagerness to touch her when he took her hand. Then his lips on hers, his hand on her waist as they walked out of the church, stood on the steps and posed for the photo.

18

QUIN

JUNE, 1988

Lunchtime the next day, Quin went to Tom's office armed with a notebook. She hoped her navy-blue suit and fake pearl earrings with a matching necklace were corporate enough for a lunch with a CEO.

"Ready?" he said, putting on his suit jacket. He stared at her and frowned before turning away to pull out a draw.

"Here, this looks better," he said, handing her a leather compendium with Solid Rock embossed in gold on the front.

"Oh, I couldn't take yours."

"It's not mine. It's the new merchandising. All staff will get one, but you can have this. First rule, Quin, is that you've got to look the part, then play the part, then be the part."

She ran her hand over the leather.

"Now you look the part," he said, his eyes drifting from her face to her neck to linger above the neckline of her blouse.

Then he glanced at his watch. "Let's go." As she followed him out of the office, she flung her tatty notebook on Deb's desk.

When she got into Tom's new red Ferrari, the fresh leather smell caught her by surprise and she coughed.

"Yeah, it's a bit strong," he said, starting the engine.

"It's okay."

On the way, she took notes as Tom chatted about the client and his business. "He's not going to have much collateral, but I want you to work out a way of getting the deal across the line so it looks good on paper."

The car idled at the lights, and he turned to look at her. "Do you think you can do that?"

"Yes."

She didn't quite know what that meant. Did he want her to lie or massage the information perhaps? She'd heard Larry use that term. "Massage the information" so it looks like an acceptable deal to satisfy the auditors and the regulatory bodies. This must be what Tom meant by playing the part.

Lunch was at an expensive restaurant, one she and Pete could never have afforded. The food was delicious and she made small talk and smiled. Then the conversation turned to business. She took down notes, and the client handed over his draft financial statements. Tom dropped her at the office, and she got to work. She took the financial statements, put together a deal and submitted it. There was an unsecured component, and she wondered whether Larry would approve it. By the time she was ready to go home, it was back on her desk and approved. No questions. She'd played her part yet she didn't know if she should be happy or worried. She decided on being happy.

The following Monday she met Tom at the airport. Her first business trip interstate to Sydney. She was nervous and excited. When they boarded the plane, he helped her with her overnight bag, and she bumped into him when she sat.

"Sorry," she said, cursing herself.

She pulled out her compendium and pen, but he put his hand on hers. "Let's not talk about work on the plane. We're going to be flat out when we land, so put it away and relax." He removed his hand.

"Oh, okay."

He closed his eyes.

"Big weekend?" she said.

His green eyes flashed at her before he smiled. "Is it that obvious? Man of my age should be slowing down. Is that what you think?"

"No, no of course not. What did you get up to?"

"Attended the footy in the corporate box, then stayed out a bit too late. And then had to drive down to Hammondville to see my poor old mum. An eight-hour round trip is a bit much." He looked at her to see her reaction. "You?"

She wondered how much to tell him. "I went to my boyfriend's place and, yesterday, watched my brother play footy. Nothing much."

"I hear your boyfriend is Pete. Is that true?"

"Did Deb tell you?"

"She might have let something slip."

This was news. Maybe Pete had said something to Deb. She shouldn't have been surprised. Deb was extremely perceptive.

"Pete's a nice bloke, and I've got big plans for him." He looked at her. "And you."

"Really?"

"The company's expanding rapidly, and I need people I can trust right by my side."

The scent of his musk aftershave overpowered her. She coughed.

"You can count on me, Tom."

"I'm glad."

It was exhilarating going out with Tom in the weeks that followed. They took clients to expensive restaurants. She was by Tom's side at cocktail parties on yachts, in seaside mansions in Portsea and, once, even flew by helicopter to Hammondville.

Tom told Larry to distribute Quin's clients to the others so she could be available solely for him. She got a substantial pay rise and a new title, Relationship Executive, writing up all the deals Tom was acquiring. The after-hours work meant she had to defer her studies, and she only saw Pete on weekends.

*

"I'm going to Sydney tomorrow," she said to Pete when they were lying in bed Sunday morning. "And staying overnight. Then we go to the Gold Coast to get a deal with a consortium of investors. So, I probably won't see you until next weekend."

"Tom's really bringing in a ton of business."

"Ten million in the last month. You're not upset, are you?"

"That he didn't pick me to go with him? Hell no. I've got more than enough on my plate now that the deals are landing on my desk. You're doing a great job, you know."

Why did she feel as though he was giving her a work-performance feedback session?

She propped herself on one elbow. "So, you don't give a stuff that you won't see me until next weekend?"

He wasn't smiling. She was joking but wondered if their relationship was waning. Pete seemed to care more about work since she'd started her new job, happy that she was handing the deals off to him and building his client portfolio.

"Of course, I'm going to miss you. But I guess I'll be so busy it'll go fast." He rolled off the bed. "I'm going to take a shower first. That okay with you?"

She slumped back into the pillow and wondered if he was jealous of her success.

*

One evening when she got home late, Ben and Nan were sitting at the kitchen table strewn with papers.

"What's going on here?" she asked.

"I'm gunna buy two video stores in Hoppers Crossing. I was showing Nan." Ben's face was flushed with excitement.

"It seems a great opportunity, love." Nan looked at Ben and patted his arm. "It'll get Ben out of that garage."

"How much?" she said, throwing off her heels.

"Thirty thousand for both of them." Ben leafed through a flyer and held it out for Quin.

"Mmm," she said examining it. She handed it back, then opened the oven to take out the plate Nan had left her. "I'm not sure it's prudent to buy two stores. Just get one to see how it goes. You can assess the cash flow, build up the business, then after that, buy another one."

"Stop being a stick in the mud. I want to get ahead. It's a licence to print money, and I don't have to justify it to you just because you think you're a big wig in a crummy building society. If you were any good, you'd be working for one of the major banks."

She scooped up the crusted mashed potato on her fork. "Calm down. I'm just trying to give you some sound financial advice. How are you going to pay for these two businesses?"

"I'm going to borrow the money and hopefully that's where you come in. Get me one of those cheap deals you keep raving about."

"I think it's a good idea. I'm happy to mortgage my house," Nan said.

Quin chewed on the tough lamb chop. "Thirty thousand dollars is a lot to pay off."

"Stick in the mud," he muttered. "I'm not actually asking your permission, but I'm buying both stores, and if you don't want to organise the finance for me, then I'll go somewhere else. I'm not holding a bloody gun to Nan. She's the one who said to get two."

Quin gave him a withering look. "Video stores are great

businesses. Okay, let me finish eating, then you can show me and Nan the figures, and we'll sort something out."

Nan looked at Ben. "See? I told you if Quin thinks it's good, then it will be. She's looking at businesses all day. Isn't that right?"

Quin nodded.

19

LUCILLE

1939

Lucille hummed as she pulled out the weeds in the front garden of their newly built home in Camberwell. She'd been shocked when Max had surprised her with the new home just before their wedding, ten months earlier.

"How can you afford it?" she'd asked walking around the three bedrooms, visualising them filled with their children.

"When Mum died the bank sold the house but there was a little left over which came to me."

"I remember that you said something about that. But how was that enough to buy a brand-new house?"

He'd smiled. "I invested the money on the share market and I made quite a bit. So I sold them and here we are. Do you like it?"

"I absolutely love it. Everything is brand new, even an inside bathroom and toilet. What a luxury."

She sat back on her heels, wiped her face with a handkerchief and admired the freshly mown lawn and the rose bushes dotted across the garden beds. Once bare-root stems, planted in winter, they now held a lovely display of pink and white blooms. She'd loved Aunt Mavis's rose garden when she'd stayed there after her mother died. There was one thing missing. A purple rose like the one Aunt Mavis had grown. She'd loved its colour and scent and one day she would find it for her own garden and plant it right near the front door.

"Hello!" Mildred yelled from next door, her large arms full of shopping parcels. Lucille waved back, then wiped the sweat from her face with a handkerchief. Mildred struggled to open her white picket gate and Lucille got up, ready to help, but Mildred seemed to manage. Lucille liked her neighbour, who was the mother of five sons. When the time came, she hoped Mildred would be a source of knowledge, perhaps even a mother figure to help her with her own children.

She glanced at her watch. Max would be home soon from work. It was high time she got ready to cook dinner. How she loved married life, looking after the house and him.

The potatoes were mashed and beans boiled by the time Max came home, breathless with excitement.

"Petal!'

Ever since she'd started growing roses, he'd begun calling her Petal. She loved how it sounded.

"Guess what?"

With one eye on the chops, she glanced at her husband's flushed face.

"I got a promotion."

She squealed. "Darling, that's wonderful." She flew to him, smothering him with kisses.

Max laughed. "Now that's what I call a homecoming. I should get a promotion more often."

Lucille let him go and moved to turn the chops over in the pan. "Sit down, dinner's just about ready. Tell me about the promotion?"

"I'll be working exclusively on the pesticide research."

"Does that mean more money?"

Should she have asked about the money? It wasn't her business. When she needed money, Max gave it to her, which was different to Pa, who'd given her a set amount each week for housekeeping and bills and never asked questions. But Max did. He was careful with money, which made her feel uncomfortable for asking. Still, he wanted her to go shopping, to splurge on anything she needed, get the purple rose she badly wanted, but he had no idea what things cost. Although, she would need to buy some new dresses soon and wondered how to broach it.

He nodded and looked into the pot. "I think so. I'm starving."

"It won't be long. Now you're getting under my feet," she said, guiding him to the kitchen table. "Why don't you tell me about the job?"

He tugged on his shirt sleeve, a tell-tale sign of his anxiety.

"What?" she said.

He looked up and tilted his head to one side. She took off her apron and hung it on the hook behind the door.

"Out with it," she said. "There's something else isn't there?"

"No, not really. I have to join up, that's all. This thing in Europe is hotting up."

She sat at the table and stared at her plate, her appetite gone.

"But I won't be going anywhere. The Defence chaps are interested in the research and want us to work for them."

"Harvey too?" She picked up her fork and buried the beans under the mashed potato.

He laughed. "Even Harvey. I'd love to know what Geraldine says when he tells her."

"Me too," Lucille said, remembering how angry Geraldine had been at dinner a few weeks before, when they'd discussed the likelihood of war. Germany had issued the order for one hundred Jews per day to be deported from Germany, and Harvey had argued that Hitler needed to be stopped, forewarning that Britain and Australia would have to get involved too. "It's not our fight," Geraldine said. Lucille had silently agreed.

"She won't like it," Max said. "I reckon it'll mean less travel though, so I should be home more."

"Well, that'll be good. I'm sick of you going to Canberra all the time. Now, I have some news too." Suddenly, Lucille felt like a young girl overcome with shyness.

His eyes widened, he leant forwards. "You found the purple rose?"

"No," she said, smiling. "But you're going to have to increase my housekeeping."

He sat back in his chair, his hands crossed in front of him on the table, looking mortified. "Haven't I been giving you enough?"

"Not enough to feed an extra mouth."

"Is Pa coming to live with us? I've been saying all along he should. It's not good for him to be alone."

She leant over and patted his arm. "No, you goose! I think we might be having a baby."

He jumped up and grabbed her around the waist. "A baby?" He kissed her so hard she was breathless.

"It's only early days. I'm going to the doctor tomorrow. But I'm fairly certain. I'm tired and feel a bit odd."

"Odd? Are you all right?"

"Yes. I smelt the milk today, and it turned my stomach. That sort of thing. I should expect to be a bit queasy. That's what I've heard anyway."

"A baby. God, I love you. You've made me so happy," Max said. "Our own little family. We need to celebrate."

"We need to save money now," Lucille said, laughing. "Let's just have an early night instead." She winked.

*

By the fourth month, Lucille hated being pregnant. She'd celebrated her first wedding anniversary with her head in the toilet bowl. She'd also declined Bethany's invitation to celebrate her engagement to Patrick. Mildred made some herbal tea for her but confessed to having had easy pregnancies. Lucille was so exhausted, sometimes all she could do was lie on the bathroom floor.

Max's prediction about staying in Melbourne had been wrong. He was away more than ever and had little idea of what she was going through.

"It'll pass. That's what Geraldine said. It's usually for three months," Max said, one evening.

"How would Geraldine know? She's never had a baby," Lucille snapped. "The doctor said I might be one of those women who are sick for the whole pregnancy."

They'd argued when she finally found out that joining up meant soldier's wages, not the big increase they'd both expected. She hadn't been able to buy the purple rose. Instead, she'd scrimped and saved just to buy maternity clothes.

She knew Max tried to understand, but no matter what he did, it seemed wrong to Lucille. She felt guilty afterwards, but he honestly couldn't know how she felt. No-one could. Alone and feeling sorry for herself, she wondered why she was being punished by this wretched child. Her grandmother's warning swirled in her head.

*

By early September, Lucille was sick of herself. Her bulging stomach, discomfort and tiredness made her irritable.

"Max, the tea you made was dreadful," she said, waddling her bulk into the kitchen. "Did you at least boil the water? I need another cup." She replaced the tea-leaves in the pot and put the kettle on to boil. "How can you make a bad cup of tea? It's not a difficult job. It's the one thing I need first thing in the morning before I get out of bed. And today of all days, when I've had hardly any sleep with this child constantly kicking me, you manage to make the worst cup of tea I've ever had."

Max's head was in the newspaper, his own tea untouched.

"Did you hear a word I said?"

"Uh?" he put his paper down and looked at her as if he hadn't noticed she was there.

"What's wrong?" she said.

"We're at war."

Lucille carefully eased herself onto the chair, forgetting about the tea. "I don't understand." Then she saw the headlines on the front page and shivered. *Britain and France at war with Germany. Australia pledges full support.*

"We missed Menzies's announcement. He was on the wireless last night when we were out for a walk. I can't say I'm surprised. We've given them enough warning. Since Hitler invaded Poland on Saturday, there's no other choice." Max dragged his hand over his face.

The baby kicked furiously, as if objecting to the news.

"If we're at war, what do you think will happen here?"

"I don't know. According to the newspaper, General Motors have pledged support with machinery and men. They're not looking for volunteers yet." He pushed the newspaper towards her.

"But you're already in the army. Will you need to go?"

"No. I shouldn't think so. The work we're doing is of utmost importance, so I reckon they'll want us to keep doing it." He got up and leant over to kiss her. "Don't worry. It'll be fine."

She frowned. "I'm not sure researching pesticides will be the most important thing to the government right now."

His face fell. "It's more important than ever. One day, I'll be able to tell you."

The country came first. Maybe she was just being paranoid, guilt chewing through her? She should be a better wife, stoic and dependable, not prone to hysterics like the stories she read in the Women's Weekly.

"Don't worry. I'll be staying put. I have to. We've got a baby coming." He smiled weakly. "I better get going. I'll see you later."

She was unsettled after he'd left, sure now that there was a war, she'd see him even less. She cried, sorry for herself. "I'm just fat and ugly," she sobbed. No wonder he wants to be away. The baby kicked again, and she soon forgot about the war. Her back ached and she rushed for the toilet.

20

QUIN

NOVEMBER, 1988

Quin organised the finance and Ben bought the two stores. The businesses did well. Sometimes, she and Nan helped out on weekends.

"I've banked the weekend takings today." Ben sat on the couch, looking like a cat that ate the cream. "It's the most we've done."

"Oh, that's wonderful love." Nan stopped knitting. "It must have been because there was a mature face behind the counter, recommending the old movies."

"Yes, it must have been," Ben said. He kissed Nan on the cheek.

"That's great," Quin said, grinning. She liked it when her brother was in a good mood.

"I've decided to invest the profits in those non-withdrawable investment shares in Solid Rock you keep talking about so we can make more money," Ben said.

Quin nodded. "Good idea. The rates are great now – up to eighteen per cent."

"The mortgage interest rate has been rising. Shouldn't we pay off the mortgage with it?" Nan said. "I was always taught to pay with cash and never go into debt unless it was for a house. And the idea was to pay it off as quickly as you could."

"What for? It's not the war years. You're getting a cheaper mortgage rate. You use the bank's money to make money. Everyone's doing it," Ben said.

"Non-withdrawable? What if we need the money?"

Ben rolled his eyes. "It's like a term deposit. We're not going to need the money until I'm ready to buy a house next year. Or do you want to get rid of me already?"

Nan looked aghast. "Of course I don't. You're being silly now. But I can't help worrying."

"You explain it to her." Ben looked at Quin.

Quin drummed her fingers on the table "I know you're worried about your house, but it's okay. It's like this. You invest at eighteen per cent, but we lend you money at fifteen per cent. You're ahead by three per cent. Ben is doing the right thing. The mortgage is interest only, so he only needs to pay the interest and that leaves the rest of the profits to invest. Do you get it?"

"I suppose it makes sense … I guess."

Quin watched Nan closely. "Okay?"

Nan nodded.

"Glad that's settled." Ben said. "What's for dinner?"

"It's ready. Come on." Nan heaved herself up from the

couch, and the three of them went into the kitchen. Ben talked about new movie releases coming up, and Quin told them about a new deal she'd put together for Tom.

"The minestrone needs salt," Nan said, sprinkling liberally.

Quin looked at Nan. "It doesn't. And too much salt is bad for you. Remember what the doctor said about your blood pressure?"

Nan shrugged. "Hmmph." She put the salt shaker down. "And how's Pete going? When are you going to bring him home for dinner?"

"Nice change of subject," Quin said, rolling her eyes.

"Poor sod, going out with you." Ben grinned and wiped his bowl with a slice of thick white bread.

"What are you paying those girls to go out with you?" Quin said.

"They pay me," Ben said. "I am, after all, what's called a catch, now that I'm on my way to my first million."

Quin laughed and so did Nan.

"Pete's good, but we're working such long hours we only get a chance to see each other on weekends."

Nan smiled. "You were always a hard worker, even at school."

Ben looked up. Quin tensed, hoping he didn't decide to have another competitive swipe at her for being the better student.

"And you're a hard worker too, darl," Nan said quickly.

"Huh, yeah." Ben's mind seemed to be elsewhere.

"Pete got a promotion the other day. He's going to work on corporate deals for Tom."

"Really? That's so nice for him."

"Tosser is what he is," Ben mumbled.

"Shut up, you dipshit. What is your problem with Pete?"

Ben narrowed his eyes. "Nothing. Actually, there's nothing specific. He's probably the best of a bad bunch of losers you've been with."

"Well, well, well. My big brother actually approves."

Ben grinned.

"Ask Pete over, and I'll make my special pot roast," Nan said.

"I will. You know his promotion's a big deal. Tom set up a new department to write large commercial loans, and Pete's heading it. Solid Rock had only lent money to small businesses up to now, but the big money is in larger loans. It's so exciting."

"When are you going get promoted again?" Ben said, leaning back in his kitchen chair, picking his teeth. "You're already on the boss's good side." He winked. "Maybe you should sleep your way to the top."

"You really are a disgusting, sexist pig. I sure hope you don't expect that from your female staff."

Ben's eyes widened. "I'm only joking. Chill will ya?"

"No-one's laughing. Are we Nan?"

Nan put a bowl of chocolate pudding in front of her brother. "It's not funny, Ben. You should know better. I didn't raise you to talk like that. I hope you treat your female staff with dignity and respect."

"I do, Nan. I do." Ben looked suitably chastised. "It was just a joke," he muttered.

"Anyway, I just got promoted," Quin said. "Remember?"

"Ben, the chair! How many times have I told you not to lean on it like that?"

"Sorry." Ben sat back.

"I'll leave you two to do the dishes. My show's on," Nan said.

"I'll wash, you dry," Quin said, clearing the dishes.

Ben picked up the tea towel. "You know we could do much better than we are? If we use your staff discount, the three of us could borrow a hundred thousand and invest in more of those Solid Rock non-withdrawable investment shares. What do you think?"

"But Nan would have to re-mortgage the house, and the debt would be up to a hundred and thirty thousand."

"Yeah, I know. But we'd make a lot more money. We'd earn at least eighteen thousand in interest, and that'd help to buy our own houses and build our wealth."

Quin laughed. "You've really been thinking about this?"

With the tea towel in one hand and a plate in the other, he looked at her. "Yeah, I have. Nan will go with it, especially if she thinks it'll help get ahead."

"Let me look into it."

Her brother made sense, and she did want to buy her first house as soon as possible. She'd just paid off the personal loan she'd got when she went overseas, before she started at Solid Rock. The idea began to take hold.

*

Over lunch the next day, she discussed it with Pete.

"Sure. That's the only way to get ahead. My parents mortgaged their house, and the three of us invested in QRP Property Developers and in Solid Rock shares. They're doing huge developments on the Gold Coast. Tom organised a seminar last year for staff, and QRP were there telling us about the opportunity to invest. It's only been a year, but I've got a great return. Everyone's got some money in it. Now I'm doing another loan for them. They're going gang busters. Tom is best mates with the QRP directors, and he's got a bit tied up with them too. He wouldn't steer any of us the wrong way. The other thing you could do is borrow using the shares as collateral, but you'd have to go to one of the major banks to get a loan. We don't do that here. Not yet anyway. The best bet is to use someone's house as collateral for the loan, maybe use your nan's?"

Quin frowned. "That doesn't seem right somehow."

Pete laughed. "It's business. What do you think? All these jokers are doing it."

"Who? Isn't that insider trading?"

"Insider trading? Nah, it's nothing like it. We're not using knowledge to buy shares in a company?"

Quin raised her eyebrows. "No? I think as the account manager you know what the company is doing, so surely buying shares in it and lending the client money is insider trading."

Pete laughed. "Was that in the last unit you studied? Listen, it's fine. No-one's going to jail. QRP is one of the accounts I'm getting in my new job. I bought my shares before I had them to manage. It's perfectly legit. I'll be able to keep close tabs on our investments. So there's no need to worry. Look, if you don't feel comfortable, diversify your investments between investment shares in Solid Rock and QRP. And if you don't want to use your nan's house as collateral, you could borrow using the shares as collateral. The only thing is the banks will call up the loan if the shares go down by too much. It happened last year when the shares crashed. It was a bit of a debacle – people losing everything and jumping off buildings. The best bet is to use someone's house as collateral for the loan. There's no way a house will ever go down in value. It just doesn't happen."

Quin chewed her lip. "Yeah, that might be the way to go. Ben wants to do it."

"Now you're thinking. You two go in together and make the repayments interest only." He leant forward and kissed her. "So, do you want to go and see that new James Bond film tonight?"

When Quin went home, she told Nan and Ben about the strategy for investing a hundred thousand. And even though Nan was nervous about it, they told her it would set them up. And that's what convinced her.

*

The next morning, Quin took a deep breath and walked over to Geoffrey Pelanter's desk. She'd prepared the loan application but she needed a favour. He wasn't well liked in the office and his leering stares made her uncomfortable. Harry High Pants was his nickname, in honour of the way he wore his dark-brown gaberdine trousers. His mullet haircut made his stocky neck look short as it nudged over his grubby collar.

"Geoff, I need you to do a valuation for me, please."

While Geoff assessed and approved loans, he also did property valuations. Nan's house was in his allocated area.

"And hello to you to, Quiny. Still going out with Pete? You know I'd be a better catch."

"I don't think so. Now can you do a valuation or not?"

"Depends. What do I get in return?"

"How about your job?" She crossed her arms. "Or I could check with Warren, and he can tell me who else could do the valuation."

Janie smiled and nodded, mouthing, "Bastard," before going back to her typing.

"Now don't be like that. Where's the property? A drive-by all right?"

Quin gave him the address. "When will you go out?"

"I reckon I can get there tomorrow. But I've got a big deal I'm working on and need a title search."

"I'll do your title search."

"Attagirl."

"And that's all! You're lucky I have to go to the Title's Office tomorrow anyway. Give me the details."

Back at her desk, she drew up the loan application with Ben, Nan and herself as joint applicants. She completed their financial details. Once she knew the value of the house, she could work out how much they could borrow, provided it was under eighty per cent of the value of the house. She sat back and looked out of the window – a perfect spring day, cloudless.

*

The valuation for Nan's house came back two days later. Geoff brought it to her himself.

He held the paper file. "It's an all right house. Thought you might have lived somewhere better."

"What makes you think I live there?"

"Just a hunch. Maybe when I was stopped out the front of the house, a little old lady had a chat to me." He looked like he was enjoying himself. Quin wondered why Nan hadn't mentioned it.

"Geoff, get in 'ere. And bring the Hatcher file with you," Larry hollered from his office.

"You better get going then, hadn't you Geoffrey? And thank you for the valuation." Quin smiled her sweetest smile, enjoying his look of panic.

He threw the valuation on her desk and scurried to the other side of the office.

Quin opened the file surprised at the amount: $165,000. The mortgage for Ben's two video stores was only thirty thousand, and if Nan increased the mortgage by another one hundred thousand, they would have a really good investment. She wrote in the amount and dropped the file into Warren's in-basket for approval. Then she headed out to meet Tom and a client in Collins Street.

21

LUCILLE

1939

Patricia was born on 15 December 1939. Lucille held Patricia in her arms and wondered why her baby looked so ugly. With screwed up eyes on a red wrinkled face, she looked more like an old lady than the cute baby she'd hoped for. The magazines had said she'd fall head over heels in love with her baby, but so far, she'd felt nothing. Still, Patricia seemed to be perfectly normal as far as she could tell.

"Do all babies look like this?"

The nurse looked up as she tucked Lucille's bedsheet in. "Of course. I'm going to let your husband in now that you're presentable. He's been making such a fuss to see the baby. Really, he should be looking at her in the nursery. Who knows what germs he has?"

"Germs?" Lucille suddenly wondered if she should have kissed her daughter.

"I'll be back shortly to take the baby to the nursery so you can rest."

The child nuzzled against her and made a sucking noise.

"Rightio. I won't tire her." Max swept in and closed the door tight. "She's like an army general." In a few short strides, he was kissing her.

"Do you want to hold our new baby?"

"Can I?"

"Have you washed your hands?"

"Of course, I have. That old battle-axe wouldn't let me in otherwise."

He took his daughter, and Lucille watched his face transform, smiling and cooing as he held Patricia.

"Next to you, she's the most beautiful little thing I've ever seen."

Lucille laughed. "Even as scrunched up as she is? She doesn't look very glamorous right now."

"She's just perfect. Are you all right?"

She nodded. "Good, now that the pain is gone."

"Your father's out there. Do you want him to come in?"

"Go get him, then you better leave before the nurse comes back. You're meant to look at her in the baby nursery."

Max looked up sharply and frowned. "She's my baby, and I should be able to hold her anytime I like."

"I'm just warning you. Matron is fierce about the rules."

"You leave her to me. I'll get your father. He's desperate to see you and our new little miss." He handed Patricia back and left.

Lucille stared at her baby. "God, how am I going to look after you? I've never even had a pet. But then I did have a baby for a father, so perhaps I can."

*

By the time Lucille went home, she'd forgotten all about how hard the pregnancy had been. Just holding her little girl, breathing her in and cuddling her close made it all worthwhile.

She fed her with precision timing, as she'd been directed by the hospital. Six in the morning, midday, then six at night. She took her out in a pram for the recommended daily hour of sunshine. Patricia was the perfect baby for the first two days, then she cried. Constantly. She hardly ever slept and neither did Lucille. The only time the child stopped crying was when she was fed, and then she slept long enough so Lucille could wash the never-ending nappies and throw something together for dinner. The days seemed to fly and yet she'd done nothing.

Patricia was two weeks old when Max went to Sydney for work, warning her there were more work trips likely. Not that he could do much to help her, Lucille reasoned. He tried his best, walking Patricia up and down the hallway, in the pram, but the baby wasn't easily subdued. Max had a job to do, and so did she, except hers was done with little sleep.

*

It was a warm day, and Lucille dragged herself from the house with the screaming baby. As she navigated the pram down her verandah steps, Mildred came out of her front door and waved. Lucille waved back happy to see Mildred's smiling face as she marched over out of her garden and into hers.

"I've been meaning to pop over and see the little one. How're you going, love?"

Lucille nodded. Patricia cried harder.

Mildred touched her arm. "You do look tired, love. But that's babies for you. May I?"

Lucille nodded as Mildred reached into the pram and picked up Patricia. "There, there, little one. What's the matter?"

"She just cries all night and all day. I'm at my wit's end," Lucille blurted, fighting back tears.

Mildred put the crook of her thumb in Patricia's mouth, much to Lucille's horror. Had the woman washed her hands?

"How often are you feeding her?"

"Three times a day."

Mildred's face turned red. "What?"

"That's what they told me in the hospital," Lucille hurried to say. Mildred's mouth was still open in dismay, as if Lucille had mortally sinned. "Have I done something I shouldn't have?"

Mildred shook her head. "Goodness, no. See how she's sucking on my thumb? Come back inside and feed the lass. She's crying because she's hungry. That's all. You're just hungry aren't you?"

Bewildered, Lucille opened the door for Mildred and

Patricia and followed them inside. Why on earth would her baby be hungry after only four hours?

"Don't take any notice of those nurses. Half of them don't have kids and haven't a clue."

"You mean that's all that's wrong?"

"More than likely."

She was surprised how Patricia opened her mouth greedily, searching for her nipple. Mildred was right.

"How about I make you a cup of tea?"

Lucille nodded gratefully, then remembered the mess of dirty dishes in the sink from the night before, not to mention her breakfast bowl and cup. Whatever would Mildred think of her? Too late, she was trapped in the chair with a baby attached to her, and Mildred had already disappeared. She listened to water running, the sound of clattering dishes and then the kettle's whistle.

"Please, make yourself a cup too, Mildred." Lucille yelled out. "Don't mind the mess. I was going to clean up later." Patricia squirmed. Time to burp and swap sides.

Mildred soon came back with two cups of tea, then leant over to peer at Patricia. "When she cries, check her nappy, feed and burp her, and you should have a much happier time of it. Feed her when she wants it."

"I can't begin to thank you. I don't know anyone who's had a baby. I just followed what the nurses told me."

"If you need anything, just yell out. Goodness knows, I've had five of my own. And one set of twins. That was hard work. All boys. Eighteen, that's the twins; nineteen;

twenty-one; and twenty-two. I would have loved a girl, of course. The eldest joined up, and the other boys followed."

Patricia had fallen asleep, and Lucille gently put her into the pram.

"My husband joined up last year. But he's in the science area doing research."

Mildred frowned. "I don't know much about that. But you mark my words. They'll all be off overseas before we even know it."

"Oh, my husband won't be going."

"I hope for your sake he doesn't." Frowning, Mildred looked at her watch. "And I hope this war is over before they do get shipped out." She stood, collected both cups and took them to the kitchen.

"Oh, let me take those …" Lucille said, trailing behind her. Mildred was already washing the cups and saucers, and Lucille took in the spotless kitchen. "You didn't need to wash my dishes, but thank you."

"All done, love. No bother at all. Hardly anything. I better get going. Now, if you need anything just holler."

Lucille smiled wearily. "I will. Thanks for your help."

"You get some rest while she's sleeping. Don't fuss over the housework. That beautiful little girl is the most important thing right now."

*

Mother and baby settled into a routine. Max was away a lot, and when he was home, he seemed distracted. "I'm sorry, Petal. The research is getting more urgent, and I can't help working the long hours. Let me hold the baby while you do something else."

"I'll change her nappy first, then you can hold her."

"Show me and I'll change her."

Lucille looked up sharply. "You change her?" She chuckled. "You'll probably stick her with a pin. No, you relax darling, and I'll get her ready for you."

He didn't protest as he slumped into the armchair. Soon, he gently held his daughter and spoke to her in a whisper. "How's my beautiful girl?"

Lucille folded nappies on the dining table and watched Max turn Patricia's face towards him.

He ran his finger under her chin. "It's your daddy." He frowned. "Are all babies like this?"

"Like what?"

"She doesn't seem to be, well … I don't know how to describe it. She just looks blankly at me."

Lucille barely trusted her voice not to betray her worry. "She's just tired that's all. She's only two months. Babies don't do anything until they're at least six months old. They just eat, sleep and fill their nappy. They don't know what's going on in the world, and they're not interested. I'll put her down for her nap." She reached for the child.

Max shrugged and picked up the newspaper. "If you say so. You're the expert."

But she wasn't. There was something about her child that didn't seem right. She couldn't put her finger on it. Since she'd learnt to feed her properly, the baby had seemed content enough. Too content. Some days she was hard to wake. And Lucille was worried. On other days, she seemed normal enough. But neither she nor Max knew what was normal and what wasn't, and she felt foolish asking Mildred.

A few days earlier, she'd taken Patricia to the baby health centre sister, where she was weighed and checked. Lucille let out a long breath when the weight increased on the scales, but not enough it seemed. The nurse was officious with little time for her, and Lucille didn't like to ask questions when the waiting room was so crowded.

The nurse told her to stop breast feeding and turn to the bottle. Dismissed, Lucille stared at the other babies in the waiting room. One baby, dressed in blue, stared back and smiled at her, and she stopped on her way out.

"How old is your baby? He's beautiful."

The baby wriggled in his mother's arms.

"He's just over two months old. Such a handful. Doesn't stay still. I reckon he wants to get going."

"He's certainly lively."

Lucille's own baby lay quietly in her pram, staring into space.

"She's a cutie. Does she sleep?"

"Yes, most of the time, actually."

"Gee, I wish mine did. I'm worn out if truth be told. Oh, that's me she's calling. Nice talking to you."

Wheeling the pram down the street, Lucille was deep in thought. Patricia was a good sleeper now and so well behaved. Not like that other little boy. All was well. She only had to feed Patricia a bottle and the weight would pile on.

*

A month later, Max burst through the front door calling for her.

"I'm in the kitchen," she called out, wiping her hands on the tea towel. "Patricia's asleep so don't go in and wake her."

Max clumped down the hallway and stopped in the doorway, stretching his arms to touch the top of the door frame. His lips formed a thin line. "I'm going."

She fixed her gaze on him. "Going?" Her body shook, already responding to what she knew he'd say.

"Yep." He cleared his throat. "I got my orders today. I have to ship out to England. Back to Oxford to work on the research with the Brits."

Lucille slumped against the sink. This was the news she'd feared most. The newspapers and magazines were filled with hurried weddings and farewells to soldiers shipped overseas. "To work on research? Of a pesticide?" she snapped. "I know you think I won't understand, but it makes no sense to me that researching some stupid pesticide is important when we're at war. Just tell me the truth. Are you going to fight?"

He ran a hand through his hair. "No. I'm not going to fight. It's research for the war effort, and it's top secret. I can't tell you any more than that. It's important enough for them to want me to join the team there."

"Admit it, you're a little bit excited, aren't you?"

"About the work? I am, I suppose." He looked wistful.

"About leaving you? No. I wish I could take you with me. But I can't."

"When do you have to go?"

He avoided her eyes, pulled at his shirt cuff. "The ship sails tonight at nine. I don't have any choice."

"God." She turned around and put her hands on the sink, hiding her tears. The last thing she wanted was to be one of those wives who made it difficult for her husband. Women had an important role in supporting the war effort by giving their husbands strength for what they had to do, so the papers said.

It was already five o'clock. She'd had a long day with Patricia, feeding her every two to three hours, trying to get her to smile and getting no response. He came up behind her and kissed the back of her neck. "I'm sorry, Petal."

She turned around and they held each other for a long time. Finally, he let her go. "I've got to pack."

There was nothing she could say as she finished preparing their meal, fighting for control over her tears.

They ate hurriedly, in silence. Then made love. She clung to him as if she would never let him go. Eventually, he grasped her hands and lifted them away, rising to shower while she lay there allowing the tears to escape.

"What's the time?" he yelled from the bathroom.

She wiped her eyes with the back of her hand and threw on her robe. "It's almost seven thirty."

"Hell. The taxi will be here in ten minutes."

She watched him dress in his army uniform, his hair still

damp. When he was ready, he turned and planted his lips on hers, sliding his hands inside her robe quickly, grasping, before letting her go.

"Where's my baby girl?

"She's still asleep."

They crept into Patricia's room, and he leant down and kissed his daughter, then straightened to watch her, as if etching her image into his mind.

"Take this." Lucille pushed a photo of herself and Patricia into his hands. "And come back to us."

He kissed her. "I will, my darling, I will."

The taxi's impatient horn interrupted them. And then he was gone.

22

QUIN

DECEMBER, 1988

To celebrate her four-thousand-dollar bonus, Quin bought a dress for the work Christmas party and invested the rest on non-withdrawable shares in Solid Rock. With the high interest rate, she calculated she could have enough for a deposit to buy a house in about two years.

On the day of the party, she carefully dressed in her new black halter-neck dress and high-heeled sandals, leaving her long hair loose.

Nan looked at her proudly. "Darl, you look gorgeous. Don't you think your sister looks good? Ben! Get your boots off my coffee table."

Ben put his feet down. "Yeah, yeah. She looks nice."

"Keep watching your precious Charlene. She's about the best you're going to get," Quin said with a smirk.

Ben ignored her, his eyes glued to Neighbours.

"Now, now. Be nice." Nan lowered her voice. "He's taking the break-up with Suzy really hard."

A car horn beeped outside.

"He doesn't seem heartbroken to me. I've gotta go. Taxi's here. I might be staying overnight at a friend's house so don't wait up." A guilty lie, because Nan never approved of her sleeping at Pete's.

"Aren't you taking an overnight bag?" Nan said.

"I've got a toothbrush. I don't need anything else."

She kissed Nan goodbye.

*

"A champagne?" Pete asked, picking up a bottle of champagne from the ice bucket and filling her glass. The waiters placed an entrée of smoked salmon topped with caviar in front of her and she made small talk with Warren's wife. After a main course of lobster, Quin gossiped with Deb about what everyone was wearing and Pete was engrossed in a conversation with Larry. He'd hardly said a word to her all night.

"Attention everyone."

A hush came over the room as Tom stood, smiling. "Thank you everyone for coming. I only want to say a few words. Firstly, we've had a good year, and I want to thank you for the hard work you all put into the company."

"Geeze, he's smashed," Deb whispered to Lucille. "Look at him swaying."

"Secondly, an extra special thanks to the partners, wives, and girlfriends here tonight. Your support has been invaluable. Thirdly, I want to wish you all a happy, healthy and safe holiday season, and hope you'll be ready to hit the ground running for a bumper year in 1989. Here's to Solid Rock."

"Here, here."

The DJ started and people moved to the dancefloor. Quin downed another champagne, then got up and headed over to Tom, who was alone, his tie loosened. He looked tanned and trim. She touched his elbow and smiled when he saw her.

"That was a really nice speech," she said. "I just wanted to thank you for tonight and for the opportunities you've given me this year."

"You've earned it." His eyes moved over her cleavage, then to her face. "Would you like to dance with the old boss?"

Quin laughed. "I don't think you're that old."

He laughed. "Compared to you, I'm old. When you turn forty-two, you wonder what the hell you've done all your life. Don't let that mistake happen to you. Come on."

He took her arm and led her to the dance floor, joining in the Nutbush with everyone else. He stumbled with the steps, and Quin suppressed a giggle.

"Watch me," she said, above the din. He nodded and grinned when he got it right, acknowledging Quin's smiled encouragement. "Very good," she mouthed. He winked and concentrated on the steps.

"Whew, that was harder than I thought."

"It's a workout," she said.

Someone came up to shake Tom's hand, so Quin went

back to her table and poured another champagne. "Deb, who's Tom's partner?"

"That woman in the black backless dress. She's sort of a girlfriend but not really."

"What do you mean 'not really'?"

"He's a player."

"A player?"

"He's divorced, likes to play the field, if you know what I mean. He does look good though." Deb sighed. "I guess when you look like him, and you're as rich as him, you can get whoever you like. Apparently, that current one is a top model."

"Really." She looked at the woman. "She seems a bit old to be a model."

"It's the cocaine," Deb said, lowering her voice. "But you didn't hear it from me."

Quin hid her shock.

"By the way, keep that to yourself. Not good for the boss's secretary to be spreading tales."

She nodded. Deb was drunk and Quin was too, but she was having a good time.

"Pete, there you are," Quin said. "Some of the oldies are going." She turned to wave at them— "See ya, Waz, Liz"—then looked at Pete. "Are you happy to stay? They're moving us into the bar upstairs."

Pete looked at her. "I'm a bit tired."

"Come on. You haven't danced with me once."

Pete shrugged. "Sure. Why not?"

The room cleared and they headed upstairs. The music was even louder, the room hotter. She danced with Pete, Deb and even Geoff. It was two-thirty when she looked at her watch.

"Come on, another dance?" she said to Pete who was slumped in a chair.

"It's late. I need sleep."

"One more."

A cheer went up from the crowd.

"Oh my god. Look at her!"

Quin pushed her way towards Deb, who was on the bar dancing. Then Tom jumped up to join her, and before she realised it, Deb pulled her up, and she was dancing on the bar too. She spied Pete talking to Larry, again. After the song finished, the three of them bowed and jumped down. Tom held Quin's hand. "Let's get some air." He pulled her out of the bar, down the backstairs and into a laneway.

"That was fun," Tom said. "I haven't danced on a bar for years."

She raised her eyebrows and laughed. "Really? I thought you looked quite comfortable."

"You looked right at home yourself."

She leant against the graffiti-covered brick wall, enjoying the cool. He pulled a joint from his pocket, lit it and handed it to her.

She took a drag and held it in her lungs. "Since when does the boss carry something like this around with him?" she said, exhaling.

"Just for recreational use," he said, swaying. He grinned, his teeth white, face handsome. "Having a good time?"

She nodded, took another couple of puffs before handing the joint back.

"You've a lovely smile. I guess I never see it at work. People are different when they're out of the office." He touched her necklace. "New?"

She reached to touch the ruby, her hand brushing against his. "It was my mother's. I wear it only for special occasions."

She watched as he flicked the joint away and smiled. "I'm honoured you think this is a special occasion."

"A bit wasteful, don't you think?" she said, her eyes on the burning butt.

"I've got a lot more. Don't worry."

Then he leant in and kissed her. His lips were soft, his breath tinged with alcohol, and she kissed him back. Thoughts of Pete flashed in her mind as Tom's lips moved to her neck, moistening her skin like steam. She should stop this, but he'd pinned her against the brick wall. His tongue plunged into her mouth, and her arms went around his neck. Her eyes closed, her head spun. His hands were under her skirt, pulling at her underwear, which fell to the ground as her body pressed into him. Did she want this? He lifted her, and she wrapped her legs around him. His face buried into her neck, her breathing rapid, everything else forgotten.

When he finally pulled away and zipped up, he gazed at her as she pulled down her dress.

"Guess we better go in," he muttered.

"Yeah. I'll go in first," she said. She was nauseous, and her legs wobbled as she left him smoking another joint.

The upstairs bar was still hot and noisy. She found the bathroom and threw up. Feeling better, she left to search for Pete.

"There you are. I've been looking all over for you," Pete said. "Are you all right? You look a bit pale."

"Not feeling too good actually."

"I'll take you home, if you like. Back to my place?"

"Okay," she said.

"We better say goodbye to Tom. Anyone seen him?"

"I think he's gone," Deb said.

*

The next morning, Quin's body ached. Her head was heavy, and her mouth tasted as if she'd eaten Ben's socks. She found her toothbrush and brushed her teeth first, before jumping into the shower. The hot water hit the front of her and she was already beginning to feel better. When she turned, she winced from a stinging pain on her back. She twisted around. "What the hell?" she said. Her back was red raw. "How?"

Then it began to come back to her. Tom. "Oh god, I fucked the boss."

She remembered the taxi drive home with Pete. He'd been all over her. What was I thinking? she wondered. I like Pete not Tom. It's my fault. I should have stopped it. I'm a grown woman. I should have said no. She tried to think. It hadn't even been good, not like it was with Pete. How could she face Tom? Maybe with luck he'll have forgotten. What a disaster.

Pete was in the kitchen, whistling. "Do you want eggs?" he yelled out.

"Ah, no."

"How about some toast?"

She stared at her back in the mirror, her head pounding. Pete couldn't have seen it.

"That would be good. Thanks," she yelled back.

She was careful to do her bra up over the graze on her back. Where were her undies? She dropped her dress over her head and pulled it down. Wiping away a smear of mascara from under her eyes she opened the bathroom door and searched the bedroom and her handbag. Then with a sinking feeling, she remembered they might be where they'd fallen – in the laneway. She closed her eyes, sick at the thought of what she'd done.

"Hey," Pete said as she came into the kitchen. He kissed her, then handed her a plate with toast. "There's marmalade, vegemite or jam on the table. Take your pick."

"Thanks."

"Tea or coffee?"

"Um, coffee. And a couple of Panadols if you've got any. What time is it?"

"A little after twelve."

"Jesus!" she said. "That late?"

"Relax, we've got all day."

She spread a smattering of vegemite on the toast and bit into it. "My head is pounding."

"I'm not surprised. You put a lot of champagne away."

She looked at him. "What's that supposed to mean."

He looked puzzled. "Nothing. Just that you had a good time. It was nice to see you let your hair down."

"I had to dance with someone. You were too busy talking to Larry, all night." Was she trying to pick a fight with Pete to cover her guilt?

"Now don't be like that. I'm not much for dancing and I did dance a little."

"Yes, I did finally get you on the dancefloor" she said, rubbing her head.

Pete put a cup of coffee in front of her—"Here you go, beautiful"—then sat in the chair opposite.

She ran her hand through her hair. "I've no make-up on, I'm hungover and feel like shit, so I know that's not true. But it's nice of you to say so."

"I mean it. You don't need make-up. You have an inner glow."

She almost choked on her toast. "Now you're just bullshitting me. Inner glow! The only glow here is the one you've got from getting me into bed with you."

He grinned. "Well, you were a bit too drunk, I'm afraid, and I don't take advantage of women who can't participate and enjoy. Of course, if you've got time, I'll happily oblige now."

She smiled. "I'm sorry. But I've got to go."

Her deceit added to her headache.

He followed her, then pulled her to him for a kiss. She wriggled out of his grasp, her heart aching with guilt.

"Can you call me a taxi?"

"You sure you don't want to stay? We can spend all afternoon in bed."

She feigned a laugh. "No lover boy. I promised Nan I'd take her to watch my brother play in the cricket final. If I don't go, I'll never hear the end of it."

He pouted, pretending to look hurt until she kissed him.

"Okay. I'll call you a taxi."

When the taxi arrived, she grabbed her handbag and blew him a kiss. "See you Monday," she said.

*

On her way to work on Monday morning, Quin went back and forth about what she'd say to Tom. She'd even rehearsed her approach with an apology: she was drunk, and it just happened; there was nothing to it, no hard feelings; she hoped it wouldn't get in the way of their work together.

When she arrived at the office, she immersed herself in work. Every so often, she thought about what to do and found herself staring out of the window, feeling sick about it. And now there was a document that needed his signature.

She stood at his open office door. He was on the phone, his foot balanced on an open drawer as he leant back in his black leather chair, his shirt sleeves rolled up over his tanned arms.

He smiled and waved her in. A burning heat crawled all over her. He tucked the phone between his neck and shoulder and held his hand out for the document. Quin stared at a scuff mark on her right shoe.

He put the phone down and looked at the document intently. Here was her chance. He asked a question or two, picked up his fountain pen, then signed his name with his usual flourish.

"There you go," he said, handing the paperwork back. "Good job."

Her feet seemed glued to the spot, her heart beating.

"Was there anything else?"

"No. That's it."

In the end, she chickened out. He hadn't said anything about what happened, so neither would she.

23

LUCILLE

1940

Lucille kissed her sleeping baby, breathing in her sweet, powdery scent before touching her chubby cheek. A contented child in sleep, yet listless when awake, no matter what she did to coax a response. Without Max, the weight of responsibility crushed Lucille.

Picking up a dirty nappy, she was completely overwhelmed by a wave of nausea and rushed to the bathroom to throw up again. As she slumped next to the bowl, she prayed Patricia wouldn't wake up. Max had been gone for five weeks and the last few days had turned into a pattern of vomiting and trying to look after her baby. She was sure she was pregnant but unsure how she felt about it. Calculating that Patricia would turn one when the next one was born, she couldn't think how she'd cope when she was barely struggling to survive with one child. Remembering that last night, when Max had left, she wished they'd been more careful.

In the waiting room of the baby health centre, among a dozen other mothers, Lucille chewed on a nail. She lifted Patricia up and cooed as she always did, searching her daughter's face for a smile or a look of recognition. As usual, Patricia stared blankly ahead then slowly closed her eyes, as if life was already too hard for her.

Lucille smiled at another woman who was holding a wriggling child. "It's time for her morning sleep," she said, explaining her daughter's inactivity.

The woman smiled back. "She's beautiful."

"Thank you." Buoyed by the comment, she beamed and kissed Patricia's cheek.

Lucille's name was called, and with Patricia in her arms, she gathered her things and went in.

"She's doing very well. Her weight's perfect for four months," the Sister exclaimed with a wide smile. "I'll see you in two months for her six-month check-up."

Relief. Before Lucille could ask about what was really on her mind, she left the nurse with a hurried thanks, and with Patricia on her hip, threw up that morning's breakfast in the nearby toilet.

Despite her queasiness, Lucille's confidence about Patricia soared as she left the centre and pushed the pram home. "Did you hear that, my beautiful girl? You're doing very well."

Patricia's response was to fall asleep.

The next day, her spirits tumbled when she awoke early

with nausea. After throwing up a couple of times, she managed to shower and dress before she coaxed Patricia awake at nine o'clock.

"Come on, we're already behind schedule with Mummy not feeling well. Wakey, wakey. How are you going to grow if you don't wake up for your feed?" She picked her up and held Patricia close. "Come on then, here's your bottle." She pushed the teat into Patricia's mouth and was relieved to see her suck.

The wireless played a song and Lucille hummed. After a while, she took the bottle away, lifted Patricia over her shoulder and patted her gently on her back until she burped. Then she propped her on a pillow in the pram while she cleaned the kitchen, all the while glancing at her daughter.

She wiped her hands on her tea towel and drew her face close to the baby and then away. "Why don't you do something? You don't smile, you don't look at me. All you do is eat, poo and sleep. Can't you be like the other babies and give me a tiny smile?"

Patricia had slid down the pillow and fallen asleep. Lucille sat at the table with her head in her hands and sighed.

A few weeks later she went to a new doctor. Her previous one had been called up like so many others. Doctor Brandon was old with a grey goatee, which he played with as he spoke. He confirmed she was pregnant again, about eight weeks, he reckoned. She didn't bother to tell him about the worsening morning sickness, knowing there was nothing he could do about it. But she did ask him to give Patricia a check-up.

Surely, he'd know if something wasn't right. He went through the motions of checking Patricia, announced that babies develop at their own pace and, within five minutes, led Lucille towards his office door to navigate her way through the crowd of patients still in his waiting room. She was no wiser about whether her daughter was all right.

*

Max's letters from London were filled with details about blackouts, rationing and how hard the work was. Waiting for the postman's whistle each day was a highlight. Ripping open the letters and eagerly reading them, made her miss him more. How could she tell him that she was miserable? She couldn't tell anyone. It wouldn't be right when everyone missed their loved ones. Mildred missed her sons and worried about them desperately. It was better to pretend that all was well.

Pa and Mildred never knew how much time she spent in bed, a bucket next to her, sometimes too weak to get up. If they'd seen her bedroom, with stinking nappies, and the kitchen, a mess of baby bottles and teacups, the cupboards almost empty, they might have twigged. But Lucille was adept at telling them at the front door that the baby had just gone down, and she'd been up all night. "Could you come back later? I need to catch up on some sleep."

Then one morning Lucille woke with a start. It was eleven o'clock, but she slumped back under the covers. How could she have slept in for so long? Patricia had been unsettled at midnight but after a feed, she'd gone to sleep. Patricia! Why hadn't she cried for her bottle?

She threw off the covers, stood dizzy and queasy, then stumbled into the baby's bedroom. Patricia had kicked off her covers and was perfectly still. Lucille reached into the crib and recoiled at the coldness of her baby's blue-tinged skin, as if she'd touched a live electric wire.

She nudged her gently at first, then more vigorously. "Patricia, Patricia. Oh god, please wake up." She quickly wrapped her in a woollen blanket, snatched her up, and ran down the hallway and out to Mildred's house, screaming and hammering on her neighbour's front door.

"She won't wake up," Lucille said, sobbing. "Look." She unfolded the blanket from Patricia's face and held out her cold, stiff baby.

Mildred crossed herself, muttering, "Holy mother of god," as she put her arm around Lucille and led her into her lounge room.

"Why won't she open her eyes?" Lucille held her child tight.

"I don't know," Mildred said gently. "I've rung for the doctor. He'll be here very soon."

"Wake up, wake up, wake up," Lucille kept muttering over and over, rocking back and forwards.

When the doctor finally arrived, Lucille clung to her child, only allowing him to touch Patricia with his stethoscope.

"I'm afraid, Mrs Doomsbury, she's gone."

Lucille looked directly at the doctor. "No, she can't be. Please check her again, and do it properly this time."

She noticed the doctor looking at Mildred and then at her.

"She's gone to God, love," Mildred said, wringing her hands.

"Do it," Lucille said, coldly to the doctor. Her heart beat wildly. She didn't know this man, had never seen him before. How did she even know he was a real doctor?

He touched Patricia. "She's not breathing and has no pulse," he said. "I know this is a shock, Mrs Doomsbury. Your daughter has died."

She looked down at her baby's waxen face and lifeless body. "She can't have died. It's not possible." Her stomach had twisted into hundreds of knots, and her arm stung from the injection the doctor was giving her.

"This will make you feel a little calmer," the doctor said.

Energy seemed to leach out of her as she slumped on the couch, quietly sobbing, not letting go of the stiff bundle in her arms, but staring at the plump cheeks, once rosy, and the limp curl of new brown hair, never to be tied in plaits.

"You poor dear," Mildred said rubbing Lucille's back.

"It looks like the baby's been dead for at least ten hours." The doctor scratched his head and crouched in front of Lucille. "Where's your husband?" he asked.

Lucille couldn't tear her eyes from Patricia's face in case she woke up. She opened her mouth, but the words wouldn't come.

"Called up," Mildred said.

"Along with everyone else. She'll need a bit of help getting on her feet and organising a funeral."

A funeral? Lucille clenched her eyes, wishing they would both go away. She didn't want to hear what they were saying. All she wanted was her baby back. How could she have left her to die on her own? Her sobs worked back up again.

Mildred's hand was warm on her back. "You can stay here, love. Your Pa will make the arrangements. You don't have to do all that."

Why couldn't she stop crying?

"The undertakers will come to prepare the body," the doctor said, glancing at his watch as he collected his bag, then walked towards the living room door. "She'll be in shock for a while, but the sedative I've given should last for around eight hours, and it'll settle her down. Try to get her into bed." The doctor turned and glanced back at Lucille. "And tell her she can have other children."

Other children? A guttural scream came from somewhere deep. "No!" she wailed. "I want my baby back."

Mildred wiped her face with a handkerchief, like she would a child. "There's nothing you could have done. Sometimes, babies die. It happens," Mildred said gently. "You take your time with your Patricia, and I'll make a cup of tea. Okay? The doctor's getting a message to your Pa." Mildred's voice cracked, and she groaned as she heaved herself up from the couch.

Calmer, Lucille nodded and resumed watch over her baby.

After a while, someone in a suit and tie gently lifted Patricia from her arms, leaving the blanket empty on her lap.

Her head heavy, she allowed herself to be put into a large bed in a room with toy planes displayed on the window ledge. She slept.

*

The early morning sunshine seeping through lace curtains bothered Lucille when she first woke. Somewhere music played on a wireless, a kettle whistled, a car engine started up, a child outside cried. She closed her stinging eyes, lost in a fresh haemorrhage of grief, wondering how she'd learn to live again or find joy in anything.

A gentle knock at the door and Mildred poked her head in. "Just checking if you'd like a cuppa, love. How're you feeling?"

Lucille's eyes filled with tears. "My baby. She's gone, hasn't she?"

Mildred nodded and came into the room. "Yes, she has, love. These things happen. No-one really knows why. I'm so sorry." Lucille allowed Mildred's hug, closed her eyes and sniffed in the comfort of the woman's lavender scent.

When Mildred let her go, she pushed Lucille's hair out of her eyes, the same as Ma had done when she was little, whenever she'd been upset. "It'll be all right," Ma had said. Lucille tried to gulp down the sobs.

"I've got a visitor for you. It's your Pa. Do you think you'd like to get up, have something to eat?"

She nodded. "I'll get dressed first," Lucille said.

"Come into the kitchen when you're ready, love."

Pa's expression was grave. He stood abruptly, lifting his hand then dropping it, awkward as usual.

"I've got some toast with some nice homemade apricot jam?" Mildred said, leading her to the chair opposite Pa. "And a strong hot cup of tea."

"I'm sorry," Pa said. "She was such a dear little thing." His voice cracked, and his jaw clenched, stifling back emotion. "I've come to stay with you for a while," he gulped, "to help with the arrangements."

"Thanks," Lucille said. They watched as she forced herself to take a bite of toast slathered with jam.

Pa coughed. "Um, would you like me to write and tell Max?"

"Oh god." Lucille covered her face with her hands and sobbed. "I have to do that."

Mildred broke the silence after a while. "I had a miscarriage and now look, five strong strapping lads."

Lucille peered at Mildred through her tears. "You were a good mother. You never lost any of your boys."

"You'll have more children. Even the doctor said so."

"I'm already pregnant." Lucille closed her eyes. "Excuse me." She ran into the bathroom and brought up the toast.

She wiped her hand across her mouth and lay on the cold floor. Mildred tapped on the door and offered a glass of water. "How far along?"

"Eight or nine weeks? I can't keep anything down, I'm so weak and dizzy all the time. I just stayed in bed, and now she's dead because of me." Lucille howled and banged her head hard on the bathroom floor.

Mildred grabbed her arm and helped her up from the tiles. "Listen, love. You've got to carry on. Come on now, clean yourself up. You don't want your Pa seeing you like this."

Lucille splashed her face, then leant her hands on the washbasin, her face dripping.

Mildred handed her a towel. "You can't wallow in your own self-pity. You have to look after yourself for this new baby. I know it's hard. But I'm here to help you and so is your Pa. He's waiting out there for you."

"You're right," she said wearily. "I just don't know if I can do it."

"You will. It'll take time, but you'll do it."

They walked out of the bathroom together, Mildred's arm around Lucille.

Pa was still waiting in the kitchen. Lucille returned to her chair, her body limp, her mind numb. How much help would Pa be?

"You know, we always wanted a brother or sister for you. It was the saddest day to lose your mother and then your brother," Pa said. "You have the chance I never had. You're the most precious and best thing that ever happened to me."

Lucille blinked away the tears and stared at her father. He'd barely acknowledged her growing up, lost in his stupor of grief and drink. Like her, she thought. This must have been how he'd felt. Her fear grew. She wouldn't let herself turn out to be like him.

*

The constant drizzle mixed with Lucille's tears, and a cold wind caught the dirt she dropped from her hand, blowing it into the air before settling onto the coffin in the grave. Pa took her by the elbow and steered her into the warmth of the car and then home.

She'd tried many times to write to Max, to tell him that she had somehow lost their daughter, until finally, she found the right words. But she couldn't tell him she was pregnant; it seemed as if she were offering a consolation prize. In the weeks following, she waited for a reply that never came, and it tormented her. Was he angry and upset? She couldn't blame him if he was. She'd been a bad mother.

Lucille took to her bed, to rest for the baby, she said. She listened to the sounds of the house, the wireless music, the murmured voices of Pa and Mildred, dishes being washed, children outside playing. With every passing day without a word from Max, she became even more morose. How her life had turned. She resented the baby kicking inside her.

Weeks later, she heard the slam of the front door flyscreen and hurried footsteps along the hallway and into her room.

"You awake?"

"Yes." Lucille opened one eye.

Pa drew open the curtains and smiled. "This might cheer you up, love. A ship's come in. There's some mail."

"Really? For me?"

Lucille bolted from the bed and Pa nodded as he handed her a large bundle of letters. "I'll make us a cuppa."

She nodded then rifled through the letters, putting them into postmark date order. They were all from Max. She ripped open the first letter, postmarked and sent before he'd received the news about Patricia. She read the next one and the next until she got to the one that made her tears mingle with his on the page.

24

QUIN

AUGUST, 1989

Quin was lying on the couch in front of the television when Ben grabbed the remote control.

"Hey, I'm watching the news," Quin said. "I want to see what's going on with the pilot's strike. I'm going to Sydney to sign up an important deal on Thursday."

"Guess you'll have to drive your new Mercedes instead. Just because you're a high-flying executive, you think you own the TV?" Ben said.

"It won't be long before I move out and get my own TV and my own space." She made a face at her brother.

"I've had a hard day too you know, and I want to watch Sale of the Century. One of my customers is on it, and he's also one of your clients."

Quin raised her eyebrows. "Really?"

"Yep. Remember Costa? He owns the hardware store."

She nodded. Her brother was secretly proud of her. She'd

heard him on the phone with one of his cricketing mates. "Listen, my sister is a big wig at Solid Rock. Get a few dollars invested. You won't look back, mate. Use the bank's money, mate. Not your own. Listen, I'll get my sister to talk to you. Get the finance cheap and invest it big. Paying a return of nearly eighteen per cent. No-one else can do that. It's 'rock solid', get it?" He laughed at his joke.

"Okay. Let's watch it, then."

"Sale of the Century!" Ben yelled, just like the voiceover guy. "There he is. That's Costa. Now shush."

"I never said a word," she said.

Quin guessed many of the answers the quiz host asked. Nan always said she should go on the program. But she was far too slow.

An ad came on for Solid Rock. "It's the latest one," Quin said. "What do you think?"

"Is that the newsreader, Bryan Horgler?

"Shh."

The ad ended and another came on.

"Yep. That's Bryan Horgler. Doesn't he come across well? He wasn't cheap though. Tom reckons we're going to spend a million dollars this year on advertising. Can you believe it?"

Ben shrugged. "Too much, if you ask me."

"It's not, when you look at the profit we just made. Eleven million isn't anything to sneeze at. At least we're not like Puntley Mortgages. They're haemorrhaging funds at the moment. No-one is keeping their money in the banks when we're offering eighteen per cent. That's why it's all coming to us."

"I suppose. Shush, Costa's back. He's gunna go for the car."

"Well, I've got a life. I'm going to Pete's." Quin went to her bedroom and changed, humming one of her favourite songs: "Like a Prayer" by Madonna. She picked up her keys and went out to the driveway to her gleaming silver Mercedes. It startled her each time she saw it. She couldn't believe a girl like her could afford a car like that. Technically, she couldn't afford to buy it outright, but the neighbours didn't know that. With salary packaging she got it on a novated lease. Less tax and more for her, Pete said. She looked into the numbers and agreed. She explained how it worked to Ben, and he too leased a car through his business, except his was a BMW.

She opened the door, got in and breathed in the new-leather smell. The engine purred as she backed out of the driveway and headed to Pete's, mulling over what he'd asked her. He'd bought a terrace cottage in Carlton, and since she spent many nights there, he'd asked her to move in. She hadn't said yes straightaway. She worried about Nan. Ben was going to buy a house and had begun looking. She didn't want to leave Nan on her own, especially since her health scare – a minor stroke nearly four years ago. Was that what had kept both of them at home? Nan had recovered well and insisted she was fine. Both Quin and Ben could have moved out years ago.

But there was something else.

She wasn't one hundred per cent sure about her feelings for Pete. He'd never said he loved her. She was a modern woman – did she need to hear it to know? But then she hadn't said it to him either.

Then there was the encounter with Tom and it still bothered her.

A month into the new year, vacancies were announced in the Corporate Finance Department. Larry was promoted to head it. Pete was promoted too. He now managed all of the clients Tom brought in.

Soon after, Larry called her in and told her Tom wanted her to be in the team, on his floor. It was the way Larry said it that worried her. It was Tom not Larry who was promoting her. Was this called sleeping your way to the top she wondered? It nagged at her. She could handle the job; after Pete, she'd brought in the most business in the last twelve months. Surely, she'd won the job on her own? It had nothing to do with that night.

But the look on Debbie's face told her otherwise. The woman knew something – she constantly raised her eyebrows each time Tom called Quin into his office. Quin wasn't even attracted to Tom. If anything, she was in awe of him. She loved it when he asked her opinion and included her in top level meetings.

Then within six months in July, she was promoted again. Now she managed several staff in the conveyancing area, was on the compliance committee and had a small portfolio of high-value clients. It was a lot of responsibility, but she loved it. Tom believed in her. Still, if it had nothing to do with their encounter, why didn't she feel comfortable around him? Why did she feel indebted to him somehow?

Rain drizzled onto her new car, sending beads of water down the windscreen. The traffic stopped, and she peered ahead, drifting back into her thoughts.

It wasn't as if Tom had done anything. There was never a suggestion of anything further. Even if he'd tried, she'd have said no. He'd been drunk and so had she. He'd probably forgotten all about it. Her lack of confidence had hijacked her. That's all. That's what Nan had said years ago. "Honey, if you were as confident in yourself as Ben is, you'd have nothing to worry about."

She shook her head and turned up the radio. It was in the past. She was being paranoid and stupid. She should forget about it. Pete believed in her, supported her and pushed her. He did love her; she knew it and she loved him.

*

"I can't believe how much stuff you've got," Pete said, picking up the last of the boxes.

"I've only got a few. Stop your whingeing." Quin squatted as she unpacked and grinned. "I can go home, if you like."

Pete grunted as he lowered a box. He leant over and kissed her. "I guess Nan's not too happy?"

Quin pursed her lips. "No, she's not. She keeps telling me that it's a sin. How will she be able to hold her head high at the bowls club when her granddaughter is living with a man and isn't married?"

When she told Nan she was moving out, her grandmother was pleased, but Ben was pissed off. He wanted to go first. Though when Nan found out Quin was moving in with Pete, she changed her tune, and her disapproval almost killed Quin.

"Nan, it's not like in your day. Isn't it better to live with someone before marriage? It's almost the nineties, everyone does it. If it doesn't work out, then there's no messy divorce. I just move out again."

"It's not right. You don't bring Pete here. I hardly know him."

"I know him. Surely that's what matters? Besides, we live so far away, and I'll be closer to work."

"I'm not cut out for all of this. It's too much. I would have liked a wedding before I died."

Quin rolled her eyes. "You're not going to die before you get a wedding. Now stop. I'm happy. Pete's a nice bloke. It's not like I'm leaving the country."

"And when you did go overseas, I was beside myself with worry."

Ben's look said, "You asked for that.'

"Besides, Ben is still here. And I'm not far away. I'll be over every week for one of your roasts. And I'll bring Pete."

"Humph," Nan said.

Ben pulled her aside. "Listen, for what it's worth, I hate you for leaving first, but I envy you too. Not too sure about Pete."

"What do you mean?"

"He seems a bit up himself. But you know him better than me."

"Yeah, I do, and he cares a lot about me. Stop pretending to be the overprotective older brother. As if you care."

Ben gave her a hurt look. "Hey, I can look out for my little sis."

"Since when?"

Ben shrugged. "Yeah, you can look after yourself. If you like him, then that's all that matters."

She grabbed her brother and hugged him.

"All right, all right. That's enough," he said, pushing her away. He grinned. "I'll settle Nan down. She'll come around."

25

LUCILLE

AUGUST, 1940

Lucille wasn't sure if it was the letters from Max, which were coming more regularly, or the fact that she no longer felt as sick now that she'd found a way to tell him about the pregnancy. Somehow, she had a renewed energy and no longer stayed in bed. Instead, she went shopping with Mildred or took long walks. Pa continued to stay at her house, coming home in the evenings after work. On the weekends, Pa took her and Mildred for drives in Max's car to pick berries or to picnics in the hills. In the evenings, the three of them were glued to the wireless, listening for news of the war praying for it to end. Bombing raids on London heightened their worry.

Mildred received a telegram. Her youngest boy, Sam, had been wounded. Lucille was ashamed to admit to herself she was glad the telegram wasn't for her, but she said nothing when she told Pa the news.

Pa's face dropped. "Where is Mildred?"

"She went home early, saying she couldn't eat."

"I better go and see her. God, she must be beside herself over Sam."

"Don't you want to have dinner first? She's made us a stew."

"I can't eat now."

Pa left the house in a hurry. Could there be something going on? Pa and Mildred? They were both widowed and alone. Why hadn't she noticed before? She'd been too caught up in her sorry self. Pa hadn't drunk in months, and he'd looked after her when she needed him. She lifted the curtain and watched him hurry down the path towards Mildred's front door, his face furrowed in worry. Lucille smiled. She'd grown to love Mildred, and she'd be good for Pa. Perhaps it was time for him to find happiness.

*

There were many days when Lucille regretted the child growing and kicking inside her. Her grandmother's words pounded her head daily, haunting her. Was her grandmother right? If she hadn't married Max, would her life have turned out differently? She had to pluck up the courage and ask the doctor.

"Not sure. These things happen," the doctor said. "It could have been her heart."

Lucille twisted her white, embroidered handkerchief around her finger. "There's something else. My husband and

I are cousins … first cousins. Do you think that might have something to do with her death?"

The doctor frowned. "I don't know. The fact that you are cousins could cause issues."

"Oh no," Lucille exclaimed, her hand resting protectively on her belly.

"But only in very isolated cases. For example, if you both carried a defective gene, then there could be complications, but it's highly unlikely. Some babies don't form the way nature intended, and often it's nature's way of weeding out the weak so that the strong might survive." The doctor reached out and patted Lucille on the hand. "This one has a healthy heartbeat and is doing all the right things. Rest assured. I'm sure this will be a good child." The doctor stood. "It's mostly society's convention that frowns on first cousins having a child. Old wives' tales and the like. Now go home and rest, Mrs Doomsbury."

Lucille felt a little better, until that night, lying in bed, her grandmother's words came back to her – marrying your cousin could cause defects. She snapped on the lamp next to her bed and looked at the wedding photo of her and Max. This will be all right; it has to be.

Harry arrived on 15 December 1940 exactly a year after his sister's birth. Just this fact worried Lucille and, although she wasn't superstitious, she felt it was a bad omen. The doctor declared him strong and alert with a sturdy heartbeat, and Lucille lay slumped on the pillows allowing the relief to wash over her. She wished Max was with her. She'd done it. She'd produced a healthy child, she told him in a letter.

When she brought Harry home, he actually looked at her, and she felt an intense love for him. He fed well, in fact too well. Exhausting her, he cried for more milk and she gave him the bottle.

Mildred came in and helped for a few days until she received another telegram. Two of her boys had been killed and one was missing. Lucille and Mildred cried together. Pa tried to help, but in the end, Mildred decided to go to her sister's house in the country. She was so distraught that Lucille suggested Pa drive her.

Pa frowned. "Are you going to be all right?"

Lucille smiled. "Of course. I have my little man, and he's doing well."

"It's a long way, and I'll be away for a few days. Are you sure?"

"Of course." Lucille kissed Harry. "Look at him; he's as healthy as an ox."

Pa smiled at his grandson, who started crying for his next feed. "And he's got a healthy set of lungs on him too."

The day after Pa and Mildred left, Harry stopped feeding. He fussed and cried. He was two weeks old and wasn't himself.

"What's going on?" She rocked him, pushed him in the pram, tempted him with the bottle, her finger and her nipple. He wailed as the hours went on, inconsolable. She couldn't bear his crying and put her hands over her ears until he exhausted himself.

The next day she took him to the doctor.

"Mmm. He has a sore throat and a minor fever. That would explain why he's off his food."

"Is his heart all right?"

"Mrs Doomsbury, the heart quickens when you have a virus. There's nothing to worry about. Just keep him warm and try to give him some water. If he's worse in two days, bring him back."

"Shouldn't you listen to his chest?"

The doctor looked annoyed. "I know that you're worried in view of your last baby. But he'll be perfectly fine. Good day."

Lucille shuffled out of the clinic and shivered. She looked at Harry, he was too quiet. As he stared at the side of the pram, his eyes began to close. Perhaps she was over-reacting, like the doctor said.

At home she hugged and kissed him. "Please god, don't let what happened to Patricia happen to Harry."

The next morning he woke up, crying. She changed his nappy and tried to give him water. He refused, screaming louder when she put him in his crib. "Stop crying!" She put her hands over her ears again. "Just stop crying!" The nearby window was open. She had an urge to throw him through it. If he were outside, she wouldn't hear him. Instead, she left him crying and paced the lounge room with her hands over her ears again.

"Stop it! Stop it!" she screamed as she crouched on the floor. "I can't stand this."

Her heart thumping, she ran through the house and into his room. The crying must stop. She looked at the open window and back to the red-faced infant.

"You took Patricia. You're nothing but the devil," she screamed, clenching her hands so hard her nails dug into her palms.

But something stopped her from picking him up. She didn't trust herself with him. Her hands trembling, she turned and ran out of the house and down the street.

Eventually, she slowed to a walk, then stopped for breath, gasping and puffing. A woman passed by and stared at her. Lucille was barefoot and still in her nightgown. She sat on a park bench and wept. And after she was done, her arms were like lead weights, her head heavy.

When she got home, Harry was asleep. She bent over and kissed him, whispering, "I'm sorry, little man. I'm a terrible mother. I don't deserve you."

When he woke, he took some milk. What a relief! She looked at him closely, goosebumps spreading like an electric current through her body. There it was – the vacant stare, just like Patricia.

That night. She brought him into bed with her, her chest tight and dread shrouding her, keeping her awake. She read the bible and prayed, something she'd never done.

26

QUIN

1989

Tom didn't like what the ad agency had produced and asked staff across the organisation to come up with something. Larry asked Quin and Pete to brainstorm ideas for a slogan in the conference room.

"Look, it's got to be catchy but earnest," Pete said.

"Are you trying to make a joke?"

Pete looked dumbfounded and frowned. "What do you mean?"

"Earnest, like earning, a play on words. Get it?"

"Huh, yeah I suppose."

Pete obviously had no idea what she was talking about, so she let it drop. That was the thing about Pete, he had a gift for numbers and could sniff out a good deal but sometimes he was humourless.

"Okay, let's think." Quin sipped her tea. "What about

being money wise, like water wise. You know how there's a lot about saving water."

Pete nodded and tapped his pen on the table. "Yeah, go on."

"How about something like … 'Solid Rock for smart people who are money wise', or something like that."

Now Pete chewed on his pen. "Maybe. What about: 'You can trust us at Solid Rock'."

Quin raised her eyebrows. "I don't think Tom wants something that sounds false. Or how about, 'Put your money with us, it's a rock-solid investment'."

"Mmm, maybe. Not sure. There's stuff going on now. People are really worried about Puntley Mortgages. They're almost insolvent. And what about Harker Wills Insurance going under? There are others looking shaky, and then there's that bastard Dellana who ripped off millions of taxpayer funds. I reckon Tom'll go for something like, 'You can trust us at Solid Rock.' The name says it. It's solid and stable." Pete wrote down his idea.

"I don't know. Let's keep thinking."

They threw a few more ideas and thoughts around.

"I'll be back. I need a loo break. Do you want another cuppa?" Quin gathered her cup and Pete's.

"Yeah, okay," Pete said, doodling on his pad.

When Quin returned, Tom was talking with Pete.

They both looked up at her.

"G'day Quin. I was looking for you. Can I have a word about the Halloran deal when you got a sec? I want to run over some of the figures. I had dinner with Arty last night, and I reckon we'll need to get them more dough for that project."

"Of course, I'll bring the file."

Tom nodded to Pete. "Good work!"

*

The next day, in a meeting, Tom spoke. "I'm pleased to announce the new slogan has been found. It's going to be 'Solid Rock – rock solid for smart people who are money wise'." Everyone clapped and Quin wondered why Pete hadn't told her.

She hadn't submitted the slogan. She thought there were at least two more days before the deadline. Pete must have submitted it for her. She was pleased. Her slogan. She couldn't wait to tell Ben and Nan.

When the meeting ended, she noticed Tom pat Pete on the shoulder. Pete looked very happy with himself and she wondered what was going on.

She caught up with Pete at lunchtime. "You want to grab some lunch?"

He shook his head. "Nah, I'm going to work through. Can you get me a sandwich or something when you go out?"

"I was just going to the cafeteria."

"I'll have a meat pie then." Pete looked at the file on his desk.

"Did you put my slogan up for me?"

He didn't look up. "Yeah, something like that." He began adding numbers on his calculator.

"It looked like you were taking the credit for it. But I've got that wrong, haven't I?"

"Huh," he looked at her. "What does it matter?"

"It was my slogan and my idea."

He shrugged and screwed up his face. "Was it? I thought we both worked on it together."

The noise of the office seemed to fade. "You know full well that the slogan was mine."

"It's no big deal. Look, I've got to get this to Tom in an hour. Do you mind?"

"Get your own bloody meat pie." She spun around and left.

*

Quin was fuming when she slipped in behind Deb in the food queue in the cafeteria.

"If looks could kill?" Deb said. "What's going on with you?"

Quin shook her head. "Nothing." She put a salad roll on her tray, paid and followed Deb to a table nearby.

"I can tell it's not nothing. Spill."

"Pete," Quin said.

Deb smiled. "I did warn you not to get mixed up with someone from work."

"It's not a relationship thing."

"Really?" Deb smirked. "Tell me what happened."

"You know the slogan?"

"Yeah. The one that Pete came up with." Deb took a mouthful of salad.

"No!"

Deb stopped chewing and frowned.

"I mean, yes, the slogan. But not that he came up with it. I did!"

Deb swallowed her mouthful. "You mean that slogan is yours? That bugger told the boss he had a brainwave."

"Wait till I see him tonight. I tried to confront him about it, but he pretended he hadn't done anything wrong."

"This is what happens."

"Yeah, yeah, I know."

"Trouble in paradise. I suppose he leaves his towels and socks all over the floor too?"

Quin stared at Deb. "How the hell did you know?"

"Because all the girls who have been with him have complained what a slob he is. Never picks up after himself. Never helps out."

"Yes, that's right. I work all day, even longer than him sometimes, and I walk into a pigsty. He can't be bothered. Says he's too tired."

"Yep, I'm not surprised. You want my advice?"

"I think I can handle it from here, Deb. Thanks."

"I reckon you should dump him while you can."

"I'm not going to do that now. We just need to have a long talk to reach an understanding. You don't break up with someone just because they're messy."

"And they steal credit for your work." Deb raised her eyebrows. "I wouldn't put up with that."

And perhaps that's why you are alone, Quin wanted to say to her friend. She and Pete would clear the air tonight when she got home. But for now, she had to get back to work. The company report had to be finished before her meeting with the auditors, who were signing off their part. All she had to do was run her eye over the final document then give it to Tom for final approval before issuing the press release.

After lunch she met with the senior auditor, James Hamilton, who gave her his company's signed report to read. The words about Solid Rock described it as a *strong, competent business investing in quality mortgage businesses, mostly residential homes across the country.* She frowned. She remembered James raising his eyebrows at the number of mortgages in a place called Hammondville, a large country town. His advice had been to spread their risk exposure across geographic locations, not focus on one town. Still, he must have been satisfied.

She read on. *Properties are assessed by qualified authorised valuers.* She frowned again. Qualified? They're just lenders in a car driving by and working out the value by looking up the sales of three similar properties. What about all the commercial property? She flipped through the ten-page booklet. There was nothing. She was uneasy as she sat back in her chair and stared out of the window. She'd forgotten about Pete and the slogan by the time she got home from work late that night. She was exhausted anyway and Pete was already asleep.

27

LUCILLE

1941

"Lucille!"

Pa's voice jolted Lucille awake, but when she tried to sit up straighter in bed, her body wouldn't move. Her eyes seemed glued shut and she had to will herself to wake.

"Lucille, where are you?"

"Here," she rasped. Harry lay perfectly still in her arms and she tried to move again. Her heart raced and she shivered. She lifted her right arm to get some feeling back until it began burning with pins and needles.

Pa's footsteps came closer until she sensed he was in the doorway of the darkened room.

"Lucille?"

She grunted and flung her arm across her eyes when he turned on the light.

"What's happened?" he whispered, stepping so close she

could smell the scent of the summer air still clinging to his clothes.

He touched her arm, then Harry. "Oh god," he muttered.

"He's so very cold. Why is he cold, Pa?" she said. She'd folded in the blankets around her and her baby.

The next was a blur. A cup held to her lips, she gulped cool water, inhaled the doctor's sour breath, winced at the sting of a needle plunged into her arm, before falling into a fitful sleep.

She woke hours later, her mind foggy, and slipped out of bed to visit the nursery. The baby would need feeding. Why was the crib empty? She scrambled on all fours, looking for Patricia or was it Harry she'd lost? Her body trembled and her screaming took hold.

"It's all right. I'm here," Pa said.

"They're gone because of me," she wailed, her heart aching.

"Shh," Pa said. "There, there. It'll be all right."

After she'd quietened, she looked at Pa, surprised that he had his arms around her.

She pushed him away, and underneath her fatigue grew a curdling rage. "This is your fault," she spat. "I don't know why you're even here. If it wasn't for me you'd have been dead. You should be dead, not my Harry, not my Patricia. You made my life miserable."

Pa recoiled from her, his face twisted in confusion and anguish. "What do you mean?"

"I thought I'd done something wrong when Ma died and

you abandoned me. I tried so hard for you to love me. But you never did." She was bawling. "Everything I ever loved has been taken away from me. You're the only one left, and you never cared."

"That's not true, love. I … I'm sorry about Ma. I didn't realise. You seemed so … so capable."

"Capable? A nine-year-old capable? You're pathetic."

"But …"

"And you left me again, when I needed you most."

"But you said you wanted me to take Mildred."

"Just so you could have fun with her," Lucille hissed.

"No, it's not like that. She lost her two sons. I took her to her sister's house. Don't you remember?"

"She's lost two boys? So what? She's got others. At least she got to see them grow up. What's she got to complain about? And now she's got her claws into my father. You're disgusting." She clenched her fists, her broken heart beating hard.

"No, love."

"Don't you call me love. Get out of my house. I never want to see you again."

"It's the grief talking. That's all. I'll get the doctor."

"Don't you dare. That doctor is a charlatan. He didn't believe me. He didn't listen. I knew there was something wrong with my boy. Get out!" Lucille screamed. "Get out!"

She watched her father disappear from the room before she slid to the floor, holding on to the leg of the crib and burying her head into the carpet.

"Why?"

She dragged herself back to bed, where she sobbed, wiping her eyes and nose on the sheet. Then she slept. She didn't know what time it was when she woke, but found a sandwich on her bedside table. She groped for the glass of water and gulped it down, unable to stomach the food, then slumped back into the pillows to sleep again.

*

There were voices and words like "severely ill" and "funeral", but it was as if she were in a dream. Someone fed her soup and water. Someone took her to the bathroom, washed her, changed her nightgown, put her into clean sheets. Sometimes she screamed and thrashed about, pulled at her hair, scratched her arms and ripped her nightgown.

Then one day she woke and stared at shadowy stripes falling across the brown blanket on her bed. Two small windows, metals bars on them, white walls. Where was her floral bedspread, her floral wallpaper? She rubbed her face and sat up.

"Max," she murmured. Then louder. "Max!"

She swung herself out of the bed and looked down at her nightgown, course and rough in her hands. Definitely not hers. A robe hung on the back of the door, and as she shuffled towards it, the door opened.

"You're up." A woman in a starched white uniform smiled at her. "I'm Sister O'Reilly. How are you feeling, dear?"

"I'm …" Lucille frowned. "Where am I?"

"You're in hospital. I'm not surprised you don't know. You've had quite a time of it."

Lucille rubbed her aching head. "My baby?"

Sister O'Reilly grabbed the robe and helped her into it. "The doctor will be along shortly. He'll be very pleased you're up. Are you hungry? I'll get you something."

The nurse led her to a worn timber table and gently sat her in a hard wooden chair. The effort of getting out of bed had sapped every ounce of her strength, yet, her stomach rumbled and she nodded.

"Ah, that's a good sign indeed."

Lucille stared through the bars on the window – sky, tree foliage.

"What's the date?" she said.

"Why it's April fifteenth, 1941."

Lucille tried to think, to remember, but her thoughts were scrambled.

"I missed my twenty-first birthday."

The nurse looked at her watch. "Your father usually comes in every day after lunch time. I'm sure he'll be pleased that you're up."

Lucille nodded. Then she wondered where Patricia was, and touched her soft breasts and her flabby tummy. "I did have a baby, didn't I?"

The nurse nodded. There was a knock at the door. "That'll be your breakfast. Then the doctor will be along to see you."

Suddenly, Lucille was ravenous, but there was no knife or fork. She turned to ask the nurse, but she'd disappeared, so she ate the boiled eggs with her hands, hungrily dipping the toast into the yoke, then licking her fingers.

She sat back in her chair while the nurse removed the breakfast plate. "Well done, Lucille. You finished everything."

While she drank her tea, the nurse returned.

"This is Doctor Bromhill, Lucille," Sister O'Reilly said.

A man in a tweed suit and bow tie sat in the chair opposite her.

He smiled. "Your appetite's back. That's an excellent sign."

Lucille took in the thick-set man with a moustache as he wrote in his notebook.

"She's asking about her baby," Sister O'Reilly said.

"Yes. My baby," Lucile said. "I think I've left her somewhere, with someone, but I can't remember who."

"Mrs Doomsbury, baby Patricia died last year. Do you remember?"

She tilted her head to watch curling brown leaves fluttering from the large elm tree outside the window.

"My precious girl is gone?" She then leant on the table with her head held between her hands. "My boy too?"

"Yes. I'm afraid so."

"It's my fault," she said, looking up into the doctor's eyes. "I was a bad mother."

"I believe you have what we call postpartum psychosis, a condition some mothers get after they've given birth. Your father arranged for you to come here to rest and get well."

"How long have I been here?"

"Nearly three months."

Lucille looked from the doctor to the nurse, trying to remember. How was it possible to not remember three months of her life? Yet she couldn't. "So, it's like jail for being a bad mother. Good! I deserve it."

"No. It's nothing like that, Mrs Doomsbury. You've been very sick. You couldn't help it. But you will be well again. With the power of positivity, you will be out of here in no time."

"I have to tell my husband about Harry." Lucille looked at her scratched hands. They shook so much when she lifted them, she immediately pressed them onto the table. "He's in London, doing important work on pesticides. For the war, you know. He thinks I don't know, but I overheard him one day, saying it was to poison the Germans, and that was the only way to stop the war." She clapped her hand across her mouth when she saw the look of surprise on the nurse's face. "Oh no! I shouldn't have said that. It's top secret."

"Mrs Doomsbury, your husband is aware of what's happened to your son and was on a ship returning to Australia."

"He's coming back?" Lucille's heart lifted. "Please don't tell anyone what I just told you. You won't tell, will you?"

"Of course, Mrs Doomsbury." The doctor looked at the nurse and she nodded.

Lucille was relieved. Max would be so disappointed in her.

"Mrs. Doomsbury. I need you to concentrate on what I'm going to tell you."

"Yes?"

Another nurse had come into the room. She was tall and solid. Lucille had to concentrate on the doctor, so she stared at his brightly coloured bow tie.

"Unfortunately, the ship was struck by a torpedo and sunk. Your husband has been listed as missing. I'm very sorry."

It came rushing back. She doubled over. Now she remembered, and she didn't want to. She'd ripped the curtains, thrown furniture and shattered crockery after she read the telegram. She suddenly noticed the bandages on her arms. "What are these for?"

"You hurt yourself."

"Oh."

She remembered. The knife she'd slashed across her arms. She'd wanted to die and still did.

"I think I'd like to lie down now, please."

"I'll organise some medication for you. It will help you to sleep, and I'll see you tomorrow."

She nodded without looking at him. Then vomited egg all over the floor. Both nurses held her up, her strength gone.

"Sorry," Lucille said as the nurse helped with her robe. She slipped her bare feet in between the cold rough sheets. When had the bed been made?

The tall nurse brought the medicine to Lucille's lips, and she gulped the sweetness down. "Try and sleep now," the nurse said, gently touching her on the forehead.

She closed her eyes.

Their footsteps on the linoleum floor faded away with their words. "Poor, poor woman."

28

QUIN

NOVEMBER, 1989

Quin clung to the lift railing as it glided up to her floor. She dreaded the day ahead of her.

"I knew it was too good to be true. We need to get our money out, Quin," Nan said, the night before when she rang.

"It's fine. It's perfectly safe," Quin said.

"Dot told me there's a run-on Solid Rock. She went to the branch, and there was a queue a mile long. She told me to get all my money out."

"There was a lot of people trying to withdraw their cash today, that's true. We're not sure why, because everything is good. The company is in good shape and there's nothing to worry about, Nan."

That's what she'd been saying all day yesterday to clients and staff. The phones had been ringing non-stop. Solid Rock was in good shape, at least it was when she'd last inspected the company's financials.

The lift door opened and as she reached her office, several phones had begun ringing. It was going to be the same again today.

Tom called all the department heads together late that afternoon. He had circles under his eyes, and he seemed to have aged overnight. "Thanks for all of your hard work today. We think one of the big banks spread a rumour that we're in trouble. There's nothing for anyone to worry about."

"How do you know, Tom?" Quin said, chewing her thumbnail.

"I rang a few of our clients who had taken their money out, and they all went to one bank. Apparently, they'd got a phone call from staff at that bank basically lying to them that we're going under, and even though the rate was nowhere near as good as ours, they got spooked. It's as simple as that." Tom ran his hand through his hair. "It's the tall poppy syndrome in this bloody country."

"No bloody wonder," Pete said. "The politicians don't know how to run a bloody chook raffle, let alone a state. The unions are running everything. Just look at the public transport stoppages every two minutes."

"As soon as someone outshines everyone else, they're pulled apart."

"Which bank was it?" Quin asked.

"I'm not going to say but I'll be ringing that CEO to tell them to pull their head in. Tell everyone it's all under control.

Suffice to say, I don't expect any staff to be withdrawing their own money."

Everyone nodded in agreement. As Pete, Larry and Quin were leaving, Tom called them back.

"Close the door. How much do you reckon we've lost so far?" Tom asked.

Larry looked at his notebook. "Nearly, thirty million."

"Shit!" Tom sat heavily in his chair and leant on his desk, head in his hands. "It'll be all right. We'll ride it out. But none of this can get out. Do I have your word?"

Larry and Pete looked at each other and nodded.

Quin froze. What about Nan's money, her and Ben's money? What was she going to tell them? It wasn't like she'd lied to them or everyone else. But now she knew what the real situation was. She thought of her staff, and the reassurance she'd given clients. She felt sick.

"Quin?"

The three men looked at her, waiting for her agreement.

She tensed, fighting to contain the tremor snaking through her. "Sure," she said. Tom's deceit was now hers. He had all the power, and she had none. She'd looked the part, played the part, and now she was part of the whole deception. She nodded.

Pete said. "It'll blow over."

Tom stood. "Well, we've got work to do."

They were dismissed, but on the way out, Tom yelled out to Deb to get the State Treasurer on the phone. Quin wondered what that conversation would be like.

*

At home that night, Pete played with the peas on his plate, and Quin ate only because she had to. They watched the news, featuring Solid Rock as a minor news item.

"What do you reckon?" Pete said.

She shrugged. "I'm worried. I've never been in this situation before. I thought this sort of stuff only happened in the Great Depression or in Third World countries. Thirty mil is a lot to go flying out the door in a couple of days. We can't sustain the outflow if it continues. Hopefully, it'll stop."

"At least the non-withdrawable securities can't be withdrawn, but I'm dreading tomorrow."

Their whole life was tied up in those securities. No-one could touch that. She breathed a sigh of relief.

The next morning, Pete left for work while it was still dark, and Quin wasn't far behind. She decided not to drive in, opting for the tram to avoid traffic.

In the newspaper that morning was a statement by Solid Rock, reassuring depositors their funds were secure:

The company has sufficient liquidity to meet all deposits. There is no reason for people to withdraw their funds. Solid Rock has extensive lines of credit supported by banks. The Registrar of Building Societies, which is the government's regulatory body for all building societies, has confirmed with us that Solid Rock has adequate asset backing and is extremely well managed. There is nothing to be concerned about.

Quin lifted her gaze from the newspaper and scanned the faces of the other commuters on the crowded tram. Everyone had their head in the news. Some looked worried and others looked smug. This was wrong. She'd seen the accounts a day ago. Their liquidity was low. Hell, there were barely enough funds to meet any more withdrawals. She dreaded the day ahead.

Larry and Pete were in Tom's office when she arrived.

"I've read the statement in the paper. It's a blatant lie," she said.

The three men looked at her.

"Don't be naive, Quin," Tom said.

"As of last night, we won't have enough liquid funds to last out the day." Quin stared out the window. "What are we going to tell the staff, and more importantly, what are we going to tell our clients?"

And she needed to tell Nan and Ben to get all their money out, today.

The phone rang. Tom picked it up and gestured for them both to leave.

"What the hell is going on, Pete?"

"Don't you worry your pretty little head about it. We've got it sorted," Pete said.

"What? Don't dismiss me. I'm part of it. We've got to tell the Registrar the truth or this whole thing will blow up in our faces. We could lose everything."

Larry looked at Pete, frowning as he walked back to his office.

Pete took her elbow. "Go tell the teams that we're limiting

withdrawals to one hundred dollars per depositor … just for today only."

"Bloody hell. Clients are going to go berserk. I hope you know what you're doing."

"We do." Pete patted her on the bum. "It'll be fine." He left her outside Tom's office and headed to the lifts.

Too late to tell Nan and Ben, she thought. Hopefully, they could withdraw funds tomorrow. She should check with Tom if the limit would be only for one day. His door was ajar, and she stopped when she heard him still on the phone. She didn't intend to listen, but his voice was raised.

"Listen, David. All I'm asking is for some time and some funds to shore us up. A couple of days tops. We're good for it. Surely your bank should be able to help us out. Yeah, I know. You know what the media is like. They find any way to discredit us. You know you can't trust those bastards. They say anything to sell newspapers."

Quin sighed.

Tom's line rang at Deb's desk. Deb wasn't in, and Tom was still on the phone. Quin answered.

"Good morning, Solid Rock. Tom Doomsbury's phone."

"G'day. I'm after Tom. Can you put me through?"

"May I ask who's calling please?"

"Bob Carmine."

"Minister Carmine, he's on the other line at the moment. I'm Quin Schmidt, head of operations?" She took a deep breath. There was only one thing to do. "I know he wants to talk to you too. There seems to have been a misunderstanding."

"You bet there was. What the hell game are you playing there? You cowboys better sort this out. You can tell your boss that the government is not going to take the blame for your total incompetence, and we're not going to back your funds with any sort of guarantee. You got that?"

"Yes, Minister Carmine. I'll pass it on. For what it's worth, we're working through the issues and feel confident that our position will be satisfactorily liquid."

What was she doing lying to the minister?

"Good! It better be."

He hung up.

"Who was that?" Tom yelled from his office.

Quin went in and told him about the conversation with the minister.

"Why the hell did you tell him that? Now it looks like I lied."

He had lied.

"I didn't lie. We are working through it. Pete told me that we're limiting withdrawals to one hundred dollars a day."

"Yeah. To buy us time. I'm going to do another press release. Deb! Where the hell is she? Find Deb. And close the goddamn door."

Deb was putting her bag under her desk. "He wants you in there."

"Is he in a foul mood?"

"He sure is. The shit's hitting the fan."

"Bugger. It was too much to hope for a good day."

"It'll be a long time before you're going to get one of those."

Quin glanced at her watch: seven forty-five. It was going to be a long day.

An hour later, she had a copy of the statement on her desk. She checked downstairs and the reports weren't good. Clients were complaining about the limit. One kicked the door down of the branch in Hammondville. She read it through.

Vicious rumours and speculation have been circulating and we, amongst other financial institutions, have not been immune. I can categorically tell you that these rumours are not true. In fact, we have had an extremely successful six months posting a half-year profit in excess of $15 million coming after a yearly profit for 1989 at $25 million.

There is absolutely no reason to withdraw funds and you have my personal guarantee that your funds are safe with Solid Rock.

Tom Doomsbury
Managing Director and Chairman.

The statement did little to stop the run and they were forced to allow the limit to increase to $1000.

*

The next day, Tom called a meeting with Pete, Larry and Quin.

"I'm selling off the mortgages. The auditors are breathing down our neck, and it'll buy us time."

"Who's the buyer?" she asked.

"We're going out to market. I want the three of you to make sure each loan is squeaky clean. And I don't care how you do it. No bad debts. We should be able to offload them and get back at least $100 million. That'll keep the politicians and the auditors off our back."

"By when?" Quin asked.

"Yesterday," Tom said. "Go!"

Quin got every staff member in the office to check the loans, the documents and the security to make sure everything was in order to put them out to the market to sell. The team worked until midnight.

She checked the outflow of funds the next morning. The $30 million had grown to $80 million. The statement had made no difference.

Ben rang. "I tried to get some money out, but the limit is still at a thousand. Bloody do something, will ya?"

"Look, calm down. Most of our money is in the non-withdrawable investment shares, and that's safe. Just take out what you can to run the stores. It should blow over in the next day or so. Okay?"

Was their money still safe in the shares? In reality, she wasn't sure.

Larry reported back on the loans. "I don't know how some of these are going to be offloaded. So far, we have $50 million clean enough for sale. But we've got bad debt building. There's a lot of clients wanting repayment holidays."

Quin twirled her pen. "Yeah, I thought it was a tough ask."

Deb buzzed her. "He wants to see you and Larry for an update."

She rolled her eyes. Her job had become a hodgepodge of duties. Larry should have been in charge, but Tom seemed to want her involved in every little thing. It had been nice at first, but now that everything had gone pear-shaped, she didn't like it. She was involved in the accumulation of lies, and there was little she could do about it, except hope to hell they could survive.

Quin took a deep breath and went in.

"It's not good," Larry said.

Tom scratched his head. "Those mortgages have to be sold. Today. Get me the $100 mil. I'm counting on you. The auditors are coming in this afternoon."

"We'll try, Tom."

"Don't try. Get it done. Now where the hell is Pete?"

*

A few days later, Larry and Quin had $68 million ready for sale, and the auditor held a meeting with them.

They sat around the conference table, Deb taking notes, Quin, Larry, Pete and Tom ready to hear what the auditor had to say.

"Solid Rock looks to have been well managed. So, congratulations. The run on deposits has cost you big time, as you well know. Bad debts are rising, but the retail portfolio looks fairly solid. The commercial stuff you have is dubious – high risk at best. You're only getting profit via fees from lending money. The problem is that the Building Society

Act stipulates that you need a minimum of 7.5% liquidity to continue lending. If you go below that, we need to call in the liquidators. You're sitting on eight per cent, which is not enough for you to start lending. It's a vicious cycle you've got yourselves in. If you don't lend, you don't make money. And if you don't make money, your profit, along with your liquidity level, will continue to plummet."

So nothing they didn't know. Quin sighed. How were they going to get out of this mess? She felt sick thinking about the investment shares and how much money her family had tied up.

"I see. Thanks. Quin, get Morgan Brown Advertising on the phone for me. We're going to do an advertising campaign and get our funds back. Pete and Larry, start writing more loans," Tom said. Then he walked out of the office. The three of them looked at each other.

"That's a good plan," Larry said.

Quin nodded. "I hope it works." She was a little more comforted by the strategy. Surely, the government couldn't afford to let them fail.

29

LUCILLE

JANUARY 1942

Ignoring the sweat dripping off her face, Lucille lifted the soft, dark soil, letting it run through her fingers. Next to her was a pile of weeds and she sat on her haunches to admire the cleared flower bed and her purple rose. It was covered in buds except for one which had opened overnight. She pulled it closer and breathed in its perfume.

Two women in army uniform strolled past, arm in arm. She couldn't help but stare at them. When she ventured out to the shops, there were more women in uniform than she'd ever seen, and she wondered what their life was like.

It was a new year. A time for new beginnings, the doctor had said. She'd given the baby clothes and crib away to the local baby health centre. Knowing someone else could use them, made her happier. It was a positive thing to do, she thought, reminding herself of her doctor's words: "Look for positivity in everything you do."

She wiped the sweat off her forehead with a handkerchief – Max's. She looked at his initials that she'd sewn in the corner as a Christmas gift. She missed him. It had been more than a year. It was time to clear his things from the cupboard, but she wasn't sure she was ready. Perhaps after the garden. New beginnings.

Why did it still hurt so much?

She hoisted herself up and reached for the spade, pushing it hard into the soil, attacking the roots of a thistle, lifting it out and throwing it onto a pile of other weeds. Puffing, she leant on the shovel and noticed two new plants. Tiny buds were beginning to form on each of them. They might be azaleas she thought and wondered if Pa had planted them. She sighed, remembering their last meeting.

He'd taken her home from hospital. She could have forgiven him for putting her there – she'd been very sick; she knew that now. Except now he was drunk again. He needed her, he'd said. But that meant going back to her old life with him. Making sure he was okay, cooking, cleaning, staying under his control. She couldn't be around a drunk, she'd said. They'd argued. He'd fallen over in his haste to leave. She hadn't the strength to look after him, when she struggled to look after herself. She couldn't be the strong one.

That was three months ago, and she hadn't seen or heard from him since. They'd both spent Christmas alone and miserable. But the new year was a new beginning.

Her throat tightened. *That's enough.* She swallowed and picked up the pile of weeds, taking them to the compost.

Then she gathered up her tools, put them away and went inside to the cool of the house.

As she washed her hands and cleaned the dirt from under her fingernails, she peered at herself in the mirror. A few grey hairs had sprung up in the middle of her part. She'd be twenty-two in a week. She was a woman, lost and alone. The girl filled with excitement and anticipation for the life she'd envisaged was long gone. What was she to do now?

The memory of her grandmother's words pounded her head. "Leave me alone. At least I've known the love of a man and my babies," she said defiantly in the mirror. "I've no regrets about that."

She turned on the wireless and put the kettle on. The Japanese threat was spreading through Asia. They were already in Papua New Guinea. The Americans had torpedoed a Japanese submarine at Midway Atoll. It had been the first time the Americans had sunk an enemy vessel. She'd cheered. Max's ship had been torpedoed and sunk by a Japanese submarine, and how she'd prayed it was the same one the Americans had attacked.

She pulled out the tea cannister and snapped off the wireless. There was a knock at the front door and she was surprised to see her old friend Bethany standing on the doorstep in a khaki drill shirt dress with matching hat.

"Hello, Lucille," Bethany said, smiling.

"God, look at you. Have you joined up?"

Bethany nodded twisting herself around. "What do you think?"

"Amazing. It's so good to see you," Lucille said, hugging her friend. "Come in. I've just boiled the kettle. You'll have a cup of tea, won't you?"

Bethany removed her hat and put it on the hallway stand. "I sure will."

"I've seen so many women in uniform in the last few months."

"Well, there are no men now to do the jobs. They need us. I saw Loopy Liz yesterday and you should have seen the look on her stupid face."

Lucille laughed. "God, is she still around? I thought she'd have married and disappeared."

"She's still living at home, so Mum tells me. Works in a factory."

"Really? Sit down. I desperately want to hear what's been happening to you."

She hadn't seen Bethany since she'd married. Patrick had joined up and they both moved to Brisbane two years ago.

"I'm sorry I haven't been writing. I thought, since I'm here on leave to see Mum and Dad, I'd come and see how you are."

Lucille led her into the kitchen and grabbed another cup. "Milk?"

Bethany nodded and sat at the table.

"Your parents? Are they all right?"

"Yes, they're fine. Just getting old, that's all." Bethany waited until Lucille sat. "I heard what happened ... with your babies." She reached across and patted Lucille on her hand. "I'm really so sorry and wish I'd known sooner."

Lucille pulled her hand away and fidgeted with her wedding ring. She hated the look of sympathy and pity. "It's been horrible. But I'm all right now. Just getting on with things." There was an awkward silence. "What about you? The uniform?"

"When Patrick joined up, I was so bored at home on my own. And it was really hard to make friends in Brisbane. So, I thought, why not join up? Patrick was all for it. And they needed more women. Still do. The Japs are advancing so fast it's hard to know what's going to happen." Bethany sipped her tea, then looked at Lucille. "No word about Max?"

Lucille reached into her pocket for her handkerchief and blew her nose. "No. I suppose you heard that he was coming home and his ship was sunk?"

Bethany nodded. "He might have survived, you know."

"When they reached the place where the ship sank, there were no survivors. I think I just have to face it. Actually, I have faced it. Max is gone, that's all there is to it."

"How are you managing, you know … financially? If you don't mind me asking, have you applied for the War Widow's Pension? You'd be entitled to it."

"Officially, he's only been listed as missing."

"Then you're still getting his pay? I don't mean to pry, but I wondered."

"He was sending some money. Now, every so often, I

receive a money order. I think from one of his superiors in London."

Bethany frowned. "Oh."

"To be honest, it's a bit tight."

Lucille had always kept a small amount of cash aside from the housekeeping money Max had given her before he left. She'd tucked a lot away in a jar, just like she'd done when she was with Pa. But now she'd used up almost all her ration coupons and had almost spent her savings. Pa had told her to apply for the pension, but she hadn't the courage to face it. Getting a handout from the government was for poor people, not for someone like her. But then perhaps she was poor.

She clutched the handkerchief in her hand. "I should try to get the pension. It's been over a year. But I don't feel right."

Bethany touched her arm.

"On the other hand, I need to do something. I've sorted out the house. I'm reclaiming the garden from the weeds. I don't really know what to do with my life. What do you actually do?"

"I'm a driver at the moment, and there'll be opportunities to learn other jobs, like being a wireless operator. Luce, it's amazing."

"Did they teach you?"

"Yes. The training is intense, and you have to have your wits about you. But now I'm driving army trucks filled with all sorts of things. The other day I delivered boxes and boxes of rifles. Can you believe it?"

Lucille smiled at her friend. "I want to do something like that."

"Join up, Luce. They need more women, and they pay you. It's a wonderful feeling having your own money. Working more than occupies my mind." Her shoulders slumped. "And stops me worrying so much about Patrick."

"Where is he?"

Bethany bit her lip. "He's somewhere in the Pacific. There's hardly been a letter for the last few months."

"I'm sure he's okay."

"Yes. You're probably right."

Lucille drummed her fingers on the table, her mind in an excited whirl. There was nothing for her in Melbourne. She couldn't sit around feeling sorry for herself any longer. But what if Max somehow survived, came home and she wasn't there? Could she risk it? *He's not coming home.*

"Do you think I can come back with you and join up in Brisbane? Or do I have to join here?"

Bethany clapped her hands and squealed. "Yes. They desperately need more recruits. I go back in three days on the train. Come with me and join up. We can be together. Keep each other company. I'd so love that."

Lucille smiled. "I think I'm going to start a new life. God, I've got a million things to do."

Bethany stood. "You sure have so I'll go now, then pick you up on Thursday. Dad will drive us to the station."

"That'd be great. Thanks." Lucille hugged her friend. "God, I'm excited."

She wouldn't apply for a pension. Joining up, she'd earn her own money and do something worthwhile. Fight against the Japs, who'd taken Max from her.

The next day, she visited Pa and told him she was joining AWAS – the Australian Women's Army Service. He nodded and said little, but his hands shook as he reached for the beer bottle.

"Do what you have to do," he said. "I don't need you. I can get on fine by myself."

She hated seeing him like that. But it couldn't be helped. She needed this.

"Will you be all right?" she said.

He stared at her, his eyes hard. "Of course, I'll be all right. Why wouldn't I be? I don't need you, and you don't need me. That much is clear. Now get out so I can listen to my radio serial."

She closed the door behind her, tears filling her eyes.

30

QUIN

MAY 1990

As she jogged, Quin glanced at the mosaic of an unusually early frost across the park. Tendrils of fog lifted as the sun emerged, and she puffed hard, making her way onto the back streets of Werribee.

Deposits had flowed in over the last few months to keep Solid Rock going, but she worried whether it would be enough for the long term. The economy was stuffed. No-one had cash and those who did, paid off debts or invested in the big banks, which were safer. Every week, another company went under. The newspapers were baying for blood, searching desperately for someone to blame, and the politicians ducked for cover. But Tom had reassured the staff they'd weather it. There'd be no bonuses, but neither would there be job losses.

She and Pete had been fighting so much she'd moved back home. "It's probably for the best," he'd said. She didn't know when their relationship had soured. Was it because there was nothing to say after working long hours seven days a week? She couldn't remember the last time they'd touched each other. Working and living with someone was hard, especially when they were both irritable and worn out.

When she'd moved back, it was the permanent frown on Nan's face she noticed the most. Nan seemed worried all the time. Quin tried to reassure her that their money was safe. It was the everyday accounts that had been drained.

"Nan, stop cleaning and come in and watch Sale of the Century with us," Quin called out.

"I've got too much to do," Nan yelled back.

"What's going on?" Quin asked Ben.

He shrugged. "Search me. She's been like this for ages. If you'd visited more often, you'd have noticed."

"I'm here now. So, you're no longer the favourite." She smirked at Ben's withering look. "Why haven't you asked her what's wrong?"

"I tried. But she said she was fine."

"Maybe she's not well?"

He raised one eyebrow. "Ya think? I hadn't thought about that."

Quin shook her head. "Hopeless! Let's talk to her together."

Ben nodded and turned off the television. They walked into the kitchen and stared at Nan.

"What?" Nan said.

"Sit down," Ben said gently. "We'd like to have a family meeting." He looked at Quin, who nodded.

Nan wiped her hands on the tea towel, and Quin noticed how red they were. Her fingernails were chewed down to the quick and her fingers were cracked. Dark bags sat under her bloodshot eyes.

"What's wrong?" Nan said to Quin. "Are you sick? Is it about Pete? I know a breakdown of a relationship can be very difficult, but you'll get through this."

"No, no I'm fine." Quin reached out and touched Nan's arm. "We're worried about you."

"Yeah, we're worried," Ben said.

"You seem … on edge. I've been home for two days, and I've hardly seen you sit down to relax. I heard you last night, walking around the house. What's wrong?" Quin squeezed her arm gently.

Nan's eyes darted around the kitchen and she rubbed the back of her head. "I'm not sleeping too well, that's true. I don't want you to worry about me. You've got enough on your plate, working long hours. I'm so proud of you both." Nan looked from Quin to Ben.

"We're fine," Quin said. "Aren't we?"

Ben frowned. "Yeah. Don't worry about us. We're on top of the world. Now let's talk about what's worrying you."

Nan pulled out the chair and sat busying her hands by straightening the lace doily in the centre of the table. "It's just that things are so bad at the club."

"The bowling club?" Quin frowned. "Is that what's going on?"

"Partly. You know Madge?"

"Best friend Madge?"

Nan nodded. "Yes. You probably don't remember, but she was the treasurer, and she's got herself into a bit of trouble. She's been caught stealing money from the club."

Quin clapped her hand over her mouth. "Madge? That's unbelievable."

"Why? And how much?" Ben said.

Nan swallowed. "She took a couple of thousand to help her daughter pay her mortgage, to stop the bank foreclosing."

"Jesus," Ben said. "I wouldn't have believed it. What's going to happen?"

"I've been worried sick about it, trying to work something out. I think I've convinced the president to let her pay it back. We're holding a raffle and a sausage sizzle to help her get the money. But it's made me think about my own situation."

Nan leant back with both hands on the table. "Things are not good. Let's face it. I've lived through hard times during the war. It's tough when you have nothing, and I don't want you both to be in that situation. Ever. I don't feel comfortable about the debt we have on this house. There! I've said it. I never have. But this thing with Madge has rocked me."

She looked at each of them in turn.

"I'm still making more than enough money to pay the mortgage," Ben said. "This will all just blow over, and we'll be richer than ever."

"Nan, it's okay," Quin said.

"We're both working and making good money. Very good money. The investments are doing well. We made nearly twenty thousand last year, just by having money invested." Ben leant back in his chair, lifting the front legs off the floor.

"But maybe we should take our money out of the term deposit and just pay it all off. I don't feel comfortable about having such a large debt. Quin?"

Ben and Nan looked at her. "The money's tied up, Nan. We can't just withdraw it. Ben's right. His two businesses are doing well. Between Ben and I, we're covering the mortgage payments easily, so there's nothing to worry about."

"But can't you just withdraw our money? Give them notice or whatever they need? You said yourself that it was just a glitch a few months ago."

It was better not to go into details. The more Quin explained to them, the more questions they'd ask, and it wasn't simple to explain. The money was actually a share in the business. It wasn't like she hadn't tried. Larry had already told her it was important the shares weren't withdrawn. How could she tell them the truth?

"It's not as easy as that, Nan." Quin looked at her watch. "It's a bit more complicated. Now I want you to stop worrying. Why don't we do a fundraiser at the footy club for Madge and her daughter? Ben, what you do you think?"

"Yeah, good idea."

"And I'll see if I can do something to refinance her loan for her. I'll ring Madge, if you like."

"Okay," Nan said reluctantly. "That would be good.

You're the expert. I trust you both to know what you're doing."

"It's all going to be fine," Ben said. "You got the two of us raking in the big bucks. Soon we'll be able to get a mansion in Essendon."

Nan laughed. "I'm not moving."

Quin kissed her and left the table. As she grabbed her keys to go to Pete's to pick up some of her things, Ben grabbed her arm at the front door.

"You better be right. There's a lot of angry people out there wanting their money."

She shook his hand off. "And it will be all right. Trust me. I've got to go."

Ben's comment worried her. It would be all right. Tom promised it would be.

31

LUCILLE

1942

Lucille held Bethany and let her sob. The telegram lay on Lucille's kitchen table. Patrick had been killed in Papua New Guinea.

She recognised her friend's anguish too well, her body rigid, Lucille held back her own pain trying to wrap itself around her, to penetrate, to get in. Finally, they let each other go and Lucille led her friend to the chair.

She felt Bethany's eyes, following her around the kitchen. "I'm sorry, I shouldn't have unburdened myself." She blew her nose. "Mum and Dad … you know were … well, sympathetic." She sniffed and wiped her eyes. "But I can see that my coming here has made this worse for you."

Lucille didn't understand until she put her hand up to her face and was surprised it was wet. She wiped her tears and poured the tea. "It's all right."

At least her friend knew for sure her husband was dead. Some words were better left unsaid.

*

Three months later, Bethany and Lucille were on their way to their new post in Alice Springs.

It was a long journey by train, the scrub and red-dirt landscape rolling by hour after hour. When they finally arrived, Lucille was greeted by a blast of heat and someone handed her a glass of cold orange juice and a slice of cold watermelon. That first day they were issued with salt tablets, together with a ration of two beers for the week and a new kitbag. They walked into cement-sheet barracks, fitted with louvred windows to let air circulate. As they were shown to their bunks, the concrete floor crackled underfoot with dirt from last night's sandstorm.

"Mmm, springy," Lucille said, grinning as she pushed down on the thin mattress. "This will do just fine." She brushed sand off the bed.

She looked closely at her friend fidgeting with her bag's zipper. After that day, back home in Lucille's kitchen, Bethany hadn't wanted to talk about Patrick. "I'll be fine. I'm tough and there are people worse off than me. There's a war and we just have to get on with it."

"Are you okay?"

Bethany turned and nodded. "Yeah, I am. What about you?'

"I feel like a new woman," Lucille said searching in her kit bag. She changed into a fresh khaki drill dress, then held up a tropical raincoat, rubber boots and a man's slouch hat. "I didn't think it rained here. God, am I expected to wear these?" She now held up a pair of overalls.

"That'll be very becoming." Bethany bent to lace up her shoes.

"I like the hat." Lucille plonked it onto her head. It had a ribbon band and the Rising Sun badge at the front with the brim pinned back.

"It suits you," Bethany said, smiling as she put her own hat on.

"And shorts? I can't wear these."

Bethany laughed. "I didn't get any of those. Why are you so special?"

"Perhaps because I'll be outdoors, and you've been promoted to a luxurious corrugated tin office?"

Bethany nodded. "Yep. That's why."

After unpacking, they shoved their kit bags into the small wardrobe provided and sat on the wire stretchers made up with bottom and top sheets. "I suppose we won't be needing blankets up here."

"Not yet," Bethany said. "But we better watch out for redbacks and snakes. I heard from one of the others that they like to get in under the sheets."

"Urgh." Lucille shuddered. "So, our worry is not dying from the Japs bombing us, just a sting from a spider or a bite from a snake."

Bethany smiled. "Too right. Except spiders bite too."

That night, Lucille wrote a long letter to Pa, describing the trip and the place she now called home.

The servicemen and women all worked hard. Besides being a driver, Lucille was taught how to service and repair trucks and jeeps. She worked long, hot hours under vehicles, often lying in dust. The overalls were very comfortable and liberated her from the constraints of a dress. Bethany was indoors working on signals.

In their downtime, they did their laundry, played basketball and made tie-dyed hessian bedspreads to brighten up their barracks. They spent their evenings at the outdoor cinema or at dances. Picnics were popular, as were camel rides, and Lucille squealed when she rode one for the first time. She enjoyed the camaraderie of the other women who knew nothing about her life before. Bethany swore she'd never say anything, and they never talked about it. Since Patrick's death, Bethany had also thrown herself into her work, but Lucille sometimes heard her cry quietly at night.

Despite all the letters she wrote to Pa, she never received a single reply in ten months. "Why don't I ask my mother to check on him? To make sure he's all right?" Beth asked.

"No!" Lucille said. "He's in a huff with me. That's all. I'm sure he's fine."

*

It was late August 1944, when Lucille got the telegram telling her Pa was in hospital. It had only been the third time she'd heard from him in two years. He'd sent a card on her birthday, saying he was fine and wishing her well, yet he'd hardly acknowledged her birthday growing up. Now he needed her. Her commanding officer gave her indefinite leave, and she travelled back to Melbourne fretting about what she might find.

She gasped when she saw him. He'd aged terribly: his yellowy skin sagged, dark circles sat under his eyes and he was hunched. He looked eighty, not fifty-three. Liver cancer the doctor said. He'd need constant care. As she gently held his bony arm, her guilt for leaving him grew. She would take him back home with her.

It was a sunny spring day. As she helped Pa from the taxi, he stopped and looked at her garden. "The roses are coming along," he said.

She hadn't noticed earlier; cleaning and organising the house had taken her attention.

"They are, aren't they?" she said, as a butterfly landed on a nearby Azalea bush.

"The azaleas are just about done. They'll need a trim."

She had never seen them flower. "You planted them, didn't you?"

Pa wheezed. "For you. I took care of the garden so it would look good for when you came back."

She swallowed the lump in her throat. She hadn't even noticed how manicured it was.

"Thank you, Pa. It's beautiful."

"Thank you for the letters. I didn't know what to write back. But I enjoyed hearing about your adventures."

Lucille squeezed his hand.

They stood for a moment gazing at the roses blooming in colours of pink, purple and red. Lucille thought of Aunt Mavis and her garden and wished Max were with her to see how much it had changed.

"I'm glad, Pa. I guess we better get you inside."

She settled into nursing Pa, until one rainy Monday morning, when Pa was barely conscious, the doctor shook his head and told her there was little time left.

She laid next to him, her head on his shoulder and cried, "Pa. Don't leave me. I've got no-one."

He put his hand on her head. "You've got your whole life ahead of you, love," he whispered. "You're the best thing that ever happened to me."

He'd loved her in his own way, and she'd loved him.

The next day, he died.

32

QUIN

JUNE, 1990

Quin grabbed a coffee from her usual cafe and drove to work. She hadn't seen Pete much since she'd moved back to Nan's. Now that she was on a different floor, it was easier to avoid him. Or was he avoiding her? She sipped her coffee as the car idled at the lights. She hadn't been heartbroken, hardly affected actually. Was she devoid of emotion? Or had their relationship merely run its course? What she did know was that work had consumed her, had stopped her thinking about where she was in life. There was no time or energy to think about Pete. Surely, that wasn't a bad thing?

She pulled into the carpark under the building. As she rode the lift to her office, she thought through her plan for the day. It was only seven, so it would be peaceful for an hour or so before the rest of the office staff arrived. Time to concentrate without being disturbed.

She walked past Deb's empty desk, peered into Tom's

office. He wasn't in either. Then she noticed her office door was closed. She always left it open for the cleaners. Perhaps they'd closed it for some reason.

She opened her office door.

Tom was sitting in her chair at her desk, his hands clasped in front of him.

Pete was in one of two chairs near the door, head lowered, shoulders slumped. A security guard leant against the wall and stared out of the window. She stood frozen on the threshold, her mouth open.

"Come in," Tom said, grimly.

Heart thumping, she remained in the doorway.

"Sit down." He gestured to the only other vacant chair next to Pete, and she plonked herself into it, her mind racing. She couldn't read Tom's expression as he opened a manila folder in front of him. There'd been talk of job cuts. Was she about to lose hers? Could Ben manage the mortgage payments on his own?

"What's going on?" she said, trying to be business-like.

Tom held a piece of paper in his hands. "I'm disappointed, really disappointed."

"I don't understand. What the hell is going on? What's he doing here?" She stared at the security guard.

Tom gestured for the guard to wait outside. After he'd gone and the door was closed, Tom leant forward and gently shook his head. He took a deep breath. "I'm letting you go."

Her head spun as his words hit her.

"Why? Is it because the company is going under? Because

of the second run? I know it made things worse. I thought we'd weathered it, haven't we?"

"It's not that," Tom said. "It's what we found. I can't have people around me I can't trust. I don't understand it. Didn't I treat you right? Promoted you, gave you this nice office, paid you very handsomely. Gave you authority to act on my behalf with a $5 million approval limit. There's only me, you, Larry and Pete with that kind of limit. And now"—he shook his head—"to find that one of my most trusted employees could do this to me. If you needed help, I would have thought you'd have come to me. But to find"—he pursed his lips—"that you have stolen from me. You've let me and everyone here down."

She reeled. "Stolen? I haven't—"

"How do you explain this?"

Tom pushed a bank statement in front of her. She leant across and took it. Her name was on the top. Numbers swirled in front of her eyes. She blinked twice and the large number remained the same. Deposited 25 May, three weeks ago. The day after she moved out of Pete's house.

"This is not my account."

Tom raised his eyebrows, and she was too afraid to look at Pete beside her.

Her mouth was dry. "You've got to believe me. I've never opened this account, and I don't know how that money got there."

"Don't make this any worse by denying it. Pete, give me the rest of the file."

Pete silently pushed another manila folder across the desk towards Tom.

"Your signature is all over the paperwork. A $2 million loan to a property developer who doesn't exist but turns out to be you."

It looked like her signature on the document. "I've never seen any of this." Her hands trembled, her chest tightened and she could barely breath.

"That is your signature?"

"Yes. Well, it looks like my signature. Pete?" she said, wishing he'd at least look at her. "You know I'd never do something like this." He folded his arms and stared out of the window.

"You've signed everything. You personally approved it." Tom drummed his fingers on the desk. "Your signature is on the entries, and the funds are in a bank account with your name on it. The police have confirmed it."

She was in shock. How? Why?

"The police?" Her voice cracked. "I don't know what to say other than I didn't do this. Please, Tom. You've got to believe me. I did *not* do this. I don't know who did, but it's not me."

"The investigation is conclusive. You need to pack up and go. And Quin, I have no choice than to put this into the hands of the police who have warned me that the penalty for something like this could be jail. You'll need to pay everything back plus interest."

I must not cry, I must not cry, Quin said to herself. Her heart pounded but somehow, she stood and grabbed her briefcase. She opened it and took out two manila folders, files she'd been working on, and placed them on the desk. "I won't be needing these."

Tom got up. "I'm disappointed. You had an amazing future with me. You'll need to return your keys to Pete."

Tom left, and she handed Pete the keys to her office, her security tag and her car keys.

"I'll fix up the lease. Your car's downstairs, isn't it? In the usual spot?"

She nodded. Then stared at him, blinking back tears. "I didn't do this. You've got to believe me."

Pete sighed, refusing to look at her. "You could have talked to me. No wonder you were argumentative and wanted to end it."

She was stunned. Argumentative?

"You were the one who was always in a foul mood," she said. "You're the one who told me it wasn't working."

He looked at her now and narrowed his eyes. "Who the hell are you? You have a warped idea of what the truth is. You dumped me. You hated living in my house. It was too small, too old, too out of date. I never would have believed that you could do something like this. Little did I know that behind that pretty face was a sneaky, lying bitch. It's all been a charade, hasn't it?"

She was so confused. She hadn't liked his house, that was true, but she didn't remember it like that. Her mind was a fog. What was wrong with her that she couldn't remember? The paperwork looked like it had her signature. Had she signed something without looking at it? Many times. The pile on her desk was always high. She trusted her staff. Maybe she shouldn't have. She was numb.

As Quin left her office, Deb was arriving – her smile fading quickly when she saw the security guard escorting Quin. Everyone knew what that meant. Someone was being sacked. Quin couldn't bear to think about the gossip that would spread. They'd talk about how suddenly she'd risen and how hard she'd fallen. Deb averted her eyes and slid into her chair.

Quin looked straight ahead. "I'll take the stairs." She couldn't bear to meet staff coming onto the floor from the elevator. It was more private and less humiliating to take the stairs.

When she was out on the street, she breathed in the still, cold air and wrapped her coat around her. She looked up at the corridor of tall buildings lining the street and began walking. She threw her briefcase into a nearby rubbish bin and wandered the streets in a daze. Eventually she went home. What was she to say to Nan and Ben?

*

"That fucking bastard. You've been set up for sure." Ben paced the floor, clenching his fists. "And fucking Pete. He's had a hand in this. I never trusted him. He's a sneaking, conniving bastard."

"Ben! Language!" Nan said.

Quin had cried for hours in her bedroom when she got home and explained everything to Nan. Then Ben had come home, and she'd told him. Now all she could do was cry in her grandmother's arms.

"It'll be all right, love. Just pay it all back."

Ben ran his hand through his hair "How much do you owe?"

Quin sniffed. "I actually don't know. All I saw on the statement was two million in what was supposedly my bank account. The loan was for two million."

"Well, it's pretty simple. Just return the two million."

"I have to pay the interest on it, Ben. It'll be at least fifty thousand. Maybe more. I don't know."

She burst into tears. She couldn't bear thinking about it.

"We've got the interest money between us, love. We can give back what we made. Ben can sell the two businesses. It'll be all right," Nan said.

"I can't sell my video stores. What am I going to live on? I've just signed an unconditional contract to buy a house. Remember? I have no money."

"We'll get the money out of the term deposit and pay off the interest you owe and …" Nan's face dropped. "That won't help, will it? Because we'll have to pay the mortgage with it."

"I'm sorry, but I can't deal with this right now. I've got a raging headache." Quin got up to go to her room. "I'll figure it out."

"Ben, we will do whatever we have to for your sister. She could go to jail."

The word jail pounded in her head like a sledgehammer.

Jail, jail, jail. She threw herself onto the bed and lay there. She must have dozed off because she woke with a start. The phone was ringing. Now it stopped. Seven-thirty in the morning. She'd slept in her clothes all night. Everything's normal, she thought. It was a bad dream.

"She's okay, but she can't come to the phone right now. As you can appreciate, it's very upsetting for everyone. I'll get her to call you when she's up to it." Nan's voice sounded shaky.

Not a dream then, she thought, and the knots in her stomach tightened. I've got to think, she said to herself. Someone has set me up. But who? She rolled over and thought about what to do first. Then she sprang out of bed, showered and dressed in jeans, jumper and boots. Ben had already gone to work when she entered the kitchen and kissed her grandmother good morning.

"How are you feeling, darl?" Nan looked like she'd had no sleep.

"I'm okay."

"How about a cup of tea and some porridge?"

Quin shook her head. "I don't feel like anything. I'll get a coffee later. Who was on the phone?"

"Someone called Deb. I said you'd call back. Who's she?"

"A friend," Quin said. She wouldn't ring Deb or deal with any of her staff. Though they probably meant well and wanted to know if she was okay.

"I'm going to try and sort this out. I'll be back soon," she said.

"What about a piece of toast?"

"Later," she said, running out of the door at nine o'clock.

*

When she stepped off the train in town, there was a lightness in her footsteps. There, in front of her, was the building where she'd spent the last three years. Her career was now in tatters, but she would start putting things right. She turned left instead of the automatic right she would have taken if she still had her job. She glanced at her watch. Nine forty-five. She walked into a small branch of Solid Rock and asked to see the manager.

Fifty minutes later, she left and found a payphone to ring Pete.

"Can you meet me for a cup of coffee?" Quin said.

"Sure. Where are you?"

"Meet me at the place we used to go for lunch. Oh, and can you get me a payout figure for the loan?"

He met her half an hour later in a coffee shop on Elizabeth Street.

Pete leant towards her as if to kiss her, then stopped himself. "Old habits, hey. Two cappuccinos," he said to the waitress. "How are you?"

"Shithouse. What do you expect? Do you have the figures?"

"Yep." He pushed a piece of paper across the table.

She picked it up and raised her eyebrows. "That much?" She sighed.

"I tried talking Tom out of calling the police. Have they called?"

"No. But I suppose they'll ring me at Nan's place at some stage."

"That's a good sign. Maybe Tom's changed his mind."

He moved his hand towards hers, and his touch was so gentle, her heart melted, just a little, remembering their days together. "Maybe if you go to the branch and at least pay back the $2 mill. Then all you've got is the interest. There'll be no need to call in the police."

"I hope you're right. I've already done it this morning. I was surprised that the account hadn't been stopped. Now all I have to do is find some way of repaying the interest."

Pete nodded. "He won't need to go to the police then."

She pulled her hand away when the waitress arrived with their coffee. "But I don't know why I've had to fix this. It's actually me who should be going to the police. Someone forged my signature." She looked for his reaction, but his face was deadpan.

"Yeah? It sure looked like your signature. I don't want to believe it. But it's hard not to. I just don't know what to think."

He avoided meeting her eyes and her stomach tightened with resentment. "When did you know?"

He lifted his head and tugged at his collar as if it were tight. "Honestly? Yesterday. Tom called me when I got in. He asked me what time you'd be expected. Then he told me. Larry had alerted him, and the auditors got involved.

Apparently, there was an investigation. Then yesterday, he asked me to stay. That's the story."

He didn't sound convincing. He concentrated on shredding the empty sugar packet. He seemed nervous. Was he scared?

Quin narrowed her eyes. "Pete. What's going on?"

"Solid Rock is going down. The liquidators arrived this morning. It looks like we're going into receivership. They're going over everything with a fine-tooth comb. They're really worried about all the commercial deals I did. The ones Tom gave me to write up. Now, my head is on the chopping block. He wanted them all approved, and they were."

Pete rattled on and on about how worried he was, about the different loans he'd written. She saw him for the weasel Ben said he was. Why hadn't she listened? Pete didn't care about her, had never cared.

She got up. "You don't have the threat of going to jail over your head. You're not being framed for something you never did. At least your whole life isn't ruined. Is it, Pete?"

He looked at her as if he was seeing her for the first time.

"And for the record. You dumped me. Don't try and manipulate that in any other way, making me think it was my fault. I reckon you can get the coffee this time. I don't have any money left."

She had the figures. Now she had to work out how she'd pay it back.

33

LUCILLE

1945

The view of Darwin Harbour, strewn with the wreckage of ships, soured the taste of the mango in Lucille's mouth. They'd been given lunch by personnel from the Australian Small Ships Company before she and her unit were taken out on a harbour tour with other military personnel. It was the second day of her posting in Darwin and she'd spent the morning exploring the town. Bethany had been posted to Townsville and Lucille wished she were with her.

"See that spot over there?" the captain said, pointing. "A yank ship with over six hundred men went down."

"Bloody Japs," an Australian soldier muttered.

Lucille shivered in the heat and moved away from the others as the reality of the war hit her.

Nearby, an olive-skinned American soldier, who must have been over six foot three, hung over the railing and moaned.

"Are you okay? Would some water help?" Lucille asked, hoping he wasn't going to throw up.

He nodded, and she thrust the glass she'd got for herself in front of him.

He gulped the water down. "Thanks," he drawled. "I thought it'd be okay, but seeing where she went down is still a shock."

She was puzzled. "Were you on it?"

He breathed in and sighed, his eyes not leaving the spot. "No. My brother was."

"I'm so sorry," Lucille said, gently touching his arm.

"It's okay, ma'am. I feel stupid now though."

"I thought you were feeling seasick."

He smiled from his great height, and she couldn't help compare his stature to Max's. "Now, I'm really embarrassed to have ruined your cruise."

"Not at all."

He gave her back the glass. "Ma'am, forgive my manners. I'm Sergeant Hank Martino."

"Lucille Doomsbury. Are you stationed here?"

"I surely am. And you?"

"I've just arrived from Alice Springs."

He cocked his head and grinned. "G'day."

She smiled. "You're okay then?"

"Thanks again," he said, nodding.

"I'll leave you to it."

She left to give him privacy and get herself a fresh glass of water. As the boat moved away, she enjoyed the gentleness of the breeze and the blue of the water – a refreshing change from red dirt. She'd been seconded to Darwin as her skills as a mechanic were second to none, if her CO was to be believed. A knitting mechanic, they called her, just because she'd knitted a few odd garments. She smiled thinking that reading a knitting pattern was not much more complicated than putting an engine back together again.

The captain pointed out another landmark. "See the wharf? They built it on the wreck of the Neptune, bombed by the Japs three years ago." The ship was still lying on its side. "Forty-five men died."

All eyes were on the wreck, but when she glanced at Hank Martino his eyes were on her.

*

Lucille was at a dance when she saw Hank again some months later. He tapped her on the shoulder. "Lucille?"

"Yes," she said, smiling. "Hello. How nice to see you again."

"Howdy," he beamed. "Wondered if I'd see you again. I made a right fool of myself on the cruise."

"Not at all."

"Would you like to dance?" he said.

"Yes, I would."

They danced to a couple of songs, then sat out in the moonlight and talked. Hank was a broad shouldered and powerfully built man. She was strangely drawn to his large green eyes, high cheekbones and flawless olive complexion. They discovered they were the same age: twenty-five. From

San Diego, he'd grown up on a ranch with three brothers and had Mexican and Italian heritage. He hadn't been home for two years, but he'd been close to the brother who'd been on the ship.

"Matt reckoned my nose is as crooked as a dog's hind leg," he said, touching his nose.

Lucille laughed when Hank explained it was from a somersault gone wrong – jumping off his garage roof onto a mattress when he was fifteen.

When she told him she was a mechanic, he slapped his knee. "Goddamn! Well, I'll be. *I'm* a mechanic, or I was before the war messed it all up."

"Really?" she said.

"We could be husband and wife mechanics with our own business. You, for the ladies and me for the men."

Her smile faded.

"I don't know what came over me. I'm stupid sometimes. I get overexcited about an idea and rattle off without so much as a single thought."

"It's okay, Hank. I'm actually married."

"Oh, I just assumed on account of you not wearing a ring."

She looked at her hands—"I can't wear any jewellery because of my work"—and rubbed at a grease stain under her thumb. "My husband is missing. Or has been for more than four years, and I'm beginning to accept that he must be dead."

She looked at Hank. "It's funny, but it's the first time I've said that out loud to anyone."

"I'm sorry about that."

"I'm sort of used to it now. It's been a long time."

"Do you think you'd like to see me again if I haven't scared you off with my stupidity?"

"I think I would. And I don't find you stupid. I find you … refreshing."

They both laughed. "First time a lady's called me refreshing."

Later, back in her bed in the barracks, she thought about Hank. He was gentle like Max, but not as self-assured, like her. She remembered his eyes, the way he looked at her, different from Max, yet there was something enticing about him. She felt equal to him. Did that mean she hadn't felt like that with Max? Had she looked up to her husband because of their age difference? Then she sat up. Had she seen Max as the father figure she'd always wanted? Is that why Hank appealed? Because he wasn't? She lay down, fiddled with the engagement and wedding rings hanging from the chain around her neck and thought about Hank's lips. What would it be like to kiss them?

Over the following months, Hank and Lucille saw each other whenever they had time off. When he first tried to kiss her, she turned away. She couldn't, she told him, not yet, and he nodded, understandingly. They didn't ask each other questions. It was easier that way. The war would be over soon, and he'd have to go home. But he awakened something in her. It was time to move on and accept that Max was gone. She removed the rings from her chain.

She kissed Hank first, and after the second kiss, she stopped comparing him to Max. She wondered if there was a future with Hank, after the war. The Germans had surrendered a week before and rumours circulated that it wouldn't be long before the Japs were beaten. It was a matter of time, everyone said, especially after two thousand bombs were dropped on Japan's oil storages in Oshima.

Hank said he loved her on the day the first atomic bomb fell on Japan. They were in a house on the outskirts of Darwin. It belonged to an Australian Hank had met, although Lucille suspected he'd won the right to use it during a poker game. She didn't ask questions.

He wanted to marry her and begged her to come to the States. She didn't know what to say, so he asked her to think it over. Maybe this was all she could hope for, she thought as she kissed Hank deeply.

She enjoyed his company and really liked him, but was it love? He's a good man, she thought. He's kind and gentle with a great sense of humour. Then there was the matter of him being American. First a cousin, then a Catholic American of mixed descent. She wished Bethany was here, but she was still in Townsville. Her signalling skills were needed there. But Lucille knew exactly what Bethany would have said. She'd say no.

Home held nothing for her. Lucille had been given her discharge orders. The war was over. She was no longer needed. She wanted to stay in Darwin, but the jobs would go to returning soldiers. "A woman can't be a mechanic", she was told. No-one seemed to think it was unfair. "That's just the way it is". And she saw the sense of it.

She and Hank travelled to Sydney together before he shipped out and she returned to be formally discharged in Melbourne. They walked hand in hand around the harbour and the city streets.

It was their last morning together. They were in bed and he wanted an answer.

She sighed. "I'm not sure."

"Look, I know the paperwork about Max needs to be sorted out. It's painful, I get it."

It wasn't that, although the finality of a death certificate would be difficult. Could she make a life with Hank?

He leant in closer, his breath on her skin. "I love you too much. We'll get married here and go back to the States to start our own mechanic business."

She pulled away and lay on her back. "I don't know."

He sat up and looked at her. "Or here's another idea. You don't have to go live in another country. I'd happily live here. I'll still have to go home and get stuff sorted, but we can marry when I return. Or we'll marry tomorrow. What about it?"

She closed her eyes. It was tempting, and what Hank was offering could work.

"We'll make a fortune, have babies and grow old and happy."

She suddenly got up from the bed, put on her robe and paced the floor.

"Baby, tell me what's wrong?" Hank leant on one elbow watching her.

She stopped pacing. She had to tell him. "I can't marry you. I can't give you all the things you want. It wouldn't be fair. I'm sorry." She couldn't bring herself to explain that she didn't want children. Ever. He wouldn't understand. How could he? She barely understood it herself. But she couldn't go through another pregnancy, another child, another death. He deserved to have what he wanted.

He sat on the edge of the bed with his head in his hands, elbows on his knees. "So, your mind is made up?" he said.

"Yes." She hesitated. "I'm sorry."

She went to the bathroom and dressed quickly, and when she came out was surprised to see him lying on the bed, his arm flung across his face.

"I'm going now."

He sat up. "Come here."

She sat beside him. "I want you to take this. My address in the States, in case you change your mind."

She took the envelope, kissed him on the cheek and left, not trusting herself to say anything else or to turn around and leap into his arms.

34

QUIN

1990

Things were moving fast. The public clamoured to get their money out. By the end of June, the liquidators gave a statement: "All funds are frozen, and mortgages secured by homes will need to be settled either by refinance or repayment."

"What the hell does this mean?" Ben said, waving the letter they'd received. "They're calling up the mortgage. All our money is tied up with them. This is fucked."

"Ben! Your foul language isn't helping." Nan's mouth was set in a tight line, her lipstick leaching into fine wrinkles around her mouth. "Quin, what does it all mean? Do we have to sell the house?"

Quin's head thumped as she read the letter, then let it fall to the table. She sat. "We have until 30th September to repay the entire mortgage."

"Even though Ben's still meeting the mortgage payments?" Nan looked grim-faced. "I don't understand."

She felt Ben's eyes boring into her. "Why don't you explain why we got this letter, and why don't you tell us how you're going to get us out of this mess?"

Quin's hand shook as she picked up the letter again and looked at Nan. "The liquidators of Solid Rock treat mortgages like assets they have to sell off, so that's why we got this letter. The mortgage documents we signed mean they can do this any time they like."

She took a deep breath and watched the disbelief spread across Nan's face. "Because our investments are frozen, we don't have the money to repay the mortgage so the only thing we can do is to try to get it refinanced with another bank."

"Refinance? What the—"

Nan raised her hand to Ben. "Is that feasible?"

Quin nodded and glanced at Ben. "I think that's the only way."

"All right. Then that's what we'll do," Nan said, rubbing the back of her neck.

"And how do you reckon they'll refinance the mortgage when only one of us is working? You haven't got a job yet," Ben said to Quin.

"I'm looking, okay? Keep your shirt on. It's hard."

When Ben slammed his fist into the table, she jumped. "What's hard is being in this mess in the first place."

"That's enough!" Nan said. Quin felt like she was ten

again. "Stop it, both of you. I've had enough of the constant bickering. We'll all go to the bank in Werribee and get it organised tomorrow." Nan looked at both of them. "Are we agreed?"

Quin nodded.

"This is all bullshit," Ben said.

"Ben!"

"Yeah, I'll do it," Ben said, his contempt for Quin all over his face. "I'm going out."

The next day, they visited two banks and submitted applications to refinance the loans, one for $30,000 for the video stores and the other for the $100,000 they'd used to invest in non-withdrawable deposits with Solid Rock. Ben's income was thankfully enough to make the repayments. They just needed a valuation on the house to confirm the value was at least $150,000. It looked promising.

A week later, one of the banks rang and spoke to Nan.

Ben had just come home for dinner before he was due to work the evening shift at one of his stores. Quin was at the kitchen table writing out an application for a job.

Nan's face looked pale as she walked into the kitchen.

"What's wrong?" Ben said.

Quin looked up in alarm. "Are you okay? Sit down."

Nan slumped into a chair, her elbows on the laminated table, and rested her head in her hands. "It was the bank on the phone. The valuation came back."

"That's good. What did they say?"

"They said they can't help us."

"What? Why?" Ben said.

"My house is only worth $120,000. They said the market's dropped, and unless there was more security, they were in no position to help us. They also said that the original valuation was overinflated."

"Jesus," Ben said. He leant against the wall.

Quin put her arm around Nan. Her eyes flitted to Ben. She'd read in the paper a day ago that home prices had fallen significantly in some areas.

"We'll just go to another financial institution. Those big banks are shit," Ben said, grabbing a beer from the fridge.

"Yeah. That's what we'll do. They're probably being very overcautious. Someone will lend us the money." Quin hoped it was true; otherwise, they'd have no choice but to sell the house. And if they did that and didn't get the right price, they wouldn't have enough to pay out the amount owing on the mortgage.

In the weeks following, they had no luck in getting a refinance. Another letter arrived from Solid Rock, reminding them of the September deadline to repay the entire amount or the house would be forcibly sold. Quin couldn't bear to see Nan's face. She'd aged. Nan never said anything to her, was never reproachful. Quin was solely to blame and there was no escaping the fact.

By the beginning of August, the wheels had been put into motion to sell. The day when the house was put on the market was one of the worst days for all of them. Nan and Pop had built it in 1952, raising Quin's mother in the modest brick house. Ben and Quin had lived there since 1973 after their parents had died. Quin wandered around the house. Their dog Billie was buried out the back under the lemon tree. She ran her hand along the back of the garage wall where their heights, along with their mother's, was marked with paint.

The real estate agent who signed them up for the sale confirmed that at best, the property was worth $120,000. He was doubtful that he could get it sold for any more as values in their area had continued to drop.

"I'm sorry, Nan." Quin huddled on the couch, shocked.

"Sorry, isn't going to cut it." Ben stood in the doorway. "Not only do we lose our home. But the money I owe has to be paid back. Now you tell us that the hundred thousand that you said, and I quote 'is just like a term deposit' is now fucking worthless. 'Cos it turns out that it wasn't a term deposit but an actual share in Solid Rock. And now it's under receivership the shareholders are likely to get absolutely nothing. Have I got that right?"

Quin swallowed hard to keep the nausea in her stomach from rising. She nodded but didn't look at her brother.

"So, the highflyer has fallen from great heights. Hasn't she? And now I've had to put down a $5,000 surety for bail in case you flee the fucking country. This is all bullshit."

"Settle down, Ben. It's bad, yes. But you don't see me bellyaching and crying about it. What's done is done," Nan said.

"Yeah, it's done all right. And we have to suffer too." He

looked up at the ceiling and held his arms out. "Jesus. I forgot. I have to sell both video shops for next to nothing to at least keep our heads above water. Then, I'll have to find some stinking low-life job that I'm gunna hate."

"Remember, this is not Quin's fault. She's a victim of fraud."

"Nan, perhaps you don't know her as well as you think. How do you know if what she's told us is anything but lies? Your precious granddaughter is more than likely going to jail. Face the fact."

"Just stop it, Ben. Stop it right now." Nan held her hand to her chest. "I don't want to hear any more about it." She got up and went to her bedroom.

"See what you've done?" Ben said, lowering his voice. "No sausage sizzle is gunna be run to help any of us out of this. Now we've all gotta declare bankruptcy."

Quin couldn't stop the tears. She sniffed and blew her nose. "It's all a terrible mistake. I'm sorry, Ben. How many times do I have to tell you how sorry I am? I've ruined everything. I get it. But I could go to jail. I need you more than ever. Please."

"Oh, and by the way, Nan didn't want you to worry, so she didn't tell you she was kicked out of the bowls club 'cos everyone down there has lost their dough 'cos of you. Your eighteen per cent for deposits in a shit-can lured them all in, and now they blame our whole family. But don't you worry. I'll find us a house to rent and keep a roof over our heads. No thanks to you. So, little sister, I wipe my hands of you."

He lowered his voice. "I don't want to see you, talk to you or hear a word from you."

Quin sobbed. "No, Ben. Please. We have to stick together."

His lip curled. "You disgust me." He turned around and slammed the front door leaving the house in silence.

He was right. It was her fault, all of it. If only she'd listened, respected Nan wishes when she first asked her to get the money out. At least then, Nan might have had a chance of keeping her beloved house. But no, she'd been a smart-arsed upstart who thought she knew better.

*

According to Nan, if a person has done nothing wrong, justice will prevail.

It had been three months since Quin had last talked to someone from the Fraud Department at the local police station. She'd told him what had happened. He'd nodded and thanked her for her time and said someone would be in contact in due course. He didn't know what might happen next, except that enquiries were ongoing.

It had been excruciatingly slow, and despite her follow up, no-one could tell her anything. She relaxed, hoping the matter had been dropped.

She was surprised when she was called in to speak to two detectives who suggested she come with her legal representative. One of Nan's friends recommended Jan Papras, supposedly one of Victoria's top lawyers who'd saved a number of high-flying businessmen from going to jail.

Quin wondered how she'd be able to afford her. It was a relief to find out that Nan's friend happened to be Jan's mother, and she agreed to represent Quin for free.

Jan was business-like in her expensive blue suit and her perfectly shaped eyebrows. Quin gazed at the two detectives whose names she immediately forgot upon introduction. One was young with a wispy moustache on his thin upper lip. He wrote while the other detective, a nuggety man in his forties asked the questions. He was businesslike about the $2 million loan.

"You paid this money back on 20th of June?"

"Yes, as soon as it was brought to my attention by Tom Doomsbury."

"You recognised that it was your account, and then proceeded to return the funds. Why?"

"The account had my name on it but it wasn't mine. I mean I didn't know about it. But I wanted to fix things because Tom said the loan needed to be repaid."

"The fictitious loan?" The man frowned.

"Yes."

God. Should she not have done that? Even Pete had agreed that was the right course of action.

"And that is your signature?"

She studied the withdrawal slip put in front of her and nodded. "Yes, that is actually my signature."

"It's odd that the account wasn't stopped. You could have taken those funds and fled the country."

"But I didn't. I wanted to fix everything."

Then they pulled out a number of new documents. More loan applications purportedly approved by her, none of which she could recollect.

"I think I'd have remembered these loans." She flipped through the files. "A $1.5 million loan for a used-car yard in Hammondville. I've never seen this file before."

"But that is your signature recommending approval on the application. And that is your signature as the approving officer and your signature on the voucher entries. Is it not?" asked the detective.

Why was her signature all over the paperwork? She swallowed back the lump in her throat. "It looks like my signature, but it's not."

"Was this normal practice for a staff member to be able put together applications with their own recommendations. Then to approve it and fund it?"

"Of course not. The practice was that the loans officer would take the details from the client, verify the information and then submit it to a senior officer with a recommendation. The senior officer would approve or decline. The conveyancing section would take care of the funding once all approval conditions and mortgage documents had been agreed and signed by the client."

"In these cases, every signature is yours."

He pushed the mortgage documents across to her.

"It's not my signature. Are these properties even real addresses?"

He shook his head. "Nope. All fictitious."

He gave her three bank statements, different accounts in her name with a single deposit equal to the loan amount of each fraudulent transaction. "These signatures look exactly like the one on the slip that you verified earlier belonged to you."

Quin held her head in her hands. "I've had these accounts with Solid Rock for years. I thought I'd closed them. See? There were no funds in them. I can't explain it, but I didn't do any of this."

"Why do you have four accounts that you don't use?"

She shrugged. "I think I opened one to save for my overseas trip when I was eighteen or nineteen. I had another one I opened to save for something else, I don't know. They're old, and I just never got around to closing them."

"Miss Schmidt, the total loans here are almost ten million dollars."

Her head pounded. "No."

"Do you still deny that you were involved in writing any of these bogus loans?"

She took a deep breath and looked at him directly. "I categorically deny everything. I don't know anything about them. I swear to you. I did not write up the applications, I did not approve them, I did not sign the vouchers and transfer the funds. I don't know what else to tell you."

She looked at Jan who sat next to her, grim-faced. The interview was terminated, and Quin was left alone in the small airless room while Jan made a few phone calls. Her stomach was in knots.

Later, Quin read over the typewritten statement she'd made and signed it in front of Jan, whose face betrayed nothing. No sympathy, no hope, no judgement.

Quin chewed her nails. "What do you think?"

Jan's gaze darted to Quin's bitten down fingernails. She put her pen down and lifted her eyes to meet Quin's. "It's not great. You might get away with a six-month jail term."

Quin held herself very still, balling up the tissue in her hand, determined not to cry.

"It's not like any of the money was used. Just moved around. That's what I could argue."

Quin sat up straighter. "That's it." It suddenly made sense to her. "That's exactly why it was done. You get it, don't you?"

Jan frowned. "I'm afraid I don't follow you." She looked at her watch and gathered her paperwork to put into her briefcase.

"No wait, Jan. Solid Rock was in trouble. It has been for almost a year. Do you remember there was a run on the funds when depositors were pulling out their money, late last year? And then it happened in March again?"

Jan picked up her pen. "Yes, I remember. I got my money out in time."

"Well, we badly needed funds to come in. We sold more home loans, but it wasn't enough, so we raised more funds by doing an advertising campaign. So, they must have decided to write up fictitious commercial loans, deposit the funds into Solid Rock to get the liquidity level up so we couldn't be shut down. Don't you see? The books were inflated by the assets and liabilities, but there was no actual money. To the investors and auditors, it all looked above board. Even when the registrar looked at our accounts, there was nothing untoward. Do you see?"

Why hadn't she thought about this sooner? She guessed she'd been too absorbed in trying to save Nan's house.

"Yes, I think I do. So, you're saying someone in the company wrote fake loans, deposited those loan funds into accounts carrying your name, and they somehow forged your signature to do it? So, on the books there was no real money, but the balance sheet for Solid Rock looked better."

"Yes, that's it."

"And you reckon you had nothing to do with it, yet they made it look like it was you? Who would be so desperate that they'd frame you?"

"I don't know."

"A disgruntled staff member?"

Quin sat back in her chair. "No, I don't think it would be someone junior." Should she name, names? "Pete Martin, Head of Corporate Lending was my boyfriend until a few weeks before this all happened. And then there's Tom Doomsbury himself."

Jan narrowed her eyes and took out her notebook. "Tell me about Pete's job."

Had he broken up with her to create some distance so he couldn't be implicated?

She remembered when Pete claimed her jingle idea as his

own. She never did press him about it. "I think he was a bit jealous of me. He took some of my ideas and passed them off as his own. But would he do something as serious as this?" Quin shook her head. "I don't think so. I've never seen him do anything underhanded or unethical. He was ambitious, but I don't think he was dishonest. On the other hand, Tom Doomsbury wasn't beyond stepping over the line. He lied to the minister. He approved loans left, right and centre. He'd go out to lunch, and by the end of the day, he'd have written a couple of details on a napkin and given it to me or Pete to put an application together. I'll admit some of the stuff approved was shaky. But he was a man you couldn't said no to. He'd lie to his own mother if it got him what he wanted."

Jan scribbled furiously.

"Thanks, Quin. I'll see what I can find out."

Quin shook her hand, hopeful that the mess could be sorted.

The more she thought about Tom, the more convinced she was that he'd done this to her. He'd used her, promoted her to be his bunny. He could easily have put the loan documents together, opened the accounts. He could have done everything all on his own, shoved it under her face to sign as an urgent deal that had to go ahead. She'd have done it without question. Because he was the CEO.

The court case was scheduled for 15 January 1991.

35

LUCILLE

OCTOBER, 1945

The trip back to Melbourne was long and boring. Lucille re-read the back of the photo Hank had given her. "I love you. I've loved you since that day on the boat. Remember? Please, please change your mind." She missed him. But it was best. She wasn't prepared to try to give him children, and that was all there was to it.

A plan began to take shape in her mind. She'd sell Pa's house or continue to rent it out. She'd have an income at least while she looked for a job. Perhaps she could open her own mechanic business to service women's cars. She had Hank to thank for the idea. After all, cars were in her blood. Her father had sold them for years, even built one himself. Or maybe she could do what she'd wanted before she married: become a teacher. The possibilities, together with the freedom to make her own choices, excited her. There was nothing holding her back. She brightened up, and by the time she reached Spencer Street station in Melbourne, she was brimming with ideas.

She went immediately to the war office where she was formally discharged. Then she went shopping and bought tailored pants. After months of working in overalls, she wasn't prepared to wear skirts and dresses alone.

The taxi driver helped her with her luggage and shopping. With an armful of groceries and six months of mail collected from the post office, she unclipped her front gate. The garden was overgrown, and she chided herself for not getting anyone to check on the place. But there hadn't been time, and she'd lost touch with the neighbours.

She opened the front door and instead of mustiness, she encountered fresh cigarette smoke and the faint sound of music coming from the back. Someone was in her house. Quietly, she put everything on an armchair and grabbed the fire poker before tiptoeing down the hallway.

A grey-haired man, partially obscured by the wall sat at the kitchen table, his back to her. He held a teacup – her teacup – and flicked ash onto the saucer.

"What the hell do you think you're doing in my house?"

He flinched.

"How dare you break in and use my things." Lucille held the poker in front of her.

The man, slowly, painfully, moved his bony arm, then twisted his scrawny legs and shrunken body so he was at right angles to her, his neck turned last, stiffly, showing a gaunt, hollow face.

"Lucille," he whispered.

A flicker of recognition. It couldn't be. "I, I don't know who you think you are, but you need to leave."

"Have I changed that much? It's me, Max."

Her heart pounded. "Max? Is this a cruel hoax?"

Max is dead. Her mind raced. How did he get in? Only Max knew where the key was hidden outside.

With the help of a walking stick, he stood and held out one arm. "It's me, Petal. I'm back."

"Dear god. It can't be." Tears filled her eyes. "Is it true?"

When he smiled, she looked into his eyes. "It is you," she whispered, dropping the poker.

She went to him, his skeletal body pressed against her.

"God, how I've dreamt of this moment for nearly five long years," he said, finally letting her go. "Let me look at you. Still the most beautiful woman I know."

He held her at arm's length, not saying anything as their eyes roved over each other, until she pulled away.

"I think I have to sit down. This is such a shock," she said.

Sitting at the kitchen table, she watched him holding the cigarette, the smoke curling around his spindly fingers as he picked up his teacup. "Why didn't you write?"

"I did," he said.

"Oh god, I only picked up the mail today from the post office. I haven't been around since Pa died, six months ago."

Max gasped. "He died? I'm so sorry to hear that. Lots of things have changed."

"You've a lot to catch up on."

She cooked him a meal and they talked.

When the ship was torpedoed, Max had almost drowned, but hanging on to debris, he drifted to a small island. It was a blow to find the Japanese occupied it, but he managed to remain undetected for several months, living in caves and surviving on mangos and coconuts. While foraging for shellfish, he was caught by a lone Japanese soldier, and kept on the island under guard for more than six months until a Japanese ship picked him up and transported him to a prison camp in Sandakan, North Borneo.

"What was it like?"

He shook his head. "There were other Australian and British chaps already there building an airfield for the Japs. The food rations weren't much, and the work was back-breaking." He lowered his eyes, and she touched his clammy hand, encouraging him to go on. She had to know. "In the end, they must have known things were looking grim for them. They made us march through the jungle to a place called Ranau. There were a couple of hundred of us in the first group, even those who were sick. If you couldn't go on, you were shot on the spot."

"Oh my god. How far was it?" she asked, her voice quiet.

He sighed and shrugged and seemed to shrink. "It had to be more than a hundred miles." He closed his eyes. "By May this year, there weren't many left. Three of us escaped into the jungle. I was lucky. A local native family took me in for a couple of months and looked after me." He lifted his head, his eyes watery. "I don't know why I survived. Maybe months on that island made me tougher." He rubbed his hand through his greying hair and blinked. "They were all good men, Petal, they were all honest, hardworking men. None of them deserved to die like that." He wiped his eyes with the back of his hand.

"The only thing that kept me going was the thought of you and what you'd gone through. Our babies gone and me not being here." His voice cracked. "I had to get back to you."

She sniffed and dabbed her tears with her handkerchief.

"I got through it," she said, blowing her nose. "We both did." She looked at the food on her plate untouched, her appetite gone. "You're here. We're together now. That's all that matters." Telling him what happened to her seemed pointless and insignificant.

He nodded as he fumbled for another cigarette and the matches. His fingers trembled so much, she leant over and lit it for him. She cocked her head and raised her eyebrows.

He chuckled. "I know. I only took up smoking when I got out. A Yank shoved one in my mouth when I was rescued, and I took a liking for it."

She kissed him again and tried hard to push aside all thoughts of Hank and the life she'd planned.

36

QUIN

JANUARY, 1991

GUILTY.

The room seemed to spin.

Quin heard the word, "sorry" from Jan. "I really thought you'd get off. It'll go quick." But the buzzing in her ears only got louder. Someone gently held her arm and led her away. She turned and searched the crowd behind her and found Nan in tears, being comforted by Madge. Deb was there and so was Janie. Ben was nowhere to be seen – he'd made good on his promise and avoided her at home by staying with his new girlfriend, Sandra.

Guilty.

The word echoed inside her head. The cold metal handcuffs cut into her wrists. Waiting in a small cheerless room. Camera flashes momentarily blinded her, the crowd outside waiting for a glimpse as she was led into the back of the van. A corrective services officer told her to mind her step as she got in. Inside it was dark and dank, smelling of urine, perhaps from last weekend's drunken louts and yobbo hooligans. When she sat on the bench, she couldn't tell if it was clean or not. The only light came through a small window in the back door. She was utterly alone.

Guilty.

Jan had tried. The theory about the fictitious loans being used to prop up the balance sheet for Solid Rock was plausible but not provable. The prosecutor painted her badly as a woman hell bent on success at any rate. Driving fast cars – hell, she'd only had her Mercedes for less than twelve months – living the high life. She still lived at home. A woman who forced her little old grandmother to mortgage her house to invest in Solid Rock, knowing it was worthless. She was painted as a ruthless woman who lured old people at the local bowling club to invest their life savings in Solid Rock.

Pete hadn't showed up in court. He hadn't even rung or seen her since the day in the cafe. And Tom was battling the demise of the company, but she was sure he would have been happy that her case had knocked Solid Rock's plight right off the front page. The papers said, as a senior executive, it was her fault that people had lost money. No doubt, courtesy of Tom's media friends, he'd somehow avoided any blame. When she'd arrived at court, people hurled abuse, called her ugly names, and blamed her for losing their money.

The van moved and she swayed. Her mouth dry, she thought about where she was going, holding onto the hope that Ben would relent and visit her once he heard about her sentence. She remembered their last conversation.

"I've had to sell up the video stores, and now Nan's house, no thanks to you. There's no way to pay off the remaining debts, so we all have to declare bankruptcy. You sicken me." He hated his new job as a warehouse storeman, and he hated her. That much was clear.

Guilty!

The van sped up. They must be on the freeway. The smell and heat stifled her.

I've never done anything wrong in my life, she thought. Never even had a parking fine. "A law-abiding citizen, who worked hard, studied, and looked after her ailing grandmother" is how Jan had described her. That's why she got a light sentence. Jan said that, given all the evidence, she was lucky.

You try going to jail for something you didn't do, Jan.

The van sped up and despite the smell and the dark, she dreaded the end of the journey. She didn't want to get out to see what was waiting for her. She wished she'd drunk that glass of water on the table while they read out the verdict. It took five minutes for the judge to dismiss the jury and read out his sentence.

Eight months. Guilty.

So long to wait to see the river, to go to a cafe with her friends. What friends? Her friends had well and truly deserted her. She only had herself to blame. They lost a lot of money and blamed her. Even her relationship with Pete was more about work and sex. He never stood by her. She didn't think he'd even believed her when she'd told him she didn't do it.

I'm twenty-eight years old.

She pressed her hands to her eyes, to stop the tears. The van stopped and a car pulled up close behind. She peered through the window. A Mercedes, like the one she'd had.

She read in the paper that morning that Lou Bromhill got five years for bribing a politician. And Solomon Connolly got two years jail for secret commissions for Connolly Mortgages, which lost $315 million of people's money.

Yet so many others got off scot-free. Why am I the scapegoat?

The van took off. Quin swayed again, setting her feet apart to keep her balance. It was difficult to sit on the hard bench seat side on.

Finally, the van stopped. If only she'd thought to check the time when they'd left. She peered at her watch in the dim light and made out two thirty in the afternoon. What did it matter where the time went? She was rigid, trying to control her fear. The engine turned off and both front doors slammed. Footsteps on gravel before the rear door opened and Quin blinked in the brightness.

"Come on then. We're here."

She grabbed her handbag then bumped her head hard on the roof before stooping over to get out. The female officer held her arm as she stepped down onto the road. The sun on her back felt soothing against the thud of her heart.

This is it.

A magpie swooped over their heads and landed on a large

eucalyptus tree, its trunk smooth and pink. The structure looked like a school building with grey corrugated iron walls and black trim around the windows. Except for the rolls of barbed wire curling along a high wire fence surrounding the buildings, the prison looked modern, clean and ordinary.

The female officer led Quin through a gate into an asphalt yard, then through a black door and into a sparsely furnished room. A grim-faced woman with greasy hair dressed in a blue uniform stood behind a scuff-marked counter. A couple of metal chairs were lined up against a wall. The handcuffs were removed. Quin had expected to see someone big and burly like in the TV show, *Prisoner*. But she wasn't in a television show. She was in a prison.

"Here's the paperwork for Prisoner Quin Schmidt," the officer said to the woman.

"Beryl," the woman called out. A door opened and a large-breasted, squat woman, who must have been Beryl, came out and stood behind the counter.

"Okey dokes. I'll take it from here. Thanks," Beryl said.

"Good luck to you, Schmidt," the officer said and then was gone.

"Okay, Schmidt come this way." Beryl barely looked at her, but Quin studied her large muscular arms. "Feral Beryl" came to mind as she was led into a stark room with nothing but a table, and a shelf containing clothing and plastic bags.

"Put ya bag on that table there. Then take ya clothes off," Beryl said.

"All of them?"

Beryl nodded and Quin put her handbag on the table, then shook as she took off her white blouse.

The other uniformed woman from the room came in and stood as if to attention near the door and watched. Quin spied the dull metal of a gun on her hip.

"You'll be warm soon enough. And your underwear too." Beryl turned to get two large plastic bags. "Size?"

Quin was down to removing her knickers and looked up. "My size?"

"Who else, sunshine?"

She stood, fully naked, cold and shivering as she handed the final item to Beryl.

"Eight," Quin said folding her arms. The designer label maroon suit she'd picked out to wear to court was lost on Beryl, who folded it carefully enough before she shoved it into a clear plastic bag with Quin's underwear.

"Your shoes and your watch too."

Quin handed over her Prada shoes, the ones she'd bought when she got her promotion. The most expensive shoes she'd ever bought in her life. Jan had told her to look her best, that once the trial was over, hopefully, she could get on with her life. She honestly thought she'd be free, having dinner with her grandmother and Ben, celebrating a victory. She was so wrong and so was Jan.

Guilty.

So exposed.

Beryl snapped on a pair of gloves. Quin looked at her in alarm.

"Lift your arms, open your mouth." Beryl peered in.

Quin did as she was told, waiting in terror to be hit or even worse. She screwed up her eyes and cringed.

"Listen, we don't like this anymore than you. But we gotta do it. Bend over."

Fighting the blast of queasiness, Quin felt the gloved hand. When she was little and scared, she closed her eyes. She learnt to find another place to escape to in her mind. If she couldn't see, she didn't feel what was happening. Like the car accident. She'd been in the backseat with Ben. They'd been fighting and the next thing she knew, she was hanging upside down with a sharp pain in her arm. Her dad was covered in blood and her mum was screaming. Then, she took herself away to a happy place at the seaside, jumping across the waves. But now, she struggled to find anywhere to escape to.

"Nothing smuggled up there," Beryl said.

She heard the other woman snigger. "There wouldn't want to be."

"You can stand up now."

Quin's teeth chattered. She caught the bundle Beryl threw at her.

"Get dressed." Beryl turned around, grabbed a slip of paper and wrote on it.

Quin slipped the bottle-green track suit pants over the brown underwear they'd given her and finished with a green t-shirt and windcheater.

"What size runners are ya?" Beryl said.

"Um, seven and a half."

"What did I tell you, Mon? Ninety per cent of women are seven and a half," Beryl said, grabbing the brown runners.

"Yep," Mon said, her voice husky. She looked bored, as if she'd heard this story a million times.

"Here you go, Schmidt. Sign here." Beryl pushed the piece of paper across the table. "This is to say what we collected from you today, and when you get out, you'll get it all back."

Quin nodded and scanned the list of her possessions.

Guilty.

37

LUCILLE

NOVEMBER 1945

Max had many ailments. He'd recovered from malaria in a hospital in Malaysia, but the tropical ulcers that had eaten away the skin on his legs took longer to heal. Worse was what was going on in his head. He couldn't bear to be alone.

"Where are you going?" he asked, following her with dog-like devotion.

She turned and smiled. "Just to the bathroom. I won't be long, then I'll make you some lunch. I'm going to fatten you up so you'll be back to your normal self in no time."

"Oh," he said, his shoulders relaxing. "That'd be nice."

"Now go and sit down. Okay?"

"Okay," he said, turning around and hobbling to the kitchen.

Who was the stranger in her husband's body? His vitality gone, consumed with sadness, he stifled her with his suffocating need. She dared not think about the plans she'd made on the train. It had only been a dream. She wondered whether to tell him about Hank. It never seemed the right time, and she knew it would add to her broken husband's pain.

That first night, when their tears had dried, they made love. For her, it wasn't the same. Holding his skinny, ravaged body and running her hand on the ridges of raised skin along his back unnerved her. His hunger for her revolted her, but she tried her best to satisfy him. Afterwards, he cried, and she held him close until he fell asleep. "We'll get through this," she whispered, not daring to think how.

The next morning, as she watched him put on his shirt, she glimpsed the scars clearly. "What happened to your back?"

He waited a beat. "Sometimes I had to crawl through thick undergrowth in the jungle, and the scratches took a long time to heal."

He turned around, and she was careful to keep her face composed. He was lying; the scars were too thick to have come from branches.

He smiled gently. "I'm glad I'm back, here with you."

"I'm glad too."

Her ideas for building a life on her own were put aside. She didn't really mind, she told herself. She wanted to look after him. Though, wiping his sweating brow after a nightmare, avoiding his flailing arms in the night and holding him close to calm him, exhausted her.

His confidence to do the simplest of things had gone –

the act of trying to tie his shoelaces often ended with him throwing his shoe against the wall. He scared her.

She read accounts of what prisoners of war had endured from the Japanese. She tried coaxing him to tell her more about what happened. She wanted to understand his pain. But he couldn't or wouldn't. He'd given statements for the War Crimes Trials. The victims had been told not to talk about it, that it wouldn't help, he'd said. He wanted to forget and build a new life.

"Do you hate them?" she asked.

Max lifted his head. "I did for a long time. But their soldiers were treated badly too. Their superior officers killed them if they were too sick to work. There wasn't much difference between the ordinary Jap soldier and us. At the end, I figured I must have been one of the few lucky ones. I left a bit of my hate back there in that camp. After I got picked up by the Yanks and arrived in Darwin, I gave up on it all together. And I figure it's useless to me now."

Lucille clamped her hand over her mouth. "I was in Darwin too. If only I'd known. But then, I was in Sydney on leave for a month."

They worked out they'd missed each other by a few days when she'd left for Sydney.

"I wish I could have seen you. Those last days were tortuous, just knowing I was back in Australia but not home. Tell me about what you were doing in Darwin."

She explained her job, the heat, the dust and the damage.

"Did you … did you see anyone?"

"What do you mean?"

He looked out of the window. "You thought I was dead. Four years is a long time and … well … I wouldn't have blamed you if you'd gone out and had some fun."

She hadn't expected his question, and she shouldn't have hesitated, but she did. It was time to tell him. Only a few days ago she was with Hank, in his bed. How could she put her husband through more pain?

She kissed him. "I knew you'd come back. I felt it somehow."

He turned his head and smiled.

"We've both changed, but we'll work on getting back to the happiness we once had. Do you think you can do it?"

He nodded. "I'll get there. Being with you makes me feel a hundred times better than I was."

Lucille said nothing. If he no longer hated the Japs, she wouldn't either. Thinking about her babies and the hospital she'd been in, she understood why he didn't want to look back and relive it all.

*

In the following weeks, she vowed to be a good wife and help him heal. His pallor changed. He stood taller and walked with a steadier gait, and it heartened her.

Within six weeks, he'd put on weight, thrown away his walking stick and was ready to go out.

"Are you tired?" he asked. "How about we go to a movie tonight? You've been run off your feet looking after me."

"I'm all right," Lucille said, folding the washing. She was, in fact, hiding her exhaustion.

"You need to eat more too. I'm putting it on and you're taking it off." He grinned.

"I'm fine. Now if you want to be useful, roll these up for me." Lucille threw a pair of socks at him.

She'd lost her appetite weeks ago, putting it down to worry about Max, and she'd missed her last period.

Max looked at her, his eyes narrowing. "And you look pale."

"Do you mind terribly if I pass on the movie? I think you're right; I am a little tired and a lie-down would be good."

"We can go another time."

She made it to the bathroom, threw up, then lay down. A heaviness settled in her chest, and her stomach knotted in fear.

Max came into the bedroom.

"I think it was something I ate," she said.

"Do you think you might be pregnant?"

She shrugged. "Don't know."

Of course, she was. Even though the morning sickness wasn't the same as with the others.

Max sat on the bed. "I know you don't want any more children. But if you are, this one will be different."

"I'm sure it's just an unsettled stomach. That's all."

She could tell from the look on his face that he was worried.

They'd discussed not having any more children the first week he'd returned. She'd been careful to please him and had even grown used to the scars. But the idea of another baby terrified her, so she'd told him how she felt.

Could she cope now if something went wrong?

The next day, without telling Max, she visited the doctor who confirmed her worst fears. Pregnant. She had to get rid of it.

Max was at the bank when she returned home. She ran a bath with scalding hot water. Before she undressed, she poured a tumbler of gin. Then she downed it in one gulp bringing tears to her eyes. She got into the bath slowly as the water burned into her feet, then spread across her lower half. She barely tolerated the pain, waiting for something to happen. If what she'd heard was right, this would get rid of the child. But after a while, the water grew cold and she got out. Perhaps it took an hour or two? Still nothing.

The next day she drank herbal tea. Apparently, that helped to get rid of a baby. It didn't. The day after that, she drank cod liver oil and wandered through a cemetery walking across graves. That would surely do it. It didn't. Eventually, she gave up. The baby wasn't budging and when she told Max, the joy in his face helped ease her worries.

*

Lucille washed a plate in the sink while Max sat at the kitchen table reading the paper. Like old times, before the war when they were young with no idea how their lives would change. Max's health improved enough for him to go back to his old job. Lucille felt fitter too and was now resigned to the idea of the child growing within her.

Max's nightmares subsided and he seemed happier. He'd never drunk before the war, but now he'd taken to having a beer every night after dinner. It relaxed him, he said, so Lucille, remembering Pa and his battle, tried not to worry.

"Is it nice to be back working with Harvey again?" Lucille asked.

He looked up at her, surprised. "He resigned last week. Didn't I tell you?"

"No!" Max's forgetfulness worried her. She'd told him that Bethany had married an American and gone to live in California, yet yesterday, he'd asked after her again. "Why did Harvey leave?"

"He decided to work in his father's business."

"Oh. And what about you? Are you happy being back?" Distracted, Lucille swiped at a blowfly with a fly swatter.

"Yes. It feels like I've come home. I'll miss Harvey, but the work is better. You know, we're going to try to eradicate those," Max said.

"What?"

"The blowfly. Well, more precisely, the sheep blowfly."

"Can you get rid of it sooner rather than later?" she said, laughing.

"Seriously, we're going to see if we can do it genetically. Pesticides can only do so much. Imagine if we could sterilise the male blowfly. They'd die out."

"But you spent so long on the development of pesticides."

He held his head in his hands. "It was to be used as a chemical weapon. Even now, I can't bear to think about all that work we'd done and what they did with it." He lifted his head and sighed. "No, this is more important and, I reckon, in the long run, more effective."

Lucille mashed the potatoes thinking about what he'd said. She didn't press him in case it brought on anything more painful.

"What have you got there?" she said.

"Share certificates. Thought I'd start buying some more shares with my backpay. Harvey's given me a few tips. His father is in finance."

"Oh," she said, remembering what shares were. "Backpay?"

"Yeah, didn't I tell you? I got backpay for the time I was away."

"Hmmph. It would have been handy for while you were gone."

He looked up from the paper. "I suppose it would have. But you were okay? Weren't you?"

"Yes. I got paid for my work in AWAS. It kept me going." She couldn't help the sarcasm that crept into her voice.

Max seemed not to notice, rattling on about what shares he'd get as he studied the paper.

"I almost forgot," he said, reaching for his wallet. "Here's the housekeeping money."

She stared at the money lying on the table as if she had been paid off for the work she'd done to get him back on his feet. The backpay annoyed her too. She'd gone without and was forced to join up but she kept her thoughts to herself. It belonged to him. If he wanted shares, then who was she to question it?

"I thought we were getting a new lounge suite." Their current one had already been old and tattered when they'd bought it second-hand before the war.

"Huh," Max said, still absorbed in the paper.

She picked up the cash and put it into her purse. Maybe she was just edgy. The baby kicked, and she thought about what the doctor had said earlier that day when they'd visited the top obstetrician in the city. He'd reassured them that the pregnancy was progressing well. "It's going to be a big baby," he said.

"The fact that you're no longer sick must mean something," Max said. "I've got a good feeling about this one. And you're glowing."

But she was uneasy. How could she feel relaxed and calm about this child when two had already died under her care? But that wasn't what terrified her most. "This might not be your child, Max!" she wanted to scream. What if the child looked like Hank with jet black hair and olive skin? They'd been careful, but she'd heard condoms weren't always foolproof. But that last night they had been careless. How could she explain that? She felt sick. She shouldn't be having this baby.

The baby kicked again as she served dinner, and all she could do was smile at her husband.

38

JANUARY, 1991

Quin had a small, stiflingly hot room within a cottage. There were three other rooms, each with its own bathroom. Unlike a normal cottage, there was no common area, like a lounge or kitchen. There were several cottages like hers, each connected by covered walkways.

"You're lucky you're in a low security prison. We opened it last year, so everything's new and clean. You make sure you keep it that way," Beryl said. "Probably nicer than the shit box you lived in before."

Mon sniggered.

Shit box? Where did Beryl and Mon think she was from? Then Quin reminded herself. She was scum according to everyone, no better than anyone else here.

"Dinner in the dining room at five thirty, lockdown at six thirty, breakfast at seven sharp. You start work at seven thirty every day and finish at four thirty. No days off. And for that you get four dollars a day."

"Work?" Quin said, raising her eyebrows. She hadn't thought about what she'd be doing. For some reason, she thought she'd be reading and watching television to pass the time until she could leave. Get her manicured nails dirty for four dollars a day? She opened her mouth to protest and tell her jailers she'd earned more than the two of them put together in a single month.

"Yep, work, sunshine. You'll be in the kitchen for two weeks and then out in the garden tending the vegies and weeding."

"What?"

Beryl laughed. "Look at 'er face, Mon."

Mon's bored, hard face broke into a smirk.

Beryl pulled one of Quin's hands to her. "These'll be rough and scaly by the time you get outta here. Won't they Mon?"

A grin slowly spread across Mon's horse-like face.

"Can you cook?" Beryl asked.

"Not really," Quin said, pulling her hand away.

"It's your lucky day 'cos you're gunna learn. And some day, you'll make someone a nice little wifey." Beryl cackled at her own joke. "Everyone oughta know how to cook, isn't that right, Mon?"

"Yep," Mon said, picking something from between her teeth.

"The others will show you the ropes when they get back."

After they left, Quin stood alone in the small room.

Somewhere cicadas started up. She had no idea what the time was. She peeled off her windcheater and scanned the dull grey room. She found a clear plastic cup on the bathroom sink and rinsed it out before filling it and gulping down the chlorine tainted water. It was better than nothing. No mirror, no soap, no toothbrush or toothpaste. She used the toilet – at least there was toilet paper. As she washed her hands, she made a mental note to ask about toiletries.

The single bed had a plastic sheet and a pile of bedding on the end. She set about making it, trying not to think of the women before her and the yellow-stained pillow. She didn't dare look under the plastic mattress protector.

When she was done, she splashed water on her face, then lay down. There was no other place to sit. She had nothing but the prison clothes she wore – the uniform marked her as someone she never thought she'd be. She stared at the stark grey concrete wall and the white ceiling – pockmarked with someone's frustration. Somewhere a baby cried. A magpie chortled and the cicadas seemed louder. She put her hands over her ears. Could she tolerate it here for eight months? What choice did she have? She was nothing but a convicted felon.

She didn't know how long it was before she heard voices, then footsteps. She leapt up and peered through the bars of the aluminium window. A group of women dressed in the same green as her, were walking towards her cottage.

She sat back on her bed and waited. Someone dragged their feet, another laughed. Her door remained open so she could see who came down the corridor. She stood when she saw a red-headed woman come towards her.

"A new one. G'day," the woman said, walking over to her. "I'm Daisy, but you can call me Daze."

Quin went to hold out her right hand and quickly checked herself. This was not a business meeting. "I'm Quin."

"G'day Quin. This is Marcy and Colleen," Daze said, as two more women crowded through her doorway. They'd blocked any possible means of escape, and Quin shifted nervously from one foot to the other.

Marcy, with mousy brown hair, long nose, small mouth was short and plump. She nodded at Quin. Colleen was tall and slender with a hard-weathered face. Her rolled-up sleeves showed a tattoo with the name Carey on it. The women looked to be in their twenties, except for Colleen; she looked closer to forty.

"New girl," Colleen said. "We were all new once." She didn't smile. "What sort of name is that?"

"It's a family name," Quin said, ready to explain the history of it. "It's—"

"Like a surname?" Marcy said.

Quin nodded.

"What are you in for?" Colleen said, cutting off any further explanation.

"Fraud and theft," Quin said.

Daze whistled. "What did ya steal?"

"I didn't do it. I was framed."

All three women roared with laughter. Colleen laughed so hard, she dabbed her eyes with a tissue.

"It's true," Quin said. "I was set up."

When Daze stopped laughing, she put her hand on Quin's shoulder. "We all say that. But we still end up in the same place."

"Bloody hell, I nearly wet myself," Marcy said. "Oh, I needed a good laugh. Seriously, how much did you steal?"

"Does it really matter?" Quin said.

Colleen pushed Quin so hard she fell backwards on the bed and just missed hitting her head on the wall. She scowled. "Yeah, it does. We all live together, and you're lucky you got in with us, instead of one of the others. We won't let nothing bad happen to ya, but ya gotta be upfront. So, let's have it."

The cicadas suddenly stopped.

Three pairs of eyes, suspicious and threatening, glared above her. The smell of their sweat filled the tiny space, suffocating her in the heat.

"Ten million."

They moved away as one and the air seemed sweeter.

Daze whistled. "Shit! Now if you're going to steal, make it big. Wish I'd done that. I stole a measly two hundred and fifty dollars, some jewellery and clothing."

"Impressive, Quinine," Colleen said. "Hope you stashed it some place safe for when ya get out."

"I paid it back."

"Jesus. What did ya do that for?"

"I didn't think I'd go to jail. But they made me pay the

interest, and I went into bankruptcy and …" Quin sniffed, unable to stop the tears. Saying it out loud had made it worse. She buried her head in her hands. She wanted them to go away, to leave her to her misery.

"We're going to the dining room in five minutes. Be ready and you can come with us," Colleen ordered. "And stop your snivelling. Cryin' does no-one any good in here."

Quin wiped her eyes with the back of her hand and nodded. "Thanks," she said, sniffing.

The crowded dining room was hot and stuffy from the afternoon sun radiating through the windows. Quin forced the mashed potato and lamb stew down. It was tasteless and tough, but she chewed, listened and watched.

"My old man reckons he's getting the kids and taking them interstate," Marcy said. "It's bullshit."

"Aren't they with carers?" Daze asked. "Surely, he don't want to be saddled with kids?"

"Course he doesn't. He's just saying it to rile me up, worry the crap out of me. If he does anything to those kids, I'll fuckin' kill him." Marcy clenched her knife and fork, stabbed a piece of lamb and stuck it into her mouth.

"Calm down, Marce. Play it cool. You lost those kids before you came in here. He's not going to get them back. The trick is to be the model prisoner, get a job when you get out, stay off the heroin and get your kids back," Daze said. She turned to Quin. "That goes for you too. Life's too short to spend your bloody life in a dump like this. No offence, Colleen."

Colleen looked up from eating. "None taken, mate. I did what I did, and I don't regret it. I got a roof over my head and buddies here to keep me going for the years I got left."

Quin stared at the tattoo on Colleen's arm. "How long was your sentence?"

Colleen tilted her head back, swung on the back of her chair and cleaned her nails with the edge of a knife.

"Life! I'm here for good behaviour 'til I die. Killed me ol' man, and after what he did to me and my daughter, I'm glad the scumbag's gone."

"I'm sorry," Quin said.

"Nothin' for you to be sorry about, Quinine. He had it coming. There's not much help in the world for women like us, and sometimes you gotta take matters into your own hands. See what I mean? You reckon you got framed. If what you say is right, you'll have to sort it out in your own way, but don't hold your breath. You'll probably never get any justice."

Quin nodded. Revenge would be sweet, but she didn't know what to do. Her life as she'd known it was already ruined, and she'd never get it back. "Thanks for the tip."

She listened quietly to the chatter until a bell sounded, then copied what the others did, returning her plate. She walked back to her room alongside Marcy for lockdown at six thirty. Marcy was in for assault and prostitution. She had two kids – three and seven – and her husband was her pimp. She'd served twelve months and had another twelve to go. Daze had ten months remaining for theft.

Back at the cottage, Quin asked Marcy where she could get toothpaste and a toothbrush.

"Listen, honey. You have to get someone to bring all that when they visit, else you buy it from what you earn. Payday is in three days."

"You mean we get nothing. No starter pack?" Quin said, wondering how she'd wash her hair.

Marcy laughed and slapped her knee. "A starter pack? You got a lot to learn, mate."

Quin heard the others laughing and assumed Marcy had told them what she'd said. It was almost six thirty, and she slumped onto her bed. There was another two hours of daylight. No television, no books, nothing else to do.

Footsteps. A clank of the lock. Now she was truly alone.

And hot. She slid the window as far as it would go – a ten-centimetre opening – then changed into a t-shirt and shorts, flung back the blanket and lay on the bed waiting for darkness and sleep to come.

The next morning, the sun streamed in through the window, baking her. She rubbed her swollen eyes. She showered in cold water, thankful that she at least didn't have to share and got dressed. The guards walked the corridor, yelling at the inmates to get up, unlocking doors. She would ring Nan to ask her to bring her things when she visited. She didn't know when that would be, but memorised a list in her head.

After breakfast, Quin stayed behind in the kitchen to report for work. She washed the dishes for fifty inmates, swept and mopped the floors, then helped to prepare lunch. She was on her feet all day, and the time went fast. By the time she finished, she was exhausted. There'd been no chance to ring Nan.

In the kitchen the next day, she asked a guard, Betty, if she could make a phone call.

"It'll cost you a dollar. The payphone's in the office." Betty nodded towards the other building.

"A dollar? For a twenty-cent call?

"That's the cost."

"I don't have any money," Quin said.

"Well, you better wait till payday." Betty's mouth set in a firm line. "Now get back to work."

*

Three days later, after dinner the women lined up at the office window in the courtyard to receive their pay. There was a kiosk where personal items could be bought, and that was where most went.

When it was Quin's turn, she received eight dollars. "Excuse me, I think there's been a mistake. I've worked for three days."

Betty narrowed her eyes and scratched her cheek. "No mistake, Schmidt. Next!"

Quin turned away and looked at the notes in her hand.

Daze whispered. "They take a cut off everyone."

"And that's legal?"

Daze nodded and made the motion of zipping her mouth.

At the kiosk, Quin got everything except shampoo and

resigned herself to washing her hair with soap. How she envied the inmates who bought moisturiser and deodorant but she had to keep enough back for her phone call to Nan.

She lined up with the others in the corridor just outside the office. There was yelling and everyone in line craned their necks.

"Nothing to see," Betty said, sweeping past to close the office door.

Daze behind her leaned in close to her and muttered. "A new recruit, I reckon."

Quin made to turn around.

"Eyes to the front Schmidt."

The line moved slowly. She would have to go back to her room shortly. Two in front of her, then one then it was her turn.

She picked up the red phone grimy with dirt and dialled. "Nan, it's me."

"Oh, darling, how are you? I'm so worried. I rang, but they said they couldn't get you to come to the phone."

"I'm fine, Nan. Are you okay?"

"I'm good. Really, I am. Don't you worry about me. I've put my name down to visit. You have to fill out a form, and then they give you a time and there's all these rules and regulations. Do you need anything?"

"Yes, Nan. I need you to bring me some underwear, socks, my pyjamas, some books …"

"Hold on. I better get a pen. Okay, I'm writing it all down."

"And Nan can you bring me a carton of cigarettes?"

"You don't smoke. Oh my god, they've forced you to take up cigarettes?"

"No, it's nothing like that. It's like currency in here, so I can barter for stuff I want."

"I'll bring you what you need, love."

"Schmidt, hurry up. You got one minute left," Betty yelled. "There's others who need to use the phone."

"Nan, before I go, how's Ben?"

"He's all right. Still a bit upset by everything. He'll get over it. He might try to visit. But I'm not sure."

"Okay, Nan. I've got to go. Love you."

"Love you too. Stay safe."

Quin blinked back tears and hung up.

"Took long enough," Daze said. "There's a queue ya know."

"Sorry, Daze. Really sorry." Quin fled to her room to wait for lockdown.

The first thing she did was brush her teeth and wash her hands with the soap she'd bought. When she was finished, she ran her tongue around her mouth. No more furriness. She was inexplicably happy, the happiest she'd been in a long time. All it took was a toothbrush and toothpaste. The Prada shoes, the Mercedes, the high-paying job had never made her this happy. She would never take small things like clean teeth for granted again.

39

QUIN

JUNE, 1992

Quin's search for the dining car was fruitless. A man laughed when she asked where it was. "A dump. That's what this train is," he said. She agreed.

On the way back to her seat, she suddenly stopped and clutched the railing overhead to steady her shaking legs. Sitting to her right, his back to her, was a man so familiar – the same fair hair, the same broad shoulders. Ben. She so wanted to reach out, to touch him on the shoulder, to hug him, to say sorry. The man turned his head … his nose, the wrong shape, the beard stubble, dark and thick. She blinked and shrank back. Of course, it couldn't be him. She returned to her carriage, carrying the familiar pain of an aching heart.

Slumped in her seat, she tucked her clammy hands under her arms to stop them shaking. Lucille's head rested against the window, her eyes closed, face creased with lines brought about by years and worry. Like Nan. Quin could see it now. What her own grandmother had done for her and Ben, brought them up, given love unconditionally. Nan had deserved more. Perhaps Lucille had too.

The train slowed, passed a rusted tin shed, a weatherboard house, through a shard of sunlight bursting through heavy clouds.

"Ladies and gentlemen," a deep voice crackled over the loudspeaker. Lucille's eyes sprang open, and Quin saw her stiffen. "Due to mechanical difficulties, there will be a short unscheduled stop at Polesford. We expect to reach Melbourne by five o'clock this evening. We apologise for the delay."

"What did he say?" Lucille asked.

"There's some sort of mechanical issue, and they expect us to reach Melbourne by five, so we're stuck here for a bit."

"That's annoying," Lucille said, looking at her watch.

"Yeah, it is. And there's no dining car, so no cup of tea." Quin glanced out of the window as the train jerked to a stop. The Polesford station sign was rusted, the platform covered in cracked concrete with a shiny new orange phone booth perched outside a weatherboard building, presumably the railway station.

"My son is picking me up. I wonder how I can let him know?"

"There's a phone booth out there you could use."

Lucille twisted awkwardly. There were passengers getting off and some lined up in front of the phone. She turned back and rubbed her neck. "I think I should call him." She leant on the back of the seat to haul herself up.

Quin scrambled up to help Lucille.

"Thank you, dear. My knee's gotten quite stiff from sitting in one spot for too long, I suppose."

Quin slung her backpack over her shoulder then held out her arm. "Just hang onto me. We'll go and line up, and then I'll see if there's a kiosk." Quin licked her dry lips. A hot cup of tea was exactly what she needed.

Lucille clutched her handbag and glanced at the case on the ledge above her. "I suppose that will be all right here?"

"It should be fine."

Quin was surprised by the strength of the old lady's grip as she led her out of the carriage.

"You're very sweet to wait with me," Lucille said.

"No problem."

Quin stamped her feet and dug her hands into the pockets of her windcheater as the wind whistled around them. The queue slowly shuffled forwards. Impatient, she tapped the shoulder of one of two young men in front of her. "Hey, do you think we could go next?" She jerked her head towards Lucille. "She's not feeling the best and can't stand for long."

Both men nodded, making way for Lucille while Quin waited.

"It's me. The train's been delayed, and they said it should arrive at five. I'll see you then."

Lucille stepped away slowly. "Thank you very much," she said to the men before grabbing Quin's arm.

"Would you like to sit over here in the sunshine where it'll be warmer? Or would you like to go back to the train?"

"Thank you, dear. Let's enjoy the sunshine while it's out. It's nice to have a travelling companion."

Quin laughed. "I'm the one who should be thanking you. If it weren't for you, I'd have been kicked off the train and starving."

"It was nothing," Lucille smiled.

"Ah, there's a kiosk. How about a cup of tea?"

"Yes, thank you, dear. That sounds wonderful." Lucille found her purse and pulled out a ten-dollar note. "A touch of milk, please. My shout. Please get one for yourself."

"Oh no. It's fine."

"Please, I insist."

"I'll just be over there. Will you be okay?"

Lucille nodded.

Here she was taking another old woman's money. Yes, it was only a cup of tea, but it didn't feel right. If Lucille knew about her, she'd probably change carriages and never speak to her again.

Quin returned with two styrofoam cups and held one out to Lucille. "I hope this is okay." She dug into her pocket and handed Lucille the ten-dollar note. "My shout. I needed to break a fifty anyway." She didn't tell Lucille that she only had a twenty but she couldn't take money off the old lady.

Lucille looked surprised as she took the note. "Thank you," she said, blowing on the tea.

Most of the passengers milled around talking, while others

paced the platform. A tall man with a newspaper tucked under his arm stared at them as he conversed with another man. The sun shifted behind cloud and Quin shivered. Did she know him?

"Perhaps we should get back onto the train," Quin said. "Now that the sun's gone."

The man with the newspaper stared. Quin glanced behind to see what he was staring at. But there was nothing but bushes. What was his problem? Was he an old client? Had he recognised her from the court case? That was more than eighteen months ago. Her chest tightened.

"Yes. It's gotten quite chilly now, and it looks like it's going to rain again."

Quin threw their empty cups into the bin. They shuffled back to the train, Quin keeping an eye on the two men while wishing Lucille would move faster.

"Are you all right?" Quin asked. "You seem to be limping a bit."

"My joints are stiffer than usual," Lucille said.

They were almost at the carriage steps when the tall man moved towards them. Her heart went wild. *Who is he? What does he want?*

"It's just the cold, I think,' Lucille continued. "I get a bit achy and—"

"You're her, aren't you?" The man, his voice low, held a bitterness that made Quin stop. Lucille moved forwards, but the man reached for her shoulder. "You're Lucy Doomsbury."

It's not me he's after. Quin's relief was followed by shock. *Is this woman related to Tom?*

Lucille's grip on Quin's arm tightened.

"What do you have to say about your low-life son? Do you know that he's cost me my house as well as my retirement, and now I have to work for the rest of my life to make ends meet?"

Quin didn't have time to think, to fear the man, to process what he'd said. "Hey, get your hand off my grandma and leave her alone."

"We know your little old grandma is Tom Doomsbury's mother, missy." The man scowled as he towered over them, his hand still on Lucille's shoulder.

Quin read the situation: an aggressive man accosting two defenceless women. "You've got the wrong person. Now if you don't piss off, I'm going to call the POLICE!"

A few people turned to stare.

"Nan, are you okay?"

Lucille nodded, lowering her face and her body suddenly hunched over.

"I said get your hand off her, you creep. Help!"

From the corner of her eye, Quin saw the two young men who'd kindly allowed Lucille to use the phone. They were walking towards them, fists clenched.

The man reeled back as if he'd been slapped. "I'm terribly sorry," he said, backing away. "I thought she was someone else."

"What do you think you're doing?" one of the young men said.

The tall man held up his hands. "Nothing. My mistake. There's nothing going on, fellas." He walked back to his friend.

Quin nodded to the young man and smiled her thanks.

"It's not her," Quin heard the tall man say.

"I told you it wasn't. As if she'd be on a train."

Suddenly, Lucille moved faster up the stairs with Quin following closely behind.

Lucille was back in her seat with a tissue at her nose. Quin picked up a discarded newspaper from the floor and studied the photo of Tom and the woman. The sour aftertaste of the black tea stuck in her throat.

She sat in the seat opposite and stared at Lucille. "What was that about?"

"I don't know."

"I think you do. Your picture is on the front page." Quin held up the newspaper. "The photo says it's Tom Doomsbury and his mother Lucy. He's the guy who lost everyone's money. That's what they're saying. You are his mother, aren't you?"

Lucille's shoulders slumped. "Yes, I am."

There was so much going through Quin's mind. "The outcome of his trial is coming up tomorrow. You're going to Melbourne for it, aren't you?"

Lucille nodded, her hands shaking. "Please don't give me away."

Her eyes and the wrinkles around her mouth reminded her so much of Nan. But this was Tom's mother. Poor woman. She folded the newspaper and tucked it into her backpack.

"Your secret's safe with me. I promise."

"Thank you."

40

LUCILLE

1946

Thomas Clarence Doomsbury was born early on 4 June 1946 on a gloomy winter day in the Jessie McPherson Community Hospital in the city. Exhausted, Lucille stared at the wrinkled face in front of her. She examined him closely – black tufts of hair and olive skin, like Hank. Guilt, sorrow, fear formed in her throat.

"What's wrong?" Max asked, stroking his son's face.

Lucille looked at her husband. "He reminds me of Harry." Overwhelmed by her lie and the reminder of her first son, she began sobbing. "Oh, Max."

Max sat on the bed and put his arm around her. "It's going to be all right. Look at him. He's strong and healthy."

Her son latched on greedily and fought out of his swaddling. His cries were high pitched, compared to most newborn babies.

At home, he settled only if Lucille held him, and she

became possessive. She lay awake for hours, listening for a cry, slipping out of bed to check on him. She spent her days holding him, rocking him and watching over him until she was exhausted.

Max tried to help. "Let me take him so you can lie down," he said one afternoon when Tom was a few weeks old.

Lucille finally gave him up, but it was like her arm had been chopped off – the cold air replacing the warmth her baby had left behind. In the bedroom, she lay exhausted, the dimness of the day poked around the edges of the heavy floral curtains.

She listened to the wheels of the pram along the hallway, the front door closing and the gentleness of Max's voice fading down the path. Lying on her side, her body tight with tension, she drew her knees up to her swollen breasts and tried to relax. She must have dozed off as she woke with a start. Her feet were like blocks of ice, her aching breasts heavy, leaking milk down her top and onto the bottom sheet. The light had faded, the house silent.

She sprang out of bed and ran out of the bedroom. "Max! Where are you?"

No answer. She searched every room, calling out, until she opened the front door to the verandah. Max was asleep in the rattan chair, a baby blanket over his chest, Tom's small, dark head nestled under his chin. She sighed and gently backed into the house to change her damp clothes.

It was a moment Lucille would remember for a long time,

and whenever things got too much, the memory of Max holding Tom helped calm her.

By the time Tom was a few months old, he'd grown too big for his bassinet. He screamed when he didn't get what he wanted from Lucille, especially when Max was at work. He cried constantly if he was left on his own and only stopped when he was in his mother's arms, watching what was going on.

"Let's see if there's some music on the wireless," Lucille cooed one day.

She laid him on the couch and moved to turn on the radio. As she touched the dial, she heard a thump and a squeal from Tom. "Oh my god!" She swooped him up and cuddled him to her. "Are you all right my angel? Mummy shouldn't have turned her back."

The cries didn't stop, and when she looked at him carefully, she spotted the rising bump on his forehead. She ran to the telephone, Tom wailing in her arms.

"Max," she said, crying. "Something's wrong with Tom."

"Now calm down," Max said. "Get him to the doctor. Do you hear me?"

She nodded trying to stay calm.

"Get a taxi. And I'll meet you at the doctors. Look, I can hear him crying, so he can't be too bad."

"But he's got a red bump on his head," she cried. "It's all my fault. I've done it again. I can't be trusted. I'm a bad mother."

"Lucille! Stay on the phone, and I'll call the taxi. Hold on."

*

Lucille waited anxiously as the doctor completed his examination, then wrote up his notes. She pushed stray hair from her puffy, swollen face, while Tom lay quietly in her arms, sucking on his thumb.

"Well," she said, breaking the silence. "It's happening again, isn't it?"

Max put his hand on her arm as the doctor looked up from his writing.

"He's perfectly fine. Just a bump to the head when he rolled off the couch. Mrs Doomsbury, babies are more resilient than we give them credit for. However, please be aware that your baby is quite advanced for his age and wants to move. He'll be rolling and crawling before you even know it."

He smiled as he got up. "That bump to the head will be the first of many, I can assure you."

"Thank you, doctor," Max said, shaking his hand.

He led Lucille out of the surgery and hailed a taxi.

*

At home, Lucille fed Tom, then put him in his cot. She and Max stared at the sleeping child.

"I can't lose another child. I just can't."

Max put his arm around her and squeezed her to him. "You won't. It was just a bump."

"The first of many" the doctor had said, but Lucille was determined Tom would have no more. She needed to do a better job of protecting him.

She wrapped him tight to keep him warm when they went out. She checked on him constantly while he slept. She watched him like a hawk when he crawled. She swept and mopped the floors twice a day to keep them clean. When he wanted to run, she tried to stop him – he might fall over and hurt himself. When his bottom lip dropped, she jumped to placate him so he wouldn't cry.

41

QUIN

1991

Quin got used to the rhythm of prison life – no thinking about the next deal or placating Tom and Pete. The stress of work and her old life of responsibility slipped away. She did as she was told, kept out of trouble and to herself. She'd found the prison library and read every night to take her mind off where she was.

She was known as the million-dollar girl, and this seemed to get respect from the other women. There was no point telling people she hadn't done it. A modern-day Bonnie without the Clyde. They all thought she had a stash in a plastic bag in a locker somewhere. The Quin of old, responsible, law-abiding, corporate executive had long gone. The old Quin, immaculately groomed and wearing the corporate façade, no longer existed. It was plain Quin: lank blonde hair fading to brown without the help of the hairdresser's bleach bottle, blistered hands, freckled face bare of make-up. She surprised herself that she no longer cared about any of that.

At night, she learnt how to tell who was crying. Mostly it was Marcy crying for her kids, worrying for them. That's when Quin rolled away and put the pillow over her ears.

Mail call and visitors day was the highlight of the week.

Daze complained: "My 'ol man can't be bothered visiting. When he was inside, I went every week. Visiting days at the men's prison were packed. Their old ladies crying, bringing them in cake, the kids. It was like a party."

"We're at the bottom of the chain. There's only one thing ya rely on a man for," Colleen said.

"What?" Daze said.

"Sex! They only think with their dick. There's nothin' else. It's as simple as that. You're outta the way, and they move on to someone else."

Quin thought about Colleen's situation – how the woman had killed the man who'd killed her girl. No visitors.

"If you got no women in your life, you'll get no visitors."

Colleen's blue eyes drilled into her. She seemed to be waiting for Quin to say something. She must have noticed her lack of visitors.

"My nan tried. She took two trams and a train. When she got here, they turned her away and told her she had to write for permission to visit. So, she wrote for permission but was rejected because she didn't have enough information. They should have told her in the first place. The bastards! She's old and stressed enough."

Colleen, Daze and Marcy let her prattle on, their faces betraying nothing as Quin opened up.

"… and she's had to deal with a lot. Looked after me and my brother when my parents died in a car accident when I was eight." Quin stopped, gulped for air, then turned away. This was the most she'd spoken about herself the whole time she'd been here. "Anyway, she's coming next Tuesday."

No-one said anything for a while. "Well, that's nice," Colleen said.

"Yeah, nice for you," Daze said.

Marcy giggled. "You're lucky. Money, good looks and a nan."

Quin turned back and stared. "No money, Marce."

*

A month had passed before Nan was permitted to visit. Quin stifled her shock as Nan shuffled in with a walking stick – grey hair uncut, her face drawn, bags under her eyes.

"Here's the things you asked for." Nan handed her a bag and Quin peeked in, pleased the cigarettes were there. "They pulled everything out and examined it. I felt like a criminal," she said, not realising her gaff.

Quin smiled. "Thanks, you're a life saver."

"How are you going love? Are they feeding you enough? You look too thin."

"I'm fine, Nan. The food's okay, not as good as yours but manageable. I did some cooking. Everyone has to. And now I'm working in the garden, growing vegetables. The tomatoes are flowering, and we've just planted the lettuce."

Nan frowned. "Are you wearing sunscreen? You've got a lot more freckles."

"They were always there, Nan. It's just that I used to cover them with make-up. And we have hats."

"I'll bring you some sunscreen."

Quin nodded. "How are you? Why do you have a walking stick?" She rubbed Nan's hand.

Nan looked sheepish. "I took a tumble."

"What? Where? Did you hurt yourself?"

"Nothing to worry about. Just a bruise. The doctor said I should use a walking stick for a while in unfamiliar places." She drew her hand away. "I am perfectly fine."

Quin didn't want to upset her, so didn't press further. "What about Ben? How is he?"

Nan shrugged. "He's good. Working hard." She broke out into a smile. "He's still with that girl, Sandra. He reckons she's the one."

"Really? I'm glad."

"Of course, he hasn't brought her home yet, but he goes out a lot, and sometimes I smell perfume on his clothes."

"You sly old devil. Snooping like Jessica Fletcher in Murder She Wrote."

They both laughed. It eased the tension and made Quin forget where she was, just for a moment. When visiting time was up, they hugged each other tight, and Quin's eyes welled as she watched her grandmother leave.

*

The next day, Quin was eating in the dining room when

Robbie, a hard-faced guard with pencil-thin eyebrows approached her. "Schmidt. You're wanted in the office."

"Why?" Quin asked without thinking, goosebumps spreading along her arms. A hush overtook the room, heads turning in her direction.

Robbie shrugged. "Get up and come with me."

"What 'ave you done?" Marcy whispered. "No-one gets called to the office."

"Shut up. Leave her be," Daze hissed. "It's probably nothing."

Everyone watched as she walked out with Robbie and the chatter resumed as soon as they'd left. Just like being back at school when a summons meant a punishment.

"Sit down, Schmidt," Feral Beryl said, not glancing up while she wrote something down on a piece of paper. The brown laminate desk was bare except for a folder, the piece of paper and an empty in-tray sitting on one side. Quin tried to read Feral Beryl's writing upside down, like she used to at work – it had been a good way to learn information that might be useful later – but the writing was a scrawl.

Nervous, she pulled the sleeves of her windcheater down over her hands. *What have I done?*

Finally, Feral Beryl put the pen down and leant forwards, chin resting on prayer-like hands. "I got a phone call that a relation of yours has passed away."

"Who?" She couldn't think of who she might be talking about.

Beryl picked up the piece of paper and read from it. "Her name is Patsy-Quin Blake. Is that a relation?"

"Yes, that's my grandmother's name." Quin was alarmed. "I saw her yesterday. Are you sure? She seemed fine."

"It says here that she collapsed last night and died."

Her breath left her. She didn't trust herself to speak, to protest, to believe. She wanted to get up, to run, to escape the stare, the silence, the indifference. But instead, she stared at the scuff marks on the linoleum floor and gripped the side of the vinyl chair with both hands to control the tremors, to keep herself upright. A clock ticked on the wall behind her. A kookaburra began its cackling crescendo of laughter.

"Sorry, Schmidt." Beryl shrugged and Quin knew she didn't mean it.

Quin lifted her head. "Who told you?"

Beryl glanced at the piece of paper again.

"A Mr Ben Schmidt. He wanted me to tell you."

"He didn't ask to talk to me?"

"No."

Beryl moved about on her seat.

Nan dead. They'd laughed together only yesterday.

"Can I go to the funeral?"

"I'll have to fill out a heap of forms and get permission. I don't know if approval will come in time."

"I have to go. For god's sake! She's my grandmother. She brought me up. Please!" Her lips trembled. She would not let this woman see her cry.

"I'll see what I can do. No promises."

Quin cried at night in the privacy of her room. Determined not to fall apart in front of everyone, she kept to herself over the following days.

On the morning of the funeral, Feral Beryl came to her while she was shovelling manure from a wheelbarrow. "You can go. Get cleaned up. Your escort will be here in thirty minutes."

Quin dropped the shovel in the wheelbarrow. "Can I wear the clothes I arrived in?"

"Nope. You go in your greens," Beryl said, walking away.

Two female corrective services officers drove her, taking no interest as Quin sat in the back seat of the car, handcuffed to one of them. The three of them slipped into a pew at the back of the church just as the service began. There were no more than fifty people spread around the small church, and she recognised some from the bowls club.

Ben got up and spoke. She should have been beside him. She willed him to look at her, but he didn't. His voice cracked, and he made no mention of Quin. When the service was over, she and the officers slipped out again and into the unmarked car. She didn't have to speak to anyone.

They wouldn't let her go to the burial and as they drove off, she peered out the car window. A young woman stood hugging Quin's weeping brother. It broke her heart.

42

LUCILLE

1949

Max was at the kitchen table, reading the paper as usual, her son banging the spoon on the highchair while she finished cooking their evening meal. Like old times, she thought. But it wasn't like old times. Tom held out a spoon which Max ignored.

After dinner in the loungeroom, Max sat in his favourite armchair with Tom at his feet. It pained her to see her son waiting like a puppy, thumb in his mouth, ready to clamber onto his father's lap while Max read his newspaper.

"Thumb out," Max muttered, lifting Tom.

Tom eagerly complied as he settled on his father's lap. Quietly satisfied, Tom had never been content in the same way with her, instead ruling her every movement in ways he knew he couldn't with his father.

Lucille looked at her husband; his hair not perfectly in place, a spot under his chin unshaven, his face pale. With

Tom quietly on his knee, Max stared at the newspaper resting on the arm of the chair, not seeing, not listening, not touching his son with his hands. Instead, his fists were clenched and his shoulders hunched tight.

Had she been so consumed by Tom that she'd failed to notice that something was wrong? Was Max resentful of the time she spent with Tom and not with him. Or did he suspect that Tom wasn't his son?

That night in bed, she plucked up the courage. "What's wrong?"

Max took a long time to respond and when he did, he looked through her as if he were lost. "Nothing," he said.

"Have I … have I done something to upset you?"

When he turned to her, his face was pained. "No. Not at all."

"Then what is it?"

"It's nothing. Just a bit of melancholy. I feel it sometimes." He flicked off the lamp.

"Is there something I can do?"

He turned away from her. "It'll pass. Just leave me be for the time being."

She was drifting off to sleep when she heard him.

"I don't know why I'm here. Why was I allowed to live when others, more deserving than me, died?" he whispered.

Her eyes flickered open, not knowing what she could do for him.

★

Lucille lay in bed one morning. She heard father and son in the kitchen eating breakfast, talking and laughing. Tom already had a wide vocabulary. She'd constantly read to him, teaching him new words each day. He was an advanced three-year-old, the baby health centre sister had said. Listening to them she felt jealous but forced herself to stay where she was. This was their time today.

She picked up a magazine and flicked through the pages, then stopped to read an ad: Teachers Wanted. She sat up and stared at the words. Training was provided. She'd wanted to be a teacher when she was at school, and if it hadn't been for marrying Max, she'd have been one by now.

Lucille daydreamed about standing in front of the blackboard and the smiles on children's faces as they learnt how to add and subtract. She closed her eyes. Perhaps when Tom went to school. Suddenly a squeal came from the kitchen. She was on her feet in a second, running.

"What's going on?" she demanded, taking in the scene of her son on the floor, crying, his father towering over him.

"I want it, I want it," Tom sobbed.

"I said he can't have another piece of cake, and this is what he does." Max raised his voice. "No, Tom. You've had enough."

"Surely, he can have another small piece?"

"No, he can't. It's breakfast for god's sake. I let him have one small piece already. He has to learn rules, and this is one of them."

Max clenched his fists and roared. "Go to your room. Now!"

Tom screamed, kicking his heels on the floor.

"Get up, boy!"

Lucille went to the child, but Max pulled her away. "No, Lucille. He's got to learn."

She looked at the red mark he left on her arm.

"Now!" Max yelled. She and Tom jumped. "Go now, Tom, or you'll get a spanking."

Sobbing, Tom stared at his father, then at Lucille. He pulled his little body off the floor and went to his mother, hiding behind her, clutching her night gown.

She put a protective hand on his head before swinging him onto her hip. "There, there," she said, wiping away tears from his blotchy face. "You can have another piece of cake." She looked at Max in defiance. "Here you are, darling."

Reaching over to the counter, she took a small piece, put it on a plate and made her way to the kitchen table.

Max slammed the plate out of her hand smashing it onto the floor. "When I say he's to go to his room, he's to go. Put him down!"

Tom sucked his thumb and sobbed. "No, dada. I want cake."

Max pulled Tom from Lucille's arms and dragged him to his room.

"But—" Lucille called.

"Stay out of it."

She squatted to clean up the remains of the smashed plate

and cake, horrified by what Max had done. She'd never seen him like this. She'd heard stories of returning soldiers beating their wives and children. Is this what it had come to? Tom's muffled crying behind his bedroom door and Max's footsteps on the linoleum floor made her tense.

"You will never do that again," Max said, his voice lowered. "The child needs discipline and rules, otherwise he'll run amok."

His eyes glistened and his hand trembled as he lit his cigarette. She knew he was fighting an inner demon from a past she hadn't been part of, one that terrified him still.

"You're right," she said, vowing never to leave them alone together if she could help it.

*

Max convinced Lucille to go out to a new restaurant, leaving Tom in the care of their neighbour, Judith. It was a rare occasion for Lucille to leave Tom, but knowing he'd be in bed asleep for the night helped her to relax.

Lucille raised her eyebrows at the extravagance when Max ordered a bottle of champagne, but she said nothing. They chatted about the weather, the house, his work, and they ate and laughed, relaxed in each other's company.

"You're still the most beautiful woman in this room." Max leant across the table and touched her cheek. "And I'm the luckiest man on earth."

Lucille sipped her champagne. "Happy anniversary,

darling. Twelve years. And to think that I'd nearly lost you." Blinking back tears, she noted his clenched jaw.

The band started up, and when they played "Begin the Beguine", he looked at her.

"Our song," he said. "Let's dance." He gulped down the last of his champagne and took her hand, leading her onto the dance floor.

She sensed his mood shift as he held her overly tight, his fingers digging into the small of her back, and she silently cursed herself for alluding to the war.

She clung to him until the music stopped, then led him to the table. "I think it's time to go," she said, picking up her shawl. He nodded, sighing as he let her take his hand.

When they got into the car, Max sat with his hands on the wheel. Lucille looked at him waiting for him to start the engine. She touched his arm. "What's wrong, darling?"

He shook his head. "I don't think I can do this anymore."

"I don't understand. What can't you do?" she asked, terrified of the answer.

He took a deep breath. "While we were dancing, I saw someone I thought I knew. He was over by the far wall, at a table with two other men. His name is Ted Morrison. We called him Horrie Morrie because of what the Japs did to him."

"Why didn't you say hello?"

He looked at Lucille, his eyes glistening. "I couldn't. I just couldn't. I …" He turned his face away. "I left him. I left him in the mud and ran. It was the one chance I had to escape, and

I took it. How could I have left him? What sort of man am I? He was the bravest man I knew. He copped beatings and humiliation from the Japs time and time again. But his spirit was incredible. When there was an air raid and the Japs were distracted, we saw an opportunity to escape, so a few of us made a run for it. We split up. I was with Morrie, but when he fell in the mud, I left him for dead. Don't you see what that's made me?"

She tensed, holding her breath as he continued.

"Go, he said. Get going. He'd catch up, he said. I stood there like an idiot when I should have helped him up from the mud. I made a split-second decision and ran. I ran and left him."

She put her hand on his arm, but he flinched, so she removed it.

"Then what happened?"

"I ran through the jungle, waiting for a bullet to hit me. Expecting to hear the sounds of the Japs. Hoping like hell that Morrie had gotten up and was running behind me. I couldn't afford to stop, to see what was happening. It was getting dark and I ran until I couldn't run any further. Just me in the jungle, using every ounce of my strength to run. I don't know how I did it. I ran until I dropped, and by then, I didn't care where I ended up. I gave up. I was ready to die, and I guess I passed out. I woke up next to a river, saw two fellows in a canoe and yelled out to them. I was lucky they took me to a village where the headman was in charge of an anti-Japanese guerrilla unit. They looked after me."

"The scars on your back?"

He shrugged. "Beatings. Some of us were put in cages for days at a time. Given water every few days, and little or no food. Beatings if we spoke, beatings if we looked in the wrong direction, beatings just for the hell of it. Captain Lionel Matthews set up an intelligence unit with some of the locals. It boosted us all. But the Japs got wind of it, and he was shot. When our chaps began bombing, we were forced to march. Many were sick, barely able to put one foot in front of the other, but march is what we had to do." His voice croaked. "Anyone who stopped was bayonetted and hauled to the side of the track. I was lucky. I still had boots, a lot didn't. And I plodded along, hoping like hell I'd make it."

He laid his head on the steering wheel and sobbed. Lucille's tears were silent. Her heart broke for him. She slid across the bench seat and put her arms around him, and they cried together for a long time in the dark of the carpark.

Finally, he pulled away, took out his handkerchief, wiped his eyes and blew his nose. "How can I go on?"

"It's been a long time. How sure are you that the man in there is Morrie?"

"I'm not really sure."

"Do you think you might like to talk to him?"

"How can I face him after what I've done?"

She took his hand in hers putting it up to her lips. "I can come with you."

He was silent, and she waited patiently.

"I'll do it." He suddenly got out of the car and headed to the restaurant. She caught up with him, and together, they stood scanning the few diners who remained.

"He's gone. I've done it again."

Lucille held his arm. "You've done nothing. You don't even know if it was him. Come on, let's go home."

As they turned around and headed to the carpark, Max stopped abruptly. "Morrie?" he called out his voice cracking. "Morrie?" he said louder. He shook off Lucille's arm and jogged to the far side of the carpark toward a man who stood frozen.

Lucille stood a little way off not able to hear what was being said but she watched as Max shook the man's hand.

Then Max turned and beckoned to her.

"Morrie, this is my wife, Lucille."

"Actually, it's Ted, Mrs Doomsbury. Morrie's just a nickname I picked up during the war," Morrie said. "Listen, why don't we go and get a drink?"

They went back inside.

"I wondered if you'd survived," Morrie said, holding a beer in his hand.

"I've thought the same about you," Max said. "What happened?"

"I got up quick smart and was right behind you. Then to throw them off, I went to the left, while you went to the right and lucky for me I ran straight into a camp full of Americans. I couldn't believe my luck." He patted Max on the shoulder and looked at Lucille. "I've had sleepless nights wondering if my mate here made it." Then he looked at Max. "By jove, I'm glad I ran into you."

Max raised his glass. "So am I, mate. So am I."

43

QUIN

1991

Quin didn't hear from Ben despite writing to him, and there wasn't a day when she didn't think about Nan. She continued to keep her head down and stayed out of the way. The other inmates had their own hell and left her alone. There were days where her longing to be anywhere but inside was so overpowering, she felt she would burst. Then a meditative reminder would sink in – the days, the hours, the minutes ahead, inside the grey walls of barbed wire with this group of women, just like her. Some days, she made plans – a job, where to live, revenge on Tom. But the latter was a fantasy. No-one could touch Tom. On those days, she reminded herself that in a few short weeks she'd be free to take back control of her life.

*

The night before Quin was due to get out, Daze, Colleen and Marcy threw her a party.

"It's not much," Daze declared, producing a mud cake from behind her back. "Ta Da."

Quin's mouth watered. "How did you get that?"

"We got home delivery. They deliver ya know," Marcy said. "Besides, I've been craving mud cake, and what better excuse?"

"But how did you get it in?" Quin asked.

Daze touched her finger to her nose. "Never you mind."

"Okay," Quin said. "I don't want you to get into any trouble."

"Stop worrying," Daze said. "They run a scanner over it for any metal bits."

"Really?"

Marcy laughed. "Look at her. Actually, we asked Beryl, and she ordered it for you."

Quin didn't know what to think, but the cake looked enticing. "I'll never forget you."

"Yeah, you will," Colleen said. "And you should. You're young. Get that money out from where you stashed it, meet a good bloke and have some babies. Forget this hell, put it behind you."

"For the umpteenth time, there's no money," Quin said, laughing.

"Let us believe there is," Daze said. "Stop wrecking our fantasy. Now let's get stuck in."

"Fuck, forgot the spoons," Marcy said.

"I didn't. Here you go." Daze handed each of them a spoon.

They sat in a circle on the floor and attacked the cake.

Quin felt their hope for her in that huddle, and it gave her strength.

Robbie, the guard came to lock up. "What's going on here?"

"We're eating cake. Schmidt's last night. Wanna a bit?" Daze said, her mouth full.

Robbie hesitated, then shook her head. "Beryl get it for you?"

They nodded.

"Get it cleaned up by the time I get back."

They stuffed the rest in their mouths, hugged Quin and returned to their rooms.

Quin cleared away the crumbs with pieces of toilet paper, then lay down. Her stomach swirled from cake and nerves. Thirteen more hours and she'd be free.

*

She'd been given her outside clothes the night before and now stood dressing carefully. Her old greens, she left in the same bag for washing and wearing, ready for the next size eight who had the misfortune to come in. They didn't allow the new releases to eat breakfast with the others, so a tray was waiting for her in the office. She was too excited to eat.

"Ya getting out," Beryl said, counting out the notes on the counter in front of Quin. "Now according to us, we owe you eighty dollars."

Quin frowned. "Eighty? No, that can't be right. It should be at least six hundred dollars."

Beryl was smug. "No, sunshine. There's expenses and the like."

Expenses? What expenses? "You never said anything about that."

"Uniforms, shoes, letting you have a television, use of the library, the cake … It all costs money, you know. Do you want me to go on?" Beryl sniggered. "Take it or leave it."

This couldn't be happening.

Beryl smirked. "We all lost a bucketful of money with Solid Rock, didn't we, Mon? The taxi's waiting. I'd suggest you get out, find some of that money you got tucked away and use it."

Quin glared at the two of them, pushed the cash into her bag and left.

The taxi took her as far as the station. Her Majesty's Prison system would not spring for anything more. On the train, she gazed around her. The stale musty smell, the brick veneer houses, graffiti on back fences and normal people in normal clothes, all seemed remarkable.

She had an address in the Western Suburbs and a phone number. Nan and Ben had moved the week before Nan had died. It didn't surprise her that the phone had rung out. Ben would be at work. Surely, he'd be over his anger, excited to see her.

The train deposited her in the city, and to kill time, she walked the streets and the lanes, gawked at the construction sites and the beginnings of new skyscrapers. She savoured a hamburger and a coffee and sat in the city square, people-watching, looking like any other office worker in her suit, enjoying the warmth of the winter sun. She couldn't wait to change when she got home to Ben's. He'd have her things.

After catching two trams, she walked along the street that would soon be her new home. An ordinary street where a reluctant dog was yanked along by a man in jogging shorts, where someone had half parked a Ford on the nature strip and a grey cat meandered in the middle of the road. A young girl in school uniform dawdled, and a car expelled excited kids into a brick house with a neat front lawn. It was a street, smelling of frying onions and lamb fat and the sounds of trucks nearby changing gears and where the sky changed colour from orange to pink to purple.

She reached number twenty-five and stood in front of the neatly kept weatherboard house, which looked like all the others in the street, built in the fifties. This was her beginning. A pot with a dead plant on the wide verandah greeted her and she grinned – so like Ben. She forgot about her feet, sore from the high heels, and knocked. No-one came to the door, no matter how many times she thumped. She peered at her watch. Five-fifteen. Perhaps he was working overtime.

She sat on the step, folding her arms to ward off the growing chill and jiggled her knee. He wouldn't push her away. He'd let her stay until she got on her feet. They'd cry together, reminisce about Nan. He'd forgive her.

It was the longest time, waiting in the dark for Ben. She

needed a toilet. Stiff from her perch on the wooden step, she stood and walked up the street to the main road, then wandered along until she found a Maccas. Relief. The smell of food forced her to open her wallet. She ate another hamburger with fries and downed a soft drink so fast she'd forgotten about the shock of the fizz. The sugar hit surged and propelled her back to the house. A car was in the driveway – a Holden ute – a come down from the BMW Ben had leased.

She combed her hair with her fingers and knocked on the door. An uncontrolled anticipation of happiness flooded over her when she heard the thud of bare feet down the corridor. The door swung open, and she stepped back. "Oh," was all she could utter. An older man, mid–forties at least, bald with a moustache, stood in front of her.

"Yes?" he said.

She came to her senses. "Ah, is Ben here. Ben Schmidt? I thought he lived here."

"He's gone to Hammondville, I think. I took the lease over from him." He narrowed his eyes. "Why?"

"Sorry, I'm an old friend. I thought I'd surprise him. No wonder he didn't answer the phone." She laughed nervously. "Do you know when he left?"

"A coupla months back."

She nodded. "You don't happen to have a forwarding address, do you?"

He looked at her, weighing up whether he should hand over the information. Quin smiled, encouragingly. "He'll be so mad that I came all this way from Perth and missed him. I'd really like to catch up." She was still a capable liar. Her face burned.

"Just a sec."

The man closed the door, and she heard a drawer open and slam shut before the front door reopened. "Here you go. That's where I forward on his mail, when I get any. There's not much. And I don't even know if he's there still."

"Oh? I might see if I can visit him."

The man frowned. "It's a long way to just pop in."

She knew where the town was. Solid Rock started there. "Oh really?"

"A good four hours by train, I reckon."

"That far? Perhaps I'll send him a letter instead. Thanks ever so much." Quin smiled sweetly.

"Good luck to you."

"Thanks."

Deflated, Quin walked along the street. It was too late to do anything tonight. She'd catch a train to Hammondville in the morning. But first she had to find somewhere to stay.

In the city, she a found a hostel, thirty dollars for the night, which was more than she could afford. The paint was peeling, the bed was hard and the pillow lumpy. But she was free. She'd buy a change of clothes at an op shop and be with Ben in Hammondville tomorrow.

44

LUCILLE

1970

Lucille was in the garden, wandering around her roses. It had been a tough day, at the local primary school where she worked as a teacher's aide. She'd spent years organising fundraisers for the primary school, then high school. Max hadn't wanted her to work. He said she needed to stay home to look after Tom. And she did. Then five years ago she was offered a paid role and loved it. She loved having her own money, her own financial independence.

"Come on," Max said, holding two glasses. He placed them on the wicker table on the front verandah and settled himself on the chair. "I've made you a gin and tonic."

"Having you home early is a nice surprise," she said, peeling off her gloves and throwing them into the basket.

"I like that mauve frock on you. It matches the purple roses."

She laughed as she climbed the stairs to the verandah. "As you know, I love mauve, and I do love roses."

Lucille took the drink and sat opposite Max. "I always feel a little sad at the end of summer."

"Me too," he said. "You can feel the nip in the air already."

They touched glasses and sipped.

"Why are you home early anyway?" Her eyes narrowed as she studied his face. "You look very happy with yourself."

"I am. I've got some news that will secure our future."

She raised her eyebrows. "Uh, oh. I've heard this before."

He feigned a look of hurt. "Now, don't be like that. It's not bad."

She stifled a chuckle. Max had toyed with a few crazy ideas. In the early sixties, he'd wanted to buy a farm and live off the land. He'd had the notion that they'd grow their own food, spin their own wool. She'd told him in no uncertain terms that she had no intention of living like a cave woman or hermit, without electricity and having to spin wool.

"What about the time you wanted us to live on a houseboat on the Murray?"

"Well, yes that was a bit stupid. But it would have been an adventure."

"Not for me. It would have been stressful with a young child, watching him every second of the day."

"Mmm. But this news is good and sensible. Those were just brainstorming ideas about living differently. I wasn't really serious about any of them."

"Really?" she said, smiling. "Okay, then let me have it."

"I bought a forty per cent share of a building society."

She choked on her gin and tonic, coughing and spluttering.

"You okay?"

She nodded and composed herself. "A building society? What building society?"

"The Solid Rock Building Society."

"The one Harvey owns with his father?"

"Yep. I bought out his father's share." Max put his glass down and leant forwards, resting his elbows on his knees. "It's a chance to build a nest egg for our retirement. And it's a great opportunity for Tom. He's nearly twenty-five and still hasn't found a job. It's bad enough that he took three extra years to finish his business degree."

"He's trying to find a job." She coughed again. "He's really a good boy."

Though Tom was young and carefree, she had to admit she'd had ambitions for him. He was smart and had dabbled in quite a few things, trying to make money. When he settled down, she knew he'd be somebody, she was sure. The time wasn't right for him yet, he'd explained. Life experience was important too, and Lucille had to agree. Lord knew, she'd had to grow up too fast once her mother died, then straight out of school and into marriage.

Max frowned. "Let's face it. He's a no-hoper." He counted off on his fingers, one by one. "He's been expelled from school, set fire to another, been caught underage drinking, cheated on his exams. And that's what we know of. He's been a constant source of worry."

Lucille's hackles went up when he talked about Tom like that. "Maybe he was looking for your attention," she murmured.

Perhaps Max had been too absorbed in his own issues – the war had screwed up his ambition and his life. He'd been resigned to work for the CSIRO, shunning advancement. Occasionally, he'd come up with hare-brained ideas that made no sense.

Max leant back in his chair. "Don't blame me for his behaviour. If I'd had my way, I would have pulled him out of school and got him an apprenticeship. You've mollycoddled him his whole life. Now he's trying to dodge the draft and probably spaced out on who knows what. The money you earn all goes to supporting him. Why would he work?"

"He does work. He can't get a proper job. No-one will hire him. There's nothing wrong with him being self-employed. Buying and selling American dollars wasn't the best idea, but at least he's been giving it a go. You know he looks for your approval all the time, but you never give him an inch. He looks up to you and always has, yet you give him nothing."

"I don't know what you're talking about."

It was like a broken record, talking to him about his relationship with Tom. He'd been hard on the boy his whole life. No wonder he'd rebelled.

"Puh! Cutting his hair would be a good start. He's probably out there selling drugs, for all we know. I don't know why you encourage him. He looks like a long-haired lout driving around the place in a combi van, wearing thongs and hippie shirts. Ridiculous. He needs to wake up to himself."

"He was making those thongs and selling them, if you remember."

Lucille did worry about Tom, but he assured her he was all right. He didn't come home often, but when he did, he talked about the farms he'd worked on up north, the places he'd been to and the money-making ideas.

"He bloody well needs to settle down and work in a good, honest job. Who knows what the hell he's up to? Once we get him settled, then all we have to do is retire and enjoy life."

"I suppose you're right. It might be the start Tom needs. But where did you get the money from to buy into the building society?"

"I sold our shares, dived into our savings and mortgaged the house. It's a good deal."

"You took our savings? Our joint savings? That was meant to be for our retirement. How could you do this without talking to me first?"

"I am talking to you now. I tried to talk to you about it a few weeks ago. Whenever I discuss money, you glaze over."

She folded her arms and pursed her lips.

"It's true. Don't give me that look."

"What look?"

"As if you're suddenly shocked. I've tried to tell you about how investing works, but you throw up your hands and say"—he imitated her now—"'It's all too complicated and boring'. That's why I look after the money and the bills."

She closed her eyes. "Well, it *is* boring. But I didn't think you'd use our savings to buy some ridiculous business you know nothing about. You're a scientist for goodness sake, not a businessman."

"It's called investing. And I've been doing it for years and doing very well at it, I might add. And if you remember, Harvey was groomed by his old man and started from the ground up."

"And what do you know about this business?" Lucille said. It was true that Max had invested on the stock market for years and had made quite a lot of money. He'd even taken the money from the sale of Pa's house and invested it well.

"I don't need to know anything. Harvey will sit on the board with his father, and they'll run it. This is for Tom. It'll be a great career for him, and he can finally use the degree we paid for."

Max reached for her hand. "There's nothing to worry about. I've done a lot of research on it. The return on our investment will be enough for us to retire, get a place on the coast and have a nice little income to live on. I'm nearly fifty-five. I don't want to work until I drop. I want to work for another two years. Then we can do all the things we said we wanted to do. We can travel the world and play golf."

He reached over and touched her face. "Come on, Petal, let me see that beautiful smile."

She couldn't help smiling. It made sense. She'd always

wanted to go to Europe, and to England, where Pa had grown up. "There's certainly a lot we could do," she said. And Tom would have a job and settle down. She trusted Max. He always made the right decisions, but from now she decided to pay more attention to their financial affairs.

*

Two months later, Lucille was surprised by Tom's excited reaction to joining Solid Rock.

"You're going to have to start from the bottom. Harvey's happy to take you on, and with a bit of hard work, you'll rise up the ranks," Max said. "And one day take over the company."

Lucille frowned. "I don't know why he has to start by being a teller. For god's sake, he's got a business degree. It's a bit demeaning."

"It's okay, Mum. It won't be for too long. I've got to understand the business from the bottom up. Everyone starts there," Tom said.

"Where are you starting then?" she said, serving mashed potatoes alongside slices of lamb.

"A place called Hammondville," Tom said. "I'm moving there for a while. Apparently, that's where the head office is."

She frowned. "That's a long way, isn't it?"

"About four hours on the train, I think."

"You're going to have to cut your hair, son." Max smiled as he handed his son a beer.

"Going to the barber tomorrow, Dad. Great roast, Mum."

45

QUIN

HAMMONDVILLE, 1991

Quin stood in front of a run-down house – paint peeling, patches of mud stuck to the weatherboards, and old sheets hanging from the grimy front window.

She nervously rolled the piece of paper with Ben's address around in her hand. She took a deep breath, picked her way along the broken concrete path, then knocked on the splintered front door. No answer. She knocked again. Finally, footsteps thudded along the hallway, and the door creaked opened just enough for her to see a young woman.

"Hi," Quin said. The door opened wider, and the woman screwed up her face as if the light hurt her eyes. Her face was pale, her brown hair pulled back in a loose ponytail.

"Yeah?"

"Um, I'm after Ben Schmidt? Does he live here?"

The girl frowned. "Jesus." She flung the door open and

beckoned Quin to follow her down the dim corridor. "Richo! Richo."

The girl's reaction puzzled her. Was Ben in some sort of trouble? The grimy carpet was covered with dirt and leaves, and the doors on either side of the corridor were shut.

The girl stopped in front of an open door towards the rear of the house.

A skinny man, twenty-something with a tattoo of an eagle on the front of his chest, was sprawled on the couch. On the television, Tony Barber's voice blared on The Sale of the Century.

"What?"

"She wants Benny."

Quin raised her eyebrows at the nickname her brother had hated. "Um, yeah. Is he here?" She squirmed as the man's eyes trawled her from top to bottom.

He sat up. "What for?"

"He asked me to look him up if I was in the area and said I could stay a while."

It was clear he wasn't there, and she fought to hide her disappointment.

He narrowed his eyes. "When?"

"What do you mean when?"

"When did he ask you?"

Quin hesitated. "A while ago. Is this the right address?"

"It is," the man said.

"He's obviously not here, but do you know when he'll be back?"

Richo and the girl looked at each other. "He ain't comin' back."

"Oh. Do you know where he's gone? Where I can find him?"

The girl started crying.

The man scratched his head. "Um. He won't be back. I'm afraid he's dead."

Quin let go of the ball of paper, and her backpack slipped off her shoulder. Her legs buckled and she gasped for air, moaning.

"Listen, you better sit down." Richo was on his feet. "Shels, stop ya snivellin' and getta cuppa on. She's gone pale."

Shaking violently, Quin allowed herself to be led to an armchair, where the man pushed off a startled cat.

"Here you go. It was a shock. He was a nice bloke, screwed up in the head, but a good bloke."

She tried to slow her breathing, to stop the rising hysteria, her disbelief, her tears. "You're definitely sure?"

"Hell, yeah. The cops made me identify 'im. It was pretty bloody awful. Never wanna do that again, ever. Shels, where's the tea?"

"Comin'. Keep ya shirt on."

He grinned. "I ain't got one on."

Quin blinked. "I have to know what happened. Tell me everything."

Richo turned the television volume down. "Not much to tell. One minute he was here, and the next thing we knew, the coppers were banging on the door. They said he went off

Jumper's Bridge. He seemed all right, the last time I saw him. That's what I told the coppers."

Shels came into the room and thrust a cup of black tea in Quin's hand.

"When did it happen?" Quin asked, nodding her thanks to Shel, who sat cross-legged on the floor, patting the cat.

"Monday. Who did you say you were?"

She gazed at the ceiling and closed her eyes. The day before she'd got out of jail.

"Sorry, I'm Quin Schmidt, his sister."

"Oh," Shel said.

"Ah, you're a sister," Richo said. "We knew it musta been a relative when we saw the same last name on the letters. Look he had a car, but it was old, and I had to sell it in a hurry to pay for the funeral. I'm sorry about that, but we couldn't get hold of ya. We wrote, or I got Shels to write. The coppers rang and said you weren't there and couldn't be found, so I had to make decisions. Okay?"

Quin nodded. "That's okay. Thank you." She sniffed and wiped her eyes with the sleeve of her windcheater. "What address did you use?"

"Shels, where did you send the letter?"

"Um, a jail, I think. Figured ya must have worked there."

Quin nodded. No need to tell them otherwise.

"Pity you didn't get here earlier. The funeral service was this morning. Just a small one, mind, at the funeral parlour. He's being cremated. It was cheaper than a plot, the funeral guy said. But listen, you might be able to stop it if you wanna get hold of 'em and do something else instead."

"Oh." Quin blinked. "No, that's all right." She didn't have money to live on, let alone find a plot for her brother. She held her head in her hands and let the tears come, trying to understand why her brother was dead.

"Listen, I was plonked into this, and I shouldn't have been. He paid up his rent until the end of the month. You can stay in his room if you want."

Quin sniffed and turned her gaze to Richo. "Thanks. I'd like to go to his room now, if you don't mind." She had to get away from Richo and his incessant talking. She put her cup on the floor, grabbed her backpack and stood.

"Shels, show her the room."

Shels had snuck off.

"Shels, where the fuck are ya? Shels?"

"It's fine. I should be able to find it."

The final round was on and Richo turned his attention to the television. "What? Oh, yeah. First door on the left as you go back down the corridor towards the front door."

There were three doors on the left and three on the right. "Near the front door?"

"Yep."

She opened the door to what she assumed was Ben's room. There was a double mattress on the floor. The only bedding on it was a sleeping bag – she recognised it was his from when they'd gone camping years earlier. She sighed as she threw down her backpack and sat on the mattress. She turned on a lamp that was on the floor and gazed around the room: a poster of Iggy Pop on the wall, which Ben must have brought from home; a suitcase lying open in the corner; and an empty pizza box under a wooden table. Tired and head thumping, she lay back and stared at the ceiling, chewing her lip so hard she tasted the metallic taste of her own blood. The air was stale and musty with a hint of the spicy aftershave he wore for special occasions. Entirely alone and lost, she couldn't help feeling this was all her own fault. Deep down was another niggling thought. Why did her brother come to this town?

After a while, she got up to find the bathroom. It was next door and clean enough.

The sound of the television drew her back towards the lounge room. Richo was still glued to the screen. In the kitchen, Shels was at the table, reading a hard-cover book. She didn't look up when Quin found a glass and filled it. There were no dirty dishes, and while the sink was stained, it had been wiped clean. The green laminate on the benches was peeling as was the paint on the kitchen cupboards. The yellowed fridge hummed, and a dog barked outside. She glanced at her watch. It was almost seven-thirty, still light because of daylight saving.

"Ya can make ya self a tea if ya want," Shels said. "There's cups in the cupboard above ya head and tea on the counter.

"Thanks."

"Sorry about your brother. He was a nice guy."

"He was."

"Fuck!" Richo shouted. "He missed it, the moron."

Shels glanced towards the lounge room.

Richo thumped into the kitchen, his feet bare and jeans hanging. "Some people shouldn't be on a show like that."

He opened the fridge, pulled out two beers and held one out to Quin. "The fucker could've won. I wouldn't have missed it."

"Thanks," Quin said, taking the beer.

Shels stopped reading and cocked her head towards Richo. "Ya did. Ya froze."

"Yeah, but it was a hard question. Not easy like that dickhead had."

Quin flipped off the lid and drank. It felt good. "You were on that show?"

Richo downed the stubby before he looked at her. "Bloody oath, I was. Won ten grand, year ago."

"Oh, that's impressive." She sipped. "I hope you don't mind me asking, but I was just wondering. Was there an autopsy done? It seems awfully quick to have a funeral."

Richo stared at her. "The coroner was here for another one and did a quickie and the coppers said it was hunky dory. Someone saw him go over. Jumper's Bridge is kinda the place to go to top yourself. There's been quite a few." He looked at Shels for confirmation.

Shels nodded.

"Lotta people lost all their dough to that mob Solid Rock. Ya know, it started in this town way back when?" He looked at Shels. "The sixties, I reckon. Anyway, barriers are goin' up next week, too late for Benny boy though."

Quin picked at the label on the stubby bottle and sighed. "How did he seem to you?"

Richo opened the fridge door and stopped. "Your brother kept to himself a lot. He never said much. But he'd watch Sale of the Century. We'd have a few beers, watch a bit of footy. The usual. Not much else to tell."

"He loved Sale of the Century. Thanks for looking after him."

Richo closed the fridge door and turned to her. "Look, the other reason we did the funeral so quick was that it was cheaper to do it with someone else."

Quin frowned. "What do you mean?"

"Another bloke jumped the day before, so they said that since Benny had no-one, he could tag onto that funeral. The other guy's parents had no money either. There's only one funeral place here, and they've been a bit busy. The young ones jump, the oldies use shotguns or drugs. That's the fact of the matter."

"I see," Quin said. "That's horrifying. All because of Solid Rock?"

"And the recession," Shels piped up. "No jobs, no money. That's what it's like in a country town like this."

Richo reached into the fridge and brought out a pot, which he put on the stove. "Yeah, the recession. Listen, you probably should talk to the coppers tomorrow since they were looking for you."

"I might do that."

"Ya, hungry?"

Quin shrugged and Shels reached for three bowls and spoons.

"What are you studying?" Quin spooned lentil and green bean soup into her mouth. It was the best meal she'd had in months. "This is delicious by the way."

"Sociology," Shels said. "Richo cooked it last night. Have some bread."

Quin reached across and pulled two slices of fresh white bread out of the packet and dunked a piece into the soup. "Are you a cook, Richo?"

"He works at the Koffee and Kettle. The breakfast and lunch shift." Shel licked her lips and grinned.

"I suppose there's no jobs around that you know of?" Quin asked.

"We need a kitchen hand. Can you wash dishes?" Richo said, his mouth full.

"Yeah."

"Then you got a job."

"Really? When can I start?"

"You can start right now with these dishes." Richo roared with laughter and Shels giggled.

"I'd be happy to clean up." Quin gathered the bowls.

She felt better with a full stomach.

"Start tomorra mornin' at seven at Koffee and Kettle. It was Benny's job anyway," Richo said, finishing his beer.

Shels was back reading her book.

"Thanks, I appreciate it."

46

LUCILLE

HAMMONDVILLE, 1980

Lucille loved the ocean view from her kitchen window and never tired of it. She was glad they'd sold up in Melbourne and moved to Hammondville to be near Tom. It was a pretty town, and the investment in Solid Rock had grown so well they could afford to travel every year. Tom had done well at Solid Rock, earning several promotions. When the head office relocated to Melbourne, five years ago, Tom had moved too.

"Mum, where's Dad?" Tom called out as he let himself into the house.

Washing dishes, Lucille smiled when she heard her son's voice. "In here, darling," she said wiping her hands.

She hugged her son, kissed him on the cheek and stepped back. "Let me have a look at you." Looking at Tom reminded her of Hank. She pushed the memory away. "Why didn't you call? Do you want something to eat? Are you staying?"

Tom stared at her. "No, Mum. I'm not staying, I'm not hungry and I need to find Dad. Do you know where he is?"

"He's playing golf. Why do you want to see him and not me?"

Tom's shoulders dropped. "Mum! It's not like that. For goodness sake, it's business. I need to talk to him about Solid Rock." He raised his eyebrows and cocked his head. "Something you wouldn't understand or even be interested in. Okay?"

"I see."

Tom and Max ignored her when it came to discussions about money and investment. Leaving her out, hurt her, but what they didn't know was that she always listened. She still had her own bank account from wartime, and even though she should have told Max about it, she never had. She was proud that the bank balance had grown over the years, just from putting aside coins in jars and tins. She was sure Max wouldn't have cared but having something for herself had become important to her.

"How long do you reckon he'll be?"

She looked at her watch. "He'll be home for lunch. About one, he said."

Solid Rock consumed her son. In ten years, the business had emerged as a strong contender in the country, supporting farmers with good returns for deposits and providing loans to those who needed funds at reasonable interest rates.

"Do you want me to drive you to the golf club to wait for him? We could have lunch there."

"No, I have to see a client on the way back."

"You're not staying? It's a long way to come and go, darling. I'll make you a sandwich. You've got to at least eat."

"I don't want anything." He looked at his watch. "Dad'll be home in a few minutes. I'll just wait."

"What about a cup of coffee or tea?" She put the kettle on.

He shook his head and paced, picked up the paper, then flung it down and looked at his watch. Lucille cast her mind to find something to keep his attention.

"So, how's Jenny? When are you bringing her back to Hammondville?"

She liked his wife. There had been numerous girlfriends, but Tom had married Jenny six months ago.

His lips set in a straight line. "She's fine … I guess."

Lucille looked at him sharply as she poured herself a cup of tea.

"You guess? What happened, Tom?"

He shrugged and played with his car keys. He wouldn't look at her.

"It didn't work out. That's all. I'll have coffee after all. Have you got any cake by any chance?"

"You've broken up?"

"Yep. She left me."

"God, why?"

He shrugged. "She found someone better, I guess."

He stood limply while she wrapped her arms around him. "I'm sorry, love."

She sighed, won over by pity for him. She made the coffee and found some left over Christmas cake.

"This is so good. You make the best cake, Mum." He smiled showing off his perfect teeth and sad eyes.

She didn't press him any further about Jenny, keeping her worry to herself.

$$47$$

QUIN

1991

The next morning, Quin woke with a jolt, remembering her brother was dead. She'd slept fitfully in his room, lying on his mattress, surrounded by his things. Now her entire body ached as she pulled herself up. She'd come to Hammondville for his forgiveness and his help. Her eyes stung and it occurred to her that his death had benefited her somewhat. Apparently, she had a job, Ben's job, and now his room.

Someone called her name, and she hurried out of the bedroom, met up with Richo and they left for the cafe.

The work was easy, washing dishes, chopping onions, tomatoes and shredding lettuce. She let her mind wander as she settled into the rhythm of her duties.

"You seem to know your way around the kitchen," Richo said.

Quin stopped chopping. "Yes." She continued.

"Right," Richo said. "It shows."

Her eyes welled up. "If you don't mind, I need a bit of fresh air." She wiped her eyes with her forearm.

"Sure."

She went out the back door, cried for a minute then pulled herself together and went back to the onions.

Three days later, she built up the courage to go the local police station after work. They didn't tell her much more than she already knew: Ben had jumped off the Goanna Gorge Bridge, they were sorry for her loss, there'd been five suicides in the last year and she could be assured that the anti-jump barriers were going up in the next week. There was no comfort in their words.

She found the bridge – ornate iron railing on both sides; an endless procession of cars and trucks containing blank-faced drivers going back and forth, oblivious to her grief. Her body a deadweight, she stood in the middle of the span, adding the bunch of flowers she'd picked from the side of the road to three bouquets of dead ones.

Had he peered over before he climbed on the railing and jumped? She tried not to think what might have been in his head during those last minutes. She forced herself to look, then gasped, putting her hand to her mouth. Jagged rocks, brown tufts of shrub clinging in spots, a ridge of flat-faced rock plunging towards a slip of gurgling water. She turned away and trudged back to the house, exhausted and grief-stricken.

In the days following, she went through the motions. Say hello, goodbye, make tea, drink water, remember to eat, go to work, buy some clothes from the op shop, put one foot in front of the other. Go home, lie on Ben's bed, stare out of his window, try not to think.

Richo and Shel let her be.

It was a fragile holding pattern for a couple of weeks. Moving out of it was too horrifying to contemplate.

Then one afternoon, Quin sat on Ben's bed and looked at the state of the room. She found the energy to clear away the pizza boxes, used coffee cups, mouldy apple cores, then wash the linen and get some order into the room. Clearing the small wooden table, she found a receipt for $3000 for the sale of Ben's car, and one for $3,800 for the funeral. Richo's name was on the funeral receipt. He'd never said anything about the money. He'd given her a place to stay and a job and now this. She'd have to find a way to pay back the extra eight hundred dollars, and knowing that weighed heavily on her.

Then she found the letters. A neat pile. On top was an envelope addressed to Ben in her handwriting. The letter she'd sent telling him that she was getting out of jail and that she was coming. She took a deep breath and turned it over. Still sealed. He hadn't even seen it. If only he had. She put it aside.

The next envelope had her name on it, no address and was completely sealed. She flipped to the next one, again addressed to her. There were several like that, all sealed, never posted.

She curled up under the sleeping bag and stared at the pile of letters. Hands shaking, she opened the first one from the bottom of the pile, dated the week she'd been sent to prison. It was Ben's handwriting, scrawled across a ripped page from a spiral notebook.

Quin,
You've ruined my life. I hope you know that.
Ben

Crushed, she lay back on the mattress, staring at the ceiling, imagining how he must have hated her. She opened the next one, dated a month later, No greeting, no name, same scrawl and same spiral notebook paper.

We can't afford the rent, so Nan and I have to find another place.
Thanks a lot for saddling me with all of this.

The next one was two months later.

If you think I'd visit you, you've got another thing coming.
I can't believe you came to the funeral and showed your dispicabel face.

Dispicabel. She remembered the spelling contests they'd had when they were young. She'd always won, and now she wished she hadn't. She drew in a deep breath, readying herself.

The next one read:

I hate you.

Yep, that hurt too, Ben.
The one after read:

It's so hard on my own, without Nan. At least I have Sandra.
I don't know why she puts up with me.

Oh, Ben. Where is Sandra?
The next one.

Sandra and me are off.
She doesn't want to be with some loser like me, she said.
Hope your happy.

I'm not, Ben. I'm very sad. If only I could have told him.

Don't bother going to the new place, I've sold or given away everything and I've sub-leased the house.
I have to get away from all of Nan's and your stuff.
It's not fair, I had to do this all on my own.

Why didn't she write to him more than once when she was in jail? Another reason she was a selfish bitch.
She opened the next one, undated.

Dear Quin,
Do you remember the fundraiser when you said that you'd

forgotten what Mum and Dad looked like? You asked me if I still remembered, and I said I did. We've never talked about it, and maybe we should have, because I remember. I've always remembered and spent years trying to forget.

You were being stupid, whacking me in the back seat with your Barbie, trying to get me to play the voice of Ken. You were Barbie. Sometimes we played a story that you made up. Anyway, I didn't want to play. We were on our way to the beach. We were on school holidays, and I desperately wanted to learn how to surf. Dad said he'd teach me. I kept asking Dad when we would get there. Is it soon? Will the waves be high?

She dropped the letter, lost in a memory. She'd hit Ben with her Barbie, deliberately scratching the doll's high heels down his arm. She didn't know it'd be so sharp, and Ben yelped in pain, blood streaming from the gash. Her father had turned his head and yelled.

Her hands trembled.

Her mother had twisted around in the car. The slap stung. "For goodness' sake, why can't you be a good child?" Her mother's last words.

Quin held her breath, trying to shake off the memory. Her hands shook so much she could hardly pick up the letter to read the rest.

I screamed, and Mum and Dad turned around.

But I kept on and on about it. I wouldn't let up about how I wanted to go surfing to get away from you.

Dad turned around again, so didn't see the semi-trailer coming around the corner. I did. I saw it. It was my fault.

That's why I've always been a shit. Because sometimes it let me off the hook, to shift the blame to you.

Your loving brother, Ben.

Quin touched the words on the page, bleary eyed and hollow. Could she read the last letter? It was dated the day of his death. She unfolded the page slowly.

Dear Quin,

I'm in Hammondville. I thought I could get some closure or even forgiveness about the accident, that's what the counsellor told me. Yeah, I've been seeing a counsellor on and off for a few years now. I should have told you, but I was too ashamed to tell anyone. I should have been stronger for Nan and for you. I talked you into mortgaging Nan's house. It's my fault we lost everything. You tried to do the right thing, and I took everything out on you.

I found the spot where it happened, just before the bridge.

It turns out that it's made me feel a whole lot worse about myself.

You'll be right. You've always been smarter than me. You'll bounce back. If you ever get this letter, promise me you'll carry on for the two of us. I wish I could, but I can't.

Your loving brother x

P.S. The accident wasn't your fault. Forgive me.

She dropped the letter, tears streaming down her face. No, Ben. It was my fault. Dad turned around to stop Mum. There were no seat belts then. I had moved over to you and wiped your arm, crying, sorry, trying to be good, trying to avoid Mum's slap.

48

QUIN

JUNE, 1992

The train's shrill whistle made her jump, and Quin craned her head towards the far end of the platform. The last of the stragglers had boarded. The carriage vibrated and jerked forward, the platform giving way to a mass of thistle and bracken fern, then weedy pastures and old windmills standing like sentries guarding empty dams.

She shot a glance around the carriage. The other passengers had moved elsewhere, perhaps in search of the non-existent dining car, or off the train. Quin was alone with this brittle-looking woman who had her eyes closed, whose angular cheekbones pushed through sagging skin. A woman bearing little resemblance to the son she'd brought into the world. Her mind raced. What were the chances of her being on this train, sitting opposite? Was she ashamed and mortified about Tom? Perhaps her expectations, her hopes and dreams for him had been shattered, just as Nan's had been destroyed by her.

"I know him," Quin blurted, smoothing her sweaty hands down her jeans. "Your son."

Lucille's eyes sprang open.

"I worked for him."

"And you lost your job?" Lucille sat up straighter, immediately interested.

Quin nodded, then focused her gaze on the misty drizzle that had started, not trusting herself to speak.

"I'm sorry about your job."

Quin shrugged.

"The recession has been tough for so many people. Did you manage to get another one?" Lucille asked.

"Yeah, sort of. It's been hard."

"I can imagine."

At first, she thought Lucille was mocking her. What would this woman know of hardship? Look at her in her comfortable warm coat, the expensive diamonds on her shrivelled fingers.

"The government hasn't handled things terribly well," Lucille said.

Quin stared at her. How dare she start in on politics. What about what her son had done?

"I imagine you're worried about Tom and how things are going to go tomorrow," Quin fired back.

The look of surprise on Lucille's face, gave her satisfaction. Did the woman think she didn't know that her son was waiting for the verdict, that she and everyone else hoped would turn out to be a lengthy jail sentence? Did she think that a woman like Quin didn't know? That she hadn't been following the court case like everyone else, where everyone believed the prosecutor when he claimed that Solid Rock's accounts were mostly a sham, designed to create an illusion that the company was solvent? Did this woman know that no-one believed Tom's denials and his explanation that the accounts portrayed a fair position?

"Yes. I'm very worried." Lucille was grim-faced. "He seems to be taking all the blame. It's the tall poppy syndrome. The big banks ganging up on a small operator like Solid Rock, and then there's the government who seem to have escaped any responsibility."

Quin looked at her sharply, her anger rising. "Is that what he told you?"

"Well, yes I have spoken to him." Lucille suddenly looked as though she'd said something she shouldn't have. "And I've been following the case in the newspapers. It's so one-sided, anyone can see that." She sat forward, looking confident. "The company was highly successful, and if the run on deposits hadn't occurred, the company would still be around today. As a teller, it must have been terrible for you when that happened, having to deal with all of those angry clients."

A teller? She tried to ignore her growing irritation, wondering why so many people thought that women couldn't hold any other position in a bank or building society. "Tellers copped a lot of abuse, but Tom didn't run the company very well, so it was only a matter of time. He cut corners. Many of the securities he took were just holes in the ground and weren't worth anything."

Lucille raised her eyebrows. "What job did you say you held?"

"I was Tom's Head of Operations. I worked closely with him."

The shock was evident on Lucille's face and she stared at Quin, no doubt re-appraising her and her second-hand clothes.

Quin tilted her head and smirked. "He made some very risky deals, which in the end were hardly worth the paper they were written on. He raised a bucket load of money selling those non-withdrawable investment shares, conveniently letting clients think they could get their money back, which of course they couldn't, especially now the company is insolvent."

Lucille nodded, her face miserable. "It was terribly unfortunate. I'm afraid I was an enthusiastic unpaid recruit for Solid Rock, telling everyone I knew to borrow and invest in those shares. Perhaps Tom was misguided."

"Misguided?" Quin spat out the word. "Is that what you call it? People invested all their life savings. I don't know about you, but I feel incredibly guilty for selling those bloody things. My brother and my Nan lost everything, and so did I. I've barely a cent to my name."

"I'm really very sorry. If it's any consolation, Tom and I lost our money too."

Quin lowered her eyes, squirming under Lucille's gaze of sympathy. It was only now she noticed how frayed Lucille's coat was, the woollen beanie and the bag she'd clutched on her lap, so worn the colour had faded in parts. "I'm sorry you lost your money, but I'm not so sure Tom has lost much. How do you know that he hasn't got money stashed somewhere offshore in some little tax haven?"

Quin pulled the newspaper from her backpack. Allegations that Tom was like all the other crooks who'd stolen millions, had taken hold in the media. The court prosecutor claimed the restructure of the business in the days before the company was declared insolvent was done so that Tom could avoid any personal liabilities. That he'd pulled out ten million of his own money. Where had the money gone? Tom denied any wrongdoing and said it had gone to pay off a loan. The prosecutor claimed that Tom had changed the name of the loan from his name to that of Solid Rock so that depositors would wear it. Tom denied it. It was a legitimate part of a restructure, he'd said.

Lucille looked taken aback. "Oh, he hasn't got any money. He's been honest about that."

Quin shook her head. How could she tell Tom's mother what her son was really like? The woman was clearly delusional, no doubt fed by Tom's lies, just like everyone else.

"You've probably had a lovely life and don't know hardship. And I know you're his mother, and it would be hard to hear, but he's definitely dishonest and unethical."

"I don't know why you'd say something so hurtful. Perhaps

you're just a disgruntled employee?" There was a coldness to Lucille's voice.

"I probably am. I not only lost my job, but I'll tell you something else. Your son defrauded the company by writing fictitious loans, and he framed me for some of them. I ended up going to jail."

Lucille fixed her gaze squarely on Quin. "That's quite an accusation. I presume you have proof."

She blinked. "Well … no, I don't."

"Hmm." Lucille flicked off a piece of fluff from her coat and folded her arms.

"Just because I don't have proof, doesn't mean it didn't happen." Quin pushed, unsure why she was so desperate for this woman to believe her. "And that's the unfortunate bit. Nothing has been proven, and I will never get a chance to clear my name."

Lucille's eyes seemed to soften as she listened.

"Do you know my nan died because the stress was too much for her? And my brother"— her voice cracked—"killed himself." She was losing control. Why couldn't she shut up? "I have no other family, I live in a rundown share house, I've a mountain of debt and no decent job because no-one will employ an ex-con. The only job I could get, and I count myself lucky, is a job as a kitchen hand in a cafe in Hammondville. Now I've got two days off to go to Melbourne, just to get some satisfaction in watching your son go to jail tomorrow."

Lucille blinked. "I'm truly sorry about what's happened to

you. Really, I am. But I can't think how my son is responsible for any of that."

Quin swallowed and took a deep breath. "Let me tell you about Tom, some of which you would already know and some you won't. On the plus side, he did care about his people, but the catch was that he wanted his pound of flesh. I worked night and day and so did everyone else. He rewarded me handsomely, promoting me beyond my capabilities so he had me on side. I did anything he asked."

Her rising voice sounded whiney, but she couldn't stop herself.

"And he was a womaniser, taking advantage of anyone in a skirt." Why had she thrown that in? What did that have to do with anything?

Lucille stiffened, and Quin couldn't tell whether it was because she'd said something the woman didn't know or whether she was surprised that someone else knew.

"Besides that, he was ruthless and never hesitated to lie his way out of anything if it got him what he wanted. He's not the type of person you could say no to. And maybe I can't prove it, but he definitely did something to defraud the company because he wanted everyone to think the company was solvent. Unfortunately for me, I was framed to take the focus off the company and ended up in jail for it. Lucille, I went to jail for something I didn't do. And I hope to hell he goes to jail tomorrow and rots there."

Quin trembled. The rattle from the train seemed louder. Melbourne's outlying suburban sprawl came into view: brick veneer housing, graffiti-covered factory walls, wire fences littered with plastic bags.

"He told me the big banks were trying to bring him down," Lucille said, softly.

"It wasn't a well-run business."

"That's what it says in the papers."

"He was delusional. He was spending everyone else's money."

"It could have been anybody in the company writing those loans, and I don't understand how that would make the company look solvent. I'm sorry, but that doesn't make any sense."

Quin swallowed. "It could only have been me, a guy called Pete, or Tom himself. It definitely wasn't me, and I'm fairly sure it wasn't Pete. We were the only ones with the authority to sign off approvals and funding of those amounts. My signature was forged – I sure as hell didn't do it. The loans were paid into Solid Rock accounts in my name, and that made the balance sheet look healthy to the regulators. Tom had a lot at stake. Pete and I didn't – we were mere employees. So, I'm fairly certain your son did it all on his own. His plan would have worked too, if all the depositors hadn't wanted their money back. That was the one thing he couldn't manipulate."

"Sadly, you're not the only one to tell me home truths about my son. I've received a lot of abuse from ex-staff and friends and even people like you whom I don't know. I've been told that my son is a murderer and that he's destroyed people's lives. You're very much mistaken if you think I haven't known hardship, because I've certainly weathered my share. As for writing these fictitious loans, I believe you wouldn't have done it. My son is no angel, and tomorrow he will take responsibility for his part. Still, he's my son. A mother can't wipe away years of love. I just can't do it, no matter what he's done. But I wonder Quin, what part did you play in what's happened, and can you find some peace?"

Quin stared at Lucille, her anger subsiding. "I blame myself for everything that's happened to me. Every minute and every hour of every day. But there's no going back. As my nan said, what's done is done."

49

LUCILLE

JUNE, 1992

Tired and drained, Lucille got off the train to find a nugget of a man in a blue chauffeur's uniform holding a sign with her name on it. He'd been careful not to use her surname.

"I'm Lucille," she said.

"Mrs Lucille Doomsbury?"

"Yes. Where's Tom?"

"He's been delayed and asked me to collect you," he said, taking her bag.

Lucille grunted, annoyed at her son. Her tolerance was wearing thin. Then again, he might not have wanted to be out in public, she reasoned. Grateful that the chauffeur didn't rush her and her stiff knee, she followed him to a black sedan.

As she was driven through the streets of Melbourne, she rested her weary head against the cold window. The wet, darkening streets looked even greyer than when she'd last visited, two years ago. That was the last time she'd seen Tom.

Her mood was contaminated with the sickening feeling that the car she was in was propelling her towards a confrontation she'd delayed for too long.

She had to face the fact that the love she once had for her son had soured and that she was being forced to face the accumulated facts of her life – the bad choices she'd made. Yet, there was a tiny semblance of hope, deep inside her, that perhaps it had all been a mistake. She wasn't ready to condemn her son, despite what Quin had said. She felt sorry for the girl, and she felt sorry for herself. Her words to Quin swirled in her head. What part had she herself played in what happened? She'd enabled Tom, encouraged him, even applauded him. Hank's son.

It wasn't long before the car pulled up in front of a renovated Victorian weatherboard house in Carlton, where the driver asked for payment. No wonder Tom hadn't come, she thought irritably as she handed over cash. Then she checked her grumpiness; she had to pull herself together for his sake.

Tom opened the door. "Hi, Mum." He looked tired and pale in a blue t-shirt and dark tracksuit pants. "How was the trip?"

"It was all right."

He bent his tall frame down, brushed her cheek with his lips and took her bag. He stank of cigarette smoke and alcohol.

"I'm glad you're here. It's been too long. Come in."

"Two years."

He frowned. "That long?"

He'd promised countless times to visit, and she'd been constantly disappointed by the grovelling apologetic phone call. The last time, on Christmas day, a flat tyre was the excuse. At least his short phone calls were regular enough. They'd argued when she'd complained how she hadn't seen him for months. He'd lost his temper. "Stop being a bitch," he'd said, he was under enough pressure without his needy mother getting stuck into him.

That had stung.

"Whose house is this?" she said, following him down the polished floors of a long hallway.

"It's a rental. I had to sell the other one."

The "other one" had been a large modern mansion in Kew, overlooking the river. Another thing he'd not told her.

"What about the house in Sorrento?"

"Sold a long time ago."

Was Quin right? Had he stashed away money? "What happened to the proceeds?"

His eyes flashed in sudden anger. "Ploughed back into Solid Rock to keep it afloat. What do you take me for?" And just as suddenly his mood softened. "This is your room."

He opened a door off the hallway and put her bag on the floor next to a large bed covered with a pale-green floral doona with matching pillows. At least, he'd prepared for her. "You've got your own ensuite too, just through there."

He seemed eager to impress.

"Nice," she said, peering through the door. The room was

light and airy with new carpet and a large fireplace. "Is this your furniture?"

"I got rid of my stuff and rented it fully furnished. It's nice, isn't it?"

She nodded, taking off her beanie, scarf and coat and leaving them on the bed. Probably sold his furniture, was her first thought, but she kept that to herself.

"Come on," he said. "I'll show you the rest."

He nodded towards another closed door off the hallway. "That's a third bedroom where I've put a lot of my stuff. It's meant to be a study."

"You know your father rented a house just like this one before we were married, same style and layout."

"I think you've told me that before," Tom said. "A lot of the houses around here are like this. Same set up. So, the trip wasn't too long?"

She didn't answer. He knew it was long. He's trying to make conversation, putting off her inevitable questions.

"And this is the kitchen and the family room. All open plan." He waved his hand towards a long couch and two armchairs.

There was floor to ceiling windows and French doors opening onto a small paved courtyard. "It's quite comfortable."

"It looks it. It's nicer than my house." She waited for him to explode, to tell her how much her whingeing about her house was getting him down.

Instead, he leant against the kitchen sink. "It's only a rental, as I said. So, the trip wasn't too long for you?"

He seemed nervous. She sat at the breakfast bench and noticed an empty whiskey bottle and glass.

"It was okay, but I need a cup of tea."

"Rightio then."

Max used to say that.

"I'll put the kettle on."

"Shall I make it?" she said, getting off the stool.

"I am capable of making you a cup of tea," he sniped.

"Okay." She hoisted herself back onto the stool. "How are you, Tom? You look tired. Have you been sleeping?"

"I'm all right. I don't sleep much, but I get by. Nothing to worry about."

"Really? I'm extremely worried. How could I not be? I've been following the court case in the newspapers."

He flicked the switch on the kettle, then swung around to face her and sighed. "It's a witch hunt, and they're looking for a scapegoat, Mum. It's as simple as that." His hair, previously black but now speckled with grey, was well cut. His green eyes once adoring, bored into her.

"So you've been telling me. Are you saying none of what's been reported is true?"

He shrugged as he turned from her to put the glass in the dishwasher and throw the whiskey bottle in the bin under the sink. He poured the boiled water into a mug with a teabag. "Do you take milk?"

"Yes." She wondered why he didn't know, then couldn't remember a time when he'd made her a cup of tea.

He put the milk carton in front of her before lighting a cigarette, his hands unsteady. The use-by date on the milk carton was three days ago. "Thanks," she said, sipping the tea black.

There were deep lines around his eyes and mouth. The chicken pox scar on the side of his cheek seemed to radiate from his pale face. A memory from when he was almost one came to her – his first steps with her hands hovering to stop him from falling. "He has to fall now and then," Max had said, but she couldn't bear for her son to cry. "He will not get hurt," she snapped back. "You're walking, Tom. Good boy." She clapped and so did he. A mother and son moment shutting out the world.

A different mother and son moment now. She wondered how many of his difficulties were her fault. Max had been right; she'd spoiled him and indulged him. The tea suddenly tasted bitter, and she pushed the cup away.

"Who's looking for a scapegoat? The government?" she said.

He avoided her eyes and drew back on the cigarette. "Everyone," he said, smoke billowing. He paced in front of her.

Lucille watched her son carefully. "I met a young woman who said she worked with you."

His shoulders tensed. "Oh? Who?"

"Her name was Quin."

He stopped his pacing, his expression strangely alarmed.

"She helped me on the train when there was some trouble."

He looked relieved. "That's good." He resumed pacing and smoking.

"Do you know her well?"

"Yeah, she worked for me." He stood in front of her resting a hand on the island bench. "But she let me down, and I had to let her go. She'd been a good worker too. Pity."

Her son was lying. No-one knew him better than she did. "She told me you framed her by writing fake loans and that she went to jail for it."

A flicker of fear, then he composed his face and crossed his arms. "She told you that did she? I hope you didn't believe her."

"I don't think your troubles will be over tomorrow, Tom. She says she has proof that you forged her signature and that you were the one who did the loans."

Lucille knew there was no proof. Why was she testing his honesty? Was it to help him or to help her? Deep down she prayed like she always had, that it wasn't his fault.

"Bullshit." He reached under the bench for a full bottle of scotch.

"Is it true?"

His hand shook as he poured the alcohol, spilling some on the bench.

"Well, is it?"

He drank deeply. "What do you think?"

She studied him. He avoided her eyes, looking shaken. It

was enough to tell her that he had lied, and that he was scared. "I don't know what to think. What's going to happen?" She spread her hands on the bench.

He ran his fingers through his hair, his cigarette still alight, ash teetering.

"I'll get out of it, Mum. I always have. And Quin is a nutcase. She's just a disgruntled employee."

He was probably right. He'd got out of every scrap. How could she forget when he'd set fire to a school building? She'd believed him when he said it wasn't him. And she wanted to believe him now. He was expelled anyway. He'd forged his school reports and they'd only found out by accident when Max ran into one of his teachers. He hadn't even been attending school. Lucille never believed it, always defending him – her boy was only fifteen.

She'd pleaded with Max to pay for him to get into university and use Max's old boy network. Then there was the incident where Tom's wife had found him in bed with another woman, one month into their marriage.

Lucille shut her eyes, trying to stop the horrible memories, but they kept coming: Tom taking a mortgage on the cottage. "Why get a mortgage from one of these big banks?" she'd asked him. "Trust me," he'd said. "It's better. Don't worry. The loan is to invest in your future." And she'd blindly signed the documents. He'd never told her what happened to the proceeds of the first house she and Max had bought. He'd said it was going into an investment for her. She'd never seen any paperwork. But she knew now what she hadn't wanted to know then. Should she say something now about the valuer? The administrator had said no-one was likely to get their money back.

"It's just that … money's tight. I needed a lot for my defence team."

She sighed. "I don't need my money back."

He continued pacing, absorbed in his own problems. Her son would never know and understand the dark places she'd inhabited in her life. She'd never told him, resisting the urge to garner sympathy for the loss of her other children and her nervous breakdown.

"I saw Stan at the station."

Tom placed his hands on the bench, opposite her. "Stan?"

"Stan Briggs in Hammondville. You were once friends with his son, Sammy?"

"How was he?"

She hesitated, wondering if she should remind him that Stan and everyone else in Hammondville blamed them for Sammy's death. Should she tell him about the eggs smashed on her front door, the blood of some dead animal smeared along the fence? Or should she protect him from that? Deep down, she knew she was protecting herself from his lack of interest. "Let's just say he wasn't pleased to see me."

Tom stubbed out the cigarette in the ashtray. "I guess that's another friend lost."

"It's not a lost friend, Tom. Sammy is dead."

"I know, Mum. I feel bad about it. Don't try to make me

feel even more guilty," he snapped. "It's not like I pushed him."

"The Hammondville Times accused you of murder."

"That's preposterous, and you know it."

"Stan said you got Sammy into too much debt, and that the life insurance policy you sold him wasn't worth the paper it was written on."

"Let's not get into this, Mum. I need someone on my side, now of all times. I thought I could depend on you for support." His eyes bored into her.

"They said in the paper that you were a cowboy, and that the company was grossly mismanaged."

"That's just bullshit from a left-wing rag. I helped people. You know me. What they're saying is slanderous and untrue."

There'd been so many lies. Maybe she'd encouraged his arrogance and belief that he could do anything. She'd been so blind to his faults, Max had said. How could she continue to deny who her son really was?

"Are you going to jail? Is that what's going to happen tomorrow?"

He cleared his throat and rested his hand on the sink. "I hope not. Barry, my lawyer, thinks it'll be all right but ..."

His voice caught and suddenly he was her little boy again, crushed, face contorted, a sob escaping. She rushed to him and held out her arms. He took a deep breath and buried his head into her shoulder, and once again, her motherly love overtook her.

"It'll be okay," she said, rubbing his back like she did when he was small. "It'll work out." Why did she say that? This man, her son, a monster, the paper said. Ruining lives by his lies, his empty promises and deceit. "The cause of death and destruction," one journalist had said. She'd seen it with her own eyes in the town she'd called home for years.

This was her fault. She'd created him, made him who he was.

He pulled away from her and wiped his eyes with the back of his hand. "You need to be prepared in case,' he said. "That's all. Richard Connolly got jail and I might too."

"What did he do?"

"He ran Connolly Mortgages, and he breached his duties as director."

"And did you?"

"No, Mum. I didn't." Tom dragged his hand through his hair but didn't look at her. "It's all been one big mistake."

"But the paper said the company owes more than two billion dollars. Hammondville is up in arms. I can't even walk down the street."

"I know, Mum. Why didn't you tell me about the eggs thrown at the house?"

If he knew, why hadn't he checked on her?

"I … I didn't want you to worry."

"You can't live there. You'll have to stay here. I've paid the rent for the next twelve months."

"Live here? What about my cottage?"

He turned away and stared out of the window.

"Tom! What have you done?"

"I've sold it."

"Oh my god! You've left me with nothing, Tom, nothing." Her heart pounded. "How could you?"

He turned and stared at the floor. "I needed the money in case of an appeal. I'm sorry. Listen, it's a loan, and when I get back on my feet, and I will, I'll pay it all back with interest."

The money would never come back, that much she knew. Just like the day Max gave Tom their shares in Solid Rock so he could own it outright after he'd bought out Harvey. She shook her head. "And what do you suppose I'm going to live on in the meantime?"

He looked at her in surprise. "The pension. What else?"

She folded her arms. "And what are you going to live on?"

He raised his eyebrows. "I thought we'd live here together until I got myself sorted."

"And if you're in jail?"

"That's unlikely, but if it comes to that, I'll appeal. And even if I did have to go, then it would only be for a short time. You'll be here when I get out."

"What if I don't want to be here? What if I have other plans?"

He smirked. "Huh, what other plans?"

"I thought I might like to go to Uni and study."

Her son laughed. "That's ridiculous at your age. You can barely look after yourself."

Underneath her tiredness brewed a curdling rage. "What if

I decide to go back to Hammondville and rent my own place? What if I don't want to financially support you?"

He looked at her, stunned. "Now don't be like that, Mum. I don't know what the hell has gotten into you. You'll be here. This is the best place for you." He looked at his watch. "Now, I've got to see Barry to talk over a few things. There's some food in the fridge if you're hungry. Help yourself."

She could see it all so clearly now, what she couldn't before. She clenched her fists, nails digging into her palms, her anger erupting.

"Clearly, your so-called pleas that you needed me were just a ploy to get me out of the house in Hammondville so you could sell it. Just another one of your lies, Tom. Isn't it?"

He was almost at the door to the hallway, and his shoulders tightened as if she'd hurled a rock and hit him in the back. He stopped and half-turned, his face cold, his eyes empty.

"You're a real bitch, you know that? You're absolutely pathetic. Thank god Dad's not around to see you like this."

He continued up the corridor, and she heard the lock click as he stepped out and slammed the front door behind him.

Tears streamed down her face. She wished Max were with her. He'd have known what to say to their neighbours and friends in Hammondville. But he'd have been heartbroken, and she was glad that he hadn't lived to witness it. It had been five years since he'd had the heart attack in the bathroom. It pained her to think about him dying alone. They'd had a fight about Tom, as usual, and she'd stormed out and went to the bowls club. She couldn't even remember what the fight was about. Tom blamed her for not being home. He'd always sought his father's approval, his love and his acceptance.

She'd never wanted the aggravation, the heartache, the pain, the worry and the sacrifice. She knew that from when she'd had Patricia and Harry. Her intense love for Tom just happened and it grew, never letting her go as it snuck into her soul and her very being. And now she was at a loss to know what she could do about it.

Her grandmother had been right after all.

50

QUIN

1992

Quin wished Lucille luck before watching her disappear into the crowd at Spencer Street station.

Alone again and anxious, she hoisted her backpack over her shoulder and walked in the opposite direction, out of the station, and onto a waiting Number 96 tram. She paid her fare and slumped into a seat, wrapping her arms around herself to keep warm. She was tired, hungry and sad. Skyscrapers loomed out of the drizzle as the tram moved down Collins Street, and she twisted in her seat as it passed the building where she'd once worked. All traces of Solid Rock were gone, replaced by the garish signage of a newly formed telecommunications corporation. She leant back and sighed. It was strange returning to a place now foreign to her.

The tram trundled along. The ding of the bell startled her each time passengers got off. The lights from the streetlamps catapulted reflections across the wet road. She took a hair tie from around her wrist and, after running her fingers through her hair, tied it up in a high ponytail. She found her lip balm in her backpack, stuck her finger in, and ran it around her dry lips before smacking them together. She was ready, and the tram stopped directly in front of the street she wanted.

The terrace cottage in North Carlton looked the same from the outside. She walked up and knocked on the fly screen door.

"Hello," she said when the door opened.

"Ah, hi.' His eyes flicked past her.

"Do you think I was followed or something?"

He frowned. "Where's your car? So I can give you a parking permit."

She gave him a withering look. "As if I could afford a car. I caught the train."

He nodded. "Oh. Come in."

"You don't look too delighted to see me."

"Of course I'm happy to see you. It's just that I expected you hours ago."

"Yeah, well the train was late."

She followed him into the lounge room. Nothing had changed, including the floral carpet and mustiness. Pete's shirt hung loose; he'd lost weight.

"I'll order some pizza. That okay for dinner?"

She threw her bag onto the floor. "Yep."

While he rang and ordered, she sprawled on the couch as if it had been only yesterday that she'd lived there.

"It'll be here in fifteen. Margherita still okay? It was your favourite."

He remembered. She couldn't help smiling. "Yep."

He had two beers in his hand and handed her one. Then he settled into the armchair opposite resting his elbows on his knees. "Where've you been?"

"In the country."

"That's what you said in your telephone message. But where, exactly?"

"Hammondville. Trying to find Ben, actually."

"Did you find him?"

She sighed and took a long swig, letting the cold liquid slide down her throat, then nodded. She put the bottle on the floor and pulled both legs towards her wrapping her arms around them. "He topped himself."

"Oh, Jesus."

For some reason, it all poured out of her, and she wiped her eyes with the back of her hand. It was a day for confessions.

"He was a nice bloke," Pete said.

She appreciated the fact that he didn't try to comfort her with a hug. He sat on the edge of his seat, his hands joined together, as if in prayer.

"He never liked you," she said.

"Really?"

Quin nodded. "Afraid so. Told me you couldn't be trusted."

"Oh." He scratched his head.

The pizza arrived, and they ate and drank another beer.

"Look, I'm sorry I didn't visit you in jail. It's just that … well, everything was blowing up."

"Yeah, I suppose it was pretty tough trying to save yourself."

His head jerked up. "I'm really sorry about everything that happened. I did everything I could to help you."

She stared at him. "Did you? Did you really? I went to jail for something I didn't do. But then you know that already."

"I tried my best. I told him you didn't do it. You know what Tom was like, he'd never listen. He threatened me with the sack."

"Did he?" She shifted, pulling her leg under her.

"Have you heard that I testified against him?"

"I've been out of jail for some time now, so yes, I read the papers about how he forced you to approve those worthless loans."

He stared at her. "Why are you here?"

"I need someplace to crash and figured you owed me at least one night's accommodation."

"Sure. You can stay here as long as you like. I'll sleep on the couch."

"Thanks. I'll take the couch. But it won't be that long. I'm just here to see Tom's slimy face when the judge tells him he's going to jail. Then I'll be out of your hair."

"I hope he goes to jail too. But people like that often don't. He's got a lot of powerful friends."

"He'll go. The public want blood, and I reckon that's what they'll get."

"Do you mind if I come along with you in the morning?"

"To court?"

"Yep. Then I've got to go to work. I've got an appointment at twelve thirty."

"Work? Where did you get a job?"

"Palace Home Loans. I've been with them now for about six months."

"Really? Doing what?"

"I go out to clients' houses and take their home loan applications."

Quin screwed up her face. "Go to their houses?"

"Yeah. Clients ring up looking for a home loan, and I go and visit them. At night mostly but sometimes during the day. Once I left Solid Rock, I did some contract work for a bit and then found this. Actually, Waz put me onto it. They're a start-up, but I reckon they've caught onto something. They sell the deal to one of the banks for a percentage, and there's nothing on the books. I get part of the percentage and a part of the fees."

"Sounds interesting."

"They're looking for people. Why don't you have a chat? I can set something up for you."

"They're not going to take me. I've got a record. No thanks to you."

He looked pained. "I don't think that's fair. I tried. I really did. But I know I was a coward, and you deserved better." He lowered his head. "And it's nothing compared to what you went through, but I live with it every day too."

She wondered what it was that she'd ever seen in him.

"I know I can't make it up to you, but I can get you an interview. Their HR department is pretty sloppy. They'll never check. Believe me, you'll get a job. And I can be your referee."

At his feet were the remnants of the shredded beer bottle label he'd slowly picked off.

"I'll think about it."

He was trying hard, and she already knew she'd take the job if she could get it. It was the only way to start again.

The next morning, Quin and Pete pushed through the crowd and into the court building, only to be turned away. They found themselves in a large room with everyone else and had to watch the proceedings on a television screen rigged up on a wall, too far away to hear. Her stomach churned when she saw Tom's face. She thought she saw Lucille. Everyone stopped talking when the judge appeared on the screen.

Quin's heart beat wildly. Seeing Tom go to jail might well be the happiest day she'd had for quite some time. Except her view became obstructed by the people jammed in front of her. Her frustration grew as she tried to jostle for position, but it was hopeless. She and Pete had been pushed to the back.

The judge began to talk.

"God, what's he saying?" someone asked.

"He reckons Doomsbury is partly to blame for the billion-dollar collapse. He was arrogant, excessive and greedy, and he deliberately flouted the Building Society Act."

"No kidding."

"We can't hear up the back. Speak up."

The person who was relaying the information raised his voice. "Something about irresponsible lending. That although what he did was wrong, the government's lack of foresight and control over the building societies was unconscionable."

"Hear, hear," another voice said from behind Quin. The crowd murmured in agreement.

"Yeah, the government is shit."

"This is hopeless. I can't hear a bloody thing."

"Shut up. We can't hear."

"God, he's going on and on," a woman complained.

Quin put her hand on her stomach and glanced at Pete, his neck stretched towards the screen. The crush of people around her seemed to close in, suffocating her. She was a fool to have come. She should have stayed in Hammondville and watched it on the news.

Then from the front there was a roar.

"Fuck!"

"What's happened?" Quin said, her heart beating.

"He's got a fine of three hundred thousand."

"The bastard!"

A woman wailed. "He took my boy."

"That sucks."

"I live in a shack."

She felt Pete's hand in hers. She turned to look at him, tears in her eyes.

"I'm sorry. I really hoped he'd go," he said.

She bit her lip, let go of his hand and fought her way out of the crowd. Outside in the fresh air, she sat on a concrete step, her face pressed into her knees, and sobbed.

51

LUCILLE

1992

Lucille was seated a few rows behind Tom when the judge read his verdict. She'd had a sleepless night preparing herself for the ruling that her son might go to jail, yet desperately hoped he wouldn't. The court erupted and people around her yelled, shouted their displeasure or agreement. It was hard to tell which. She was dumbstruck and confused. She might have been hard of hearing, but she was sure of what she'd heard. A slap on the wrist with a fine. The sale proceeds from her cottage would no doubt be used to help pay for it.

Tom was thumped on the back and congratulated by men she didn't know. There seemed to be a lot of them. She was anchored on the hard seat, not knowing what she should do. Tom couldn't wipe the smile off his face, and he gazed around the room until he caught the eye of a slim, blonde, young woman and winked. She blew him a kiss.

Then his eyes found her, and he grinned. Lucille smiled

back weakly, fighting the rising nausea and shame. He looked the happiest she'd ever seen. And she wondered if he had any remorse as she sat, incredulous that he'd got away with it. Somehow, what he'd done to so many people had become the government's fault. He would walk away and go on to deal again without so much as a backwards glance at the devastation he'd left behind.

The court was emptying and an official gestured for her to leave. Tom was surrounded by people. She hoisted herself from her seat and limped out of the doors towards the exit. Finding a bathroom, she splashed water on her face and rested her hands on the sink to steady herself.

"I suppose you're happy?"

She lifted her eyes. It was Quin, coming out of a cubicle. She looked drawn and tense, her eyes red. "It makes me sick to think about all the people he's hurt," Lucille said.

Quin shook her head as she washed her hands. "I know. I'd hoped he'd go to jail, but these guys hardly ever do. If he'd broken into a house and stolen a television, he would have got a couple of months. If he'd been black, it probably would have been a few years. It's just the way the system is."

"Hmm. You're probably right," Lucille said as the image of Sammy Briggs's dead body coming up from the water sprang into her head. Who was responsible for his death? His parents had screamed at her. Her head spun.

"Are you all right?"

"What?" Lucille blinked.

"Do you want to hold my arm? There are seats just outside where you can sit for a while."

Lucille nodded.

Quin helped her to a wooden bench, then disappeared. A chilly breeze swept through an open door at the end of the corridor of the old building, and Lucille sat in a daze.

"Here you go." Quin held out a styrofoam cup filled with steaming tea. "A touch of milk, just the way you like it," Quin said, smiling as she sat on the bench next to her. "Are you okay? I can get Tom if you like."

A few sips of the tea seemed to revive Lucille. "No need. I'm much better. It was very sweet of you to bring me this." Here was a woman she barely knew who cared more about her than her own son. "I just need to sit here for a bit. But you go." Her heart ached and tears pricked her eyes.

"I'll just wait a bit longer, just to make sure you're okay. Then I'll have to get going. I've got a job interview."

She reached out and put her hand on Quin's arm. "And here I am holding you up. I can't thank you enough for your help."

"Oh, it was my pleasure. I feel a bit bad about yesterday. I was pretty rude, and … well, I shouldn't have taken my frustrations out on you."

"I don't blame you. You weren't the first, and you won't be the last. I'm afraid, I've had my head in the sand, and only now am I seeing things that I couldn't before. You're a good and kind person, Quin."

This girl had shown a kindness towards her that she hadn't

experienced from anyone else she'd known in the last two years. She didn't need to, and shouldn't have, but here she was, sitting next to her and feeling bad about what she'd said. A plan formed in her head. "I wonder if you'd indulge me and come and have lunch with me tomorrow … if you're free."

Quin hesitated.

"My shout."

"Ah, well …"

She could tell Quin was trying to come up with an excuse.

"There's something I want to give you."

"You don't need to give me anything."

"It's nothing much. Please?"

Quin nodded. "I suppose I could."

"There's a little cafe on the corner of Lygon Street and Faraday Street. Why don't we meet at twelve?"

"All right. Thank you. Are you okay now? I better get going."

"Yes. Much better. Tom will be wondering what's happened to me." They both stood. "I'll see you tomorrow."

Lucille went outside and found Tom. She doubted he'd even missed her.

"There you are. Are you right to get home by yourself?" he said.

She nodded. "I'll see you back …"

Her voice trailed off as he was whisked away by two men. "C'mon mate, there's a lot of celebrating to do. The car's waiting."

A black stretch limousine was on the curb, and the blonde

woman she'd seen earlier was already inside sipping champagne.

*

The next morning, Lucille found a newspaper on the kitchen bench. A ray of sunshine lit up the photo on the front page – Tom with a glass in one hand, his other arm around the blonde woman, dancing. 'Disgusting' read the headline. She sighed.

Next to the newspaper was a scrap of paper with Tom's scrawl across it.

Mum, I'm really sorry, but I have to get away. Just for a while. The house is yours, as I said, for the next twelve months.

Love you, Tom.

She read and re-read the letter again. This man, she didn't know. This man, who showed no remorse, who partied last night at a restaurant with his team of lawyers, paid for by her and others he'd devastated.

She made herself a tea and found two pieces of bread left in the packet. She rummaged around in the empty cupboards and fridge. He'd left it to her to shop for groceries.

Sitting on the couch, she forced down the toast and read the paper, most of which was about the government's lack of corporate regulation and the state's reluctance to do anything about it. There was an article, however, at the bottom of page two – a group of depositors were taking her son to court. He must have known.

She couldn't think about him now and threw down the paper to get ready. She had a lot of things to do.

*

Quin was already at a table in a corner of the busy café.

"Hi," Lucille said, taking off her coat. "Glad you found a table for us."

Quin smiled. "Gee, I envied that coat on the train."

"It's warm but very old. I see you have one now."

"One of the things I did yesterday was to buy a coat so I can cope with this winter."

The waiter came up and took their order. Coffee and a ham and cheese toasted sandwich for each of them.

"And how did you go with the interview?"

"It was more of a chat than an interview. I wasn't really dressed for it. But I must have done okay since they asked me to start on Monday."

Lucille smiled. "That's marvellous."

Quin told her all about the job as a mobile lender. "It'll be pretty easy work, but at least it's a start so I don't have to go back to the café in Hammondville. I rang up this morning and told them. They weren't that happy to be honest; I was supposed to be back tomorrow. I feel bad that I left them in the lurch."

"There's lot of people looking for work. Don't feel too bad about it."

"That's true."

"It looks like things are changing for you."

"I hope so. I'm thinking about doing some study. I started

an accountancy course, and I think I need to finish it and see where it takes me. But first, I have to find somewhere to live."

Lucille frowned. "Where are you staying now?"

The food arrived.

Quin spoke with her mouth full. "I've got a couch at a friend's place." She swallowed. "Sorry, that wasn't very polite. My nan would have had a fit."

Lucille smiled, wiping her mouth on a napkin.

"Actually, at an old boyfriend's place. But I don't want to stay there too long. I'll have to find somewhere, buy some new clothes and get myself organised."

"It's a new beginning for you." Those words reminded Lucille of what she'd said to herself when she'd got out of hospital all those years ago.

"You know, blaming myself was eating me up, and I really wanted revenge against your son."

"I don't blame you, not one bit."

Quin cocked her head. "Sorry, it must be very painful for you to hear that. But that's the way it is."

"I know. There are many people who wanted him to go to jail. I wish there was something I could do, but I can't." Lucille sipped her coffee. "You know, there's going to be a class action. Maybe we can get some of our money back."

"You can't get blood from a stone. The only way anyone will get anything is if they put pressure on the government." Quin sighed. "I suppose Tom's pretty happy with himself this morning?"

Lucille slid her spoon around the cup to collect the

cappuccino froth, thinking about the punishments Max gave to Tom when he was young and how she'd tried to stop him. She'd let him off, and he took no responsibility for what he did. That was her fault.

"Lucille?" Quin leant towards her.

"Sorry. What did you say?" She licked the spoon.

"I said, I bet Tom's happy this morning."

"I wouldn't know. I haven't seen him since yesterday at the courthouse."

Quin raised her eyebrows. "Oh. I thought you would have been with him celebrating."

"No. He's not likely to drag his old mother around town. Besides, it seems he's left."

Quin frowned. "Left? Left Melbourne?"

Lucille nodded. "I believe so. It doesn't appear he has any remorse. But I have plenty for the two of us." Lucille brought out an envelope from her handbag and slid it across the table. "This is for you. A small gift. It's not much, but it's a token of how sorry I am for the way he wrecked your life and for how you've helped me. Now I want to help you."

"Oh," Quin's hand fluttered to her neck. "I'm very touched, but you don't need to give me anything." She glanced at the envelope.

"You can open it."

Quin ripped the seal, and as she pulled out the thank-you card, a cheque slipped onto the table. Her eyes widened. "I can't take this. It's too much."

"It's only two thousand dollars. But it should be enough to

get you started. Get a new wardrobe for work perhaps, pay for those books. I won't take it back."

"I don't know what to say." Quin's eyes filled with tears. "You've been so nice to me. Even though I said some horrible things about your son."

"You weren't lying about him. I confronted him about what you said, and … well, I think you're right. You also made me face some things I should have a long time ago."

Quin jerked her head up. "I was right? He did frame me? Did he say that?"

"He didn't admit anything, but I know him well enough to know when he's lying."

Quin wiped her mouth on the serviette and sat back in her chair. "I don't suppose we can take that as a confession? But still, it puts my mind at rest that my theory was true."

"And for what it's worth, I know you didn't do anything wrong. I believe you, and I hope that means something and that you can find some peace. My husband was a POW and he found that, to get on with life, he had to let go of his hatred for the Japanese. It's the only way."

"You're right. I know that's what I have to do," Quin said, holding the cheque.

"I also happen to have a spare fully furnished room you could use, rent free, where I'm staying."

Quin narrowed her eyes. "Really? Aren't you staying with Tom?"

"Tom's made arrangements for me."

"I don't want to impose."

"No imposition. You'd merely be keeping an old woman company until you found your own place."

"Thanks, Lucille. Except for my nan, no-one has ever been as nice to me as you."

"And no-one has been so nice to me since Solid Rock collapsed. So, I guess we're even." Lucille smiled. "So, what do you think? Do you want to keep an old woman company for a while?"

Quin nodded, wiped her eyes and smiled. "I'd love to keep you company."

*

Lucille walked down the street in the sunshine. Even her knee felt better. She'd made some decisions. Giving money to Quin was a small step. She had more than enough to look after herself. Her years of saving first began when it was Pa and her. She'd hidden the money just in case she needed it. And at times she had. She collected old jars and tins and hid them under the rose bushes. When she joined the army, she'd opened her first bank account, dug up the money and watched her balance grow as she continued to add to it. It had grown to nearly five hundred thousand dollars over the years. She'd always felt guilty not telling Max or Tom about it. For some reason, she'd kept it a secret.

Just in case she needed it. And now she did. Perhaps she'd buy a house or unit when she was ready and invest some in the stock market.

But for now, she'd change her will.

March, 2002

SEXUALLY TRANSMITTED DEBT CAN BE A FINANCIAL SURPRISE.

FINANCIAL STRAITS TIMES – PETA JACOBSON

Kim Green was in a sound relationship and wondered, after ten years with her husband, Steve, why they were struggling to make ends meet. She and her husband had a home loan of $150,000 for ten years, and nothing had been paid off. Her husband's business was growing, he said, and the mortgage was increased to $200,000 to help pay for the expansion. She trusted her husband, until one day, she opened a letter addressed to her from the bank, telling her that her house was to be sold because payments had not been made for almost twelve months. It turned out Steve had a gambling problem and had lost the business without telling her. She was left responsible for the debts he'd accumulated. She hadn't taken an interest in their financial affairs, leaving it up to him.

Kim is one of the many who have sought help from The Women's Money Managers Foundation (TWMMF), according to CEO Quin Schmidt. "When a partner leaves you with full responsibility for a joint loan, this is known as a sexually transmitted debt. It might not start out malicious or intentional, but the result can be devastating. And it can be something small like a joint credit card or personal loan, or as big as a home loan or business loan." Ms Schmidt, a certified financial planner, explained that she helps many people like Kim who have unwisely trusted their partners or children and found themselves in financial hot water.

Ms Schmidt should know. She was one of those people who had a large loan and lost her grandmother's house during the recession of 1990. With the help of her mentor and friend, Lucille Doomsbury, Ms Schmidt set up TWMMF in 1993.

Mrs Doomsbury explained that women of her generation were not used to having financial independence. "We waited for our husbands to hand out the housekeeping, praying it would be enough to feed the family. It was the husband's job to manage money, and it was the wife's job to manage the children and the house. But actually, we did know how to manage money. We had to be frugal, especially during wartime. We signed whatever was put in front of us and blindly trusted our husbands to do the right thing. And mostly they did."

Incidentally, Mrs Doomsbury is the mother of Tom Doomsbury who is still at large after fleeing overseas to Spain in 1992. Authorities are pursuing him on charges relating to billions of dollars lost as a result of the Solid Rock Building Society collapse in 1990.

"But you can be held responsible for debt, not only by husbands but by children too," Mrs Doomsbury said. "My son left me with debt when he fled. My house was sold to pay for the $300,000 fine he incurred. I haven't seen my son or heard from him since. His shameful actions are one of the reasons I invested with Quin in this business. I went to university, obtained a Bachelor of Business and decided to give something back, and helping to educate women in financial matters is one way to do it. I hope no-one goes through what I went through."

According to Ms Schmidt: "We run free workshops to show how to be financially independent and avoid sexually transmitted debt. It can be one of the hardest conversations to have with your loved one. It's not just partners; a lot of elderly parents have become liable too for their children's debt and this can have devastating consequences. While it's predominantly women who are affected, we've had a few men approach us when they found out their wives had gambled away everything."

"Many women had implicitly trusted their partners and were shocked when money disappeared. We conducted a survey. Thirty per cent were surprised by their loved one's spending habits, and an astonishing sixty per cent had no idea that they were individually responsible for the debt incurred by their spouse or child once they signed a mortgage or guarantee," Ms Schmidt explained. "The best thing you can do is get separate legal advice before signing any joint mortgage, guarantee or credit card application."

At the time of writing, more than three thousand people, mostly women have sought advice from TWMMF.

Mrs Doomsbury, 82, has no intention of retiring. "I'm interested in each case and find that women over seventy are keen to talk to me about their situation. Most of them have no superannuation of their own and find it difficult to ever be financially independent. You know it's very humiliating holding out your hand for money like a beggar to your partner, and it increases the power imbalance. I learnt how to invest in the share market and set up my own superannuation fund in 1992. We've helped so many people and have a team of financial planners and specialists who provide tailored advice for each client."

"Lucille's amazing," Ms Schmidt said. "Sometimes, our clients need a cry, a hug and a cup of tea. Or a detailed financial plan, which Lucille explains simply and clearly. She's remarkable and a true inspiration."

"It just shows that learning to become financially independent can happen, no matter how old you are," Mrs Doomsbury said.

Have the conversation and understand each other's finances to make sure you avoid a financial surprise.

Acknowledgements

I have many people to thank for helping to bring my manuscript to life.

Thank you to Peter Lingard who patiently workshopped and read the manuscript over many months, providing valuable feedback in a gruelling Melbourne lockdown during the COVID-19 Pandemic in 2020.

My immense appreciation goes to the Phoenix Park Writers Group, Eleni, Sylvia, Sue, and Jill who helped me find the story. Many thanks to the Chicken Writers Group, Ara, Mia, Annie, Adam, Nikki and Kathryn who kicked me along, challenging and probing to bring the story to life. In particular, a special thanks to AJ Collins, my brilliant copyeditor, whose suggestions made my sentences sensible. My thanks also to Don Pozzuto and Colin Denovan whose sharp eyes picked up the many things I missed.

My love and thanks to my mother, Yolande who taught me that to have control of your financial independence is to have full independence and control of your own life. Her suggestions helped immensely. My aunt Dora, whose memories of life in Melbourne during the war helped shape my character, Lucille. Finally, Con who listens and reads my work providing me with encouragement, wise counsel and valuable feedback.

To my family and network of wonderful friends, thank you for your patience and understanding, for your interest and for listening. It means a lot to me.

Finally, thank you dear reader for buying or borrowing and reading this book. I am truly honoured that you've taken the time.

About the Author

After many years in corporate life, S.C. Karakaltsas found a passion for writing historical fiction about little known times and places.

Climbing the Coconut Tree, released in March 2016 was inspired by a real-life double murder on a tropical island in the Central Pacific in 1948. In 2017, she released *Out of Nowhere: a collection of short stories* and has short stories published in the Lane Cove Literary Award Anthology and the Monash Writers Anthology. In 2018, *A Perfect Stone,* based on a child escaping the Greek Civil War in 1948, was published to much acclaim.

S.C. Karakaltsas lives in Melbourne, Australia with her husband and elderly cat.

Would you like to know more?

Drop by and say hello at sckarakaltsas.com.